Exceptional Praise for the Romances of Miranda Jarrett

"Miranda . . . . powerful, moving love . . . . me period meticulously . . . . characters, and it pays off in st . . . . . . adore."
— Meg Grant, WCAU-TV/CBS News

"There is no doubt that Miranda Jarrett knows how to bring the sting of sea spray, the bite of the cutlass, and her passion for colonial adventure to readers like few others. A sparkling talent!"
— Kathe Robin, *Romantic Times*

"A marvelous author . . . one of romantic fiction's finest gems . . . Each word from Miranda Jarrett is a treasure, each page an adventure, each book a lasting memory."
— *The Literary Times*

"Miranda Jarrett is the reigning regent of colonial romance."
— *The Paperback Forum*

"A spectacular author . . . Miranda Jarrett is the queen of eighteenth-century American historical romance . . . If you haven't read her, then it's strongly recommended that you do, because [her books] are some of the best fiction of the nineties."
— Harriet Klausner, *Affaire de Coeur*

"When Miranda Jarrett writes of love and romance, her fans eat it up. . . . She maintains a personal tradition of romances that are action-packed, thought-provoking, and emotionally riveting. . . . Richly deserves her title as one of the greatest writers of colonial romance of our times."
— *The Suburban & Wayne* (PA) *Times*

MIRANDA JARRETT

THE CAPTAIN'S BRIDE

POCKET STAR BOOKS
New York   London   Toronto   Sydney   Tokyo   Singapore

An *Original* Publication of POCKET BOOKS

A Pocket Star Book published by
POCKET BOOKS, a division of Simon & Schuster Inc.
1230 Avenue of the Americas, New York, NY 10020

ISBN: 0-671-00339-9

First Pocket Books printing August 1997

10 9 8 7 6 5 4 3 2 1

POCKET STAR BOOKS and colophon are registered
trademarks of Simon & Schuster Inc.

Front cover illustration by Darryl Zudeck

Printed in the U.S.A.

For Meg Ruley and Kate Collins,
my personal Yankee "Dream Team":
for believing in cradles, the Fairbournes, and me.

The Captain's Bride

❧ One ❧

London, 1720

No honest man could ever accuse Captain Joshua Fairbourne of cowardice.

He'd left home for the sea on his eighth birthday, and in the twenty years since, he'd faced pirates without flinching, fought Frenchman with honor, and sailed his ships through hurricanes and blizzards and waves as high as a meetinghouse spire. But here on this warm June night, the most fearful challenge of Joshua's life loomed before him, goading him, taunting him, making his heart thump from uncertainty and sheer cowardice until his greatest desire was to turn and run and save himself.

Yet pride rooted him to the spot, his mouth growing drier by the second. He *had* to stay. As much as he longed to, he couldn't escape. How could he, considering that this was a trap of his own making?

For the thousandth time, he reached to touch the hilt of his sword to reassure himself, and for the thousandth time, too, he swore with miserable frus-

1

tration when he realized the sword wasn't there. In London, gentlemen—even gentlemen from the American colonies—didn't wear swords to an elegant supper and dance. They didn't swear, either, especially not in the company of London ladies, and with a wretched shake of his head, Joshua swallowed that one last oath. He hooked his forefinger into the tight band of linen that swathed his neck, trying to ease the fashionable neckband that was nigh to choking him.

He took as deep a breath as he could and wiped his forehead with the underside of his sleeve, where the sweat wouldn't show on the glazed wool of his best coat. It was hot here in this London garden, cursedly hot for June, and he longed for the river breezes to be found on the *Swiftsure*'s quarterdeck. That was where he belonged, not lurking here among roses and moss-covered marble nymphs that belonged to a grand lady whose name he had already forgotten, and again he thought of vanishing alone into the night while he still could.

But think of Mary, he ordered himself. *Think of all you'll have to gain, not of what you'll lose.*

He sighed restlessly and tipped his head back. He could just make out the new moon gleaming above the rooftops, and at last he smiled. It was easy to look at the moon and think of Mary, with her silvery pale hair and her round blue eyes so full of wonder and devotion. For *him,* he thought with a good measure of wonder himself, all for him, and his smile widened with pride and pleasure.

The music inside the house stopped, followed by a giddy rush of laughter and applause. The last dance was over; the time was nearly here. Joshua swallowed hard, his fingers again itching for the phantom sword as he concentrated on the figures moving inside the house and searched for the only one that mattered to him. Any moment now, that tall door to the garden would open and his fate would be sealed.

Any moment now . . .

It was the soft *shush* of silk taffeta behind him that Joshua heard first, the rush of layered petticoats brushing against the rosebushes as the woman hurried toward him. Though her footsteps were muted by the wet grass, her breathing wasn't, rapid little gasps from running, or maybe fear. Aye, definitely fear: why else would she be running so hard? He didn't want to look away from the door, not now, but experience had trained him to watch his back, and reluctantly he turned, just as the girl crashed into his chest.

He caught her as best he could, his fingers spreading over the slippery brocade around her waist to steady her. She was short and round and her hair beneath his nose smelled wonderfully of violets, all things Joshua realized in the same jumbled second. She didn't try to pull away, but stayed pressed against him like some small wild creature who'd found shelter at last, albeit a small wild creature with jeweled bracelets so heavy he could feel them clear through his waistcoat and shirt. She was a lady, then, not some wayward servingmaid. No matter how fine, how delightful she was to hold, he must remember that.

"Oh, sir," she said breathlessly, a quiver to her words. "Oh, sir, you must help me! You *must!*"

"Help you how, ma'am?" Joshua still hadn't seen the girl's face, hidden as it was by shadows, but from her voice he'd wager she was very young. Uneasily he looked back over his shoulder to the still-closed door. Did he truly have time to squander rescuing some faceless girl from her overardent sweetheart? "You say I must help you, sweet, but how?"

3

"There's no time to explain!" she cried. Anxiously, she looked back over her shoulder. "He's close on my heels, and if he catches me—oh, what he'll do if he catches me!"

Joshua didn't know who the *he* was, and he didn't care. The way she'd fluttered against his chest in fear had convinced him. How long could such a small act of gallantry take, anyway? A minute, two at most? Surely his own affairs could wait that much longer. And how could he refuse her, when she'd been desperate enough to turn to a stranger like him for protection?

Gently he set the girl down, where she promptly scuttled behind his broad back for safety. "There now. Do you think I'd let him catch you?"

"Let him?" she squeaked. "Oh, sir, I pray you won't do that!"

"Then save your prayers, lass," said Joshua firmly. "Whoever he is, I won't let the rascal harm you."

"Blast you, Belle, where th' devil are you hidin'?" muttered a man's voice crossly as he thrashed his way through the boxwood and rosebushes, twigs cracking with every footstep. "Show yourself directly, an' I won't give you the beatin' you deserve!"

"There's Mr. Branbrook now!" said the girl to Joshua in a whispered wail. "Pray, pray, do be careful! He has a most fearful, wicked temper!"

But the man that staggered into the clearing didn't strike Joshua as either fearful or wicked. Foolish, aye, Josh would grant him that, and young and drunk in the bargain, but not fearful. How could he be, with his wig sliding haphazardly over one ear and his full-skirted coat inside out?

"Show yourself, Anabelle!" the man ordered, weaving on his feet as he scowled shortsightedly into the

4

shadows. "Show yourself now, you cheatin' little chit!"

Joshua frowned, aware of how the girl had shrunk even farther behind him. He hated bullies, particularly ones who chose women as their victims.

"The lady doesn't welcome your company," he said, his voice rumbling low with effortless authority. "Clear off, and leave her in peace."

The man's head jerked up in response. "Who th' devil are you? What right d'you have to address me at all?"

"What right do *you* have to go chasing this poor lady?"

"That is between Miss Crosbie and myself, you impudent bastard," said the man warmly. "Now stand aside, or must I use force?"

This Mr. Branbrook *was* drunk, decided Joshua, else he'd never dare speak so rashly. At least he wouldn't do it more than once. Even here in the shadows, there'd be no mistaking Joshua's height and the strength that went with it. That much would be obvious; the experience he'd gained in twenty years of taking care of himself in waterfront rumshops and taverns would be only a little less evident, but far more dangerous.

Maybe the poor dandified fool was daft *and* drunk.

"You just go on now and take yourself away," said Joshua more patiently. "I told you before, the lady doesn't want your company."

"And I say it bloody well doesn't matter what the little strumpet wants," said the man angrily, shoving his hand inside his coat. "I'm the one she must obey!"

Joshua didn't answer, nor did he wait to see what this foolish Branbrook pulled from his waistcoat. A pistol or a knife could only bring trouble, more trouble than any of them needed, and with a sigh of resignation, Joshua stepped forward and deftly caught the man's jaw with his fist.

With a grunt of surprise, Branbrook staggered backward, his legs growing looser and looser beneath him until he wobbled and crumpled to the gravel path.

"Dear Heaven, he's dead!" cried the girl as she ran forward to kneel beside the man's limp, still body. "He's dead, and you killed him!"

"Hush now. I've done no such thing." Joshua frowned. Two minutes ago, she'd been terrified of the man, and now she seemed ready to mourn him like a lost brother. "He may be dead drunk, but that's all. He'll be back on his pegs soon enough, and none the worse for it, either."

"Are you sure?" she asked anxiously, gazing up at him so that for the first time the moonlight washed over her face. "Quite, quite sure?"

Joshua nodded, unable to do much else. It wasn't that she was so astoundingly beautiful, because by current tastes, she wasn't. Her face was too round, her cheeks too full, her mouth too wide to be fashionable. What stopped his wits so completely was harder to explain. She seemed to *glow* somehow, to have a brightness and animation that he'd never seen in a woman before.

But even if he couldn't explain it, he liked it. He liked it very much. Far more, in fact, than a man in his situation had any right to.

Anabelle. That was what the man had called her. Miss Anabelle Crosbie. She would have a name like that. A coquettish fillip of a name that suited her perfectly. He remembered the violet scent of her hair and the way her small, lush body had felt pressed

6

against his chest. At least Joshua could understand now why the man had been chasing her into the garden.

With an anxious little sigh, the girl sank back on her heels so her silk skirts settled around her like a flower's petals. Her French-cut gown was cherry-red brocade patterned with gold Chinese birds, a gown that would come most dear in a mantua-maker's shop, and yet she gave the dewy grass and its consequences not a thought.

"I pray you are right, sir," she said softly. "That the poor gentleman's not deceased, that is."

With a great effort, Joshua forced himself to look away from her and to the "poor gentleman" sprawled on the gravel, his eyes peacefully closed and his mouth gaping open like a hooked fish. Joshua had seen his share of dead men. Branbrook wasn't one of them.

"He's well enough," said Joshua. "I can promise you that."

"Can you indeed?" She was studying him just as he'd studied her, her gaze lingering on Joshua's shoulders with a wary but unmistakable interest. Branbrook might have overlooked Joshua's size, but she didn't. "Then can you promise me, too, that striking him was necessary?"

"Promises have nothing to do with it, ma'am," said Joshua defensively. "He was threatening you. You came to me for help. I tried being civil to the man, but he left me no choice."

"None?" Her dark brows arched upward. "Truly?"

"Not when he reached into his coat, he didn't." Damnation, why wasn't she thanking him the way she should instead of asking all these infernal questions? He didn't need to explain himself like this. He was a

7

deep-water captain, a Fairbourne shipmaster, accountable to himself and no other man, let alone a woman.

Especially not the girl before him on the grass, where she was offering him the most astounding proof of how tightly she laced her stays.

He cleared his throat, determined not to be distracted. "The truth, ma'am, is that you don't know what he had hidden away in his waistcoat, and neither did I,"

"In truth I may *not* know, not to swear upon it, yet I doubt there's much hidden about this gentleman's person that would be a threat to me." Her brows rose even higher, her dark eyes round with a mixture of skepticism and amusement, and the first hint of a smile wobbled at the corners of her mouth. "Fancy Henry Branbrook accosting me with his pocketwatch, or perhaps a wicked snuffbox!"

Biting back an oath of exasperation, Joshua bent over the unconscious man long enough to flip back his coat and find the small pistol tucked into the deep pocket of his waistcoat, exactly where he'd suspected it would be. So much for the niceties of London gentlemen. He might have worn that sword after all.

"There," he said with grim satisfaction as he held the pistol up for the girl to see. "A sorry excuse for a weapon for a man, I'll grant you that, but still sufficient to put an untidy hole in either one of us."

But instead of the gasp of genteel horror he'd expected, the girl only peered at the pistol with open fascination.

"Whoever would have guessed Mr. Branbrook would have such a thing!" she marveled. "How vastly, vastly peculiar!"

"Not if he'd chosen to use it," said Joshua drily. Gently, he shook the gunpowder out of the pistol's pan before he tossed it into the bushes. "We're lucky he didn't, considering how far in his cups the blasted fool was. Already so drunk he'd put his coat on wrong side out."

"Oh, that's for luck, not from wine. All the gentlemen turn their coats that way in the gaming room. To help change their fortunes for the better, they say." She sighed and shook her head sadly. "If only he'd have let me try to win back fairly what I'd lost at the table instead of chasing me out here, then none of this would have happened. Twenty pounds isn't so very much to lose at loo. I could have won it back in a hand or two."

"Twenty pounds?" repeated Joshua incredulously. Twenty pounds was more than many sailors earned in a year. "You lost twenty pounds playing cards?"

Her chin ducked low with contrition, her lashes sweeping across her cheeks. "Please don't scold me," she said meekly. "Grandmother will scold me royally when she learns of this, and I couldn't bear to hear it from you, too."

But Joshua himself had heard more than enough. As charming as this girl was, it was high time he left her. Past time, really. "You must excuse me, ma'am," he said with a bow. "You'll be safe now, and I've another matter that I must—"

"Oh, but you can't leave me just yet!" she cried, scrambling to her feet. "Not before Mr. Branbrook wakes! Whatever shall I say to explain myself?"

"The truth should serve," said Joshua gruffly, glancing over her head toward the house. The drawing room door had finally opened, and the first guests were beginning to wander into the garden. "He was the one at fault, not you. Now if you will—"

"But who would believe me?" she asked plaintively, her plump little hands twisting in her skirts. "Mr.

Branbrook—the *Honorable* Mr. Henry Branbrook, you understand—his father is an earl, a peer, and mine is but a viscount, and Irish as well. Oh, you must see the appalling scandal that will come of this!"

"I'm afraid I don't, ma'am, and I can't—"

"Because you're not from London," she declared abruptly, putting a far different end to his sentence than the one he'd intended. She tipped her head to one side. "That's it, isn't it? You speak very well, considering, but I knew at once you weren't English. No, no. But you are British, aren't you?"

"What the devil else would I be?" asked Joshua indignantly, irritated that she'd dare heap insults onto bold-faced ingratitude. "I'm as British as you. I was born at Appledore, in Massachusetts, true enough, but that doesn't make—"

"Then you *will* help me." Her skirts rustling, she scurried around to grab the unconscious gentleman by his ankles, throwing her whole weight against his as she tried to tug him back from the path. "Hurry! We must move him before someone comes!"

For Joshua, there was only one *someone* that mattered, and the reminder sent a quick chill down his spine. He'd no more wish to be caught here between Anabelle Crosbie and her honorable Mr. Branbrook than she did.

"I don't see what difference this makes," he said, even as he helped drag the other man back into the shadows. "No matter where we stow him, he'll still be some blasted earl's son, won't he?"

"Yes, but over there beneath the boxwoods, he won't be noticed until he chooses to show himself," she said breathlessly. "And if I'm very fortunate, he won't remember a thing about—oh, merciful dear, someone's coming!"

She craned her neck back to look back down the path and dropped the man's feet with a clumsy thud.

"Damnation, you can't stop now!" whispered Joshua sharply. Branbrook's inside-out coat snagged on a branch, and the harder Joshua yanked at it, the more tangled in the boxwood it became, while one of the unconscious lord's arms awkwardly flopped out across the grass. "You take his arm, and I'll—"

"There's no time!" she whispered urgently. "Quick, there's only one way!"

She darted forward and grabbed Joshua's arm, turning him so that his back was to the path. "You must shield me, like so," she said breathlessly, "and no one will notice Mr. Branbrook."

"Why the devil—"

"Because no one *ever* sees lovers in a garden!" She reached up to slip her little hands around Joshua's shoulders and pulled his face down to her level. Her expression was determined, her dark eyes serious. "It truly is the only way."

Before Joshua could protest, she was kissing him, her lips warm and soft against his. Perhaps she'd intended only a pretend kiss, a diversion meant for others, but Joshua knew better. It wouldn't be possible, not for her, and especially not for him.

And unfortunately, he was right. Not that he'd *wanted* to kiss her in return—damnation, he hadn't even wanted to be kissed in the first place—but when he felt the inexperienced eagerness of her lips, he felt every resolve, every denial, slip fast away. Despite her boldness, she still tasted of innocence, of the same bright, untouched promise that he'd seen in her face. His fingers threaded and tangled into the neat silken waves of her hair, cradling her face as he coaxed her lips apart and changed the perfunctory kiss into something else, something deeper, darker, and infinitely more seductive.

He broke away long enough to brush his lips over the velvety curve of her cheek, sweet and full like a summer peach.

"Oh, my," she murmured, her eyes dreamy and a blissfully surprised smile on her face. "Oh, my, my!"

She did that to him, too. She had done it, he realized as he kissed her again, from the moment she'd hurtled into his chest.

"Joshua!"

Mary's voice was shrill with shock, a single word that pierced straight through Joshua's guilty conscience. Instantly, he broke away from Anabelle, smoothing his hair and straightening his coat sleeves, and turned to face Miss Mary Holme.

Instantly, but not nearly fast enough. He knew that as soon as he saw the look on Mary's face.

"Is this what you wished me to see, Joshua?" she said, her voice icy and distant. "Is this why you asked me to meet you here?"

"Mary, sweet, this isn't what it seems," began Joshua, horribly conscious of Anabelle peeking around his arm. "This lady and I—"

"I do not care to hear your explanations, Joshua Fairbourne," snapped Mary. She stood so straight and motionless in her cream-colored gown that she might have been another garden statue. "I do not wish to hear anything at all from you ever again."

Desperately, Joshua held his hand out to her. "Don't say such things, Mary, not like that. If you'd only listen to what—"

"Good *night,* Joshua." She turned on her heel and marched back toward the house, her back an inflexible line of wounded fury.

"What a *vastly* disagreeable woman," said Anabelle. "I cannot fathom why she should speak to you in such a shrewish, ill-bred manner. Whyever do you care what she thinks?"

"Why?" Joshua's laugh was hollow. "Because this evening, in this garden, I'd meant to ask her to be my wife."

❧ Two ❧

"You cannot continue in this fashion, Anabelle," said Grandmother sternly. "I refuse to countenance such behavior in any person living beneath my roof and in the shelter of my good name. It is not to be borne, miss, not for another day or night."

"No, Grandmother," said Anabelle miserably, her shoulders sinking lower beneath the weight of her shame. "That is, I meant, yes, Grandmother, it is not to be borne."

Grandmother sniffed impatiently and thumped her walking stick on the parquet floor, hard enough to rattle the cups on the tea table at her side. She was the Dowager Marchioness of Auboncourt, and her patience was notoriously short.

"Anabelle, you are the most obstinate, willful, wicked creature I have ever encountered. It is without doubt your Irish blood. I am entirely convinced of it. Sit up, girl, sit up! One would think that you were born with a serpent in place of your spine!"

"Yes, Grandmother." Dutifully, Anabelle drew back her aching shoulders and lifted her chin the way Grandmother demanded. Chin raised but eyes demurely downcast, shoulders back and bosom high, ankles crossed and hands carefully arranged to rest in the hollow of her lap—how wretchedly difficult it was to be a lady! She hated sitting here on this taboret in the middle of the drawing room. She hated the dreadful stool with the prickly covering almost as much as she hated knowing she'd failed yet again to live up to Grandmother's expectations.

She felt a tearful tremor at the back of her throat and swallowed hard to keep it away. Back home with her father at Kilmarsh Hall or visiting her Dublin cousins or her married brothers, she'd never had trouble behaving. But here in London, where such things mattered so very much, she seemed always at fault, always acting too rashly or wantonly or unmannerly. She would never make a suitable match. She would never marry at all, and she would be sent back home, a long-toothed spinster and a disgraceful drain on her father's estate. Already she could see the unspeakable precipice yawning before her. She was, Heaven help her, nearly seventeen.

"Do you know where this course will take you, Anabelle?" demanded Grandmother as if she'd read Anabelle's thoughts. "Can you tell me that much, you silly girl?"

"No gentleman will honor me with an offer of marriage," said Anabelle promptly and as clearly as she could. Grandmother despised mumbling and considered it a mark of ill breeding. "And I shall be sent home to Kilmarsh in disgrace."

"Kilmarsh, hah," scoffed Grandmother. "More likely you'll end your days pounding hemp in Bridewell with all the other strumpets. You certainly won't be Lady Henry Branbrook, not after last night's debacle."

"No, Grandmother," said Anabelle with a desolate sigh. The unpleasant memory of Mr. Branbrook's groaning return to life and the accusations that had come with it was not a thing soon forgotten. "I do not believe that very likely."

"Most assuredly you will not attend any more assemblies or gatherings without me. I could not believe the tale I heard this morning from my friend Mrs. Everly." Down came Grandmother's stick again on the floor with a crack of fresh displeasure. "Your first mistake was to join Henry Branbrook at the gaming table. How many times must I tell you that ladies do not play?"

"But the tables were filled with ladies!" protested Anabelle. "I never would have agreed to sit down otherwise!"

"Married ladies, Anabelle—married ladies with indulgent husbands," said Grandmother sternly. "Your state is altogether different. If a gentleman sees a maiden lady so willing to lose her stake to him at the tables, then of course his thoughts shall turn to what else she may be coaxed into losing."

"It was only twenty pounds at loo, Grandmother," said Anabelle defensively. "Not even a dullard like Mr. Branbrook would believe I'd wager my maidenhead for that piddling sum."

Grandmother winced, the Alençon lace on her widow's cap quivering in sympathy with her outraged sensibilities, and too late Anabelle realized she'd sinned again.

"The playing table was only the beginning, Anabelle," she said. "How did you become entangled with this brawling brute of a man in the garden?"

"Oh, no, Grandmother, Mr. Fairbourne wasn't a

brute at all!" cried Anabelle. "He was most kind to me and protected me when Mr. Branbrook's attentions became too—too demanding. He was from a place called Massachusetts. A Scots gentleman, I believe, though surprisingly genteel in his speech."

"A Scots gentleman," repeated Grandmother in disbelief. "Massachusetts being a town near, oh, Edinburgh?"

Anabelle nodded eagerly. "While he did not tell the exact county of his residence, he was much too agreeable to have come from anywhere too far removed from town."

With considerable effort, Grandmother rose from her chair and took the handful of steps necessary to reach the globe that stood beside the window. She traced a single finger along the globe's mottled surface, her head held back so she could make out the tiny Latin writing over the curved surface.

"There," pronounced Grandmother at last, her finger jabbing at a large pale pink splotch of a country. "There, Anabelle, is Massachusetts. And there," she continued, spinning the globe a quarter turn, "is Edinburgh."

"Is it?" asked Anabelle faintly.

Grandmother tapped her finger against the globe, the sun through the window glancing green through the emerald on her ring. "It most certainly is. As you can see, there is only the small matter of an entire ocean between them."

Anabelle nodded, the only sensible course. She was nearly sure that the water beneath Grandmother's finger was the Irish Sea, or maybe the English Channel, but she didn't wish to risk a new lecture on her sorrowful lack of education.

Grandmother nodded, too, satisfied that she'd made her point, and sank back into her armchair.

"Your so-called Scots gentleman is neither a Scot nor a gentleman. Mrs. Everly confirmed that for me. He is an American colonist, doubtless but a generation removed from naked savages. Worse still, he is a common sailor—some say even a pirate."

"A sailor?" repeated Anabelle, her voice squeaking upward with surprise. "A *pirate?* Oh, I do not think it possible! Why would Lady Willoughby have invited him to her assembly if he were only a sailor?"

"He was there as a favor to some tradesman of Lady Willougby's acquaintance, nothing more," said Grandmother with a contemptuous sniff. "Doubtless she owes the man some enormous sum and saw this as a way to placate him. But you can see the sorrow that comes of such familiarity. Imagine fisticuffs in Lady Willoughby's rose garden! I understand poor Branbrook is fortunate to have survived."

"I still cannot believe such things of Mr. Fairbourne," said Anabelle sadly, her shoulders sagging once again. "An American—and a sailor!"

"Such things must be believed, Anabelle, when they are true." Grandmother dabbed at her nose with her handkerchief, watching Anabelle closely. "Was the rogue so very handsome, then?"

"He was," said Anabelle, her sadness deepening to sorrow with those two words alone. Mr. Fairbourne *had* been handsome, the most beautifully handsome man she'd yet met since coming to London. Not that he'd been like any of the others. For one thing, he'd worn his own hair instead of a wig, thick and black and gleaming like a raven's wing in the moonlight, and he hadn't daubed his face with powder or patches like all the other young gentlemen. He hadn't needed to, not with features as even and carved as his. He had reminded her of the ancient statues of pagan gods she'd seen here in London, except that his eyes hadn't been blank white marble but a startling blue.

And when she'd kissed him, he hadn't been cold marble, either. She felt warm all over again just remembering, and she looked down at her clasped hands to hide her confusion from Grandmother. She was at a loss for the right words to describe how he'd kissed her back, just as she hadn't known the proper name for that sea or ocean. Still, she sensed that it had been special and rare and something not to be found with every man, and that only Mr. Fairbourne would be able to make her feel that marvelous, magical way.

Marvelous and magical and never, ever again.

"By the light of the day, he might have been quite different, you know," said Grandmother. "Unsuitable men generally are."

"Yes, Grandmother," said Anabelle with dutiful, unhappy resignation.

"Indeed, yes." Impatiently, Grandmother tapped her fingers on the arm of the chair. "Love has nothing to do with happiness, you know. The best marriages in Britain are based on respect and suitability, not on love."

Anabelle nodded. What else could she do? She knew she'd been wrong to dream, foolish to hope. Even a Scots gentleman would have been deemed an inappropriate suitor. Grandmother had set her heart—hers, and Anabelle's with it—on at least an earl's son, and it wouldn't matter one whit that last night Mr. Fairbourne had behaved toward her with more gallantry and good humor than all the titled ninnies she'd had paraded before her combined.

And that, of course, was quite ignoring the fact that he'd been in Lady Willoughby's garden to ask another woman to marry him. In Anabelle's opinion, that

other woman had been a sorry-looking shrew, pale
and wispy with a tongue sharp as a poker, but that
didn't matter, either. Mr. Fairbourne was perfectly
entitled to chose his own wife. Or he would have been
had Anabelle not blundered into the middle of his
proposal and spoiled it all.

Lord help her, could she do nothing right?

"In a week's time, you will have forgotten the rascal
entirely. You will see how it is, Anabelle," promised
Grandmother with what, for her, was a smile, the
lines around her mouth deepening in her paint. "Now
come, you foolish child, give me your arm. I've some
things in the west parlor that should cheer your
ungrateful soul."

Anabelle helped the older woman to her feet and
guided her from the sitting room and down the long
gallery. Grandmother leaned heavily on her shoulder,
depending on Anabelle instead of her walking stick
for support across the slippery polished floors. They
made slow progress, Anabelle small and trudging
beside her more stately grandmother, who refused
both to wear the spectacles she needed or to abandon
the high-heeled shoes she'd always favored.

"With the hope that we will soon arrange a suitable
match for you, I had some of your mother's belongings sent down from Auboncourt," explained Grandmother as they crept along. "I thought a few of the
gowns from her wedding clothes might be taken apart
and made over for your own. The lace and the silks
are still like new, for heaven knows your poor mother
had no use for such finery at Kilmarsh. Outrageously
dear they were, too, even twenty-five years ago. But
your grandfather would indulge himself in dressing
his daughter for her wedding as he did in everything
else."

Anabelle didn't answer, knowing all too well that

"everything else" referred to the fact that her father, a short, stocky Irish viscount, was willing to trade an indecent part of his fortune for the lovely daughter of an English marquis, a girl he'd seen only once at a distance. Burdened with debts and embarrassments beyond his means, Grandfather had agreed, and Anabelle's sixteen-year-old mother had been wed to a man she'd never directly addressed. The cautious, complicated financial matchmaking that all such noble families made had been a complete success; the marriage, alas, had not.

That the marriage was a failure was common enough knowledge, just as it was commonly known that Anabelle's grandmother had ceased speaking to her grandfather on the day of the wedding and had not broken her silence even to ease his deathbed. To Grandmother, the marriage had been a grim and woeful debacle, a battle against her husband that she'd lost, and one that had banished her only daughter to the unspeakable wilds of County Kildare. No wonder Grandmother was determined that Anabelle wouldn't repeat such a disaster.

"I had the first trunks unpacked earlier so we could see what there was," continued Grandmother as a footman opened the door for them. "Plenty of work for the seamstresses, in any event. What a pity you don't have your mother's pretty figure or her height! Ah, well, there's no help for it now. You are as likely to grow taller at your age as I am to sprout wings at mine."

Not wings, thought Anabelle mutinously as the footman tugged open the parlor curtains, but if a pair of horns and a spiked tail suddenly appeared on her grandmother, she wouldn't be in the least surprised. She knew perfectly well that she'd never be a great beauty like her mother. She didn't need reminding, and with a dismal sigh, she wished once again she were back home. At least no one at Kilmarsh judged her too short or too plump.

And neither, she knew, had Mr. Fairbourne.

As the light spilled in through the windows, she could see how the parlor had been transformed into a mantua-maker's fantasy. Bodices and gowns and petticoats had been carefully laid across nearly every chair and table, the rich silk brocades and satins still gleaming like jewels despite the decades-old creases and fold lines. Two more trunks stood open back to back in the center of the room with their lids propped to display drifts of beautifully embroidered white linen: cuffs and neckerchiefs, fanciful aprons, and caps in the style of the old queen.

"There now, Anabelle," said Grandmother, waving her hand with a flourish that encompassed the entire room as she sat in the single bare armchair. "Surely even you must be impressed."

"Yes, Grandmother," murmured Anabelle. This time, they could agree, for not one of these beautiful gowns reminded her of her mother. She had been only six when Mama died, but the mother she remembered had always been dressed for riding, in plain dark wool that smelled of horses and the wind. Riding had been the one sure way she could escape Father's jealousy and ranting. Those were the times that Mama laughed, or so it seemed in Anabelle's memory, Mama with her wide-brimmed hat askew and bits of hay clinging to her auburn hair.

Lightly, Anabelle stroked the flounced sleeve of a gown of rose silk, shot with silver. Her mother had had these clothes made for her wedding, and her marriage had been desperately unhappy. What would become of Anabelle if she, too, wore them? Were they nothing more than silk and linen, or did they have the power to curse her wedding as well? Reluctantly, she gathered up the gown from the chair, holding it high against her body with one arm so the hem wouldn't drag on the floor.

"An excellent choice," said Grandmother with a sage nod. "With your dark hair, Anabelle, you can wear the less delicate colors. Turn now, turn! Let me see how it suits you!"

With a little pirouette, Anabelle did as she was ordered, the heavy silk swirling around her. But before she could finish the circle, she came to an abrupt halt, and with a little cry, she let the gown slip from her fingers.

"What is it now, Anabelle?" demanded Grandmother. "Have you been pricked by a pin?"

"Oh, no, no, it's just that this—*this* I remember! This was our cradle, John's and George's and Gerald's and mine!"

"Not just yours, child, but your mother's." Grandmother sighed deeply, her usual sharpness softened by bittersweet associations of her own. "The cradle was hers, and mine, and my mother's before that. It belongs to the women of our family, not the men. Your father would likely have turned it into a kennel for his wretched dogs if I hadn't insisted on having it back."

But Anabelle barely heard Grandmother as she ran her fingertips along the mellowed old oak. When she'd been a child, the cradle had sat near the hearth in her parents' bedchamber, in constant readiness to shelter the next babe that came their way. To Anabelle then, it had seemed enormous, and miraculously it had remained so, large enough for twins or even triplets. The style was old-fashioned now, the rails and turnings on the sides thick and bulbous and the rockers were the massive arches of the last century. But the fat-cheeked cherub carved into the hood still smiled with the same surpassing sweetness that echoed the contentment of three generations of mothers, and every nick and scratch in the well-worn wood held a story of its own.

"The cradle will come to you next, Anabelle," Grandmother was saying. "That is, it will once you are married and on the way to bearing children of your own. Perhaps that will encourage you to be more agreeable to the proper gentlemen."

"I shall try, Grandmother," said Anabelle softly, solemnly. She wanted babies, lots of them. She always had. Mama had sworn fervently that her children were the single greatest blessing of her life, and Anabelle had believed her. Not having any of her own, leaving the cradle empty, would be the worst part of being a spinster. "Truly I shall."

But Grandmother was already plotting the next move in Anabelle's campaign, tapping her stick while she thought.

"Branbrook may not be completely lost to us," she said, considering. "Thus far, he has been most open and honorable in his attentions to you. His mother assures me that this is the year he will be decided upon a wife. If we are fortunate, it shall be you. He would not have followed you into that garden last night if he did not have a certain regard for you."

Anabelle knew better. Henry Branbrook had chased her into the garden because he'd thought she'd cheated him at loo—which she most certainly had not, else she would have *won*—and whatever regard he'd had for her last night had not been honorable. Open, yes, but not honorable.

She sighed deeply, her hand resting on the cradle's rounded hood. She would do well to remember that she'd been sent to London to find a proper husband, whether Branbrook or another gentleman. That was the first step toward starting a family of her own. Her mother had found some measure of happiness through her children, and Anabelle would, too. She'd let the cradle be her reminder, just as Grandmother and Mama would wish it. Beginning today, now, this moment, she would truly try her best to be good and to do what was right.

Truly.

"You have much to sort out, Anabelle, much to put to rights," Grandmother was saying. "But I believe the challenge will not be too great for you, if only you learn to consider your actions and guard your impulses."

Anabelle smiled. She *would* put everything she'd unsettled back to rights. And she knew exactly where she'd begin.

"You understand how it is with my Mary, don't you, Captain Fairbourne?" Mrs. Holme wrung her hands in her apron as she watched her daughter through the window, then sighed so deeply that the whalebones in her stays creaked in sympathy. "A sweet girl is my Mary, Captain, a dear, gentle girl. How she wept last night, the poor lamb, how she suffered!"

Trapped at the window beside Mrs. Holme, Joshua found it difficult to judge the depth of Mary's suffering for himself. She looked as lovely as ever, sitting on the bench beneath the alder tree with her neat, gold head bowed over the book in her hand. That pleased him; he expected his wife to be able to teach their children to read. The only problem was that in the entire time he'd stood there, Mary had yet to turn a page, leaving him with the uncomfortable suspicion that she'd chosen the book because the color of its leather bindings complemented her petticoats.

But couldn't that be one more sign of the depth of Mary's suffering? That though she'd make a brave show of being unaffected, she was still far too distraught to be able to focus on her book?

"If you'd only let me speak to her, Mrs. Holme," he asked urgently, "I know I could explain so she'd understand what happened last night."

"Alas, dear captain, alas, no, it is not possible!" Mrs. Holme sighed and wrung and sighed again. "If it were up to me alone, I would take you to her myself, indeed I would. 'Tis far better to lance a suppurating boil, I say, then to let it fester and grow until the pain's beyond bearing. But Mr. Holme has forbidden it, and Mary herself wept again at the very mention of seeing you again. Her constitution is that tender, Captain, as tender as any lady's in London."

Joshua didn't like being compared to a boil, particularly one that was suppurating. He thought that was a bit strong even for Mrs. Holme. But he couldn't argue that Mary's constitution was tender. He'd wanted a London lady to take back home to Appledore as his wife, and Miss Mary Holme was the most genteel, the most refined, the most ladylike girl he'd ever met.

"It was the shock that distressed her so, you see," continued Mrs. Holme. "The nature of the upset, Captain. To see another woman in your arms, sir, and a woman like that Miss Crosbie!"

Joshua frowned. "Mary is, ah, acquainted with Miss Crosbie?" he asked uncomfortably. He'd not thought his situation could grow much worse, but this—this would do it. "They didn't seem as if they did."

Mrs. Holme clucked her tongue. "Nay, and a very good thing, too! But everyone knows *of* Miss Crosbie, if you take my meaning, Captain. A wild, bold girl, they say, always at the very eye of scandal. Now I don't care if she's gentry with blood as blue as the queen's, nor that she'll bring a grand portion as a bride. The truth is, Captain, that no decent gentleman will put his name to a woman who behaves commonly, and that's Miss Crosbie."

Joshua's frown deepened. Though there were many words he'd use to describe Miss Crosbie—he had the sense to repeat none of them to Mrs. Holme—*common* wasn't one of them. Not that it mattered. He'd no intention or likelihood of ever seeing Anabelle Crosbie again.

Or so he'd been telling himself over and over again since last night.

Mrs. Holme patted his sleeve. "There now, Captain, I know you've suffered, too," she said with maternal understanding. "How can you be faulted for your behavior with a little strumpet like that? My Mary will come 'round, don't worry. She'll come 'round to you again."

As if on cue, Mary turned and gazed wanly up at the window. Though her round blue eyes seemed clear of tears now, her cheeks were nearly as pale as the linen kerchief around her throat. He had done this to her, thought Joshua gloomily, he and that wretched little chit in the red silk. Instead of making Mary laugh and be happy, he'd made her cry the night through, and it wasn't something of which he was particularly proud.

He bowed stiffly toward her, and she nodded back. She wasn't smiling, but then she hadn't looked away once she'd spotted him, either. Perhaps he still did have a chance, if he could only explain to her.

"May I have a word with Mary now, Mrs. Holme?" he asked, hurriedly running his palm over his hair to smooth the waves. "Nothing to upset her, mind, but a word or two to reassure her that my intentions haven't changed. I could ask her right now if she'll have me. That would settle everything, wouldn't it?"

"Not this day, Captain, no," said Mrs. Holme, her voice an odd mixture of severity and sympathetic regret. "Perhaps tomorrow, or the day after. Then you may consider renewing your suit. But what dear Mary needs most now is time."

Impatiently, Joshua shook his head. "If I had the time, I'd give it to her, ma'am," he said. "I'd give her whatever she wants to make her happy. You know that. But I've only a week, a fortnight at most, before I'll finish taking on my cargo and clear for home."

"A fortnight, sir?" repeated Mrs. Holme with wounded doubt as her hand slipped pointedly from his sleeve. "Only a fortnight to spare for wooing my Mary?"

"Aye, a fortnight remaining," said Joshua, irritated by her feigned forgetfulness. Marrying her daughter was hardly some impulsive whim on his part; he'd known Mary Holme through her father since she'd been a child. The day he'd arrived, he'd made arrangements for the license, and it was only this last formality, Joshua's actually asking her to be his wife, that remained. "You and your husband know that as well as I do. Maybe better, since half of my hold will be filled with his goods, and at a damned favorable rate to him, too."

Instantly, an icy distance froze Mrs. Holme's cheerful, motherly face. "You would discuss trade in my front parlor, Captain Fairbourne?"

"Why the devil not?" he demanded. "You're a

merchant's wife, aren't you? Where's the shame in that?"

"Perhaps in the colonies, trade is considered a genteel topic," she said, her scorn intended to wither. "But in London, Captain, it is not, especially not in my parlor."

"You wouldn't even have this blasted parlor without trade!"

"That is between you and my husband, Captain Fairbourne," she said tartly. "Good day to you, sir."

"Now hold a moment, ma'am, and let me—"

"I believe you know the way to the door, Captain," she said, her manner growing more frosty by the second. "Or need I summon one of the servants to show you out?"

For Mary's sake, Joshua bit back everything he wanted to say. For her sake alone, he'd swallow his impatience and anger. Mary was a prize worth capturing. But once they were wed and safely back in Massachusetts, he'd never have to see—or hear—her pretentious fool of a mother again, a thought that pleased him mightily. For now, he'd have to be satisfied with a single curt bow in Mrs. Holme's direction and a final, tantalizing look at Mary in the garden. He didn't bother waiting for the serving girl to hand him his hat, sweeping it from the table in the hall himself, and he opened and slammed the heavy front door shut without assistance, either.

Front parlor, hell. He hoped Mrs. Holme was mortally offended.

He jammed his hat on his head and turned to begin the long walk back to the river. Though the Holmes' house, brick with black-painted shutters and a solid three stories high, reflected their growing prosperity, the streets around it were narrow and noisy, crowded with jumbling carts and carriages and ruddy-faced women from the country crying out the prices of the vegetables and fruit they offered for sale from their baskets.

But the peddlers' cries weren't the worst thing to crowd the air. To him, the Holmes' neighborhood smelled every bit as foul as the rest of London on a summer's day, the relentless stench of rot and filth and too many people living in too close quarters. He'd been in London nearly a month, and he still wasn't accustomed to it. God help him if he ever was, he thought glumly, and sidestepped the decaying carcass of some mongrel dog in his path. Mary wouldn't believe the difference between this and Appledore, and with a sharp pang of homesickness, he remembered the clean, sweet air that came from the bay and over the white sand and wild marsh roses and bayberries and into the tall open casements of his new house on the crest of—

"Beg pardon, sir," huffed the stout man in dark blue livery suddenly trotting beside him. "Beg pardon, sir, but could you draw up for a bit, sir?"

Joshua stopped, and with a sigh of relief, the footman did, too, his face blotchy and moist from exertion and his stockings drooping as he tried to collect his breath and deliver his message with some semblance of straight-backed dignity. "Beg pardon, sir, but my lady's wanting to speak with you."

Immediately, Joshua thought of Mary, and his hopes soared. But as prosperous as her father had become, the Holmes kept no footmen yet, especially not stout ones in powder-dusted wigs and silver-laced coats, and Joshua's hopes plummeted back to earth.

"A lady?" he asked, his dark brows settling low beneath the brim of his hat, a black match for his mood. "What lady?"

The footman was careful to keep his eyes focused somewhere around the middle button of Joshua's waistcoat. "You should not keep her waiting in this sun, sir," he chided. "'Tis not kind."

"I should not, eh?" Joshua's frown deepened, a frown that would have sent the *Swiftsure*'s crew scurrying with dread but seemed to have no effect on this poxy footman. "I'll damned well make your mistress wait until Judgment Day unless you tell me her name."

"She asked me specific to say nothing, sir," answered the footman, "save that she had a matter most urgent to discuss with you. Most urgent, sir. If you please, sir, her chariot is just there, near the corner."

Joshua's gaze followed the man's pointing finger to the waiting chariot, which gleamed like a great lacquered beetle in the afternoon sun, the pair of bay horses stomping restlessly and flicking their tails against the flies. First a liveried servant, and now a chariot decked out with gilt and some lord's crest on the door: against his better judgment and his ill humor, too, Joshua's curiosity rose. Perhaps it was some friend of Mary's, relaying a message from her to him. There'd been plenty of carriages as grand as this one waiting outside that infernal party last night.

"Most urgent, sir," said the footman again. "My lady would not ask you otherwise."

"Very well," said Joshua with a sigh of resignation. "A moment, and no more."

The footman scurried ahead to flip down the small folding step to the chariot and to open the door above it. Wryly, Joshua smiled at that useless little step, imagining the consequences if he actually tried to make use of it, and he smiled, too, at how differently the other passersby were regarding him now, openly gawking to discover his connection to the chariot. He was smiling still as he pulled off his hat and bent his head to climb into the chariot, blinking to make his eyes adjust to its shadowy depths after the sunshine outside.

At last they did, and he saw who was there. His smile toppled clear to the soles of his shoes.

"Oh, hell," he said. "Why the devil didn't I *know?*"

❧ *Three* ❧

"Not perhaps the most gracious of greetings," said Anabelle cheerfully, "but I shall accept it, indeed I shall. I did not believe you'd come at all, you know, but you did, and how *vastly* glad I am of it."

"But you, ma'am?" said Joshua, still inarticulate with dismay. *"You?"*

She laughed with delight at his reaction. "I *am* your odious 'you,' I suppose, which is to say that you am I. Or would it be you is me? Grandmother says I'm barbarously ill educated, and alas, this must prove how right she is."

"You are you, ma'am," said Joshua firmly, "and I am I, and you will never be either me or I."

Her laughter bubbled up again and she spread her fingers over her lips like a wayward child. "But you did call me you, so though I make no claims to being you, not me, I still must be you, else you must be mistaken about me. Or is it you?"

Joshua stared, almost afraid to speak. He had never

known any woman—or any other man, for that matter—who could twist and turn and tangle words around into such a knot of self-betrayal.

His words, blast her.

But staring at her didn't help, not one whit. She was leaning back against the dun-colored squabs, as close to outright lolling as she could in stays. He hadn't forgotten the bewitching effect of those stays on her person from last night, and he was sorry to see that his memory hadn't failed him.

Well, perhaps not exactly *sorry*. Her goldenrod silk gown was cut every bit as low for day as the one she'd worn last evening, though around her neck she'd twined a kerchief of black lace for modesty, weaving the ends through the ribbon lacing of her stomacher. But in some irrational fashion, the kerchief seemed to reveal more than it hid, her bosom beneath the black lace kissed with a rosy sheen by the heat in the chariot.

He tried to think of Mary instead, Mary pale and languid on her garden bench beneath the alder. But all he saw were vivid gold skirts, spilling around him like the summer sun bottled tight inside the chariot, and the tiny pointed toe of a silk mule twirling idle circles in the air.

"I must go, ma'am," said Joshua hoarsely. "Now."

Swiftly, he rose to his feet and thumped his head into the low ceiling of the chariot so hard that he toppled backward onto the empty seat. The driver interpreted the thump as a signal to start, and before Joshua could rise again, the footman had shut and latched the door, and with a scrape of iron-bound wheels, the chariot lurched forward into the street.

"We can go together," she said evenly, though her eyes continued to sparkle with silent laughter beneath the curled brim of her hat. "It is not a long journey to the docks, I know, so we must use the time wisely. At least I must, for I am the one who has erred so grievously."

Gingerly, Joshua rubbed the top of his head, already feeling the tender beginnings of a lump. It was his own fault. After twenty years of ducking his head against the low beams 'tween decks, he should have known better, just as he should have known better than to let himself be kidnapped like some cully from the country.

"Ma'am, I must ask you to stop—"

"No, no, I must ask *you* to stop first," she declared with an imperious wave, the whitework engageantes fluttering around her elbows. "You must stop your 'ma'am' this and 'ma'am' that. I am a spinster, dismally unwed, and not entitled to such courtesies. My name is Miss Anabelle Crosbie of County Kildare. A great deal less wieldy than your simple 'ma'am,' I'll grant, but since I'm giving you leave to use my name, you must do so."

Joshua sighed, wishing his head hurt less so he could think more clearly. "I am Captain Joshua Fairbourne. Your servant, ma'am—that is, Miss Crosbie."

"La, so Grandmother was wrong," said Anabelle, "and you do have a title. Captain Joshua Fairbourne! A captain, and one who wishes to be my servant, too!"

Lord help him, she was doing it again. "I didn't mean it like that," he grumbled, "as you know perfectly well. I was only speaking civilly. If I'm not careful, you'll have me trussed up like that fat little jackanapes riding outside."

"Prentiss is plump because Grandmother spoils him with sausages and sugar cakes as though he were

3 5

some old spaniel." Her gaze slid over him apprais-
ingly. "I do not believe that will ever happen to you,
Captain Fairbourne."

Joshua snorted. "It won't happen because I'd never
spend my days waiting on some woman's pleasure.
Sausages and sugar cakes! No honest man would
choose such a life."

"I suppose not," agreed Anabelle amicably. "But
then I don't believe even my grandmother regards
Prentiss as outstandingly honest. It's not really to be
expected in servants."

"Nor in the ladies of the family, I'll wager." Joshua
sighed with exasperation. "Not that you'd be in the
way of noticing."

"No, indeed." She smiled, refusing to be insulted.
Sometimes a little dishonesty was a useful thing; if
Prentiss hadn't been willing to be bribed into compla-
cency, she wouldn't be here with Captain Fairbourne
in Grandmother's chariot. "I'm too well bred to
notice anything."

She knew she should begin the apologies and repa-
rations that had led her here to him in the first place,
but she was enjoying herself in his company so much
that it was nigh impossible to stop.

She also knew she talked too much. She always had,
even as a child, and by now every other gentleman in
her family or acquaintance would have cut her off,
ignored her, or simply ordered her to be quiet. But
Captain Fairbourne was listening to her, really listening to her foolish babble; his expression was so
intense that it bordered on gravity. She could fall in
love with him for that alone. She really could. It
would be most wonderfully easy—and wonderfully
disastrous, too.

But making the trap more tempting still was Captain Fairbourne's own appallingly handsome self,

with his eyes exactly the same shade of blue as the summer sky at twilight and the wool of his coat stretched taut across the broad expanse of his shoulders. The heat in the chariot had curled his black hair in the most charmingly boyish way beneath the brim of his hat, a way that made her long to trace her finger along his brow.

He would be wasted—*wasted*—on that whey-faced tradesman's daughter he wanted to marry, while Anabelle herself would never find a suitable gentleman with half this one's attractions. She wanted to weep from the unfairness of it. Instead, she sighed deeply and began the penance she'd set for herself.

"Last night, Captain Fairbourne," she said contritely, "you did me a great favor. Now I shall try to do the same for you, by way of thanks."

"Hush, missy, none of that." Joshua shifted his shoulders uncomfortably. He didn't want any woman feeling she owed him a blessed thing, especially not this one. "You're not beholden to me for anything."

"But I am, and perhaps this way I can put it to rights." She twisted the ends of her kerchief around her finger, avoiding his eyes. "Even before I muddled things for you with your Miss Holme, your suit with her was in peril. Not from Miss Holme's own wishes or her father's, either, but from her mother's."

"That's ridiculous," scoffed Joshua. "Mrs. Holme and I have always gotten on like blazes."

"Like blazes, then, and straight to them, too," said Anabelle soundly. "Mrs. Holme is the same as every other London mama with aspirations beyond her station. To be dreadfully blunt, she wants better than you for her daughter. She will contrive every way she can to keep you from making your formal offer to Miss Holme, even if it means keeping you two apart until you sail again. And after that—ah, Captain, she has even dared to hope you lost at sea so her husband will consider another suitor for their daughter!"

Joshua drew back on the seat, shaking his head. "I do not believe it," he said flatly. "Not a word."

"No?" Eagerly, Anabelle leaned forward. "Then why else do you think your Mary was so late coming to you in the garden last night? Because her mother had thrust her into a quadrille with some banker's son, that's why!"

Joshua crossed his arms over his chest, his chin low on his chest in uneasy thought as he remembered his earlier parting from Mrs. Holme. He did not want to believe what the girl said, but he did. Damnation, he *did*.

"A quarter hour past, you could not have told my name, ma'am—Miss Crosbie," he said. "How the devil did you come to know so much else?"

"An acquaintance to us both, that is all." Anabelle shrugged impatiently, her dark eyes shining with a conspirator's excitement. She'd spent two tedious hours calling on Grandmother's dear Mrs. Everly to thank her for her concern, and in the process, she'd gleaned all manner of interesting information. "What you need to know is this: that Miss Holme will be visiting the Spring Gardens near Vauxhall tomorrow night with a party of friends."

"At Vauxhall, you say?" he demanded. "What hour?"

"If your Miss Holme is like every other fashionable ninny in London, she will go a-gaping at the wondrous cascade at nine o'clock," said Anabelle, who had herself judged the marvels of the garden's tin waterfall much overrated. "Most likely, you will find her and her friends there."

Joshua frowned, knowing he should object to that uncharitable *ninny* on Mary's account. But not only was Anabelle doing him a great favor, she was also unfortunately correct about Mary's taste in entertainments.

"If you are clever about it," she continued, "and make good use of the crush to separate her from the others, you'll be bound to have your time alone."

"And leave the blasted old—ah, that is, Mrs. Holme—out in the cold where she belongs," said Joshua. "We'll all have what we deserve, eh?"

"Exactly so, Captain." Anabelle nodded, her enthusiasm waning as his grew. "Exactly."

But Joshua didn't notice as he struck his fist against the side of the chariot with satisfaction. "Now I'm in your debt, Miss Crosbie, indeed I am."

Her smile was strained. "No debt, sir. After this we are even all, as the gamesters say."

"Then at least you'll take my thanks." He grinned, tugging at his cuffs in anticipation. "I know Mary will say yes once I can explain everything to her myself."

Anabelle's smile was quite gone now. Of course Mary Holme would accept him. How could she do otherwise? No woman with a beating heart would refuse Joshua Fairbourne, not when he smiled that half-cocked grin that was as wicked as sin itself.

"Is Miss Holme's fortune so vastly great?" she asked. "Is she such a prize to capture?"

Joshua shrugged carelessly. "Oh, aye, I wager old Holme will settle something handsome on her. But that's not why I'm marrying her."

"No?" asked Anabelle incredulously. She'd already judged Joshua to be impossibly gallant, but could he really mean to marry a woman without an eye to her fortune? Such a thing would be unthinkable in her world. "You truly, truly do not care how much she will bring you?"

"Now why the devil would I be set to marry if I

could not afford to keep a wife?" he asked, his disbelief a match for hers. "What kind of sorry husband would that make me? Nay, I've property and money of my own, thank you, and no wish to live off any woman."

"Do you love her that much, then?" asked Anabelle wistfully. Love matches were not a part of her world; they were reserved instead for the casual unions of milkmaids and haymakers, milliners and soldiers. No gentleman would ever look at her without seeing the five thousand pounds a year that she represented, and she remembered the crude jests that Branbrook had made about testing the mettle of Dublin gold. "Is that the reason why?"

"The reason I'm asking for Mary?" Joshua frowned. "You're asking if I love her?"

"Yes, I am," said Anabelle. The ruthless certainty of her life suddenly seemed unbearable to her, and a band of unalterable regret tightened around her chest, making her voice small and reedy. "Do you love Miss Holme so very much that you'd take her even if she came to you in her shift and nothing else?"

Joshua sighed, not sure of the answer she sought. She seemed very young to him, her expression turning guilelessly earnest, and he felt far too old to be here in her company. Despite her coquettishness and the seductive gown overlaid with black lace, she *was* young, a girl whose heart was pining for the intangible mysteries of love as promised by ballad-singers.

How grateful he was that boys—and men—were spared such foolishness! He'd chosen Mary not for some addlepated notions of love, but because she was both pretty and sensible, modest and soft-spoken, a sweet creature who'd bring honor to the Fairbourne name and elegance to Joshua's new house. Being

London bred, she'd be able to hold her own among the puffed-up wives of the Boston shipmasters, and just by her presence, she'd be able to smooth away the last rough edges of his smuggling past. He could already picture her at graceful ease among his fine new mahogany furniture, his gilt looking glasses, even his silver chocolate pot—all the trappings and gewgaws that a prospering gentleman could buy.

For whatever it cost him, Joshua meant to be a gentleman. In his own mind, he already was. All he needed now was a lady wife by his side to convince the rest of Barnstable County—and the world. And that lady would be Mary Holme.

But though he was certain that Mary would understand his reasons, he wasn't as sure about Anabelle Crosbie. She was watching him intently, her fingers twisting in the black lace as she waited for his answer. Damnation, why did it *matter* so much to her?

And now, even more strangely, to himself as well?

Self-consciously, he cleared his throat. "I have the greatest regard for Miss Holme," he said with a gruff formality that sounded forced even to his own ears, "and I esteem her above all other ladies. Else I never would ask for her hand at all, mind?"

"Then I wish you every joy, Captain," she said softly in a voice that held no joy at all. "But we are here at Queen's Docks, yes?"

To Joshua's surprise, she was right. He lifted the light canvas curtain and saw that they were in fact as close to the docks as a chariot—even one with a crest on the door—could comfortably go. Already he could hear the raucous babble of dockworkers and teamsters, sailors and rivermen, and smell the familiar, complicated scent of the Thames and the sea beyond. It had always been a welcome he'd never failed to relish, a call back to the *Swiftsure* and home and the life he treasured above all others. So why, then, was he hanging back now?

"I shall bid you farewell here," said Anabelle, gracefully extending one hand for him to bow over as the footman opened the chariot's door. "Farewell, dear Captain, and *adieu.*"

Gracefully done, and elegantly put, but it was plain enough to Joshua that the girl had no more heart for this parting than did he. Her round little face was empty of merriment, her eyes solemn instead of filled with the teasing laughter he'd come to expect. And to enjoy, too, if he dared be honest with himself.

Still, she held her hand expectantly before him. "*Au revoir,* then, if that is more agreeable," she said uncertainly, "though I do not believe our paths shall cross again in this life."

At last he took her offered hand, his work-callused palm swallowing her small, white fingers. "Come, I'll show you my ship."

Her eyes widened. "Now?" she squeaked excitedly. "But I cannot—I must not! Grandmother would never countenance such a thing!"

"Hang Grandmother," he said gruffly as he stepped from the chariot, drawing her with him. He was surprising her just as she'd surprised him, and he liked it. He'd surprised himself, too, but that was beside the point. "When else will you have such a chance, eh?"

"Never." In the sunshine, she blinked up at him from under the brim of her hat, her sudden grin a match for his own. "But that does not make it right, you know."

He cocked a single skeptical brow. "It didn't bother you last night."

"I told you already that last night I was vastly ill

42

behaved and bold beyond measure and that today I have resolved to reform," she said promptly. "So *that,* Captain, is not a very good argument to make."

He considered reminding her of kissing him and thought better of it. Besides, kissing her was something he, too, would do well to forget.

"You'll be able to see the *Swiftsure* from the end of this street," he said instead, contenting himself with tucking her hand beneath his arm. "Hardly far enough to be considered astray."

"Oh, quite far enough if you're doing the leading, Captain Fairbourne." She sighed for dramatic emphasis, then glanced at the footman, who stood avidly listening as he held the chariot door. "Isn't that so, Prentiss?"

"Yes, Miss Crosbie," said Prentiss without looking her way. "Lady Aubuncourt would ne'er countenance it, Miss Crosbie."

Triumphantly, Anabelle looked back to Joshua. "You see how it is with servants, Captain, exactly as I told you. I shall have to slide the rascal another five shillings to make him sufficiently blind, even for a quarter hour."

"A good thrashing would accomplish the same thing," grumbled Joshua as he reached into his own pocket. Every man in London expected his bit of garnish, from the lowest boatman to the highest minister; it was another of the things he loathed about the place. "Isn't the thieving dog supposed to answer to you?"

"Not to me, Captain, but to Grandmother, which is not at all the same thing," she said as Joshua's coins disappeared inside the footman's waistcoat. "But now you see Prentiss's scruples shall be quite put to rest."

Joshua looked down at her. It was natural for him

to do so, considering what a bit of a thing she was. "What of your own scruples, eh?"

"I haven't any," she said blithely. "That is why I've had to vow to improve myself, else no gentleman will ever want to marry me. But if you promise only the shortest of walks, the briefest of views of your vessel, then my virtue should be safe in your keeping."

"Safe as new eggs in a market basket," he declared soundly. "Come along, handsomely now, and I promise you a sight you won't soon forget."

Yet even though they'd been jesting, there still remained more than a grain of truth in what she said, a grain that began rubbing and chafing at his conscience like sand in an oyster. London wasn't Appledore, and Anabelle Crosbie wasn't some rumshop doxie he hoped to impress into eager submission with the sight of the *Swiftsure*. The rules for London ladies were different—very different. Would Mary and her parents regard these fifty paces he stepped with Anabelle as innocently as he did himself, or was he risking his betrothal yet again?

His uneasiness grew as he and Anabelle threaded their way toward the river. He had walked along this street times beyond counting and scarcely seen the modest shops and taverns and crowded rooming houses with their second floors overhanging the cobblestones below. It wasn't the roughest neighborhood near the river, not by a great margin, but with Anabelle bobbing along on his arm, the humble street seemed altogether changed. Every other woman's head turned to stare at so much yellow silk splendor in their linsey-woolsey midst, some with envy, some with admiration, all with unabashed curiosity. And as for the men—Joshua would have gladly challenged every last one of them for the hungry, eager way they watched Anabelle, like so many rapacious wolves circling one tiny sheep.

Not that the sheep minded, or even seemed to notice.

"I have been here in London with Grandmother these three months past, and would you believe that I have never seen this street?" She marveled with a wonder that no one else would share. "London is such a vastly grand place, yet I am fated to see no more of it than Grandmother deems proper and fashionable and boring, boring, *boring*. Oh, la, look at those men with the long pigtails, right down to their very waists! They look exactly like the heathen Chinamen painted on a lacquer chest at home. Exactly like!"

"They're British sailors, sweetheart, not Chinamen." Joshua pulled her possessively closer and glared at the two barrel-chested, ruddy-faced men grinning at her with their caps in their hands and their smiles full of rum. Jesus, what *had* possessed him to steal her from the safety of her chariot? "I'd wager they're on shore leave from a man-o'-war."

"Truly?" She gazed at the men with such open fascination that Joshua was nearly forced to hustle her away toward the end of the street, the heels of her mules clattering on the cobblestones as she hurried to keep pace with him. "But you are a sailor, too, yet you contrive to wear your hair clubbed and tied in a decent Christian fashion."

"That is because I sail for myself, not the king, and because I am a master, a captain, and no longer a common seaman," he explained swiftly, his misgivings by now blossoming into full-blown regret. The last thing he wished was to have to defend her against two man-o'-war seamen angry at being mistaken for Chinamen, and he began to feel a wonderful sympathy with Anabelle's grandmother. "Religious teachings have nothing to do with braided pigtails, mind?"

"I see," she said, though it was clear to Joshua that she didn't. "But if those men were to—oh, Captain Fairbourne, look! *Look!*"

They had come to the end of the street, where it dropped off to the docks and the river beyond, and the scene spread before them for once left Anabelle speechless. Beyond the leafless forest of masts of the ships taking on cargo at the docks lay the river as she'd never seen it. So many vessels were crowded together into this one serpentine bend in the Thames, so many different kinds, from tiny river skiffs rowed by a single oarsman to barges filled with troops of red-coated marines, squat little sloops with a crew of two plus a dog in the bow, to enormous ships of the line with hundreds of men clambering through the rigging. Sails of every shape and shade, some creamy white and others patched and dingy gray, billowed and filled with the light summer breeze as the ships below glided magically across the water and every ripple in the river's surface glittered silver with sunlight.

"Oh, Captain, it is *vastly* far beyond anything I could imagine!" she cried, patting her hands together with delight. "All the boats, all the sails—oh, it is so very beautiful!"

His misgivings forgotten in an instant, Joshua smiled, her pleasure magnifying his own. "Granted, today's uncommonly fair, but you must have seen the river before when you sailed from Ireland."

She shook her head vigorously, still enchanted by the ever-changing scene before her. "We crossed from Dublin directly to Bristol and Bath and came the rest of the way to London by coach. Even then, Grandmother insisted I stay downstairs on the boat the whole time, so I never had the chance to see anything.

Grandmother thinks sailors are pirates and drunkards and wretched wastrels, dreadfully common and ill-bred company."

"That's because we are," agreed Joshua, but all his sympathy for the Dowager Marchioness of Auboncourt vanished as swiftly as it had risen.

"Oh, bother, that's not true and you know it," scoffed Anabelle, giving him a little shove. "It's rather like saying all Irishmen are fools. Now which boat is yours?"

He leaned over her shoulder to point out across the water, the scent of violets filling his senses. "The *Swiftsure*'s not a boat, sweet. She's a brig. There, with the green stripe on her side and the red pennant."

"I can't see." Anabelle quivered with impatience as she tried to stretch herself taller, her heels leaving the pavement as she craned her neck upward. "I can't *see!*"

Without a second thought, Joshua settled his hands around her waist and lifted her onto a stack of wooden shipping cases unloaded in the street. If his hands lingered longer at her waist than they should, he told himself it was to steady her and not to savor the flaring curve between her waist and her hips, a curve that not even a stiff cage of whalebone and petticoats could entirely suppress. And it wasn't just violets he smelled now; it was violets mingled with the heady scents of her hair and her skin and her breath and the warm sheen that glowed on her cheeks.

"There," he said again, though this time his lips were near enough to brush against the back of her ear. "That's my *Swiftsure.*"

Anabelle obeyed and looked to where he pointed, and found she could do little else. She almost couldn't breathe, and she certainly couldn't move, not with one of his hands resting so comfortably at her waist. It didn't matter that she had all of London to act as her chaperone. It didn't matter a whit. Perched on the box, she felt as helpless as a waxworks doll, with Joshua Fairbourne standing near enough to melt her—and all her tidy resolutions to be good—into a shapeless, blissful blob.

"That's my *Swiftsure*," he was saying, the words a soft caress for her ear alone. "Ninety-seven feet from her stern to her stem, ninety-seven feet of speed and grace. You'll never find a prettier brig on either side of the ocean. I was there when they laid her keel eight years past and there when she rose up from the sand at Barnaby's yard. I know all her whims and fancies and her tempers, too, my *Swiftsure,* and I'd wager she knows mine in the bargain."

He spoke with such pride about his ship, such emotion, that Anabelle's heart swelled, too, just to hear it. Her gaze on the elegant brig with the red pennant was as intent as his own as they watched the ship tugging at her moorings in the river. He'd certainly shown no such regard for Mary Holme. But why would he share this special part of himself with . . . with *her,* who had no place in his life beyond this afternoon?

"We're of a piece, the *Swiftsure* and I," he was saying, his words weaving a spell that was somehow far more intimate than his hand at Anabelle's waist. "We're both a part of the land that made us. If you could see Appledore, you'd understand. There're silver-barked trees older than time and beaches with sand as white as Barbados sugar and marsh ponds with reeds and thrushes singing pretty enough to make you weep. The wind and the sea can blow ice and snow across dunes like the very devil, or sweet and easy as kiss my hand. We're changeable, y'see. It keeps us interesting. Oh, we can be as genteel as any

Englishman, growing roses as big as cabbage heads behind neat white fences, but the wildness of the place is still part of us, too. It's not something you city-bred folk will understand."

"But I do!" cried Anabelle fervently as she turned to face him. "Kilmarsh—the place I was born—is like that, too! It's not grand and fine like London, but full of trees and twisting creeks and green hills and wildflowers!"

"Then you know," he said simply. And he knew she did; he could see it in her face, in her wide, guileless eyes that would never lie. Was it those same eyes that had made him rattle on so? He never spoke so much at one time; it wasn't his way.

But with Anabelle, somehow it was.

Their faces were almost even as she stood on the box, the wide brim of her hat fluttering gently upward in the breeze from the river and dappling her cheeks with filtered sunlight, and he thought how unforgivably easy it would be to kiss her again, now, and seal the strange, impossible bond that kept tugging them together.

With his thumb, he brushed a loose strand of her hair back from her face. "So then you also know," he said softly, "how sweet your homecoming will be when you return."

"No," she said, forcefully breaking the link between them by looking down at her hands. "There'll be no homecoming for me at Kilmarsh Hall. I've come to London to find a husband, you see, an English husband, and his home will become mine. That is how it must be. I suppose I might visit Kilmarsh again someday, if Father decides to invite me, but it won't be the same. It can't be."

"Then you've already learned the secret of every wanderer," he said. Gently, he took her hand and with the palm open, turned it against his chest. "As long as you can carry a piece of your home here, in your heart where you can guard it best, then no one can take it from you. No one, mind?"

She stared solemnly at her hand, held an uncertain prisoner by his against the light blue sateen of his waistcoat. Perhaps the heart that beat so forcefully beneath her fingertips could guard Captain Fairbourne's memories, but was her own heart strong enough to keep Kilmarsh and every other memory she held most dear?

Then suddenly, she remembered the cradle crowned with the smiling cherub, and like pieces of a difficult puzzle finally sliding into place, she understood what Grandmother had been trying to tell her. If the *Swiftsure* was Captain Fairbourne's touchstone, his link to who and what he was, then the cradle was surely hers, just as it had been for her mother and the others before her. Like sailors, they all had been cast adrift in strange and foreign places, sent to find their way in new homes and among new families who scarcely knew them. Yet always the cradle had journeyed with them, a familiar talisman from their past, a promise for their future.

"There now, I've made you sad again," said Joshua gruffly, freeing her hand as he searched his pockets for a decent handkerchief to give her. "I wanted to cheer you, and I've only managed the opposite. Seems to be a rare new gift I have with the ladies."

"Oh, no, it's not that at all." Anabelle sniffed loudly and blotted her eyes with his offered handkerchief. "You promised me a sight I'd never forget, and you did exactly that. I won't ever forget this afternoon, Captain Fairbourne, or you, either."

"Joshua," he said. "My given name is Joshua."

The first capstan bell rang out across the water then,

overlapped by another and another and another, until the whole river seemed to echo with the sound. Then followed the church bells, slower by a fraction for being landlocked, the peals overlapping as they tolled the hour.

"End of the second watch, beginning of the third," said Joshua, self-consciously clearing his throat. "Three o'clock by a landsman's reckoning."

"And far too late by Grandmother's for me." Anabelle tried to smile, but found she couldn't. She hoped he would understand; somehow she was sure he would.

And in the perfect silence of finality, he returned her to the ground and walked her back to the waiting chariot, and the rest of her life—a life without him in it.

❧ Four ❧

"Tell me again how happy you are, Joshua," begged Mary in her soft, breathy voice as she dipped to sit in the center of the marble bench and opened her fan. "I wish to hear it above all things."

"Well, then, I warrant I'm bound to oblige," said Joshua with a heartiness he wished was more genuine.

God knows it should have been. Mary had wept with joy when he'd asked her to marry him, ending all his fears that she might refuse. Afterward, he'd been proud enough to walk beneath the groves of bobbing lanterns and pollarded trees here at the Spring Gardens with her clinging to his arm, announcing their betrothal to the world. She had never looked more lovely, the pale blue lutestring the exact color of her eyes, with tiny silk forget-me-nots in lieu of ribbons pinned into her pale gold hair and her obvious, boundless happiness the final crown.

So why the devil couldn't he feel the same way?

He swallowed, determined to try harder. "You,

Miss Mary Holme, have made me the happiest of all mortal men by accepting my humble offer," he said with the same stiff formality that he'd used while proposing. Poetic language didn't come naturally to him, and he'd labored hard to learn the right words by rote. "Happiest, that is, until our wedding day, when I will be happier still."

"Not that you will have long to wait." Mary smiled as she waved her fan languidly through the air. "I know you've explained that it can't be helped, but how people will talk of a betrothal lasting only a week!"

"Then don't listen," said Joshua, irritation creeping unbidden into his voice. "Winds and tides wait for no man, not even a bridegroom. And it's not as if we've just met, Mary. You've known me for years."

"Not *that* many years," said Mary meekly, "considering I am but seventeen."

Surprised, Joshua didn't answer at first. He'd known her years enough to count, and by his tally, she was twenty if she was a day. Her age didn't matter—he wasn't exactly new-clipped from his mother's apron strings himself—but the vain little lie did. He'd thought Mary above that.

"I'd have thought your father would have granted you some warning about my intentions as well," he said, deciding for now to overlook the question of age. "He said he would."

"Papa did hint at it, yes," admitted Mary with a wisp of a sigh. "But that was ages ago, and you've waited so long to declare yourself that I'd begun to believe he was mistaken, or even that you'd let your devotion falter."

"My devotion?" He scowled indignantly. "Go ask your blessed mother about my—"

"Hush, hush, no cross faces, Joshua, and no cross

words, either," she interrupted gently, the delicate curves of her brows arching with distress. "For my sake, please, please, I won't have you spoiling this evening."

Obediently, he forced his mouth to curve, the result more a grimace than a smile. But Mary was right. He'd no decent reason at all for being such a black-tempered bastard tonight, especially when he'd gotten exactly what he'd wanted.

Hadn't he?

Or was he plagued still by the memory of a woman that would never be his, a bold little creature in yellow silk that paled by comparison to her bright, laughing charm?

He shook his head to banish the elusive image, and with a sigh, he came to sit beside Mary on the bench.

"No, Joshua, please, be mindful of my skirts!" she cried with alarm, twitching the pale blue fabric away from him. "You'll muss them for certain! Silk goods are so dear these days, and Mama warned me specifically not to sully my gown in the crush."

At her first cry, Joshua had retreated to the far end of the bench, feeling like he'd been singed by hot coals. Now he felt merely foolish—and annoyed as well. What was the point of leading a beautiful young woman—especially one who'd just agreed to become his wife—into a moonlit rockery at Vauxhall if all she cared for was keeping her gown tidy?

"When you're my wife, I'll buy you a dozen such gowns," he said. "I won't have you fussing like this over a bit of rumple."

"Papa told me you'd be generous to me," said Mary in perfect seriousness, missing Joshua's more pointed meaning entirely, "and I thank you for it."

"Well, thank you, too," said Joshua gruffly. "I'll want you rigged out proper. You'll be the grandest lady in Appledore, and I don't want anyone saying you don't dress the part."

She smiled uncertainly, the restless fluttering of her fan coming to a halt. "Papa says that Appledore is a fine town, considering it is in the colonies."

"The finest," said Joshua proudly. "We're not so grand as Boston yet, nor Newport, but we are prospering, with nearly two hundred families in the county at present."

"Two hundred?" repeated Mary peevishly. "That is all? Two hundred families? Papa said nothing of that. I know I am to keep your house, but who will there possibly be to entertain? Two hundred families in all the county! Are there any shops to speak of, or markets or taverns or even churches? Where am I to dress in these dozen gowns you promise?"

"We're hardly savages, Mary," he said, and even as he spoke, he could hear in his mind the same words in Anabelle's cheerfully hurried, breathless voice. He shook his head again, determined to turn his thoughts to Mary instead. "We don't live in bark huts and eat marsh grass. We have shops and taverns and a market, to be sure, and a meetinghouse with a steeple by Sir Christopher himself. The ocean may lie between us and London, but we're not really that far apart."

"That is true," she said, her face alight with rekindled hope. "Because of your trade, you will sail to London twice a year, yes?"

"Most years, aye," he admitted grudgingly. His home was in Appledore and he wanted his wife to be there, too, not racing back to her wretched mama. But perhaps Mary was only fearing what she didn't know, and Lord only knew what old Holme had told her. It was his duty to make Appledore sound appealing.

Yet it hadn't been a duty with Anabelle; with her, the words had simply come, and she had understood.

He slid along the bench to her side, impulsively taking Mary's hand. "Mind that I've vowed to make you as happy as you've made me, Mary."

"I would be happiest as your wife in London," she said with a wounded petulance that he'd never heard from her before. "A fine new house is all good and well, but how am I to be your wife and hostess in a place where there is no genteel company to invite?"

"Once you see how fine a place Appledore is, you'll feel as I do," he said, slipping his arm around her waist to draw her closer. He knew from enjoyable experience that Mary found such attentions agreeable—welcomed them, in fact. "Once you're there, I promise you'll forget all about London and all about—"

"Joshua, please!" She wasn't listening, instead turning rigid in his arms. "Please set me free directly!"

"I told you, sweet, you needn't worry about your gown on my account." He might as well have been holding a corpse, so cold and stiff had she become, and he didn't like this change in her temperament. He didn't like it at all. "Damnation, Mary, you're going to be my *wife!*"

"Not until next week I'm not," she said sharply, shoving him away as she scrambled to her feet. "I've no intention, sir, of granting you any—any liberties until then. I may not be a lady of fashion or the daughter of an earl, but I am a decent, virtuous woman, unlike that slatternly Miss Crosbie you found so enticing!"

"Ah, so here are the cooing lovebirds now!" exclaimed Mary's older sister Frances as she sailed into the rockery, her woebegone husband Mr. Parker trailing behind her. They had been Mary's chaperones for the evening, and since they'd given her into Joshua's company, they'd also been the first to learn of the betrothal. "Such fire in your eyes, sister! Such passionate blossoms to your cheeks! Dare I ask what manner of mischief Mr. Parker and I have disturbed, here in this cozy grotto?"

"Precious little, ma'am," said Joshua, resettling his hat with disgust as he bowed curtly in Frances's direction. "Your dear sister here seems to be the one lady in London who fails to find the Spring Gardens a spot fit for trysting."

Though Mary glared murder at him, she still came to stand beside him, possessively linking her hands around the crook of his arm. "You promised me no cross words tonight, Joshua," she warned. "Remember, you promised to make me as happy as I made you."

"Oh, and he will, Mary, he will," said Frances, cocking her head to simper in Joshua's direction. "A seagoing gentleman like the captain—how could he not?"

Though the resemblance between the two sisters was strong, Frances's features fell a fraction shy of Mary's classic beauty. But the greater fault, at least to Joshua, was how closely Frances had slipped into Mrs. Holme's mold, not only in her mannerisms and expressions, but in the shrillness of her voice as well. Joshua had congratulated himself on choosing the sister that wouldn't fall into the mother's pattern. But from the way Mary's fingers were now tightening like thumbscrews into his arm, he wasn't nearly as certain.

"Captain and Mrs. Joshua Fairbourne," ventured Mr. Parker, his hands linked firmly behind his back. He was a dry crow of a man whom Joshua recalled seeing toiling in the Holme counting house, bound to the family both by marriage and employment. "Surely there is a pleasant, respectable ring to that, isn't there? To be wife to a sea captain?"

"No, no, Mr. Parker!" Frances jabbed her husband in the chest with her fan and rolled her gaze toward the lanterns swinging overhead. "It is because, as any clodpate must know, that sailors are all ardent, lusty fellows. It comes of the saltwater, they say. So thus it must follow that the captain here will keep our Mary happy. Is that not so, sister? No wonder you would steal him away from the rest of us like this!"

Frances laughed coyly behind her fan, while Mr. Parker nodded seriously and Mary turned crimson clear to the wreath of forget-me-nots in her hair.

Somehow Joshua kept his face impassive while he wondered how the devil he would survive the week until the wedding. The minute, the very second, that the minister declared Mary to be his, he would sweep her off to the *Swiftsure,* set his ship's sails for Massachusetts, and turn his back forever on the rest of the Holme cabal.

But the worst of it, of course, was that the infernal woman was right. His blood was roiling and boiling and seething with desires, as unsettled as if he were still sixteen instead of twenty-eight. But it had nothing to do with salt water, and nothing to do, either, with his soon-to-be bride. It was Anabelle he wanted, Anabelle whose soft, round body had melted against his as she'd opened her mouth to him, Anabelle who—

Damnation, would he never forget the little witch?

"You put me in mind of my obligations, ma'am," he said as the last of Frances's titters had finally sputtered away. "As . . . ah . . . pleasant as all this has been, it's high time I returned to my ship."

"Oh, no, Joshua, please, you can't, not yet," murmured Mary, her eyes moistly beseeching while her fingers dug into his arm. "There must be so many other people here to see, and share our joy."

"And that is the very least of it, sister," said Frances excitedly. "I have heard that there's a grand party in a booth hosted by the Duke of Richmond, in honor of a dear friend of His Grace's who's soon to wed. They say the gowns of the ladies and the airs of the lords are beyond description."

Mary gasped. "The Duke of Richmond? Here at Vauxhall tonight? Oh, Frances, we must go back through the colonnades and spy as much as we can! How much I'd give to see how the duchess is dressing her head!"

Joshua, who would give less than nothing to be privy to Her Grace's hairdresser, was nonetheless quick to recognize a path of escape when it presented itself. He patted Mary's hand, deftly easing her grip from his arm at the same time.

"I won't deprive you, sweet," he said generously. "I'll return you to the Parkers, and you can tell me everything tomorrow when I call."

"No, no, Captain Fairbourne, I won't let you flee just yet," said Frances. "If you truly wish to please Mary, and me as well, considering as we're close to being family anyway, you must fetch us lemonade. Yes, you must; I won't hear otherwise. I would send Mr. Parker, but he has not your air of command, and none of the garden servants will pay him heed."

"You are kind to think of me, Joshua," said Mary, accepting Frances's offer as Joshua's own. She darted up to kiss his cheek, a chaste hint of a kiss so virtuous that Joshua barely felt it. But it was enough to make Mary blush again as she hurried to join her sister, and enough, too, to make Joshua almost ready to forgive her.

"You'll find us outside the duke's booth," she called back gaily over her shoulder as they left him standing alone in the rockery. "And take care that my lemonade is made with double sugar, or I shall send it back."

Forgiveness vanished. What did Mary think she was marrying, anyway? Another spineless, cringing clerk like poor Parker? He was a deep-water captain, his own master, a man both respected and feared. He didn't take orders, he gave them, and the sooner Mary learned it, the happier they'd both be.

Double sugar, hell. He'd show her double sugar, all right, her and her meddlesome sister both. He'd more than half a mind to clear off now and leave them begging. Angrily, he kicked at the marble bench. The marble won, and he swore again as the pain shot through his big toe.

"Captain Fairbourne?" asked the breathy voice behind him. "Faith, it *is* you!"

He turned as quickly as his aching toe would allow him, even as he cursed himself a fool for imagining her voice—and a greater fool for believing it.

But Anabelle *was* there, not three paces away, framed by the arch of a curving vine. He had thought of her as haunting him, and tonight she did look more ethereal than of this earth, more achingly lovely than any mortal woman had a right to be. Her gown was some sort of silvery damask that glittered like moonlight itself, the skirts full and spreading around her across the lawn, and at her wrists and throat were pearls set in silver, pale and perfect. Her dark hair had been dusted white in the French style, a snowy cloud above her face crowned by a single curving black sultane that was held in place by another feather, this one made of diamonds. Mary and her sister needn't have gone clear to the Duke of Richmond's box to gawk at fashionable gowns, decided Joshua. One look and he was convinced that none of His Grace's party could possibly have rivaled Anabelle Crosbie.

"You're here," he said softly, unwilling to break whatever spell had brought her. "Why the devil am I not surprised?"

"You're a liar as well as a rascal, Joshua Fairbourne," she declared flatly, "for you're every bit as surprised to find me here as I am myself. *Stunned* would not be too strong a word for how I feel, and you, too. Vauxhall, la! Such a tawdry place! But it was not my whim that brought me across the river from Greenwich, but those of others, and so here I am."

"'A liar and a rascal,'" he repeated. "I've killed men for less than that."

"But I'm a lady, not a man, so I doubt exceedingly that I've much to fear." Slowly, she came toward him, glancing around them with open curiosity. "Why are you alone? I thought this part of the gardens was favored most by couples."

"I might ask the same of you." He felt oddly frozen where he stood, afraid that if he moved at all it would be to reach out and draw her into his arms.

"I left my company to seek the ladies' necessary, if you must know. I came back this way because I was certain I heard your voice. It's quite unmistakable, all rumbly and grumbly and strong. Doubtless your men imitate it behind your back." Her smile came suddenly, like the moon reappearing from behind a cloud in the night sky. "Did you not find your Miss Holme at the waterfall?"

"She was there, by the waterfall, with her sister." He smiled, too, though more for her frankness than for the thought of meeting Mary. "Exactly as you foretold."

"Ah, well, then you must tell me all," demanded Anabelle merrily, pouncing on his smile as permission to interrogate him. Better, far better, to ask about him than to have him do the same to her, and infinitely safer as well. "I have a right to hear it, after helping you this far."

"There isn't much to tell."

"Oh, bah, why do men say such dribble-drabble?" scoffed Anabelle. She spread her fan and began dancing a circle around him, her skirts swirling outward across the grass as she forced him to turn in place to follow her. He was so very tall, this shipmaster from a faraway blot on Grandmother's globe, larger and stronger than any other man in her experience, Irish or English, and she never tired of marveling at how beautiful such size could be.

"I expect that you, Captain Fairbourne, can do vastly better than that," she said archly. "Did the fair Miss Holme swoon becomingly? Did she tremble and fall like a sweet spring blossom into your manly arms?"

"Nothing of the sort," said Joshua defensively, though to hear her talk made him worry that he'd done the whole thing wrong. "It was a proposal of marriage, not a ruddy poesy."

"Oh, la, there's no reason they can't be the same, is there?" she continued blithely. "Did she wish to seek the counsel of her mama, her sisters, her friends, her flop-eared spaniel?"

"She would ask her wretched *dog?*"

Anabelle stopped her circling to laugh, pressing the blades of her fan over her lips. He was so wonderfully serious, taking everything she said as gospel true, his thick black brows stern across his blue eyes. She loved to gaze up into those eyes, their brilliant color and thick lashes so at odds with the weathered severity of the rest of his face, particularly now when she'd vexed him nearly to the limit.

"Perhaps not her dog, no," she said, relenting as she clicked her fan shut blade by blade. "But surely she begged for more time to consider your offer? Every maiden must, you know, even if she's been waiting for an offer for years and years. It's quite expected, a part of the matchmaking game. Hardly an easy role to play, I can assure you."

"You say that as if you've done it yourself." Though he had no right to be jealous—damnation, he'd no right to be alone with her here right now—he still hated the thought of Anabelle with any other man.

"That's because I have," she said promptly. "Twice, in Dublin, though 'tis nothing to speak of now. Yet each time, I held out my answer for nearly a month, and quite dutifully, too."

"Not my Mary," said Joshua staunchly, relieved to be able to praise his future wife at last. "She's far too sensible. A few happy tears, and she accepted."

"She *accepted?*" repeated Anabelle, with a gasp of disbelief. "This very night? She has accepted you already?"

"She has, aye," he said. "We haven't much time, not if I'm to make the crossing this year, and Mary knows that. We will marry a week from tomorrow, and clear London for home the next morning."

"Oh, that is so soon, so very, very soon!" she cried, overwhelmed by his haste. So this, then, was her penance at its most severe, a punishment more painful—and more ironic—than she could have dreamed. She looked down at her fan, straightening the blades as she struggled to order her thoughts.

"It—it must have gone exactly as you said it would," she said. "That is, once you were able to speak to Miss Holme yourself. But I will be happy for you. Yes, I must be! Now you shall have everything that you wished, won't you?"

"Aye," he said slowly. "Everything that I wished."

But it wasn't, not at all, and he knew it.

Laughter from the promenaders rippled over the maze of rocks and high hedges, and the muted songs of the Vauxhall nightingales, nearly as famous as the Cascade itself, floated down from the trees. Nearby, a woman's coyly half-hearted protest was smothered by her lover's kiss.

"I should return to my friends," said Anabelle, staring somewhere to the left of Joshua's sleeve to avoid meeting his eyes as she fidgeted with the diamond feather in her hair. "I wouldn't want them to worry."

Feathers made of diamonds, thought Joshua wretchedly, something meant to be light and insubstantial on the wind turned to glittering, costly stone: what better symbol could there be of the uncrossable distance between their lives?

"You wouldn't want that, no." He cleared his throat. "To have your friends worry, that is."

Yet still she did not move to leave, letting the silence between them lengthen with everything that was left unsaid.

"I know so little of you," she began at last, "this side of nothing, really, yet still . . . yet still . . ." She looked to him helplessly as she let her words trail off, then stumbled to another beginning. "That is the same suit of clothes you wore to Lady Willoughby's, isn't it?"

He sighed wearily. "Aye, it is. I've neither use nor wish for a score of foppish embroidered waistcoats."

"Oh, hush. I didn't mean it that way." Her smile wobbled. "Rather that I shall always remember you like this, Joshua, how you looked when I saw you first, and when you—"

"Belle?" called the man from the far side of the hedge, a voice that Joshua recognized even through the wild, irrational joy of hearing Anabelle use his given name. "Where are you hiding yourself, Belle?"

Without a pause, Joshua grabbed Anabelle's hand. "Come, back through here," he whispered urgently. "There's another way back to the colonnades."

"But Joshua—"

"Handsomely now, sweetheart, no idling," he said as he tried to lead her away. "That's the same foolish bastard I clouted on your behalf last time, and I've no wish to repeat the pleasure. Now come, hurry!"

But to his amazement, Anabelle pulled free, edging away from him. "It's not what you think, Joshua. I should tell you now that I've—"

"There you are, dearest Belle," said Henry Branbrook as he appeared in the arch, pausing a moment to pose for effect with his hand upraised before he joined Anabelle. He took her hand and familiarly traced his fingers along the inside of Anabelle's arm. "I've been searching clear to the river for you. Richmond's ordered a special punch and won't let any of us have a drop until you returned. Where've you been hiding yourself, you naughty chit?"

Though the man was not as far into his cups as he'd been that other night, Joshua's opinion of him didn't alter. His manner was arrogant and selfish, and he was as soft in his wits as he was in his belly. Stripped of his velvet coat and curled wig, there wouldn't be enough left of him to impress a goat. So why, then, was Anabelle tolerating his vile forwardness?

"I'll be there directly, Henry," she said, resting her hand over his to halt his wandering caress. "I was only just—"

"Only just coming with me, I vow." Branbrook looked hard at Joshua and gave Anabelle an ungentlemanly poke in the ribs to urge her along. "This way, my beauteous Belle. Won't do to keep Richmond's punch waiting."

"The damned punch can wait as long as Miss Crosbie wishes it to," rumbled Joshua, unable to keep still any longer. He didn't care if the other man was carrying a gun again, or if he'd forgotten that Joshua had knocked him senseless the last time they'd met. Anabelle needed him again, and that was all that mattered. "Come along, sweetheart. I'll see you back to your friends."

Ignoring how Branbrook bristled at the endearment, Joshua held his hand out to Anabelle, expecting she'd come running to his protection the way she had before. But to Joshua's surprise, this time she shook her head and hung back at the other man's side.

"I was trying to tell you, Captain Fairbourne," she said softly, and Joshua sensed that the return to formality between them meant that her news, whatever it might be, would not be good. "Earlier I wished you joy on your betrothal. Now I have hopes that you might do the same for me."

She took a deep breath, her eyes pleading with him to understand. "Last evening, I accepted Mr. Branbrook's kind offer of marriage."

"No teasing back and forth from you, was there, Belle?" said Branbrook with relish. "Nothing missish in the least. I asked for your hand, and you gave it. But then why shouldn't you take me? You know same as I that you'll end up wearing ermine tails as Countess o' Westover. No gamble to it, I say, considering how shabbily my sister-in-law's performing in the breeding line. But we'll show 'em how it's done, won't we, Belle? I'll give you a hundred guineas that nine months to the day of our wedding that you'll be brought to bed with my son. The devil take me if you aren't!"

He pulled Anabelle close before she could wriggle free, hungrily pressing his lips along the side of her neck. It was like being kissed by a slug, she thought with disgust, a wet, slimy slug with no manners. She closed her eyes, fighting both embarrassment and unhappiness.

Remember the cradle, she thought to steel herself, remember the children to come, to love and to treasure and be the joy of her life. If it wasn't Henry Branbrook, then it would be another well-bred, well-connected gentleman like him. Grandmother would see to that, and Father would agree. At least Henry was young and healthy and he wouldn't need to use her money to pay off his debts. And he wanted children, too, if for no better reason than to outdo his older brother. Perhaps that would be the bond that joined them together. Perhaps, over time, if fortune smiled upon her, she would come to love him as well.

Perhaps.

"You have my best wishes for your lasting happiness, Miss Crosbie," said Joshua, and swiftly Anabelle opened her eyes. "Though it seems it was no game for you either, was it?"

She shook her head, unable to find any words to answer. And even if she had, what would she have said? The laughable, painful truth? That she'd accepted Mr. Branbrook's offer only to remove herself from the temptation of an unknown sea captain from the colonies?

If Joshua was shocked or disturbed by her announcement, he didn't show it, his blue eyes remaining so devoid of any emotion and his voice so gruffly polite that it bewildered her. How accomplished he was at putting on such a grim, serious mask! In growing desperation, Anabelle's gaze scoured his face, frantically hunting for one glimmer of the empathy she remembered so well, but she could find none. Could he be such an expert at hiding how he felt, or was there simply, horribly, no feeling to hide?

And how long had the wide-eyed woman been standing beside him? Belatedly, Anabelle recognized her as Mary Holme, the next Mrs. Fairbourne. Miss Holme was taller than Anabelle remembered, and better favored, too, with the kind of figure that wore clothes well and gentlemen noticed. Already, she and Joshua seemed to have that complementary look of a married couple, as if no one else would suit the other quite so satisfactorily. Even Miss Holme's plain, old-fashioned gown and the foolish jejune flowers in her hair had a certain *rightness* beside Joshua's dark blue coat, a rightness that she, short, plump, Anabelle Crosbie, trussed up in modish silver silk damask and diamonds, could never hope to duplicate. Miss Mary Holme belonged with Joshua Fairbourne, while she— she belonged with the overbred likes of Henry Branbrook.

"Might I please add my wishes as well, Miss Crosbie?" murmured Mary, dipping an obsequious curtsy that sank far too low for Anabelle's rank. "And might I please say how handsomely your gown showed among the other ladies in His Grace's private booth?"

Branbrook sniffed, not bothering to stifle his smile of amusement. "Tell me, Belle," he said. "How could you possibly have come to know these people?"

"It doesn't signify," said Joshua curtly, sparing neither a glance nor a word for Anabelle, "because we don't choose to know *you,* either. Come, Mary, let us be away."

"Very well, Joshua," said Mary obediently, dropping another overwrought curtsy before she followed. "Good evening, Miss Crosbie."

"Fresh as cabbages from the country," declared Branbrook as they headed back to rejoin the others in the duke's party. "I vow that girl's curtsys belong on the stage, so comical were they, and as for the man—a surly, impudent rogue, born to be hanged. How you know such creatures is beyond reason, Belle."

"It doesn't signify, Henry," said Anabelle bitterly. "It doesn't signify at all."

"'It doesn't signify'—that's what she told me, Palmer," complained Henry Branbrook two nights later as he thumped his empty glass onto the table. "As if I were as deuced thick as one of those plaster-cast Apollos there in Vauxhall! Oh, it took me a bit to recall the bastard's face—Richmond had brewed a hellishly strong punch in Belle's honor, and we were all fairly fuddled—but I'd lay twenty guineas that it was the same fellow who nearly murdered me before."

"Then break it off, Branbrook," drawled Lieutenant the Honorable Edward Palmer, concentrating hard as he tipped the bottle and refilled his cousin's glass. It was late, very late, with dawn not far away, and the number of other blue-coated navy officers in the tobacco haze around them at the Silver Dolphin had thinned considerably. "Be rid of the little chit whilst you can."

"But I don't *want* to be rid of her, Palmer," said Branbrook peevishly. "That's the trial of it. Now that I've made up my mind to take a wife, I don't want to break it off. Anabelle's worth a good five thousand a year, and fortunes like that don't grow on plum trees, I can tell you that."

"Indeed not." The lieutenant sighed glumly. An heiress with five thousand pounds a year was not to be lightly dismissed. As the fourth son in his family, without even enough of an income to buy a commission in a decent regiment, he'd had no other choice open to him than the navy. "With five thousand to her name, I'd take her if she were cross-eyed and bandy-legged."

"But Belle's not like that, not in the least." Branbrook sighed mournfully, nestling his chin in his open hand. "She's a perfect little sweetmeat of a girl, all white flesh and pink cheeks—you know how fresh Irish women can be—and I'll wager her legs are straight enough. Won't be a duty at all, bedding a wife like that."

"Then do it, and be quick about it," said Palmer acidly, without a touch of the sympathy his cousin so clearly sought. "Get her with child and banish her to the country before she can cuckold you."

Branbrook's mouth slipped open with dismay, remaining that way a bit longer from forgetfulness. "Cuckold me!" he cried at last. "Damnation, Palmer, that's putting an overripe face on it!"

Palmer shrugged elaborately, wiping an invisible smudge from one of the brass buttons on his sleeve with his thumb. "That's what's ailing you now, isn't it? Worrying that she and this murderous scoundrel have already—"

"Stop right there, Palmer, else I'll have to call you out," said Branbrook indignantly. "I'll grant you Belle has a warm temperament—it's another of her charms, really—but she's too well bred to foul herself that way. Not to insult you, cousin, but the man's a sailor, some low sort of Jack-tar from the colonies, and Belle, well, for all that she's half Irish, she is Auboncourt's niece."

"Oh, aye, but you know how many duchesses dally with their coachmen," said the lieutenant coldly, smarting from the unconscionable reference to sailors and low Jack-tars. "In my experience, women are much the same beneath their petticoats. Even your precious Belle, I 'spect."

"I vow, Palmer, if you weren't my cousin," began Branbrook, then gulped his brandy before, for once, he'd say something he'd regret. Because Palmer took after the other side of the family, he was a good deal larger than Branbrook, and besides, the memory of how he'd suffered at Fairbourne's hands remained dismally fresh. "I wish the bastard were taught a lesson, that's all. Belle, too, now that I think on it. Make them understand that they can't play so free and fast with me."

"Even if the lady herself said it didn't signify?" Palmer winked broadly. "She might not care a fig what becomes of him, you know."

But Branbrook was too busy with his own thoughts to hear him. "Ain't there something in that line that you could do, especially since you're bound for the colonial station anyway?" he asked hopefully. "Some sort of convenient navy law that could catch him up?"

Palmer leaned back in his chair, his arms folded across his chest, hiccuped, and tried to look very stern and official. "The role of the royal navy is to serve His Majesty the King and to protect his country and his subjects," he said with more pomposity than pomp. "The role of the finest navy in the world is not to execute your personal vendettas."

"Oh, yes, yes, Palmer, quite," said Branbrook impatiently. "You know I'd never ask you to do anything in an Italian manner. But if you could just—"

"Listen to me, cousin." Palmer leaned forward, unsteadily holding his hand out to count on his fingers. "There are only three situations in which the navy might be able to help you: firstly, if your dear lady's rascally friend should fall into the path of an impressment party and find himself taken off to, oh, the East Indies; secondly, if he is an out-and-out pirate, bringing grievous loss and misfortune to His Majesty's people and property; or thirdly, if he is a smuggler, depriving the country of due revenues."

Branbrook nodded eagerly. "Impressment, piracy, and smuggling. That should suffice, shouldn't it?"

"Any one alone would," said the lieutenant with a wise nod. "Of course we'd have to catch the rascal at the mischief. The ocean is a powerfully broad place for such to hide."

"But if you took a special interest in the hunt, cousin," suggested Branbrook, "a special, *personal* interest in the name of the family—"

"Marry the lady instead," said Lieutenant Palmer as firmly as he could, finishing the last of his brandy as he reached for his hat. "Marry her, I say. I don't doubt that you can make that punishment enough to last her whole lifetime."

❧ Five ❧

Joshua stared critically at the *Swiftsure*'s furled sails, squinting up at the pattern of spars and masts against the bright morning sky.

"Not what I'd call squared, Samuel," he said to his first mate, Samuel Worden. "Not squared, but I warrant it must do for now."

"'Tis more a matter of what must be done than what will do, Josh," grumbled Samuel with the freedom born of knowing his captain since boyhood. "You'd think we were His Bloody Majesty's Ship *Swiftsure* for all the tidying you want done."

Joshua smiled, not in the least offended. He liked order, in his life and in his crew. Among merchant captains, he was known for running a tight ship, with every plank scrubbed, every brass polished, every line coiled, and every man in the crew so practiced in his skills and tasks that they came without thinking.

But then Joshua had always found survival and

prosperity were wonderful incentives. Though the *Swiftsure*'s captain and crew usually bowed to the trading laws here in London, once they were back on their own side of the Atlantic, Joshua paid precious little attention—and fewer tariffs—to any customs house. From long experience, he knew the only sure way to outrun the navy revenue ships cruising the coast was to be their superior. His grand new house was proof enough of how well he'd succeeded.

"You know my reasons, Samuel," he said mildly, "and I don't hear you complaining when it's time to pay out at the end of a voyage."

"If ever we *see* the end of this particular voyage," said Samuel as he wiped his nose furiously with a grimy red handkerchief. "We've never tarried this long on the Thames. We'll be fortunate to speak to Appledore by New Year's, and all because you decided to shackle yourself to this one woman for the rest of your mortal time."

"Only two more days before we sail, Sam," said Joshua, smoothing the cuffs on his second-best shore-going shirt with a serenity he didn't particularly feel, and hadn't, either, since the night at Vauxhall. He had another matter or two of business, after which he was to dine with the Holme family in Fenchurch Street, the final time he'd see Mary before the wedding. The *wedding:* the word alone was enough to make him queasy. "Miss Holme's dunnage comes aboard tomorrow, before the wedding, and all else is stowed and ready. Two more days—that is all."

Samuel sighed, clearly unconvinced. Though he and Joshua had been born in Appledore within a month of one another in houses on the same lane, Samuel had reached his full measure of height by his fourteenth birthday, while Joshua had continued to grow until he towered over his friend both in size and in ambition. Yet Joshua knew that Samuel remained content to toil in his shadow; not only could he leave it to the captain to weather the daunting storms of leadership and navigation, but Samuel was also in a splendid position to gather up the windfalls, be they profits or barmaids.

The profits he hoped would continue, but the days of the barmaids were definitely past, and as Samuel sighed again, Joshua wondered which he mourned the most.

"To think of you as a wedded man, Josh!" he said forlornly. "'Tis a tragedy, my friend, a great and sorrowful tragedy. You'll set the sweet lasses to weeping with grief from Halifax to King's Town."

"They'll live," said Josh, leaning his head back further, holding onto the crown of his hat as he studied the very tip of the foretop mast. "And so will you, Sam, if you could but—what in blazes is that rubbish trailing from the topgallant?"

"That?" As nonchalantly as he could, Samuel leaned backward, too. "That with the ribbon?"

"Aye, that with the ribbon," said Joshua, staring with curious horror at what looked like a nosegay of greenery tied to his pristine mast. No matter how disarrayed his life ashore had become this last week, he'd always been able to return to the *Swiftsure* and her perfectly ordered ways. At least he had until now. "That infernal bundle of sticks and leaves, for all love! What next, eh? What next? Will we all thrust leeks through our hats and set off for a jaunt to Wales?"

"It's some notion of Barker's," said Samuel, at last naming the carpenter. "He says where he was bred in Devon that—"

"Barker!" roared Joshua.

Instantly, the carpenter came scurrying up through the hatch, a mallet still clasped in his hand as he came to stand before Joshua.

"John Barker," said Joshua sternly. "Mr. Worden says you're to answer for that wretched bit of salad greens gracing the forward mast."

"Aye, cap'n, I am," said Barker earnestly. "I done it to favor th' lady bride, sir. To signify th' wedding, sir. It be a token for herself—an' for you, sir—for health an' prosperity an' babes aplenty, sir. In my village, we'd've pegged it on th' ridgeboard of your house, sir, but seeing as th' *Swiftsure* don't have no roof, not proper, sir, I thought th' foremast would do instead."

"Did you now?" As master, Joshua was always aware of his audience, both those men in earshot now and the rest who would hear the eager retelling from their friends in the mess. On board the *Swiftsure,* Joshua's word was law, with all the attendant gravity and consequences.

But judgment wasn't coming easily this time. The carpenter was a good man who had meant only good by his bridal nosegay, and he didn't deserve a reprimand. More importantly, what he said now regarding his wedding would be repeated among the crew for the rest of the voyage. He'd be a fool to turn down wishes for health and prosperity and children. And considering his very private misgivings about the marriage, Barker's nosegay might even bring good luck.

At least it couldn't hurt.

Besides, Mary enjoyed such fripperies. She'd declare the nosegay to be charming, maybe even credit it to Joshua. The thought made him happy, and he smiled at Barker, who automatically smiled in nervous return.

"Thank you, Barker," he boomed, loud enough for

every eavesdropper to hear. "And I'm sure Miss Holme will thank you, too, once she comes aboard as Mrs. Fairbourne."

Barker ducked his balding head with embarrassed pleasure. "Thankee, cap'n, and thankee to your lady," he said, his boldness waxing with the captain's good humor. "She's most uncommon beautiful, sir, is your Miss Holme. Jemmy Clarke an' me, we seen you with her, an' oh, she fair took my breath away."

"A pretty compliment, Barker," said Joshua with an uneasy heartiness, "though a mistaken one. Miss Holme has yet to see the *Swiftsure,* or you and Jemmy Clarke, either, for that matter."

But Barker refused to back down. "Mebbe not, cap'n, but Jemmy an' me saw you with Miss Holme, clear as day. She looked a little scrap o' a thing— meaning no dishonor, sir, just th' truth—with dark hair, dressed in a yellow-colored frock laced with black an' a little black hat sittin' topsides. She was standin' up high beside you t' view th' vessels on th' river. A very fetchin' lady she be, cap'n, very fetchin'."

Left speechless on his own quarterdeck, Joshua glared in silence as he fought back the images that John Barker had so lovingly described. All week long, he'd struggled to force Anabelle from his thoughts and from his traitorous dreams, too. But the memory of Anabelle was proving stronger than his will: Anabelle's merry, teasing laugh and *vastly* this and *vastly* that, Anabelle's scent mingled with violets, Anabelle's kiss . . .

"Fat lot you know, Barker," said Samuel with disgust, unaware of how he'd just come to Josh's rescue, "and cursed familiar you're being in the bargain, too. Miss Holme is tall with pale hair, and a born lady like her would likely perish before she'd go walking about the docks. Nor would the captain here do such a thing with her, neither. A-viewing poxy vessels on the poxy river! Don't he see enough of the pack of you as it is?"

"But Mr. Worden," began Barker, stubbornly bewildered. "I seen—"

"Nay, what you and Jemmy saw was the bottom of a tankard of rum, and that's the truth," said Samuel scornfully. "Now back to work with you, and no more of your disrespectful notions."

"Not another word about Miss Holme, Barker," rumbled Joshua. "Not another blessed word, mind?"

"Aye, aye, sir." Bowing to Joshua's blackest glower, Barker tugged at the front of his knitted cap and scurried back below.

Damnation, they all probably *did* imitate his voice in their mess. Why had he never noticed before how much he sounded like a menacing bullfrog?

Beside him, Samuel watched the carpenter go, shaking his head. "I ask you, Josh, where does such folderol come from?" he asked. "Is it the air 'tween decks that feeds such fancies? Your genteel Miss Holme in a black lace hat, tripping along the docks!"

"Stow it, Samuel," muttered Joshua. "Just stow it, mind?"

"Meant no harm," said Samuel without the faintest show of remorse on his freckled face. "Your innocent bride can wear all the black lace in Parma; it's much the same to me. Unless that's not quite what's worrying at you?"

With appalling clarity, Joshua realized how hideously close Samuel was to guessing the truth.

"I told you, Samuel, it doesn't signify," he said swiftly, but he was already too late.

"Lord, that's not the half of it, is it?" Samuel whistled softly and shifted closer to Joshua as he lowered his voice. "Not the lace, but the lady. Ha, you rogue, I knew you couldn't shackle yourself to only one! So how'd you arrange such a thing with old Holme breathing over your shoulder to make his daughter respectable? Who's this cunning little doxie in yellow?"

"You are dreaming, Mr. Worden," said Joshua deliberately. "There's no doxie, in yellow or any other color."

"None?" asked Samuel, disappointment and skepticism equally mixed in his voice. "You know you can trust me not to spill your secrets, Josh."

"I swear to it that there's no doxie. Will that suffice?" As nonchalantly as he could, Joshua settled his hat more firmly on his head. He *was* telling the truth. Not even Samuel would dare call an earl's granddaughter a doxie. "Is the boat waiting?"

But the doubting look on Samuel's face remained in his thoughts long after the boat had carried him to shore, and it was there still as he rocked back and forth in the hired chair on the way to this last appointment. Technically, he hadn't lied to Samuel, but the sour little spot in his conscience told him that this kind of truth wasn't a hell of a lot more agreeable.

His conscience seemed to be telling him that quite often lately, making a great deal more noise than Joshua might wish for the sake of untroubled dreams. Of course he'd been sleeping perfectly well until Anabelle had hurled herself into his chest and his life, too, but he couldn't exactly blame her, as much as he wished to. No. The problem instead lay with himself. Plain and simple, he could not forget Anabelle Crosbie.

No matter that tomorrow he was promised to marry a girl the world would judge far more beautiful and suitable.

No matter that Anabelle herself was betrothed to another man who was equally suitable, in turn, for her.

No matter that he'd always preferred tall, blond, uncomplicated women who were neither talkative nor clever, or that small, dark Anabelle possessed the latter two qualities in frightening overabundance.

No matter that he scarcely knew her at all, or that the three times they'd met had been under the most charmingly intimate circumstances, or that she'd been the first woman in his experience to kiss him before he'd kissed her, to mark him forever with her scent and taste and the yielding softness of her body and—

Jesus, he was doing it *again.*

With another muttered oath—he was swearing a great deal lately, too—he thumped his knuckles on the shiny black door before him. The door belonged to the studio and home of Alec Rowan, R.A., and in the time that it took for a servant to answer, Joshua tried to recall what Mary had told him those two letters after Mr. Rowan's name signified. The *A* must stand for artist, since painting portraits of ladies was his trade, but the meaning of the *R* eluded him completely. He did remember what was most important to Mary: that Mr. Rowan was the best painter of likenesses in all London—nay, all Britain—and that she'd been oh so fortunate to have herself sketched by so great a genius.

That sketch in *trois crayonnes* now hung in magnificent, gilt-framed splendor in the dining room in Fenchurch Street, where Joshua had both admired and coveted it. There was no doubt that Mr. Rowan had captured the exact turn of Mary's head and the languid beauty of her eyes.

To Joshua, it was nothing short of a miracle.

Massachusetts was still too near to its puritanical founders to be a place where fine art flourished; the best paintings to be found there were generally on signboards over tavern doors. Yet Joshua could recognize a quality painting when he saw it, and especially when he learned the cost of it, and there was an empty place over the mantelpiece in his new front parlor where the portrait of the new Mrs. Fairbourne would look most handsome.

Mrs. Holme, however, would not hear of parting with it. Losing Mary was hard enough without losing her likeness, too, and on the same vessel and over such fearsome seas, mercy preserve her darling!

But the great Mr. Rowan had proved more amenable. In honor of Miss Holme's nuptials, and for a fee that had made Joshua swallow hard, he had been persuaded to make a copy of the sketch. It was this bespoken copy that Joshua had come himself to claim, not trusting such a treasure to any messenger.

"Tell your master that Captain Fairbourne's here," said Joshua to the footman, a tall, regal African dressed in scarlet livery. "Look lively now, man; I haven't all day."

The footman stared at him a pointed moment longer, then with a bow and a flourish opened the door. Silently, he showed Joshua into a small parlor, bowed again, and vanished.

Restlessly, Joshua paced back and forth with his hands clasped behind his back, walking from one nude plaster-cast goddess on a pedestal to her sister poised on the opposite side of the room. He'd seen such statues before in brothels, and to his mind, they'd looked much more at home there than in this parlor that strived to be both genteel and exotic. The walls were lined with engravings of Rowan's portraits, dozens of solemn, painted faces above various antique costumes, while a large portfolio of more engravings, suggesting more poses and backgrounds, lay invitingly open on a table near the window.

A salesroom, decided Joshua, albeit one decorated more eccentrically than most, but not that different than that of any other tradesman with samples to display, and impatiently he drew his watch to check the time. Rowan had told him to call at two, and it was now half past, with no sign of either the painter or his silent servant. For Joshua, whose life was regulated by the bells of the *Swiftsure*'s watches, punctuality was a requirement, not a virtue, and with an irritated sigh, he threw open the parlor door to hunt for Rowan himself.

The small private parlor across the hall was empty, a breakfast tray still on the table amidst scattered newspapers and tobacco crumbs, but in the distance, down the hallway, Joshua could hear a man's voice that he recognized as Rowan's.

With a little *hah* of satisfaction, Joshua followed the voice, and as he grew closer to the double doors half ajar, he could hear a lute being strummed and, incongruously, the chirping of birds.

"Where are you hiding yourself, Rowan?" he called as he pushed the door open the rest of the way. "Are you here?"

"Of course I am here," said the artist grandly. The older woman playing the lute in the corner stopped with an awkward *plunk,* leaving only the sound of the linnets singing cheerfully in a bamboo cage near the tall, uncurtained windows. Rowan himself stood with his palette on his arm, poised before an enormous canvas with the life-sized figure of a woman barely sketched in place in a sepia wash. "I am here, and every right I have to be so, too, considering this is my establishment. As for you, sir, bellowing and roaring into my studio! Didn't Pompey show you to the parlor?"

"He did," said Joshua sharply, bristling not only at the painter's tone but also at the reference to "bellowing and roaring." Why did all these infernal Londoners take such offense at his voice? "And there I've been waiting for you, sir, this past half hour."

"Oh, a mere handful of minutes." Rowan swept his arm dismissively through the air, his paint-laden brush like a wand in his hand. With a thicket of sandy brows over his eyes and a velvet slouch cap on his head, he did resemble some sort of wizard, especially now as he leaned backward to study Joshua, squinting with his head cocked to one side. "A drop of nothingness in the ocean of eternity."

"Spoken like a man who's never been to sea," said Joshua with growing disgust. "Now I don't give a tinker's damn for your time, but my own is worth something dear, and I don't take well to those that squander it. I've come for my picture of Miss Holme, and damnation, I mean to have it. *Now.*"

Defensively, Rowan drew himself a shade taller. If he was not exactly intimidated by Joshua, he was at least a bit more respectful. "You're the mariner from the provinces, aren't you?" he said, his airiness easing into deference. "Yes, yes, I recall you now. A veritable Neptune! Wouldn't he make a magnificent Neptune, my dear lady? Or perhaps Homer's own true sailor Odysseus?"

"What Captain Fairbourne will make, Mr. Rowan, is a sorry stew of *you,*" called Anabelle, hidden somewhere behind the canvas on the easel. "I've seen him do it before, you know, and to a much greater man than you."

In three steps, Joshua was around the easel. His ears hadn't tricked him after all: she really *was* there.

There, yes, but not in a way that even his most eager imagination could have concocted. Standing on a raised platform beside a fragment of a plaster column, Anabelle wore no stays stiffened with whalebone this afternoon or wide hoops to swell her skirts or any of the other concoctions that fashionable ladies used to disguise their real forms. Instead, she was dressed only in a thin linen shift and a long, sleeveless robe of rose pink satin that seemed to spill and pour over the curves of her body, a body that was most obviously covered by nothing else. Even her hair was free of its customary pins, the dark waves rippling over her bare arms to her waist, held back only by a gold cord over her brow.

"Good day to you, Captain Fairbourne," she said, moving only her eyes to look at him. She remained as Rowan had posed her, one knee bent slightly, her body twisted one way and her head turned toward the other to show her profile, a giltwork bow in her hand like a walking stick. "Forgive me for not moving, but I swore to Mr. Rowan that I would stand still as death."

"You don't look dead to me," said Joshua, praying she didn't hear the strain in his voice. Dead, hell. He'd never seen a woman look more alive.

"I am most relieved to hear it," she said. "Goddesses are supposed to be immortal, aren't they? It wouldn't do to be a lifeless—umm, Mr. Rowan, who is it I'm impersonating again?"

"Diana, the chaste goddess of the moon and the hunt," said Rowan quickly. "A most honorable role for a lady to assume on the eve of her marriage."

"Oh my, yes, what better role for moonstruck young ladies hot in pursuit of every marriageable bachelor in the woods?" Anabelle laughed wryly, somehow still managing to keep her profile aligned. "Do you think I would have done better for myself if

I'd brought a quiver full of arrows with me to St. James?"

"That's not the meaning your grandmother and I intended, Miss Crosbie, nor one, I'm sure, that would please Lord Henry," said Rowan crossly, his bristling brows twitching with affronted vexation. "A portrait in the antique style must not be viewed with such levity. The primary symbolism of Diana is her chastity, her purity."

"Well then, we shall ask the captain," she said, her gaze shifting wickedly. "Do I look the very picture of chastity and purity?"

It was not a question Joshua could answer with any honesty, and he didn't. But the studiously noncommittal look he set on his face was still enough to make her laughter peal freely, and enough, too, to send one strap of her tunic sliding precariously over her bare shoulder.

"My bespoke picture, Mr. Rowan," he said sternly, barely composing his face to match his voice as he turned toward the artist. "You can fetch it now and grant Miss Crosbie a leave from her posing, eh?"

Rowan hesitated, clearly torn between his own wishes and those of the two people before him. Finally, he tossed his palette and brushes on the table beside the easel, bowed deeply to Anabelle—deeply enough that his queue flopped over his velvet cap— and left them.

Joshua smiled at the woman with the lute. The smile worked as it usually did, warming her cheeks to a deep crimson of confused pleasure.

"Likely you wish for a leave, too, ma'am," he said to the woman. "Playing away while old Rowan paints—I'll warrant that's no easy task, is it?"

"Yes, sir." Nervously, she smoothed the neat linen wings of her cap, shyly returning Joshua's smile.

"That is, Mr. Rowan's a good master, but the sittings can be powerfully tiring, as you say."

"Then go, ma'am." He waved his arm expansively toward the door. "Take your ease where you wish. I'll square it with Rowan."

"Thank you, sir, but I cannot go," she said, glancing uneasily at Anabelle, "not and leave Miss Crosbie unattended."

"Oh, pooh, what harm will come to me?" declared Anabelle, tapping the toy bow against her shoulder. "I, Diana, the most chaste and pure goddess in all London?"

"But, miss, I—"

"I vow I'll stay right up here on my little stage," promised Anabelle. "Shall that be enough? Oh, and I'll—what was it you said, Captain Fairbourne?—I'll *square* it with my grandmother. Now please leave us."

"Yes, miss." With an uneasy dip of a curtsy, the woman grabbed the lute and fled, closing the door behind her.

"Well, now, that is done," said Anabelle as the door closed shut. "But you'll have to explain to me what this squaring might be, you know, so I shall be able to do it properly."

She had never expected to see him again, let alone here in Mr. Rowan's studio, and the surprise of it had buoyed her spirits most amazingly. It was almost as if he had become her own proverbial bad penny. But now that they were alone, the memory of that dreadful night at Vauxhall lurched once again to the fore, and she wasn't sure what would come next.

And in the next second, she had her answer. "I didn't follow you here, Miss Crosbie," he said bluntly, the smile he'd given to the other woman not to be shared with her. "Don't think I did."

"I didn't," she said quickly, wishing she didn't sound so defensive.

His jaw tightened. "I came here only to claim that blasted picture, mind. I'd no notion you'd be here."

"However could you?" Now he was the one who sounded defensive, though why, she couldn't begin to guess. "You and I being in the same place once again—'tis no more than coincidence, exactly as it was at Vauxhall."

"Oh, aye," he said flatly, but she saw the little twitch of his mouth above that tight, hard jaw. "Vauxhall."

"Exactly so," she said, wondering what despicable demon had made her mention Vauxhall at all. Belatedly, she shoved the errant shoulder strap of her tunic back into place. The costume had been made for a much larger woman; if the brass brooches that held the shoulder seams together sat where they belonged, then the front of the tunic dipped far too low over her breasts, but if she tugged the front up for decency, then the brooches slid over her shoulders and the whole length of slippery fabric would fall away. If she wished to be as chaste and pure as that hideous goddess, then she was going to have to stay on the stand and keep very still.

Very, *very* still.

He cleared his throat, the deep rumble that reminded her of some great cat's purr. "So you are having your likeness painted?"

She nodded, then smoothed her unbound hair over the front of her tunic. All afternoon, she had stood before Mr. Rowan while his assistants and servants came and went, and she'd felt not a smidgen of self-consciousness. But with Joshua Fairbourne, she had become acutely conscious of how much the costume revealed of not only her body, but her body's shameful responses as well. Already, she could feel the same warm glow tingling in her belly that had been there when she'd kissed him, and he was still a good eight feet away, and cross with her in the bargain.

No, it was worse than that, for she'd felt it the moment she'd heard his voice. Having the rest of him here before her now wasn't helping, either, all broad shoulders and weathered skin and those huge, capable, lovely hands that no gentleman would ever claim.

"I've never had a proper portrait done, you know," she began, determined to keep her thoughts where they should be, "and now that I'm marrying Mr. Branbrook, I have to. He's sitting for one, too, of course, so we can be properly hung side by side, man and wife, lord and lady, in the great hall at Winchelsea Park. That's why it's to be all of me, clear down to these foolish sandals—to match the others of Harry's family at Winchelsea, you see—even though that's the most costly portrait that Mr. Rowan paints. Did you know he charges extra for showing my hands, because fingers are so dreadfully tiresome for painters?"

Joshua sighed. No matter how Anabelle was dressed, or undressed, *she* was doing all she politely could to remind him of her own upcoming marriage. He was a besotted clodpate, a hopeless mooncalf. Clearly, she had been able to forget that one wretched kiss. So why the devil couldn't *he?*

"No," he said at last. "I didn't."

"Well, true it is," she said, more rattled by that unexpected softness in his voice then if he'd bellowed across the rooftops. Why couldn't he have kept to being angry with her? That she could cope with, that she could manage without a thought, because it would mean that he had accepted the fate he'd chosen as surely as she'd accepted her own. But not gentleness, not kindness, not anything that *mattered*—that, she could not bear.

"Mr. Rowan paints only people of fashion, gentlemen and ladies," she began again, "and because they've come to think the world of him, he can tell them to do whatever foolish thing he pleases, and they will only value him more. You know, you are probably the first person ever to order him about."

"Nay, Anabelle, you must have been first," he said, and instantly cursed himself for being so familiar.

"Me?" She laughed, a gulping little nervous giggle of a laugh caused by the sound of her name on his lips. "I am far too much a coward to question such a vastly acknowledged genius as Mr. Rowan. Even Grandmother bows to his taste, else she'd never have agreed to me wearing this silly, strumpety dressing gown."

"It's not strumpety, not on you," he said. Automatically, his gaze slid downward over the satin, lingering, before returning to her face. "I like it."

Her face grew hot, and worse, she felt her breasts ache and grow strangely heavy, the weight of the slippery fabric mimicking the tracing path his gaze had taken. She could do nothing about her hideous blushing, but she prayed that at least her hair was covering the tight little pebbles of her nipples through the satin. If only he wouldn't look at her like that and listen to her with such eminent, disarming seriousness, as if what she said was actually worth hearing.

Lord, Lord, help her, why had she ever agreed to be alone with him again?

"I can tell you more of the great Mr. Rowan," she cried, desperately clutching the gilded bow with both hands before her as if it truly were a weapon. "Oh, indeed I can!"

She could hear herself racing along like a six-horse

carriage without a driver, this breathless, breakneck babbling her last empty defense against herself. "Do you know that he does not even paint his own drapery? Can you fancy such a thing, Captain Fairbourne?"

"I can believe anything in London," he said. He could believe anything of himself now, too. "But Anabelle—"

"Mr. Rowan insists that I wear all this satin, yet all he will deign to paint is this bit around my shoulders," she said, not letting him finish, or even begin. "One of his apprentices told me. Another man, a tailor–painter, will come to finish the big patches that Mr. Rowan finds too tedious to finish. Could you ever conceive of such a *vastly* dishonest scheme? I wouldn't—oh, *oh!*"

With a loud crack, the gilt bow suddenly snapped where she'd been clutching it, and with the tension of the string gone, the two broken pieces flew apart. Without thinking, Anabelle grabbed for them, and as she did, the satin tunic slithered perilously off her shoulder and over one breast. With a horrified gasp, she let the broken bow fall and looked down to clutch at the fabric, struggling to tug it back to where it belonged.

Then suddenly, his hand was there, too, steadying her, his fingers brushing over the bare skin of her arm, and with no more warning than that she was staring into the blue eyes she remembered so well, level with hers as she wavered on the edge of the model's platform.

"'Tis said that Mr. Rowan is not the only painter of fashion in London to do such deceitful things to fool his patrons," she whispered, her gaze tumbling deep into his. "'Tis said Mr. Rowan—"

"Hang Mr. Rowan," ordered Joshua as he pulled her closer.

She had never seen this look in his eyes before, an openness and uncertainty and vulnerability, too, that was so achingly a match for her own that it terrified her.

She swallowed hard, her heart pounding, as her words stumbled haltingly over one another. "'Tis said that Mr. Rowan—that he—oh, Joshua, aren't you married now?"

"No," he said as his face slanted over hers, "and neither are you."

As his lips found hers, her last sane thought was of what a sorry goddess Diana she made, for there was nothing chaste, nothing pure about kissing Joshua, nor did he put her in mind of slugs, either. Instead, he tasted of dark, mysterious things that were forbidden, of tobacco and rum and the sea and experience and most of all of himself, luring and pulling her deeper into a hot pool of need.

She forgot the immodest tunic, letting the wayward silk slide where it pleased as she twined her arms around the back of his neck, his hair curling like strands of black silk over her wrist. She forgot everything as his hands spread over her hips, his fingers pressing into her flesh to pull her against the hard proof of his own desire, and though some last tiny bit of her panicking conscience warned her of the danger, she didn't want to stop. Before much longer, she wouldn't be able to.

"Have you any notion what you've done to me, Anabelle?" he whispered hoarsely, almost begging, the heat of his breath on her ear making her tremble. "Do you *know*?"

She did, because he'd done the same to her. She felt

the same intoxicating, bewildering confusion that he felt as she sought his mouth again. His hand slid higher, and she heard the click of the brass brooch unclasp, and then how gently, oh, how sweetly, his fingers moved across her bared skin. *She* was the one who arched against him so wantonly, she was the one who trembled as she pushed her breast against his warm, rough palm, who wanted more. She cried his name with the unexpected pleasure of it, and her eyes flickered open to search for the same joy in his face.

But what she saw over Joshua's shoulder was even more unexpected, and the joy fled as swiftly as it had come.

For there, before her, she saw her own ruin.

❦ Six ❦

"Oh, dear Lord in Heaven," whispered Anabelle, the color bleaching from her cheeks as she frantically tried to pull the slippery silk back over her breast. "Oh, dear Lord, help me now!"

Though his blood was pounding in his ears, his hand almost shaking with the dizzying sensation of touching her, Joshua could guess what had happened without turning. Rowan would be there ogling her, that fancy-dress manservant, too, both doubtless summoned by that blasted woman with the lute, and he silently, heartily cursed them all as he struggled to rein in his own ungentlemanly impulses. He wouldn't be any help to Anabelle if he didn't.

"An audience?" he asked as evenly as he could, deftly helping her shaking fingers refasten the clasp on the top of her shoulder.

She nodded miserably, her eyes wide with mortification as she fumbled clumsily with the tunic.

"Idiots," he muttered. As much as he wanted to turn and look at the intruders himself, he stayed where he was, shielding her behind his body until she was decent again, or at least as decent as she could be. "Damned meddlesome basta—"

"No," she said. "No."

Her face was so pale above the rose-colored silk that he feared she'd faint, and as she tried to edge around him, he automatically took her arm to keep her from teetering off the edge of the platform. If her head was spinning half as fast as his own, then there was a good chance she might, and the last thing he wanted was to see her tumble before the others.

But then—or was it now?—he'd do anything to make things right for her. No, it was more than that. He would do anything in his power to protect her. He had kissed her, the unreasonable, irresistible impulse of a madman, and in return, his entire being had lurched out of balance. He couldn't explain it any better than that. No other woman had left him feeling like that, but then, no other woman was like Anabelle. Nothing else might make sense to him now, but that did, and at last he turned to face the intruders.

A good half-dozen faces were crowded into the doorway like playgoers in a single box. Rowan was there, of course, and a gap-toothed apprentice, holding the framed sketch of Mary like another witness. But standing before them were three elderly women, no, *ladies*—by now, Joshua knew the difference—all dressed in the rich, angular styles of years past, all three leaning heavily on the arms of their own liveried footmen in lieu of walking sticks, and all of them staring at him and at Anabelle. He'd never felt such a wave of disapproval, scorn, and outright hatred wash through a room.

Gently, he squeezed Anabelle's arm to reassure her.

"We'll weather these old she-wolves together, lass," he said, his voice low for her alone. "Together, mind?"

But to his surprise, Anabelle shook her head, then eased her arm free of his hand. She stepped from the platform, pitifully small beside him in her flat-heeled sandals, before she bowed her head and sank into a gracefully respectful curtsy, the silk puddling around her ankles and her hair sliding over her shoulders. No matter how she must feel inside, decided Joshua with growing admiration, she still had the courage to face them alone, more courage under fire than many a man.

"Good day, Lady Stanfield," she said as if they'd just met over tea, her voice shaking only the tiniest bit. "Lady Enid. Grandmother. Grandmother, I—"

"*Mr.* Rowan, sir," said her grandmother, the one in the front, her words crackling with anger as she interrupted Anabelle and addressed the artist. "Mr. Rowan, sir. I had no idea your rooms were used for common assignations. You had led me to believe, sir, that I could leave my granddaughter beneath your roof in unimpeachable safety."

Lady Stanfield sniffed, her gaze sweeping scornfully over Anabelle. "What else could you expect, Horatia, when you let the little hussy stand about in such undress before some great, lusty fellow? If you but recall her father, this tawdry show makes perfect sense."

"Entirely understandable," agreed Lady Enid in a haughty drawl. "To be sure, the girl is but half English."

Anabelle let the silk slip from her fingers, by sheer will alone keeping her expression unchanged even as she felt her world crashing in around her.

She was ruined. Eternally, unforgivably, unlamentably ruined. It would have been bad enough to have this happen before Grandmother alone. But for the Marchioness of Stanfield and Lady Enid to be there as witnesses, too, made her situation infinitely worse. Their appraisals would be both thorough and merciless. By tomorrow morning, her disgrace would be known in every fashionable parlor in London, and by nightfall, she would be welcome in none. And as for her engagement—she'd learn soon enough the depth of Henry Branbrook's affection, as well as that of his forgiveness.

She had failed again. She'd failed at *everything*. At being a dutiful daughter, an obedient granddaughter, a well-bred lady, a gentleman's future wife, even a goddess.

Especially a goddess.

Rowan edged his way closer to Grandmother, his bristling brows now turned strangely meek. "I assure you, Lady Auboncourt, that when I left dear Miss Crosbie with this gentleman—"

"He is no gentleman, sir," said Grandmother sharply. "Come, Anabelle."

"Now hold there, ma'am," said Joshua at last, with the deep quarterdeck rumble that Anabelle had come to know so well. "You know nothing about me, not even my name. You don't know if I'm a gentleman or the basest-born rascal alive. By my lights, that means you've no right to speak of me like that, any more than you've the right to treat Anabelle like this just because she's your own flesh and blood."

Anabelle nearly gasped aloud. No one spoke to Grandmother like that. She doubted even Grandfather had dared do so.

Grandmother lifted her chin, the better to look down her nose at Joshua as if he were a small, unpleasant insect instead of a man towering nearly a foot above her. "You are correct. I do not know you."

"Then let me tell you," said Joshua, his tone a commanding match for hers. "My name, ma'am, is Joshua Fairbourne, master of the brig *Swiftsure,* of Appledore in the colony of Massachusetts."

Grandmother's eyes glittered bright and hard as cut steel. "And I will tell you, you young cockerel, that I still do not know you, and never shall." She beckoned to Anabelle. "Come with me directly, you poor lamb, before this provincial scoundrel harms you any further."

Yet Anabelle didn't move. *Before the provincial scoundrel harms you further*—so that was the tactic that Grandmother would use to try to salvage her name. She would be painted as a victim, an innocent girl nearly seduced by a wicked savage from the colonies. She would be regarded with pity, not as a sinner but as a fool, and a half-Irish fool at that, while Joshua—Joshua would be treated as if he'd never existed.

Anabelle shuddered. There'd be no choice for her, of course. Grandmother was old and clever, and she knew which tales, whether truth or fiction, that would be most palatable to society. What Anabelle herself thought would matter not in the least.

"Of course the girl herself cannot be blamed for being weak," admitted Lady Stanfield with another sniff. "She has so much in her breeding to overcome."

"Here, Anabelle," said Grandmother, an edge of warning creeping into her tone. "I know you're distraught, but it is better for us now to return home, where you can rest and recover. Prentiss, help her."

The same plump footman that Joshua remembered from the day near the river came toward Anabelle, his arm outstretched in the exact balance between solicitude and respectful distance, and every bit the equal to her old bitch of a grandmother in outright insincerity. God only knew what they'd do to punish Anabelle. The way they were treating her now was bad enough.

"Nay, Prentiss, stay where you are," he ordered, and the man stopped abruptly. "Miss Crosbie, listen to me. You don't have to leave unless you want it. They can't force you against your will."

Though she kept her back toward him, Joshua saw the slight lift of her shoulders, how her long hair shivered down her back, and knew she was listening.

"Anabelle, lass," he said softly. "You don't have to go."

"Hah, and what else do you propose she do instead?" demanded Lady Stanfield, her laughter mocking. "Pray, where else would a peer's granddaughter go but to her home?"

Where indeed, thought Anabelle sadly. Didn't Joshua realize how differently the world treated men? He could spend tonight in the most notorious brothel in London, drinking and wenching until sunrise, yet as long as he could stagger before the minister in time for his wedding to Mary Holme tomorrow, he would be regarded as an honorable man of good reputation. In most circles, a last night of debauchery was even expected.

But not for an unmarried girl; never for a lady. The tantalizing freedom he was offering simply didn't exist for her, and never would. Mr. Rowan's three linnets, hopping and singing in their bamboo cage, had known more of the world than she. A lady depended on the shelter and protection first of her father, then of her husband. And as much as Anabelle might wish it otherwise, all Joshua truly had to offer her was that single, shameful unforgettable, kiss.

"Remember who you are, Anabelle," ordered Grandmother urgently. "If not for your own sake or for mine, then for the memory of your dear mother, remember who you *are*."

With a sinking feeling deep in his chest, Joshua watched as Anabelle bowed her head and walked slowly from him, now more a penitent Magdalene than the laughing, merry pagan she'd been for Rowan's brush. He watched her offer her arm to her grandmother, saw the older woman's private smile of triumph as she leaned upon her, saw how the others in the doorway parted to let them pass.

Not once did Anabelle look back to him. But this time, for the first time, she hadn't said good-bye.

And neither, he realized, had he.

With the afternoon shadows long on the walls of her chamber, Anabelle lay on her back in the center of her bed, her arms and legs like a starfish as she stared at the gathered damask canopy overhead. She had tried reading to overcome her wretchedness, she had tried fingering the spinet in the music room, she had even tried jabbing a needle in and out of the linen of her much-neglected crewelwork. Nothing had made her forget what had happened this day, because, deep in her heart, she hadn't wanted to.

With a desultory sigh, she flopped over onto her stomach, the pointed toes of her slippers drumming idly against the mattress and the bones of her stays poking into her ribs. While Grandmother had gone to call on Mr. Branbrook's mother, determined to reach her before the gossip did, Anabelle had been forbidden to leave the house for the rest of the day—an edict doubtless to be extended for the rest of her mortal life.

Yet hidden away as Anabelle was, Grandmother had still insisted that she change from the artist's silk tunic into the clothing of a respectable woman. Stays were highly respectable, even mandatory. So were stockings with garters and a heavy petticoat and a ruffled Holland cap and an open jacket and a boned, bowed stomacher, even if no one but her maidservant saw them. She sighed again, taking an empty pleasure in crushing the neat satin bows on the front of her stomacher. Satin bows were about the only thing in her life she still had any power to control.

With her chin propped on her folded arms, she could see the cradle, a silent, poignant reminder of both the past and her own future. Her future: an elegant home and an English gentleman for a husband, children and respectability, even a fair chance of becoming a countess. No wonder the angel carved into the cradle's bonnet smiled so winsomely there in the late-day sun.

But still, Anabelle wished wistfully that her mother were alive now, so that she might ask her if she had ever dared waver from the tidy destiny before her, if her mother, too, had ever kissed the wrong man before she'd married her father. It wasn't a question Anabelle could ask Grandmother, not when Grandmother had sworn that the happiest marriages were made without love. If that were so, then she and Mr. Branbrook would be the most joyfully wedded couple in the world. With a choked sob, Anabelle buried her face against her arms.

Yet even as the first hot tears spilled from her eyes, she heard the tremendous thump that echoed through the hall below. Then came another, more like some medieval battering ram pummeling the door than a genteel request for admission. With a sniff, Anabelle pushed herself up to listen, wiping her eyes with the back of her hand. She heard the servant's footsteps scurrying across the tile floor, the muted squeak of the key in the brass box-lock, and at last the caller's voice, a deep-throated rumble that reverberated through the house as easily as it would have through a Caribbean hurricane.

"I've come to see your mistress, Prentiss," said Joshua as he pushed his way easily past the footman into the hall. "The young one, Miss Crosbie. You tell her that she and I have business that can't wait."

"Miss Crosbie cannot receive you at present, Captain Fairbourne," said Prentiss, striving to regain control. "I shall tell her and Her Ladyship you called."

"Meaning both of them are here," said Joshua. Now that he'd resolved on his course, steering it seemed simple enough, once dunderheads like this footman cleared out of his way. "That's it, Prentiss, isn't it?"

Resolutely, Prentiss squared his shoulders, though the front of his waistcoat remained decidedly round. "I cannot discuss Her Ladyship's whereabouts with you, sir."

"I didn't ask you to discuss them, man, only to say whether Miss Crosbie was here." The front hall of Lady Auboncourt's London house had been designed for grand effect, and so was full of black-and-white Italian marble and gilt-framed looking glasses, and all of it, decided Joshua, as cold and hard and costly as the old woman herself. His jaw tightened as he thought again of how she'd dismissed him. He'd show her how a true gentleman behaved, which was a sight better than a lady like her.

"I don't give a tinker's damn whether your precious ladyship's here or not, Prentiss," he said. Lightly, he ran his fingertips across a bit of Greek key molding, noting how the footman winced as if he'd dared touch the dowager herself. "I still mean to speak with her granddaughter, and I mean to stay here until I do."

"But, sir," protested Prentiss. "Her Ladyship would not wish—"

"Oh, Joshua—*Joshua!*" cried Anabelle, her face upside down overhead as she leaned across the rail from the landing above. Her voice was full of frantic dismay, which was not at all the welcome Joshua desired. But she did hurry swiftly down the long staircase toward him, almost running with her petticoats bunched in her hands to keep from tripping, and for Joshua, that eagerness made up for the dismay. He'd made the right decision. Damnation, how could he have dreamed of doing otherwise?

"Miss Crosbie," he said formally, cleared his throat, and added a slight bow to be sure the thing was done properly. "Good day, Miss Crosbie. I've come to speak to you."

"You can't, not while Grandmother's not here, and you shouldn't be here either, Joshua Fairbourne, if you'd had a farthing's worth of concern for me or my circumstances!" She waved her hands before her as if shooing a recalcitrant stray dog. "Now go directly! Go!"

"Nay, missy, I shall not," he said flatly. "Not until you hear what I've come to say."

She shook her head impatiently, trying to shake away his foolishness. If Grandmother returned to find him here, she would assume that he'd come at Anabelle's bidding, and the trouble that was already simmering around her would increase a hundredfold.

But how could she possibly force a man the size of Joshua to move if he didn't wish to? He stood before her with his feet wide spread and his hands clasped behind his back, as immovable a force as she'd ever confronted. This late in the day, his jaw was shadowed by his beard, and the black hair that had been so neatly combed earlier had slipped loose from its black-bowed queue, the heavy locks falling across over his forehead. He looked rakishly mussed, perilously close to disheveled, every inch the pirate Grandmother had accused him of being.

But that, alas, wasn't the worst of it. Anabelle had brothers, three wild, charming, and thoroughly spoiled young men, and from them, she'd learned to recognize that determined gleam in a male's eyes. She knew all too well the sort of mischief that might follow, mischief she'd no intention of encouraging again.

"You *must* go," said Anabelle urgently. "Don't you understand what you've done to me already? I can't possibly see you ever again, not here, not anywhere!"

Joshua smiled then, his teeth very white. "You're seeing me right now, aren't you?"

She exploded with a muffled shriek of exasperation, and to both his delight and amazement, he realized he'd just twisted her words around to befuddle her the exact way she did to him. Now he could understand why.

"Seeing you, am I?" she demanded. "Well, *that* can certainly be remedied!"

She twisted away from him with a swirl of her skirts, and as she did, he grabbed her arm.

"Hush now, don't say it," he said softly as she glared at him. "It's my turn to speak, Anabelle. Past time, truth to tell."

He didn't believe she'd run away now, but he kept his hand tight around her arm to be certain. He reached into his breeches pocket, withdrew a guinea, and held it, gleaming, between his forefinger and thumb for Prentiss to see.

"How much silence will that buy, eh?" he asked the

footman. "Enough for me to speak to Miss Crosbie alone? Enough that your blessed ladyship won't learn of my being here?"

Prentiss sniffed, reaching for the coin.

But Joshua snatched it upward. "Your word, man, for what puny, paltry stuff that's worth. Have I bought your silence?"

"Prentiss would sell his own grandmother to the Turks for a guinea," said Anabelle, glaring as she tried to wrench free and failed. "Now please say whatever ridiculous thing you're determined to spout, so that you can leave me in peace."

"Oh, aye, I mean to," said Joshua as he tossed the coin to the footman. "But not in the hearing of our friend Prentiss here."

With her arm still firmly in his grip, he guided her across the hall to one of the pairs of tall doors that would, he guessed, lead to a parlor. Without waiting for Prentiss, he flicked the latch himself and shoved the door open. At once, he saw he'd found the dining chamber instead, an immensely long table surrounded by at least a score of tall-backed chairs. But he wasn't about to admit he'd made a mistake, and he drew Anabelle into the room anyway, shutting the door after them.

He led her to the far end of the table, away from the door where Prentiss was doubtless listening with his ear pressed to the crack. He turned the last chair, an armchair with a Flemish-worked cushion, away from the table and toward Anabelle.

"Now sit," he ordered as he released her, then, as an afterthought, softened the order. "Please."

Anabelle was not mollified. "I can't," she said with moody formality. "That is Grandmother's chair, and no one else may use it."

"Anabelle," he said, raking his fingers back through his wayward hair with exasperation. "Sit. *Now.*"

Still she didn't sit, instead frowning to the left of his waistcoat. "Are you hiding a gun beneath your coat? I vow I just saw one there, when you moved."

With an impatient sigh, he flipped back the left side of his coat to show the heavy pistol hidden beneath. "Are you satisfied?"

"You didn't have that at Mr. Rowan's studio!"

"In truth, I did." He sighed again, thankful that he wouldn't have to explain the long sailor's knife tucked into the sheath at the back of his waist, too. "You didn't notice, that was all. After that tussle with your fine Mr. Branbrook, I haven't gone about this wretched city without a gun."

"Then you're no better than he." She sank into the offered chair, her objections to it forgotten, and her feistiness, too. "Indeed worse, for you would not carry such a pistol unless you would make use of it. You truly are every bit the pirate Grandmother believes you are."

With an unhappy frown, Joshua clasped his hands behind his waist, where she wouldn't see how tightly one hand gripped the other. "I'd hoped you'd rate me a bit more highly than that."

"Oh, Joshua, you still don't understand, do you?" she asked forlornly. "Kissing you this morning was a dreadful, terrible mistake, and I could be quite, quite ruined by it. If Grandmother can't explain things properly, then Mr. Branbrook will break off with me. He'll be perfectly within his rights, you know. No one at all will fault him if he does. But I—I shall be sent back to Ireland as a hopeless, worthless old maid."

"I doubt that."

"I don't," she said with bitter bluntness. "Oh, you

men needn't marry at all. You could sail 'round the world to Bombay, if it pleased you, and begin life again as some sort of rogue pasha with a thousand houris at your beck and call. You *could*. But what choice do I have? If I do not marry, then I will spend the rest of my days at Kilmarsh, cleaning up after my father's hounds and blotting away the brandy and whiskey he spills upon himself. Or perhaps I can become a pitiable old aunt, the one whose 'misfortune' is whispered about the county, whilst I am ferried from one unwilling family to another until they, too, tire of me."

He looked down at his shoes, unwilling to see such a hideous future reflected in her eyes. "When will your grandmother return, lass?" he asked softly.

"I don't know. I suppose it shall depend on how long her repairs to my shattered reputation may take." The crumpled satin bow at her bosom trembled. "Will you let me go now?"

"Nay, but a moment longer," said Joshua. "I have a few more repairs of my own to make."

She didn't answer, but she didn't leave, either. He had intended to speak first to her grandmother in lieu of her father, but he'd come too far with Anabelle now to wait any longer. This time he'd no pretty words prepared, only the truth, and he prayed that truth would be enough.

"I came to London meaning to take a wife," he said, wincing inwardly at that clumsy beginning. "I meant to wed Mary Holme, but now I—that is, she and I—hell and damnation, Anabelle, the honest truth of it is that I've ended things with Mary, and there'll be no wedding for us."

"You've ended with her?" Anabelle gasped, her eyes wide with shock and disbelief. "Today, the day before your wedding? Oh, Joshua, how could you have been so barbarously *cruel?*"

That stung, coming from Anabelle. Joshua could be a hard man when he needed to be, a ruthless man when he had no choice, but he'd never been willfully cruel, especially not to a woman. And he'd taken the harder, more honorable path by going to her and her father this afternoon, instead of simply cutting his cable and running free for home.

"The cruelty would have been in marrying her," he said defensively. "The same for me, to put a sharp face on it, for Mary wept a good deal more when I proposed than when I broke it off."

"But to have waited this long!" cried Anabelle. "However could you have done such a thing to a woman you loved?"

"Do you love Branbrook?" he asked sharply. "You've said you'd be his wife, yet there has been nothing of his dutiful wife-to-be in how you've behaved with me."

Shame stained her cheeks, but she didn't look away. "I've never once said I loved Henry," she said, her defense as quick as Joshua's own had been. It should be, she thought unhappily, for every word had been drummed like a catechism into her unwilling conscience by Grandmother. "Marrying for love is one luxury my jointure cannot buy. For me, marriage will be a way to combine fortunes and families for the betterment of both. Love would only be an impediment, a difficulty."

"Then can't you understand that it was the same between Mary and me? Oh, I'm not so grand as you fine, noble-born folk, dripping lace like yesterday's snow," he said, unwilling to keep the edge of sarcasm from his voice, "but my reasons for choosing Mary

Holme weren't much better than yours for accepting your little lordling."

"I see," said Anabelle faintly. But she didn't see at all, or rather she saw too much, far more than she wanted to, and swiftly, before he could tell her more, she rose to her feet. "I congratulate you on your new wisdom, Captain Fairbourne, and I give you joy of your escape, if that is how you wish me to perceive it. Now if you will excuse me, sir, I must leave you and—"

"Nay, Anabelle, I won't excuse you, not until I'm done," he said, praying for the right words to make her understand. "I know I've wronged you, wronged you most grievously. 'Twas done through no ill intent, but the damage is there still, and I'm gentleman enough to know it. I won't cast you adrift alone. I mean to set things to rights, lass, if you'll let me. If you'll have me."

But from the wild, desperate look in her eyes, he knew at once that neither his prayers nor his words had worked.

"Oh, no, Joshua, please don't!" she cried, slipping around the chair, clinging to the polished mahogany to have at least some sort of barrier between them. "You must not say such things. You cannot! You may be free, but I am not! Remember that! Remember my own betrothal!"

"A betrothal you believe that puling bastard lord may have broken already!" he growled with frustration—and fear, too, that he'd lost her before she was even his to lose. "How can you trust your life to a blackguard like that?"

"You say you would marry for the same reasons as I," she said, speaking so fast that she was almost breathless. "Without the consent of my father, you will never see a farthing from him, not now in my dowry or later from his will. I will be an outcast, a pariah, worse than a sack of stones around your neck!"

"It's you I want, Anabelle, not your father's blasted guineas!"

"But you know nothing *of* me," she continued rapidly, her fingers whitening against the dark wood, "none of my ways, my habits, my tempers, and my weaknesses—"

"Damnation, Anabelle," he said, reaching for her over the high-backed chair. "Can't I be the judge of that?"

"Can you?" she asked, darting away out of his reach. "What am I left to judge, then? How soon would it be before you found another woman you'd prefer, and cast me aside the same as you have poor Mary Holme?"

He froze, his hand left hanging clumsily in midair. Anabelle had never seen such longing in a man's eyes before, longing mixed with a sorrowful conviction that his desire would forever be beyond his reach. He could play all he wanted at being invincible, and wear a brace of pistols and a cutlass, too, for all such show would convince Anabelle. She wouldn't believe it, not after she'd seen that look flicker across his face to betray his practiced, manly bluster. That look, that moment, had made him vulnerable and it had made him achingly human, and for Anabelle, it very nearly made him irresistible.

Unaware of how much he'd revealed, he let his arm at last drop heavily to his side and shook his head.

"You ask how you might judge me, and I cannot say I know," his voice hoarse with emotion. "Because the sorry truth of it, Anabelle, or the rest of the truth, anyway, is that I don't believe there's another woman in this world like you. There can't be. No matter how hard I try—and dear Jesus, how I've tried!—I can't put you from my mind. Otherwise, I never would have wronged you as shamefully as I did this morning. Marry me, Anabelle Crosbie. Marry me, and set things right for both of us."

She stared at him, too stunned to respond. Oh, dear Lord, how simple he made it sound! If she married him, nothing would be set to rights; everything would be as tumbled and confused as an overturned apple-cart.

But she would have *him*. She had never dared dream of such a rare, beautiful man as her husband, one who could say such lovely, precious things to her and mean every word. It didn't matter that he said them in his rough, strange accent, or that he'd come clear across the ocean to do so. She didn't even care if he truly was a pirate, or had a heathen red savage for a mother. She hadn't been able to put him from her mind, either. He had said nothing yet of love, but she didn't doubt that love would come for him as it already had, she realized, for her. After all, he wanted *her,* not her money or her family's influence or her breeding stock for future heirs.

Perhaps her children weren't destined to be born beneath the ancestral roof of Winchelsea Park after all. Perhaps they'd never be earls or sit in the House of Lords or be presented to court in a gown heavy with ermine. Perhaps instead she would lay to sleep in her cradle babes with eyes as blue as the sea itself and black silky curls to twine around her finger, fine, fat-cheeked babes who would grow straight and tall and proud as their father, in a wondrous land that she still couldn't find on the globe. But she would learn, because that place that was Joshua's home would become hers as well.

"Oh, Joshua," she said softly, her head and heart

both spinning at the possibilities he was holding out to her. She had never dreamed of having any sort of choice in her life, let alone one as magical as this. "What you ask—what you offer!"

She saw the hope flash in his eyes like a beacon. "Come sail with me, lass. Come with me and be my wife."

"Yes," she whispered, afraid to say the words aloud and break the spell of the moment. "Oh, yes, yes, yes!"

She ran to him and flung her arms around his neck, laughing with delight as she caught him enough off balance to make him stagger back a step.

"You surprised me," he said gruffly, lifting her into his arms.

She laughed again, burrowing against him. "I mean to do it often," she said. "You deserve it after what you've just done to me."

He kissed her then, turning her laughter into a warm vibration they shared between them. She parted her lips to let him deepen the kiss, and as he did, hungry for her, he tasted the new intimacy growing between them.

Damnation, she'd surprised him again, just as she'd promised. He hoped she wouldn't stop, either, not until he was cold in his grave.

He allowed himself another moment to savor the sweetness, then reluctantly broke away. As tempting as it was, he wouldn't let himself be trapped by her heady, breathless eagerness again until they were safely wed. "There'll be plenty of time for that, sweetheart."

"Never enough," she murmured, so fervently that he nearly reconsidered, imagining a score of wicked uses for the long dining table.

"Nay, not for us," he said instead, "for I've no wish

to meet your grandmother in such circumstances again. But I'll be back for you tonight."

"Tonight?" She looked up at him, questioning. "Here?"

"Tonight." He smiled, glad the next surprise was his. "The *Swiftsure* sails tomorrow, and I'll want you on board by my side when she does. But seeing how your family wouldn't exactly turn out to say farewell, I'll have to steal you away tonight."

Her eyes danced with excitement. "An elopement! Or is it an abduction? Oh, but whichever, how wonderfully, perfectly romantic! We shall be like the lovers in plays or stories, running away together to wed!"

"Well, aye, I suppose we will," he said dubiously. His reasons were more from necessity than some silly play; not only would the tide not wait for the *Swiftsure,* but he also doubted very much that his suit would be welcomed by Anabelle's family. If he wanted Anabelle, he'd have to take her, and soon, before her grandmother realized what was happening. One look at Anabelle's bright, joyful face, and the secret would be done. "Where is your chamber?"

"To the back of the house. The second row of windows, the third and fourth casements from the corner if you're sitting on the willow bench in the garden and look up over your shoulder. Oh, Joshua, are you really going to take me through the *window?*"

"Unless you wish the whole house to know, aye, the window would be best." He untangled her hands from around his neck, holding them firmly in his as he tried to make her listen. "I'll be back this night at one by the clock. One sharp, mind? Be dressed and ready."

She nodded. "What should I bring?"

With a mental shudder, he remembered the mountain of Mary's trunks and bags and chests that had been piled waiting in Holme's hallway. Why was it that women couldn't shift for themselves without enough dunnage to found a colony?

"One sea chest," he cautioned sternly. "One *small* sea chest."

"One small sea chest, yes," she said promptly. "And, of course, the cradle."

His eyes narrowed suspiciously. "Cradle? What cradle?"

"My cradle, of course," she said, not flinching in the least beneath his stern-eyed suspicion. "Or rather, my mother's cradle, and my grandmother's, and several others besides, far back beyond memory. I cannot leave it behind, Joshua."

"But to haul some damned *cradle* through your chamber window—"

"It is not 'some damned cradle,'" she said indignantly. "It is the one thing I cherish most from my mother, the only thing I truly must bring with me. Please, Joshua. Where else would our own little babies sleep?"

He frowned down at her, but the logistics of getting a cradle through a second-story window had been replaced in his thoughts by the far more seductive prospect of siring those little babies.

"A small cradle?" he asked dubiously. "For little babies, you say?"

"For very little babies," she promised, and leaned up to kiss him again, her breasts nudging gently against his arm.

He kissed her back, agreeing without saying a word. He was, he realized, going to have the devil's own time learning to refuse her anything.

❧ *Seven* ❧

Crouched in the shadows of Lady Auboncourt's garden, Joshua opened his battered pewter watch and tipped it to catch the faint light of the crescent moon. The longer hand had nearly crept upright; the short one hovered beside it, pointing to the first hour of the new day. The waiting was nearly done.

"Those windows—there—those are the ones, Webb," whispered Joshua to the sailor beside him. "We can rig something proper from the crosspieces, eh?"

With great seriousness, Webb shifted the coil of rope over his shoulder and patted the canvas sack with the mallet, blocks, and deadeyes for emphasis.

Joshua nodded in return, hoping the man didn't sense his own uneasiness. Ezekial Webb had sailed with him since the privateering days, and there was no one on board the *Swiftsure* more clever at contrivances with lines and traces and pulleys. If anyone could get Anabelle's blessed cradle from the window without summoning the watch here to the east side of St. James Square, it would be Webb.

But Webb was hardly the only one of the *Swiftsure*'s crew to be involved in fetching Anabelle. Beyond the garden wall sat the hired cart to carry them back to the river's edge, where the two Hallet brothers and their cousin Robert Stark would be waiting on their oars in the boat to carry them to where the brig lay moored. There Samuel Worden would be standing ready at the helm, prepared to make sail and follow the tide the minute they were on board.

They were all following Joshua's orders without question, the way they always did, but he knew that speculation and rumor were already flying wildly among them and the rest of the men left on board. Tomorrow, he thought with an inward sigh, once they were under way, he'd have to give them some sort of explanation as to why his bride was now named Miss Crosbie instead of Miss Holme, how she'd changed from tall and fair to short and dark. Exactly what form that explanation to the crew was going to take, though, was still beyond him.

Far, far beyond. How could it be otherwise, when he still couldn't explain it rationally to himself?

He clicked his watch shut. Anabelle's window was dark behind the curtains, and he nodded with approval. He'd hoped the girl would show the good sense not to light the room like a beacon. He also hoped she wouldn't become a gibbering, shrieking ninny when confronted with a bit of danger or discomfort, but that, he thought with a sigh, was likely asking for the moon. She was only a woman, and he'd no right to expect overmuch from her.

He motioned to Webb to follow, and together they ran across the walkway to the house, their boots crunching softly on the raked gravel. A narrow porch opened out onto the garden, its slate roof just below Anabelle's window. For two men accustomed to clambering through a ship's rigging, pulling themselves up along the porch's columns and up onto the roof was no challenge at all.

Lightly, Joshua tapped his knuckles against the closed window. "Anabelle," he called as loudly as he dared. "Anabelle, lass, are you there?"

No answer came, and with a muttered oath, Joshua tried to open the window. It was, of course, possible that she'd somehow been stopped, betrayed by that thieving footman, or worse, that she'd simply changed her mind. He tugged on the latch, swearing again as the bolt held fast from within. Quickly, he drew his knife, and with a few deft twists with the tip, the latch gave way.

"Anabelle?" he called again as he eased the window open. "Are you there, lass?"

Still no answer. With every nerve on edge, Joshua slid through the window drapery and into the darkened room, Webb moving like a shadow behind him. Slowly, he let his eyes adjust to the velvety darkness, making out the shapes of an immense curtained bed, chairs, a tall chest on chest. He edged along the wall, freezing for a chagrined instant as he caught sight of his own reflection in the looking glass across the room. It was all quiet, too quiet, with the queasy feeling of a trap to it.

"Anabelle?" he whispered hoarsely, unwilling to risk anything more. He hadn't put the knife away after he'd used it on the lock, and his fingers relaxed and tightened restlessly along the familiar horn grip. "Anabelle, so help me, if you're here—"

From the corner of his eye, he saw the figure dart toward him from behind the bed hangings. Instinct took over from conscious thought, and in one deadly motion Joshua had grabbed the intruder and flipped him onto his back on the bed, the knife's blade pressed close to his throat.

No, realized Joshua abruptly. Not *his* throat. *Hers.*

"Damnation, Anabelle, where were you hiding?" he said as he released her. "I didn't hurt you, did I?"

"If you didn't, Joshua Fairbourne, it wasn't from lack of trying, was it?" she demanded crossly. She rolled over onto her hands and knees on the bed, her petticoats brushing across his legs in the dark. "Twice this night already, Grandmother's maid has come on trumped-up excuses to spy on me, and I thought you were her again. Oh, if you have crushed the plume on my hat, I shall never, ever forgive you!"

He watched as she lit a candle on the stand beside her bed, her face appearing suddenly in the small ring of light. It was every bit as charming a face as he remembered, one to make climbing in that infernal window entirely justified. But he did wish she'd shown more concern in return for *him.* He was sorry if he'd hurt her hat, yet, in his opinion, in light of everything else that was happening this night, a crushed plume seemed of very little consequence.

Yet still she studied the hat in her hand, a small red beaver with the brim trimmed and cocked like a man's but crowned by a very unmannish curled pheasant's feather that she was stroking gently to assess the damage. "However did you come here, anyway?" she asked. "I hadn't unlocked that window yet."

"I unlocked it myself," said Joshua. "I have a special key that will unlock anything. Now come, I've no wish to meet your grandmother's maid, either."

She grinned wickedly up at him. "You picked the lock, didn't you? Or broke it, or forced it, or otherwise bent it to your will. Oh, my darling Captain Fairbourne, you *are* a most wondrously accomplished gentleman!"

"That he is, miss," offered Webb promptly, bobbing his head in agreement as he gazed, moonfaced and adoring, at Anabelle. "The cap'n here, he knows more than ten other mortal men put together about gettin' free of a tight spot. No matter that they'd send him straight to dance at Tyburn for breakin' and enterin' a grand palace of a place like this. No, no, he don't care, not even when—"

"Webb, shut your mouth," rumbled Joshua, shooting poor Webb a glance murderous enough to send him shrinking back into the shadows. *"Now."*

"Oh, bother, Joshua, the man intended no harm," said Anabelle, earning Webb's eternal devotion and another murderous look, just for herself, from Joshua. "You shouldn't speak so harshly to him. In truth I find his assurances regarding you rather comforting, considering the circumstances."

For a long moment, Joshua was silent as he struggled to control his temper. No one—no man, no woman, no wife—came between him and his crew. Especially not *his* wife. His word was law and must remain so. How could she mean to marry a deepwater captain and not understand so simple a fact of their existence?

Unaware, Anabelle pinned the hat back in place, cocking it rakishly over one eye before she smiled at him again, more tenderly this time. He truly was a wondrously accomplished gentleman, and wondrously handsome, too. A good man, a decent man, far better than she deserved. She hadn't meant to hide from him or startle him the way she had. She'd been as jittery as a cat all afternoon, painfully determined to have things go right with Joshua.

"Shall we go?" she said almost shyly. "I've everything ready, exactly as I promised."

But the warm smile she'd expected in return from him wasn't there. Instead, his face was dark with anger, black with an incomprehensible fury that the feeble candlelight couldn't possibly dispel.

"You tell me, Miss Crosbie," he said with cold formality. *"Shall* we go, or not?"

Beneath the intensity of that cold blue stare, she looked away, unable to let him see her pain. It was exactly as Grandmother had predicted: no decent man, especially not one like Joshua, would ever take her for a wife.

"You've changed your mind, haven't you?" she said quietly. "You've decided you don't want me after all. I understand. Truly I do. Your—your *gallantry* in offering for me was most fine, but once you had time to reconsider—"

"That's not what I meant at all, Anabelle!" he exclaimed. Angry though he was, he hadn't intended on crushing her the way he apparently had, leaving her small and forlorn beneath the combined weight of his criticism and that ridiculous hat.

"It's not?" she asked uncertainly.

"Nay, and may the devil take me if I say otherwise." He sighed, and she sighed, too. "It's only that you must remember not just *who,* but *what* I am. I'm the captain of the *Swiftsure,* mind? The captain and the *master.* I'm responsible for everyone on board, from the cabin boy to you, and you must obey me. Isn't that so, Webb?"

Webb nodded vigorously, delighted by the chance to redeem himself. "Aye, aye, Cap'n. Like gospel, your word is."

Anabelle listened gravely, swallowing her own misery. She wanted *her* Joshua, the man who had teased and laughed and kissed her until she'd seen stars dance before her eyes, not this grim-faced captain and master that seemed inexplicably tied with him. Since when was a lady wife's lot to be lumped in with that of a common seaman?

"It's for your own good, Anabelle," continued Joshua more gently. He had to remember how young she was, how unaccustomed she'd be to his ways. He reached out and brushed the back of his fingers along her cheek. "It's for your good, sweetheart, and everyone else's. There can be only one master on board, and his name is Joshua Fairbourne. But as for wanting to marry you—sweet Jesus, Anabelle, that's never going to change. Why else would I be here now, eh?"

Relief washed over her, and that glancing caress of his fingers on her skin warmed her through all her doubts and straight to her heart. He didn't wish to cast her off, at least not yet. Why else *would* he be here? As for him giving orders—he was a man, and all men liked giving orders, nearly as much as they liked being obeyed. He couldn't help being otherwise.

For now, she gave only a quick duck of a nod, accepting. She would have kissed him, too, but the awkward presence of the sailor with the odd name stopped her. She'd had more than enough of kissing before witnesses for one day.

"Good lass," said Joshua gruffly, longing for a less clumsy endearment. The easy compliments he'd always tossed the rumshop doxies and fishermen's daughters seemed unworthy of Anabelle, and for her sake, he wished he was more poetic by nature. "Now we'd best be on our way."

"Oh, yes, to be sure," said Anabelle quickly, thankful to be able to agree to something with such ease. She lifted the candlestick from the table and set it on the floor, then flipped the coverlet and hangings aside so she could pull her sea chest out from under the tall bedstead.

"Here," she said, huffing a bit as she tugged it with both hands. "A proper little sailor's sea chest, as small and tidy as ever you could wish. I know you didn't believe I could do it, but I did. 'Twas the first time in my life I've packed for myself, too."

"Here now, miss, let me light that away for you," said Webb, taking it from her and hoisting it easily onto his back. "Why, 'tis no more than a feather-weight, Cap'n! I could've carried this down without botherin' with the tackle at all."

But Joshua wasn't looking at the chest or at Webb, either.

"Anabelle," he said slowly. "What in God's great green earth are you wearing?"

"Do you like it, then?" Anabelle scrambled back to her feet, flushing with pleasure that he'd noticed her dress. Carefully, she smoothed the full, plum-colored petticoats back into place. "I hadn't the slightest notion what one wore properly for an elopement, but I guessed my new traveling habit wouldn't be amiss."

"It most certainly is," said Joshua with mingled disbelief and despair. He wished he'd had a good look at her before this, for he didn't want to criticize her again. But like every other article of clothing he'd seen her wear, this "traveling habit" was stitched and sewn to fit as closely to her body as possible and used the most damn-your-eyes expensive French goods and laces and whalebone to do so. At least her bosom was decently covered; that was the best he could say.

"Anabelle," he began with a great sigh and matching care. "Sweetheart. You cannot wear hoops on board the *Swiftsure,* or on any other Christian vessel. It is not possible."

"But I wore them on the packet from Dublin!" she protested. "That captain never once complained!"

"Then that captain was a weak-kneed cowardly bastard who risked your life to claim your passage," said Joshua soundly. "You've more yardage on your person then I have canvas on my mainmast. The first decent wind we meet will send you spinning over the side and straight to the bottom. If you even make it *up* the side, that is."

"I had not considered that," admitted Anabelle glumly. To the credit of the packet captain from Dublin, he had forbidden the ladies to walk on the deck, and when Anabelle recalled the difficulties she had maneuvering her skirts on windy days on land, she could see the wisdom of Joshua's prediction. But she was sorry to give up the new plum-colored habit, very sorry indeed. Not only was it extraordinarily becoming, as Joshua would have been bound to see by daylight, but it also had the only bodice she could fasten up herself, without a maidservant to help her.

She sighed dejectedly, fingering the kerseymere one last time. "But I understand, Joshua. I do, and I shall change directly."

"Nay, there isn't time, not if we've a prayer of making the tide," said Joshua, and as if on his command, a clock chimed and echoed the half hour from far away in the house. "Can you leave off the hoops by themselves? Is that possible?"

"Most possible," said Anabelle, turning away from the two men to lift the front of her skirts and unwind and untie the tapes that held the cage of whalebone and linen around her waist. With a wiggle of her hips, the hoops dropped to the floor, and as she stepped free, she heard the dull smack of Joshua cuffing Webb for watching her too closely. She smiled to herself, amused and pleased by Joshua's jealousy; it made up for his too-knowledgeble familiarity with lady's underthings.

"I'm left with rather a lot of petticoat," she said, leaning forward so she could see how her unsupported skirts now puddled on the floor around her. "But I shall contrive to manage until I might have them shortened."

Joshua watched as she pulled the loose skirts to one side to keep from tripping, and his mouth went dry. It was much the same effect as when she'd worn Rowan's goddess robe, the soft wool clinging familiarly to the full, plump curves of her hips and bottom.

"All I wish you to contrive now," he somehow managed to say, "is to hurry."

"Oh, I'm quite ready," she said, walking to the open window with her petticoats clutched in one hand and the candle in the other. "Mr.—Mr.—your sailor has my sea chest, and the cradle is here."

She lowered the candle so the light fell over the cradle, and it was all he could do to bite back another oath. He had never seen such a monstrosity of old oak and gnarled turnings: the wretched thing must be near the width of a whale boat. Did the women in her family really give birth to babies of such a size to warrant a cradle like this?

"That be the cradle, Cap'n?" asked Webb with open amazement. "That great piece o' lumber?"

"Aye, and what else could it be, you dunderhead?" said Joshua, his own disbelief making his voice sharp. "'Tis the one thing Miss Crosbie wished us to bring special, and bring it we will. Won't we, Webb?"

"Aye, aye, Cap'n," said the sailor promptly, sliding Anabelle's chest to the floor so he could begin unwrapping the coil of rope from his shoulder.

"He will be careful, won't he?" asked Anabelle anxiously, hovering with concern as Webb threaded the rope through the cradle's spindles to fashion a sling. "That cradle is vastly ancient."

"Aye, don't doubt for a moment that he will," said Joshua absently, his thoughts turned to sorting out the last details of their departure. "He knows he'll have to answer to me otherwise. Cover the light, Anabelle. Not even a glimmer, mind?"

He nodded as she shielded the little flame behind her cupped hands. Carefully, he eased the heavy drapes apart and scanned the darkened garden. Most likely, he was taking far more precautions than were necessary; if no one in the house suspected Anabelle was leaving, then they'd have no cause to watch her windows, either. But that overly conscientious maidservant of her grandmother's worried him still, as did the greedy footman Prentiss, and he wasn't entirely at ease about Mary Holme's father, either.

"How shall we get down?" asked Anabelle, her voice unconsciously dropping to a conspirator's whisper as she uncovered the candle.

"The same way we came up," said Joshua. "It's most obliging of your grandmother to have this porch for us to use as a ladder."

Anabelle came to stand beside him to follow his gaze, doubtfully peering over the drop to the roof of the porch, and from the porch to the ground. If he'd asked her to jump from London Bridge itself, the prospect would have been no less daunting. She didn't want to be frightened before him, especially not now, but oh, how far below the ground seemed!

"It would seem," she ventured, "like rather a great distance to fall, Joshua."

"Well, aye, I suppose it is," he admitted, glancing carelessly over his shoulder. "But I've not the least intention of falling, so you won't, either."

"You will help me, then?" Suddenly the distance didn't seem quite as far.

He looked at her, his great dark brows twisted scornfully over the bridge of his nose. "Do you truly believe I'd do otherwise? God in heaven, what you must think of me!"

"What I think," she whispered fiercely, "is that you have carried off such bold enterprises a great many times, while I have done them not at all. Not at all!"

"Anabelle," he said, slinging one leg over the window's sill. "Would it set your mind at ease to know that this is the first time—the *absolute* first time— that I have ever stolen a young lady from her bedchamber by moonlight? I'm as much a quivering maid in these matters as you. Now come, enough of this chatter. Give me your hand."

The notion of Joshua's quivering at anything was ludicrous, let alone being a maid, but Anabelle did recognize a challenge when she heard one. Biting back her retort, she thrust her hand into his, determined to neither quiver nor chatter. She followed his lead and sat beside him on the sill, staring resolutely at the leaves of the tulip tree before her instead of the gravel path below.

He smiled with encouragement, but before she had the chance to smile back, he had released her hand and dropped to the narrow roof below, as gracefully as any cat, and with only the slightest thud on the slates. He grinned up at the window, beckoning silently.

"Go 'head, miss," said Webb behind her. "Cap'n will catch you, jus' like he said."

Clutching tightly to the window frame, she looked back into the room. Webb had finished preparing the cradle and was waiting to follow her with the jury-rigged block and line in his hands, ready to lower both the cradle and her chest to the ground.

She swallowed hard, fighting her fear. Behind Webb, she could barely make out the three white rectangles propped up on the mantelpiece, the letters she was leaving for Grandmother and Father and jilted Henry Branbrook.

When she'd written them earlier in the evening, she hadn't been certain exactly what purpose they'd serve. Were they letters of farewell, or pleas for forgiveness? But what she'd realized when she'd read the letters over was that she'd neither begged nor waxed sentimental. Instead, in her loopy, sprawling hand with a splattering of hurried blots, she'd simply told the truth: that she loved Joshua Fairbourne and believed he would make her happy in ways no other man could.

She believed it and prayed with all her heart that she was right to do so. She looked back to Joshua, standing with his arms outstretched. His hat had fallen from his head, a black triangle on the lawn behind him, and the ribbon on his queue fluttered lightly in the breeze. His face was turned toward her, full and rapt with eagerness and longing for her, just for her. She swallowed hard, took a deep breath, and slipped from her old life and into Joshua's waiting arms.

He caught her easily, surprised again by how small she was against him. She hadn't wept and she didn't cry out or shriek, but he noticed how her fingers clung convulsively to his shoulders, and he drew her closer to steady and comfort her.

"Halfway there, sweetheart," he whispered into her ear. "To the ground, 'tis all. I'll be waiting again."

He began to ease himself free, meaning to climb down the column first himself and catch her again, but she held fast to him, her eyes wide and her lips pressed tightly together. Neither was reassuring. He had a horrible image of himself watching helplessly as, alone, she swayed on the slippery slates, her yards of petticoats streaming behind her as she crashed to the ground.

"I've a better notion, sweet," he said, turning himself and crouching down lower for her sake. "Lash your arms around my shoulders and hold tight, and I'll carry you down with me."

He felt her obey, her small hands clasping onto his shoulders. "Use your legs, too," he whispered, "like a little monkey on a palm tree."

Behind him, Anabelle hesitated, her fear warring with the gross impropriety of what he suggested. Like a little monkey, indeed; she was no barbarous ape, nor was he any mere palm tree. To straddle him with her legs, to hold tight to his body with such intimacy and without even the shelter of her hoops, made her face burn hot with shame.

But what was the alternative? She did not wish to be left on the roof alone while he went on without her, but his shoulders were too broad for her to loop her arms securely around them. She couldn't go back up, yet the ground still seemed far, far away.

A length of rope flopped down beside her like a snake, and she gasped. Joshua grabbed it and waved to Webb, who had rigged the rope through the cross-piece in the window frame.

"This will ease our passage, won't it?" said Joshua as he tested his grip upon the line. "A generous fellow, Webb. Now clap on, lass, and we'll be off."

She felt him try his weight against the rope, bouncing lightly on the balls of his feet. Any second, he would drop over the side, and with a muffled whimper of anguish, she buried her face against his back and wrapped her legs around his waist. As soon as she did, he jumped clear of the slates, letting them dangle like a spider on its silk thread. She felt the heavy, flapping weight of her petticoats, the rush of air rising beneath them cool over her legs, bare above her stockings, and she felt as much as heard Joshua's grunt as they landed on the ground. Yet still she clung to him, unable to let go. He was warm and solid beneath her, her one real security.

"You can let go now, Anabelle," he said, his voice strangely distant. "The ground seems quite firm beneath my feet."

"I never said I doubted it," she said quickly. She was behaving exactly like that trembling virgin she'd sworn not to be, and now that the danger was past she was once again aware of the wicked familiarity of having her legs clasped around his waist. Swiftly, she released his shoulders, intending to slide as gracefully as she could to the ground. Faith, she grumbled to herself as her shoes kicked and sought aimlessly for purchase, why did the man have to be so blessed tall, anyway?

But a graceful descent was not to be hers, nor, to her growing mortification, any descent at all. The front of her bodice fastened over her breasts with a double row of polished pewter buttons à la Marlborough, very military and very fashionable, and, as she soon realized, very much like little fishhooks. As she slid downward, the edges of the buttons snagged and caught fast in the woven braid on the back seams of Joshua's coat, trapping her there with her toes still above the ground.

"Eternal blast and hellfire," she muttered, an expression she'd learned from the stableboys at Kilmarsh. Clumsily, she twisted to one side and then the other, but instead of freeing herself, it seemed she'd only made the buttons embed themselves more deeply. "Blast these infernal *buttons!*"

She felt a low rumble beneath her and realized Joshua was laughing. "Blast you, too, Joshua Fairbourne!" she whispered fiercely. "This is all your fault, as you know perfectly well!"

"And I knew you were fond of me, Anabelle," he said, trying not to laugh, "but I'd no notion you'd grown so, ah, *attached.*"

"That is not amusing, Joshua, and you are a vile, hateful man to pretend that it is." She gave him a sharp kick in the back of his calf for emphasis. "Now *you* let go of *me* directly, or I shall scream and wake Grandmother and watch with glee as the constable carts you away to Newgate."

"Ah, Anabelle," he said with a mournful sigh, "you'll slaughter me with your affection."

He reached around and grabbed her firmly by one knee. Despite the layers of her petticoats, his grip seemed more like a caress, enough to make her squeal with indignation and try to kick him again. But as he raised her up, the buttons slipped free, leaving her to drop unattached at last to the ground.

She stumbled backward, glaring at him as she spread her fingers over the offending buttons to assure herself that none had been lost. That, and to soothe herself, too. Even through her shift, stays, and several thicknesses of kerseymere, the sensation caused by the pressing of her breasts across his back had been, well, *unsettling.*

"That was not done well," she said sharply, wishing she wasn't having such a difficult time catching her breath.

"Ah, well, I warned you I'd not done it before." He

bent to retrieve his hat from the lawn and settled it squarely on his head. "We'll see if we can better it when we board the *Swiftsure*."

She looked at him suspiciously. He was teasing her again, that was clear, and she decided to pay his foolishness no more attention than it was worth. Ships were boarded by neat little bridged walkways that ran from the dock. She remembered that from the Dublin packet, and he wasn't going to fool her into thinking otherwise.

She lifted her chin resolutely and took a deep breath to compose herself. She'd suffered a terrible fright. Yes. No one could deny it. Surely that was the reason her heart was still racing and her thighs were as quivery as jelly from holding so tightly to him. Surely that, and not—

He grinned, and all her prim indignation disintegrated along with her wits. If he could leave her feeling like this now, she thought as she flushed like a doting simpleton, what would happen when they were finally husband and wife?

Dear Lord, thinking *that* way wasn't going to calm her in the least.

Deliberately, she broke the lock of his gaze with hers, looking away in time to see the cradle hanging in the air over Joshua's head. She gasped and pointed, and he turned to reach up and guide the cradle to the ground as effortlessly as if he'd known it was there all the time. Perhaps he had; by now, it wouldn't have surprised her in the least.

She hurried forward, running her hand over the wood. Webb had lashed the cradle to the top of her trunk, before he'd lowered the two together, and as far as she could see by the moonlight, neither had suffered. As Joshua knelt down to untie the longer rope that had brought them down together, Anabelle stepped back to look up for Webb.

"Oh, no," she murmured in disbelief. "Oh, damn and blast, *no!*"

"What is it, sweet?" asked Joshua over his shoulder as Webb dropped silently to the lawn beside the cradle. "Have your buttons played you false again?"

She rushed forward, away from the open lawn and to the darker shadows beneath the porch. "Someone's lit a candle on the top floor," she whispered urgently. "I saw it moving behind one of the garret windows. A maidservant, a footman—who knows how long they might have been watching? We must leave at once, before they have a chance to warn anyone else!"

Joshua's easy grin vanished, his face growing instantly harder as he rose to his feet. "There is a two-wheeled cart waiting on the street beyond the north gate," he explained rapidly. "The driver's in my hire, a ginger-haired man in a striped weskit named Stark. If we're separated, go to him."

"Separated?" She searched his face anxiously. "But that won't happen, will it?"

"Anything can happen, Anabelle," he said sharply, "and God knows, it usually does."

"But I—"

"Go now, there's no time. You run on, and Webb and I'll follow with the cradle and the chest. Don't stop to look back, and don't you trip on those fancy petticoats of yours, mind?" He bent over her, his lips rough and quick across hers. "Go, sweetheart. Don't tarry, and mind your captain's orders."

Her captain's orders. Put that way, it didn't sound like orders at all, but a warning, a caution, proof that he cared what became of her. With a fleeting smile, she bunched up her skirts in her fists, turned, and ran.

In a dozen steps, she was across the narrow stripe of close-clipped lawn; another half-dozen carried her beyond the teakwood bench where she'd eaten sugarplums in the afternoon, eight more steps and she'd passed Grandmother's roses and the moss-covered faun that her uncle had brought back from his tour of Rome three decades ago. She saw it all in a rush as she fled the garden and her past, yet she did not stop, and as much as she longed to, she did not look back.

Captain's orders, she told herself with fierce delight. *Her* captain's orders.

The gate in the north wall was unlocked and ajar, the first time she could remember it being that way, and she edged her way through it to the street. She stopped there, breathing hard. She hadn't run so much since she'd been a girl, and she laced her stays a good deal more tightly now than she had then. Thrusting the loose pins back into her hat, she hugged the wall and stared up and down the street. At this hour, there were no passersby, no carriages, but drawn up near the corner stood a lone two-wheeled cart, the driver sitting tall with expectation.

She jumped at a thump behind her and turned in time to see Joshua and Webb lumbering through the gate with the cradle and chest between them.

"Did anyone see you?" she asked, hopping with excitement as they worked to hoist the cradle into the back of the narrow cart. "Did you hear any alarms?"

"Nay, we saw nary a soul," said Joshua, wiping his sleeve across his forehead. "Though that's not to say they didn't see *us*. Or hear us, more likely. A great African elephant would've made less noise thumping and bumping his way through that garden than us with that cradle. Here now, lass, up you go."

He lifted her up into the cart, climbing up beside her onto the rough plank that served as a seat. As the cart lumbered forward, she reached back to touch the cradle, as much for luck as to reassure herself that it had survived unharmed. She had never thought of the cradle as something that went "thumping and bumping," but then she'd never tried to move it herself, either. She realized now that most men would have refused such a request. However, she'd realized, too, that her Captain Fairbourne was vastly removed from other men.

Quite vastly.

"Thank you, dear Joshua," she said softly, not wishing for the others to overhear. "For coming for me, and bringing the cradle, and—and everything else, too."

He fussed self-consciously with the set of his hat, not looking directly at her. "I want to make things right for you, lass," he said gruffly. "And whatever it takes, I'll do it. But I do have one question for you, Anabelle."

She searched his face uneasily, wondering if she'd spoken too freely. "One question?"

"Aye," he said. "And that's why the devil couldn't your mama have left you a handkerchief instead?"

❧ Eight ❧

Joshua's gaze swept along the length of the river's curving embankment, his uneasiness growing by the second. He didn't like this; he didn't like it one bit. He had left the Hallet brothers here, with orders to wait until he returned, and now there was no sign of either the *Swiftsure*'s boat or the two brothers.

"Whatever are we doing *here,* Joshua?" asked Anabelle plaintively, rubbing her ankle where she'd bumped it climbing down from the cart. The cart, and the horse and driver with it, had left them here at this bleak, deserted spot, and now she sat perched on the edge of the cradle, her shoes resting on the rocker and her skirts pulled up to keep them from the wet, slimy river soil. She had never observed the river at this close a range, nor smelled it, either, and she rested one hand on her cheek, the better to surreptitiously mask the stench of the water behind the perfume on her wrist. "I thought we were going to your ship."

"We are," said Joshua tersely, scanning again the

black silhouettes of the vessels bobbing on the river's surface. Jacob and Asa Hallet were among his most reliable men, Quakers both, not given to being misled by rum or strumpets, and neither was their cousin Robert Stark. They were large men as well, too large to tempt the water thieves, but also too large to disappear so completely on a clear summer night. Damnation, where could they have gone?

"Then we cannot possibly be in the proper place," said Anabelle. "We are nowhere near a dock. I would think that most necessary to boarding any vessel. At least for me it is, since I am not of that saintly persuasion who can saunter blithely across the water."

Joshua swung around to stare at her, almost, she thought suspiciously, as if he'd forgotten she was there.

"Well, isn't it?" she asked. "Necessary, that is?"

He cleared his throat, unwilling to admit that he'd only been half listening to what she'd said, and that the half he'd heard made no sense to him at all. There were a few other things demanding his attention—the missing boat, the absent Hallet brothers, the danger of sitting here beside the Thames in the middle of the night.

"I told you, Anabelle," he said, his voice sharper than he'd meant it to be. "Things seldom go the way they ought."

She frowned, uncomprehending. "Even to losing one's own dock? Faith, Joshua, however do you find your way in the ocean if you—"

"Beg pardon, mistress," said Webb urgently, pointing down the river to the narrow, dark shape bobbing near the foot of the bridge. "Lookee, Cap'n, that boat there, way away. Could that be them, sir?"

Joshua narrowed his eyes, straining without his

customary spyglass to see through the night. The tiny quarter moon had benefited them when they'd left St. James Square, but its faint light offered little comfort now.

"Could be," he muttered. "But why the devil would they have taken the boat down there?"

"Dunno, sir," said Webb. "Maybe they was keepin' clear o' the pressmen, or some other mischief. But I could run along after 'em, sir, to tell 'em we be here. That is, sir, if you wish me to leave you."

He glanced pointedly at Anabelle, sitting on the cradle.

"We'll be well enough, Webb," said Joshua. "Go, but watch your back."

"Aye, aye, sir," said the seaman dutifully, and off he trotted, his footsteps making dull slapping sounds across the damp mud.

"I'm sure he'll be back directly," said Anabelle cheerfully, "and with the others, too."

She shifted her seat on the edge of the cradle, making room for him, and patted the rail in invitation. "Come, there's room enough, if we don't sink together into the mud. And look above: how many stars there are in the sky this night!"

She looked so young, the plume of her hat curling impishly over one eye, and he thought with a pang of guilt of what he'd done to bring her here. So young, and so vulnerable, too. She hadn't the faintest notion of what could become of an innocent, lovely woman like her in a place like London.

But then her London was lords and ladies, servants and coaches. She'd never needed to know of the other city that lay so near to her now along this waterfront, of low rumshops and brothels that catered to a sailor's basest needs and swallowed up countless young girls in the process. He knew; he'd seen it, and he never wished to again.

He moved closer to her, wanting to protect her from all that was evil in the world. A lady like her would expect it. And how much she must trust him already, to be able to gaze beyond this miserable riverbank and up to the stars with such open, guileless pleasure!

"The number of stars stays the same," he said, standing over her. "But more will show themselves when the moon doesn't shame them into hiding. Wait until you see them at sea, lass, away from the lights of London. You'll swear the sky is nothing but diamonds."

"Truly?" she said, her eyes shining bright as diamonds themselves. "You will show me, won't you? Oh, how beautiful it must—"

"Quiet," he ordered, his voice dropping to a rough whisper that demanded obedience. "We have company, sweetheart."

His eyes had turned hard and flinty, his whole body radiating a coiled readiness she'd never seen in him before. Swiftly, she turned to follow his gaze, rising to her feet beside him.

The three men were standing at the wall at the top of the embankment, one with his legs widespread on the top of the wall itself. From their dress, they were clearly sailors, wearing the loose striped breeches, short jackets with kerchiefs, and the long braided pigtails that Anabelle had noticed before with Joshua. But that had been in daylight, in a crowded street, not on a deserted bank of the Thames well past midnight, and these men did not remind her of the Chinamen on the lacquer chest at Kilmarsh. No, for these men were climbing over the wall, coming toward her and Joshua, intending nothing but ill.

"What have we 'ere, mates?" asked the first man, his gaze raking hungrily over Anabelle, lingering over the way her soft kerseymere skirts clung to her hips. He smelled worse than the river, of rum and the cheap scent of a low doxie. "A pretty little strumpet in a feathered hat, needful o' new companionship?"

Joshua stepped forward, shielding Anabelle. "She's a lady, you black bastard, and she doesn't need a damned thing from you."

"Then let th' *lady* speak for herself," said the sailor, with so much mocking emphasis on *lady* that his two friends burst into raucous guffaws. "Come here, darlin', let's 'ave a fair look at ye. Sure, th' jingle in my pocket should tempt ye out o' hiding."

Anabelle could feel Joshua tense, the cold fury radiating from him. She remembered the pistol hidden beneath his coat, but that was only one pistol, with one ball, which offered precious little reassurance when there were three men threatening them.

"Clear off," said Joshua, his voice rumbling with the weight of years of command. "Shove off, the lot of you."

This time the man didn't answer, nor did his friends laugh again.

"Clear off, or answer to me," said Joshua. "'Tis your choice."

Unable to resist, Anabelle peeked around Joshua's broad back. The three sailors were hesitating, hanging back with rum-fed uncertainty before the unmistakable authority of a captain's voice. It reminded Anabelle of the way haughty milliners disintegrated and quailed before her grandmother, and the irresistible comparison between the milliners and these sailors made her giggle nervously.

The first sailor's gaze immediately swung around to find her. "Ye think ye be so fine as to laugh at me, ye little hussy?" he said angrily. "Ye think yer bully boy can keep ye safe enough, do ye?"

He grabbed for her then, reaching for her arm to pull her free of Joshua, and with a frightened yelp, Anabelle ducked away.

But the sailor never came close. Joshua's fist reached him first, driving hard enough into his jaw to lift the man off his feet and onto his backside in the mud with a resounding slap. Joshua's arm was still raised when one of the other men charged forward to pound into his exposed ribs. With a sharp grunt, the two of them toppled back over Anabelle's sea chest and to the ground, rolling over and over as they struggled to strike each other.

Without a thought for her gloves, Anabelle grabbed a thick, water-logged branch dripping with muck and swung it with both hands as hard as she could against the sailor's head as he and Joshua tumbled past her. The man yowled with surprised pain, but he still managed to keep his grip on Joshua. With one of her stableboy oaths, Anabelle determinedly raised her branch to hit him again.

"Drop it, ye little bitch!" ordered the third sailor, warily watching the branch in her hand. "Drop it now, I say!"

Breathing hard, Anabelle staggered around to confront him. She had to tip her head back to see him properly, for her hat had slipped forward again, but she still had a good view of his mean, pock-marked face and the long-bladed knife in his hand.

Oh, dear Lord, a *knife*.

"Come here now, my pretty little Judy," he said, coaxing her with a quick flick of the knife through the air. "Drop yer stick an' come to ol' Bill."

He edged closer until only the cradle lay between them. His eye was on the branch in her hand, and because he was so much larger, she doubted she could swing faster than he could block her flying branch. She swallowed hard, the rush of excitement warring with fear. Though she didn't dare turn to look, behind her she could still hear Joshua and the other sailor grunting and pummeling one another. Clearly, she could expect no help from that quarter, and she prayed Joshua was winning.

"Here, girl," said the sailor, leaning toward her over the cradle. "Come nice to Bill."

With all her force, she stamped her foot on the cradle's front rocker. Instantly, one side of the cradle lurched down toward her while the ornate oak bonnet swung up, crashing with a sickening thump into the front of Bill's breeches. With a yowl of agony, he doubled over, and Anabelle whacked her branch across the back of his pigtailed head with most satisfying precision.

She felt a hand on her arm, and with a gasp, she whipped around, ready to swing her makeshift weapon again. But instead of the enemy, she met only the long, startled face of Ezekial Webb.

"The . . . the boat, mistress," he stammered, "if'n it pleases you—"

"Hell, Webb," shouted Joshua as he ran toward her. "It had damned well better please her!"

Before she could answer, he had caught her around the waist, his arm like a band of iron. She dropped the branch to loop her hands around his neck as he lifted her up close to his chest.

"Oh, Joshua," she cried, pressing closer. He was here, he was alive, and he didn't seem to be hurt. "You're all right then, you're—"

"Later, Anabelle," he said curtly, breathing hard. "There's no time now."

He was wading quickly through the water now, her overlong skirts trailing over his arm and into the river, and then, without warning, he dumped her into the boat. A small tin lantern sat before her, blinding her eyes after nothing but night. Instinctively, she scrambled to her feet, and as the boat began rocking wildly from side to side beneath her, she grabbed at the sides to steady herself.

"Jesus, Anabelle," said Joshua as he, too, grabbed the side of the boat to help keep it from swamping. "Aft with you, and *sit*. In the sternsheets!"

Bewildered by his orders, she squinted past the lantern, trying to find his face in the darkness. "But Joshua, aren't you—"

"Sit," he ordered again, making her feel like one of her father's ill-behaved dogs. "I must go fetch that double-blasted cradle of yours!"

She heard him go wading off, leaving her with only his orders and the sting of his reference to her "double-blasted cradle," but no answers to help her follow his wretched orders. What, in Heaven's good name, exactly were sternsheets? She hadn't a clue where such articles would be kept in an open boat, let alone how to sit in—or would it be upon?—them.

With a sigh, she reached down to wring the water from the hem of her petticoat, and for the first time noticed the two men sitting at the oars on the other side of the lantern. They were so evenly matched that they could have been twins, both square and very blond, and equally impassive as they watched her twist the wool in her hands.

"Good evening," she said, uncertain of what else might be proper.

Though they both nodded, the one on the left cocked his head back over his shoulder. "Skipper means for thee to sit there," he explained, his solemn expression remaining unchanged. "Aft be the back of the boat. The sternsheets be the bench. That is where thee must sit. Beside the skipper."

"Why, thank you," said Anabelle, smiling warmly. "Thank you very much."

The man nodded again. "Thee is welcome. Mind thyself, now."

"Oh, I will," she said as she made her way unsteadily between the two men and to the wooden plank that served as the best seat in the boat. She settled herself on the bench, arranging her wet skirts as best she could. "And so this is the sternsheets, such as it is. Or are? One does wonder why your high and mighty skipper can't use the king's own English so that one might understand precisely what one is supposed to do."

With a thump, Anabelle's sea chest landed in the bow of the boat, followed by the cradle, settled more carefully athwartships because of its weight. Wearily, Joshua hauled himself into the boat, leaving it to Webb and Stark to shove off, and came back to the sternsheets to sit beside Anabelle.

He set his hand to the tiller, wincing as the pain shot clear up his arm. He guessed that bastard had cracked a rib or two, and damnation, it felt like he'd guessed right. He was too old for this sort of nonsense. Come daylight, he'd be a pretty enough patchwork of bruises and scrapes—the brow above his right eye seemed especially tender—but what did he expect, brawling with a pair of drunken navy men over a woman?

He glanced at her now, his feelings less than charitably inclined. Her hat was cockeyed, the plume bent, and her hair was trailing in damp, untidy pieces down the back of her neck. There was a splotch of mud across her cheek, her skirts were covered with it, and her fawn-colored gloves were clearly ruined. Yet despite her dishevelment, her eyes were bright, her lips half parted with excitement still, and she'd never looked more damnably attractive.

"Are they following us?" she asked, looking back over her shoulder as the boat began to glide faster through the water.

"Would you care?" he asked curtly, the pain in his ribs as he leaned into the tiller shortening his temper.

"Of course I care," she said indignantly. "What a foolish thing to say, Joshua. Would I care, indeed!"

He sighed, then wished he hadn't, breaking off with his breath half drawn. "No one is following us. Nor did we leave those bast—rascals in a humor to follow anyone soon."

She grinned, pulling away a loose strand of hair that the wind had blown to her mouth. "Then we bested them, didn't we? Handsome odds, too. One gentleman, one lady—one smallish lady at that—against three great hulking seamen. *Vastly* handsome of us, I'd say, and I—are you quite all right, Joshua? Joshua?"

"Was that all it was to you, Anabelle?" He'd be damned before he'd admit to her how much he hurt, and with an enormous effort, he made himself sit straighter. "Handsome odds and rum sport?"

He hadn't fooled her. He could see the concern in her eyes by the lantern's light, but at least she had wisdom enough not to mention it. Hell, he was supposed to be the one protecting her, not the other way around.

"It wasn't exactly Donnybrook Fair, I'll grant you that," she said slowly, "but near enough for me. Not that I haven't seen my share of scrapes, not with brothers like mine. Joshua, are you sure you're—"

"What the devil would your brothers say to that sorry business just now, eh?" he said harshly. "Have you any notion of what could—nay, what *would*—have become of you if those men had gotten past me? Do you?"

She looked at him uncertainly. "I venture to say it would not have been pleasant."

"Not *pleasant?* Damnation, Anabelle, if they hadn't killed you outright with their—their usage, then you would have wished yourself dead by the time they'd done!" He broke off with painful despair, unsure how to make her understand. How could she, considering the sheltered manner in which she'd been raised?

"I know you are a lady, Anabelle," he began again, "and very young in the bargain. But what you did there with those men was reckless, dangerous beyond reason!"

"Being young and a lady does not make me either a ninny or an invalid," she said. "Joshua, I could not stand there like a block and do nothing while they hurt you!"

"I was doing fine enough on my own, Anabelle," he said, a flat-out lie that made him wince almost as much as did his battered ribs. "But by your actions, you put us both into more danger."

"*I* did?" she said defensively. "I rather thought I dispatched that man most directly! Perhaps you didn't see all that I did, but if you asked Webb here—"

"Oh, aye, and then perhaps Webb can tell me why you saw fit to laugh, too!"

"You laughed before, in Grandmother's garden!" she protested. "When my bodice buttons became so horribly tangled on the backside of your coat. You didn't think it so ill to laugh then, did you?"

He might not have thought ill of it then, but he certainly did now, with the four men at the oars pretending so studiously not to hear while remembering every ludicrous word to repeat to the rest of the crew. None of them would have understood exactly why he'd laughed then, or how he'd struggled with the alarming temptation of having her "tangled" around him. To feel her firm, plump thighs against his waist, her breasts pushed into his back as she'd wriggled breathlessly against him: it had been a miracle that all he'd done was laugh and not moan or weep aloud. Even so, he barely caught himself now from letting his gaze return wickedly to that double row of polished buttons, straining against decency there across the front of her bodice.

And he didn't need Webb to remind him of the horrible sight of his future wife—his lovely *lady* wife—flailing away with a muck-covered stick like some Billingsgate fishmonger. He'd grant that it had taken pluck, rare pluck, for her to defend him like that, but pluck alone didn't make such activity any more proper.

"There's a time that's right for laughing, Anabelle, and a time that's not," he said, sounding even to his own ears like some pompous preacher. "Those men were ready to walk away until you laughed at them. You left them no choice. They had to fight."

"Only because they were men, and drunken ones at that." Her back was as straight as a new timber, her hands clasped into tight fists in her lap. "But perhaps I have no choice, if I am to be your wife. Perhaps I must never dare laugh again, for fear of provoking some man to bloody the nose of another. It may be the only way I can keep you unharmed—and myself from becoming a widow before I'm properly a bride."

"Oh, hell, Anabelle, that's not what I want," he said wearily. He had neither the wit nor the stamina left to spar with her now, especially not before his men like this. "You know that."

"Indeed I do not." She lifted her chin even higher, imperious as a duchess, until the broken plume on her hat blew down to tickle across her nose. "No laughter from me at all, Captain Fairbourne. Not even a titter."

He looked at her hard, unable to imagine her keeping such a ludicrous pledge. He might have believed it from Mary Holme, but not Anabelle.

"Well enough, Miss Crosbie," he said finally, keeping his doubts to himself. "If you've no wish to laugh, then I can't make you do so."

"No, that is quite right. You cannot. No one can. At least no one ever *has.*" With a sigh, she glanced at him sideways, and it seemed to Joshua that her rigid spine yielded just a bit.

"You know you are going to have the most monstrous black-and-blue spot over your brow by dawn," she continued more softly, so that the others couldn't hear. "A cold compress might ease the swelling, though. It might. Once we're on your ship, I could arrange one if you wish."

He didn't answer, his face wooden. He couldn't remember the last time when anyone had been so genuinely solicitous toward him, and he wasn't sure how to respond. It had probably been his mother, before she had died and before he'd gone to sea. More than twenty years, then. But how he'd felt when his mother had tended his boyhood mishaps and illnesses, and what he felt now at the suggestion of Anabelle's bending over him, Anabelle's cool fingertips lightly upon the angry bruise, Anabelle's leaning closer, closer as he lay on his bunk—these were very different feelings indeed.

Only the bar of the tiller lay between them, a small enough barrier for him to cross. Long ago, her muddy skirts had drifted and spread over the toes of his boots, and she'd made no move to draw them back. It would be nothing, really, for him to slip his hand from the tiller for a moment to touch her hand, only long enough to let her know he appreciated her concern. He could manage that, and no one would laugh or make jests of him for it. A simple, genteel gesture of—

"Ahoy, *Swiftsure!*" bawled Webb to the ship that loomed close before them. He held the lantern up in his outstretched arm and waved it slowly back and forth for good measure. "Cap'n Fairbourne comin' aboard!"

"Ahoy, Cap'n's boat," came the automatic reply from the lookout on watch. From this distance, Joshua wasn't sure who it was, but there was no mistaking Samuel's face, lit by the lantern near the binnacle, or the eagerness with which he came to stand at the rail for his first glimpse of the captain's bride.

With practiced ease, the men at the oars pulled closer to the *Swiftsure* at her moorings, and with a barely suppressed grunt of pain, Joshua pulled the tiller over to guide them to the ship's tall, black side. With all his fancifying over Anabelle, he'd nearly forgotten his ribs, but the pressure on the tiller had reminded him quickly enough. How the devil was he going to manage boarding without shaming himself, let alone without dropping Anabelle in the process?

"In bows," called Webb next, and in tidy unison, the four long oars rose upright, dripping and glistening, before the men shipped them inside the boat and reached for the boathooks. Webb fished the first line to pull the boat closer to the ship, followed by Jacob Hallet with the second to hold the boat steady beside the row of boarding steps, the shallow grooves carved like a permanent ladder into the ship's sides. Then all four men stopped, waiting expectantly for Joshua to climb up first, the privilege due him as captain.

And to the captain's lady, too, though she didn't realize it.

"Oh, my," said Anabelle faintly, staring upward. "I suppose those little perches are intended for our feet, aren't they?"

She understood now what Joshua had meant: a second chance, he'd promised, when they'd made such a muddle of climbing down from Grandmother's porch roof. But then all that had laid beneath them was gravel and grass, neither welcoming, but neither as threatening as the black, murky waters of the Thames, lapping with cheerful menace against the side of the boat. As tightly as the two men were holding their boathooks, still the boat bobbed back and forth, up and down, against the much larger ship. Shifting from one vessel to the other and then up those perilous steps was going to be a challenge. If she lost her footing and fell, the yards of kerseymere would sink her like a stone in a millrace.

And when she and Joshua had been dangling from Grandmother's eaves, he had been quick with encouragement, ready with help. They had done it together, a team, a pair. He had even laughed and teased her into forgetting the danger.

But there'd be no teasing from Joshua now. Now he sat grim-faced and formidable, offering her nothing and expecting less. He hadn't even smiled when she'd volunteered to see to his bruise.

Where had she gone so woefully wrong? She looked from Joshua's stony face to the slippery little steps and back again, frantically trying to find the mistake she'd made with him to guide herself now. The change seemed to have come after the scuffle with the sailors on the riverbank. He blamed her for that, for causing the mischief and then being a hindrance instead of a help. She wouldn't do it again, that was certain. She'd been half jesting when she'd sworn off laughing, but she was completely serious when she vowed to herself now that she'd never again be a trial, never be a nuisance.

"Should we rig th' boatswain's chair, Cap'n?" asked Webb, finally saying what the others were thinking. "For th' lady?"

"What is a boatswain's chair?" asked Anabelle quickly. "And pray, why should a lady have one?"

Webb shifted his shoulders, clearly wishing that she'd asked the captain instead of him. He had rested one hand on the cradle to keep it steady against the boat's rocking, and he patted the carved oak now, almost as if to reassure it along with her.

"Why, a boatswain's chair's a certain sort o' convenience we might contrive," he began. "For landsmen an' ladies an' such, t' haul them up—"

"No," barked Joshua sharply. "We won't be needing a chair."

If he held Anabelle against his left side and used his right hand to manage the ropes, if he moved carefully and deliberately and didn't jerk, then he might make it up the side. No, he *would* make it. Anabelle was depending on him to see her safely aboard. A lady like her shouldn't have to be hoisted up through the air in a boatswain's chair as if she were no more than a hogshead of rum. Besides, his men were watching, including Samuel at the rail above. It was going to hurt like hell, but he wasn't about to fail before any of them, especially not at the beginning of a voyage.

He turned to Anabelle, and the wealth of uncertainty he found in her eyes only served to steel his reserve all the more. He wanted his wife to depend upon him, the way his mother had looked to his father, to trust him to make things always right.

"Are you ready, Miss Crosbie?" he asked gruffly, wanting to ease her doubts. " 'Tis only a handful of steps to the break, no more."

"No more, indeed," repeated Anabelle, convincing herself as she confronted the ship's side. Joshua wished her to do this, and so she would. It would not be so bad; only darkness and the murky water below made it seem so. With the ropes that hung down on either side to serve as handguides, climbing these steps would be easier than climbing into the treehouse her brothers had built in the oldest oak at Kilmarsh. There had been thirty-four steps to the lowest branches, without any sort of handrails, and she had survived that unscathed, and often, too. By comparison, this should be nothing.

Swiftly, she rose before she lost her confidence. Because of the boathooks, the boat did not seem to rock quite so much beneath her feet as she faced the slightly curved wall of the *Swiftsure*'s side. She *could* do this. Deftly, she bunched her skirts and flung them over the crook of her arm, the way she had as a child climbing to the treehouse, and seized the ropes with both hands. Luck made the boat rise in the water at the exact moment she reached her foot for the nearest groove, and with that little boost, she pulled herself upward.

"What in blazes?" muttered Joshua. He had looked away only a minute, lashing the tiller in place, and in that instant, Anabelle had hoisted her skirts and begun to scramble up the side like a seasoned deep-water sailor, albeit one in petticoats. Stunned, the four men in the boat stared open-mouthed at the spectacle of Anabelle's muck-covered buckled shoes and striped stockings clear to the tops of her flowered pink garters, tied neatly in double bows over the knee.

Appalled, Joshua lunged for her, only to double over, swearing, as the pain ripped through his side. "Anabelle," he gasped wretchedly, though she was now out of his sight. "Damnation, Anabelle, wait!"

But Anabelle had already reached the top, and the end of the ropes. Her head could just clear the top of the side; apparently, the next step would be to pull herself over and make a decidedly ungraceful, flopping entry face first onto the deck.

"Here, miss," said a man's voice from the other side of the rail. "Let me hand you up."

Before she could reply, he had grasped her firmly by the wrists and lifted her up the last bit of the way, almost swinging her onto the deck.

"Oh!" she said with a relieved gasp of surprise at having reached her goal. "I've done it, haven't I? I've done it!"

"Aye, aye, you have, Miss Crosbie, and most hand-somely, too." The man swept off his hat and made as showy a leg as he could in his faded breeches and homespun stockings. From what she could judge by the binnacle light, he was handsome enough as men went, though no match for Joshua. "I'll be the first to welcome you on board the *Swiftsure,* Miss Crosbie. Samuel Worden, miss, first mate. But then, doubtless you know who I am from Captain Fairbourne."

"Actually, no, Mr. Worden, he hasn't told me." Still, she smiled winningly, shaking her skirts back down as she peered over the side. "Though I'm sure he will in time. Why hasn't he followed me, I wonder?"

But Joshua had followed her, and he pulled himself up on the deck now.

"Oh, Joshua, did you see how grandly I climbed the side?" said Anabelle gleefully as she rushed to him. "Just as you wished, without any help from your silly boatswain's chair!"

"I saw it, aye," he said, every bit as grim and somber as he'd been in the boat. "I saw your climb, and a great deal more of your person in the process, too. Has the tide turned, Samuel?"

"Aye, aye, Captain," said Samuel, with a crisp show of seamanly efficiency for Anabelle's sake. "But not more than a quarter hour ago, sir."

"A quarter hour that's now lost to us forever," lamented Joshua. "We were on land a good deal longer than I intended."

From long habit, he clasped his hands behind his back and smothered his oath from the resulting pain as he looked up at the sails overhead. But the agony of his ribs wouldn't matter as much now—nor would Anabelle's outrageous behavior. Now he could overcome them both. He was back on board the *Swiftsure,* the one place on earth—or rather, on sea—where things were ordered as they should be.

"Call all hands to prepare to sail, Samuel," he said, his spirits improving with each step on his own deck. "The moment the boat is stowed, Samuel, the very moment—"

"But how else was I to climb up that sorry little ladder, Joshua?" interrupted Anabelle, the bent feather on her hat trembling with indignation. "I thought I did exceedingly well, considering. Even your Mr. Worden here said it was handsomely done. But if you wish me to be more maidenly and modest about it, faith, you shall have to issue me my own pair of breeches."

He swung around to face her, his expression studiously blank as he mentally wrestled with the image of her in breeches, though it wasn't precisely his mind that was doing the wrestling. Anabelle's scampering over the tumble-home with her skirts hiked high had been provoking enough, but Anabelle's doing the same in breeches was almost beyond imagining.

Almost, but not quite.

"I've always wanted a pair, you know," she continued blithely. "The same sort of close-fitting ones that serve you gentlemen so well. Though I've never quite resolved whether they should be bespoke from a gentleman's tailor or my own dressmaker."

Samuel coughed, an odd choking sound that proved that he, too, found the question an intriguing one. For that matter, it seemed to have riveted the attention of every man within hearing on the deck.

"Anabelle," said Joshua, his voice strained. "Miss Crosbie. We will discuss this later. Much later. We have lost a quarter hour of the tide, and I mean to make it up. Hosea, you will see Miss Crosbie to her quarters directly."

Anabelle was suddenly aware of activity surging around her, of men hurrying to obey even though not a single direct order had been given. "But wait, Joshua, please," she said plaintively. "Cannot we speak now?"

"Nay, Anabelle, we cannot," he said, turning from her to gaze up again at the sails overhead. "Later, when we're clear of Gravesend."

The tall boy Hosea appeared at her side with her sea chest on his back. "I'm t'take you t'your quarters, miss, if you please. Then I'll stow that cradle below in th' hold."

"Oh, no, please, don't do that," she said swiftly. "I should like the cradle with me, in my—my quarters."

"Truly?" The boy looked doubtfully at the cradle and back to her. "A great hulky thing like that, miss? You won't be having space t'turn."

"I don't care," she said. "It stays with me."

Abandoned after the men had hauled it from the boat, the mud-dabbed cradle looked forlorn and bedraggled as it sat in a puddle on the immaculate deck, a long strand of green weed trailing from one rocker.

Seeing it there, Anabelle herself felt every bit as extraneous and out of place, unnecessary both to the workings of the ship and to the stern-faced captain who was even now walking away from her. Lord help her, it was happening again, and she fought the bitter, growing taste of despair and panic.

She thought she'd done everything in her power to please Joshua. She had tried to follow his foolish orders, and she'd tried to be as agreeable about doing it as was possible. But it hadn't been enough. She'd prayed that by coming with him, her life would change, but it hadn't, not in the ways that mattered most. No matter how hard she tried, she still couldn't manage to please him, any more than she'd ever been able to please her father or her grandmother or even Henry Branbrook.

She looked back at the faint twinkling lights of London, and then to Joshua's broad, unforgiving back. She did not want to be left like this; she did not want to feel so achingly alone in a crowd of people.

"Please, Joshua, wait," she cried softly, more frightened now than she'd been during this whole long night. Without thinking, she slipped her hand into his arm to hold him back. "Might I stay with you?"

He didn't answer at first. But she didn't need words to feel how he stiffened against her touch, and she saw how his face tightened, blocking her out. Her hand fell away as if it had been burned.

"Not now, Anabelle," he said at last, his voice distant and his gaze fixed inward, away from her. "Later. I will call for you then."

"This way, miss," said Hosea. "Watch yourself on th' steps o' th' companionway now. You can hurt your head something brutal at sea if you don't be mindful."

"I thank you for the warning," murmured Anabelle, her gaze still fixed on the tall figure standing behind the helm. "I thank you indeed."

It was all well enough to watch her head on the steps at sea. But why, oh, why, had no one cautioned her to mind her heart as well?

"She's *run?*" demanded Lieutenant Palmer incredulously. "The little chit's bolted on you, just like that?"

"Quiet, Palmer, you damned blustering idiot!" hissed Branbrook. He glanced uneasily over his shoulder at the men and women laughing and drinking at the other tables in the tavern. He'd chosen this low place near the waterfront specifically to avoid his other friends, but even among these sailors and strumpets, one never knew who might be listening. "The old marchioness and I have managed to keep it quiet between us, but if you keep braying like a jackass, the entire world's sure to hear of it!"

"The world will hear soon enough, cousin. You can't keep something like that a secret for long." Palmer waved for another two pots of ale, barely able to contain his glee. "So who's the lucky grig who's stolen your golden bride off out from under your nose?"

"No gentleman, that's certain enough," said Branbrook glumly. "That's the only hope I have of fetching her back. She ran off only last night, you see."

Palmer leaned closer across the battered table. "You'd wed her still? You'd take her back even if this other rogue had her maidenhead?"

"For five thousand a year," vowed Branbrook fervently, "I'd take her back with another man's bastard in her belly. Besides, truth to tell, I'd grown proper fond of my Belle. We would have suited admirably."

"You astonish me, cousin," said Palmer, though if he'd been honest, and in the same unfortunate position, he'd have done the same. "I wish you good hunting in finding her."

"But that's where I'm relying on you, Palmer." Branbrook fumbled in his pockets for the thin packet of folded papers. Carefully, he spread them on the table, using his ale pot to hold one edge flat. "Took some doing, I can assure you, and more than a bit of silver into the right hands, but here you have it, just as you asked."

Palmer frowned. "I've asked for nothing."

"Oh, yes, you have!" said Branbrook impatiently. "You said before you could go after Belle's wretched sailor, you needed proof that he's a pirate or a smuggler. Well, here you have it, everything laid out to show that what's in his hold isn't exactly what he says."

"I can't be expected to go racing after some threepenny scent-smuggler from Deal."

Branbrook jabbed at the paper with his forefinger. "You study that last figure there and tell me if it's not more than three pennies."

Reluctantly, Palmer looked, then whistled low under his breath. "How did you come by this, cousin?"

"The rascal's made his share of enemies. Jilted one poor lass outright, and her some fat merchant's daughter, too." Branbrook rubbed his hand across his mouth. "You will help me, then?"

"I will." Lovingly, Palmer scored his finger beneath the value of the *Swiftsure* and her cargo, already calculating his lieutenant's share of the prize. "Come with me, cousin. My captain will wish to see this directly."

❧ Nine ❧

Joshua was dreaming, the old dream that would never leave off haunting him.

He was eight again, tall for his years, his head even with his mother's shoulder as he stood at her side. That was his rightful place now as her eldest son, now that Father was lost.

Lost. That was the word they all used, as if Father were only mislaid, like an old darned stocking beneath the trundle, instead of dead, drowned, dashed by the waves against the cruel rocks off Marblehead as his ship had broken up around him.

Lost. The men in the tall-crowned hats, the powerful, important gentlemen of the meetinghouse and the town, were saying it again, here as they stood in an awkward ring before his family's hearth.

"Twenty-five guineas is a good sum for the land, Mistress Fairbourne," said Master Webster sternly. "Times are hard. The town cannot support every sad widow and orphan of a sailor lost at sea. You must not consider too long lest the offer be withdrawn. As for this house—"

"But I do not wish to sell my house!" cried Mam with anguish. "My husband built it with his own hands, his own toil! Where would I go with my children? Where would be our home otherwise?"

The four men glanced at one another, their eyes so black that Joshua had curled his hand into his mother's fingers, fighting the sickening dread they shared together.

Master Webster frowned, smoothing the soft Holland ruffles over the front of his waistcoat. "It is unfortunate that Captain Fairbourne did not have the wisdom to provide more ably for his widow and children. But in his memory, we are willing to be merciful and generous."

Mam stepped forward, her red-rimmed eyes bright with new hope. "You will help me? We may stay here?"

"Master Godwin has agreed to grant you the cottage on his land," said Master Webster curtly. "You should be comfortable enough there. But this house and anything of value in it must be sold as quickly as possible to pay your husband's debts."

Mam had cried out, a low wail of sorrow and shame, and thrown up her apron to hide her face. Clumsily, Joshua had put his arm around her quaking shoulders, trying to stand as tall and unwavering as Father would have done.

"Don't speak to Mam that way!" he'd said, anger making him brave. "She's still grieving, and she don't need to hear such talk from you!"

"She needs to hear a great deal more, boy," said Master Webster coldly, running his appraising fingers across the polished pewter on the overmantel. "She may take the babe with her, of course, but that is all. She cannot afford to feed so many idle mouths. Your brothers will go to Mistress Hatten's farm and you, boy, you will sail with Captain Patrick in three days' time, to follow your father's trade."

Lost. Now it was their home and everything in it that was disappearing, their family torn apart and broken up just as Father's sloop had been.

"But that is not what Mam wishes!" cried Joshua, struggling against the last tears of his childhood. "None of us do!"

Master Webster's smile was as merciless and cruel as the jagged gray rocks that had killed Father. "Wishes, boy," he said, "are a luxury you can no longer afford."

And with a wild, animal howl of blind fury, Joshua hurled himself at the man and all the grief and injustice and sorrow he represented.

Lost . . .

He woke with a start and a mumble, squinting against the morning sun that streamed through the cabin's stern windows. The dream had been no more than that, only a dream, yet still it had the power to make his heart pound and sweat break on his brow as if he were once more a grieving, frightened eight-year-old—which, thank God, he'd never be again. With a muttered oath, he rubbed the heel of his hand against his eyes. Eight years old, hell; this morning he felt old as Methuselah himself.

"Well, and a fine morning to you, too," said Anabelle soundly. "Faith, what a way to greet the new day, and me as well!"

He rolled over in his bunk, swiftly pulling the coverlet with him. When last night he'd shed his clothes, soaked through by a passing squall, he'd been too tired to put on anything else and had dropped into the bunk as naked as a newborn.

"I'll make any greeting I want in my own cabin," he growled. How long had she been there, anyway? Long enough to hear him mumbling and moaning like a child over the past? "Damnation, Anabelle, what are you doing here?"

"I grew weary of waiting for your invitation," she said, leaning back comfortably in the high-backed armchair—*his* high-backed armchair. "For four days, I've been sitting humble and alone in that wretched little closet you mistakenly call a cabin, waiting for you with perfect patience whilst my food was brought in to me as if I were a prisoner. Perhaps I was. I certainly felt as one. Another day, and I would have gone quite, quite mad."

So would he, though nothing was going to make him admit it.

Not that those four days and nights apart were at all his doing. His guilty conscience would swear to that. Their way downriver to the channel had been a constant trial, plagued by rain and crosswinds and the usual crowds of ill-handled boats and ships to outmaneuver and barges to be dodged. The channel itself had been no better, gray and rough with rain that seemed to come sideways rather than down from the clouds, as was proper. Foul, dirty weather, by any sailor's standards, until the clouds had finally begun to break and scatter last night when the wind had swung around, and, exhausted, he had finally allowed himself to come below to sleep.

Yet in all that time, Anabelle had been in his thoughts, insistently, immovably *there,* no matter how hard he'd tried to banish her. He had not expected that to happen. He hadn't wanted it to, either. He'd believed that once he'd returned to the

Swiftsure, he'd be able to leave all the untidy confusion of life on land behind him in London. It had always been that way in the past, but then in the past he'd never brought along a part of the confusion with him to sea, where it could creep into his very cabin while he slept.

"I'm sorry the accommodations don't please you," he said, his voice thick from sleep and sarcasm. "Samuel gave up his cabin for you, and I'm sure he'd be more than willing to take it back. Perhaps you'd be happier slinging a hammock with the men below, or lower still, in the hold."

"Perhaps," said Anabelle, unperturbed. She swept her arm to encompass Joshua's cabin. "But I think this chamber would be vastly more pleasing. La, you must live as fine as a king here!"

"I should. I'm the captain," he said. What he felt like was a damned fool, huddled in his bunk with the covers pulled up over his bare chest like some old maiden biddy. "And it's not a chamber. It's my cabin."

Pointedly, she let her gaze wander from the broad, glittering sweep of the stern windows to the paneled bulkheads, the polished brass candlesticks swinging gently in their gimbals, the handsome furniture made from Massachusetts maple.

"And *I* am not Miss Anabelle Crosbie," she said, "but merely a provoking, meddlesome creature, come to fill your life with disagreeable sorrow. That is what you're thinking, Joshua, isn't it?"

What he was thinking was something altogether different. By her standards, she was dressed simply, in a green silk jacket above a glazed wool petticoat, a lawn kerchief around her neck and plain ruffles at her wrists. But the jacket fit to within a heartbeat, and below the hem of her petticoat, she wore another pair of the impractical little mules, their curving red heels drawing his eye like a beacon to her ankles. Higher still, would she be wearing the same flowered garters, tied twice around her plump white thighs?

Uncomfortably, he shifted himself beneath the coverlet. Oh, aye, she was provoking him, all right, though not the way she'd meant. He could only hope she wouldn't notice exactly how well she'd succeeded.

"You don't belong here, Anabelle," he said. "Not at this time of day, anyway."

"I rather think I do." She patted the battered pewter coffeepot, wrapped and tied with a cloth to keep the contents hot, and then flipped open the lid with her thumb, letting the rich, seductive aroma of morning waft toward him. "Your cook did not know the first thing about roasting coffee beans, let alone grinding them. I do believe he was using a cleaver to chop them into little bits, if you can conceive of such barbarity!"

"What I can conceive is Thomas thumping you on the head with one of his kettles for interfering," said Joshua, not entirely in jest. "You've no right telling the poor man his trade."

"I do when you're the recipient of his wares." She leaned forward to sniff the coffee herself and smiled sweetly. "A wife—a *good* wife—should always be looking after her husband's welfare, yes?"

"Well, aye," he admitted grudgingly. He did want a wife who'd look after him. He couldn't deny it. "But we're not wed, not yet, and for you to go upsetting the galley and lecturing to Thomas like he's some half-wit parlormaid in your grandmama's house—that's not how things are done at sea. Leastways not in any vessel where I'm captain."

"You are captain only as long as there's a deck heaving beneath your feet," she reasoned, "but you'll be my husband always, on land and at sea and anywhere else you choose to go."

He was losing. Again.

"Thomas is one of my people," he said, "and I can't have you flouncing about between decks, countering my orders and riling my crew."

"Oh, Joshua, pray forgive me." Her eyes grew round with an innocent surprise that he didn't believe for a moment. "I didn't realize you'd left orders regarding the hacking and chopping of your coffee beans."

"Damnation, Anabelle," he said with exasperation, "you know what I mean!"

She smiled, the surprise and the innocence, too, slipping away. "Why, yes, I believe I do. So did your cook, when I showed him how best the beans should be roasted and ground. I was very agreeable, and he did not seem to mind in the least."

Doubtless Thomas didn't, thought Joshua, not if Anabelle leaned over the way she was doing now, giving the old rogue a prospect fine enough to make his one remaining eye pop from his head.

"But I shall leave it to you to judge for yourself," she said, carefully beginning to fill the heavy stoneware mug that had survived at sea longer than any delicate saucer and cup could. "Though faith, it is beyond me to see how anyone can pour genteelly when the table's rocking to and fro."

"You're doing well enough," said Joshua, concentrating on the tantalizing aroma of the coffee and not the genteel arc it made going into the mug. Like most sailors, he preferred coffee to tea, and though his cook's regrettable coffee had always smelled like burned toast and tasted like the scrapings, it did have the virtues of being hot and black, and after a rough watch on a wet night, he'd drunk it gratefully enough. But this coffee of Anabelle's—this was the same heady scent he recognized from the best London coffeehouses, yet here in his own cabin, in his own mug, on his own table, and far, far out of his own reach.

"Here you are," she said, turning the mug so that the handle faced him. "I would bring it to you myself, but I'm afraid I'd end up splashing it all over your lovely floor. I mean your deck. I don't seem to have— now what was it that Hosea called it?—oh, yes, my 'sea legs' yet."

"Your blasted sea legs have nothing to do with it," growled Joshua. Hosea had taken away his wet clothing in the night, and though another dry shirt and pair of breeches hung waiting on the peg on the back of the door, they remained a safe harbor he'd never reach with Anabelle in between. And his coffee, that tantalizing, steaming, blissfully, wickedly black coffee, was growing colder every second. "Damnation, Anabelle, what the devil do you wish me to do?"

"You could stop swearing," she said promptly. "You won't scare me away by being cross. Cross men do not frighten me, not in the least. If you could see my father act the right royal Tartar before his breakfast, you'd know why."

"Anabelle," he said, his impatience verging upon open despair, "you cannot come creeping unbidden into a man's cabin at this hour and expect him to be ready to receive you. You're not my wife yet, and it's not right for you to be here until you are. You must leave. Now."

"Oh, pooh." She narrowed her eyes, resolutely placing her palms flat on the edge of the table. "You *are* trying to frighten me into leaving you alone,

Captain Fairbourne, and I tell you, it won't work. I'm not leaving. I am far too weary of my own company to bear it."

"Very well, then." He pushed himself upright, letting the coverlet slide to his waist as he swung his legs over the edge of the bunk. "God knows I've tried to be honorable about this, Anabelle, but there's an end to it, even with you. *Especially* with you."

But Anabelle wasn't listening. Instead, she was staring at all that the coverlet had hidden, at the dark hair curling across his chest, over the curving pattern of muscle and sinew clear to his waist, narrowing into a path that disappeared under the scrap of the coverlet that still thankfully covered his lap.

But such gratitude was short-lived. In a single powerful motion, he rose to his feet, and Anabelle gasped, her gaze snapping downward as her hand flew to cover her mouth. She would not look; no matter how tempting, she must not, and she didn't, squeezing her eyes shut for good measure. She heard his bare feet come across the deck toward her, the slight scrape of the stoneware mug as he lifted it, the silence while he drank followed by the sigh of satisfaction when he'd done.

"You were right, Anabelle," he said. "Everything you swore about not chopping the beans and such was flat-out true, and I—"

"I did not know you weren't wearing anything," she said in a wounded rush that still managed to be accusing at the same time. "You never told me that. You let me believe you slept in a shirt like a Christian, not—not in nothing."

"You believed what you wished to believe. If you'll recall, I tried to tell you, but you wouldn't listen."

With her eyes still tightly shut, she could guess that he was standing directly beside her. If she opened her eyes, she'd see him right before her, but Lord help her, what she'd *see.*

"I didn't want to listen," she said unhappily. "Sometimes I simply can't. I don't know why. Instead, I talk and talk and talk and say so much tomfoolery. No one listens to me anyway. Except you, Joshua. You always have. That's partly why I came here this morning, with a silly pot of coffee for an excuse."

"It's not silly coffee," he said gruffly. "I wouldn't drink it if it were."

She shook her head sadly, her eyes still closed. "I only wished to be of some use to you. To anyone. Oh, Joshua, these last four days have been so *vastly* hard on me!"

"Now, now, it couldn't have been so bad as all that," he said uncomfortably. He'd thought she'd been playing another one of her confounded little word games again, that was all, but now it seemed to have degenerated into something else, altogether mystifying. "All you missed topsides was a fat lot of high seas and foul weather, and me swearing at everything in sight. Sailing the ship had to come first, Anabelle."

Her head drooped even lower. "You will always put your ship ahead of me?"

"I must, Anabelle," he said as gently as he could. "If you're to be the captain's wife, you have to understand that. How else can I be sure to keep you safe for our wedding, eh?"

This was not the answer she'd wished for, not at all, but troubled though she was, she still tried to find the sunlight behind the clouds. They would not always be at sea. Soon, very soon, when they were back on land, there'd be no ship or seagoing rules to come between them. She raised her head to look at him, forgetting why she'd bowed it in the first place.

"Our wedding," she repeated softly. "You still want me to become your wife?"

"I want no one else." He smiled crookedly. "I don't believe I've ever seen you blush like this, Anabelle."

She felt her cheeks burn even warmer, but she didn't back down and look away. "That's likely because I've never had to sit before a gentleman in such *undress* before."

Undress was putting a fine word upon it. At least he wasn't completely without decency, as she'd dreaded, but he was still well beyond her scant experience. He'd yanked the coverlet from the bunk and held it loosely wrapped low around his hips, the blue-and-white homespun trailing behind him across the deck. But somehow that rumpled coverlet and the casual intimacy of it only served to accentuate his blatant masculinity all the more, and in ways that left her feeling decidedly unsettled. With his black hair untied around his shoulders, his jaw stubbled with four days' dark beard, and his legs wide spread against the roll of the ship, he really did look the part of Grandmother's fearful savage.

Except, of course, for the coffee mug in his hand instead of a tomahawk.

She looked at him more closely, at his forehead, and frowned. "You did not tend to that bruise the way I told you," she scolded. "It would be faded and nearly gone by now if you had. Let me see it more closely."

She stood, rising up on her toes to meet him as he dutifully bent before her. Lightly, she ran her fingertips over his brow, relieved to see the swelling had diminished more than she'd thought.

"Did you show it to your physician?" she said with concern. "Wounds to the head can be dangerous."

"Physician?" he scoffed. "We've no such article on

board the *Swiftsure,* or on any other vessel I've ever served on. There's not one in all of Appledore, either. Beyond a pair of midwives who see to the women, we give ourselves over to God's mercy or the devil's care, whichever suits, and tend to each other."

"How wonderfully trusting of you." She was staring critically at the angry purple blotch on the side of his chest. She balked at touching it, not only because she'd no wish to hurt him but also because, however well intended, touching his bare chest seemed alarmingly forward, almost dangerous. "This looks far more wicked than the bruise on your forehead, and I'll wager it grieves you more, too. Can you raise your arm?"

"I am not a cripple, Anabelle," said Joshua indignantly. "I've spent watch on watch these past four days and nights, haven't I? More time on deck than any other man on board. That should be proof enough, even for you."

Now that she was looking for it, she could see the awkward way that he held the mug. *Foolish man,* she thought, *foolish, brave, prideful man!*

She glanced up at him from beneath her lashes. "Then set that cup down and raise your arm."

"Anabelle, I—"

"Raise your arm," she said, "and I shall be content."

"Very well." With a thump, he set the mug down on the table. He grasped the knotted coverlet firmly with his left hand to keep it from slipping, took a deep breath, and slowly lifted his right arm.

His mouth tightened from the effort of keeping silent as the pain ripped through his side.

"Higher," said Anabelle. "That's scarcely above your waist."

He glared at her and jerked his arm over his head.

Then immediately, he swore loud and long as he flopped over, the offending arm now clutched tight against his side.

"It's your ribs, isn't it?" she said, her face twisted with concern. "From that wretched fight?"

"Nay," he gasped, dropping into the second chair. "I did it picking posies in a meadow. Grant me a moment here and I'll be well enough."

"No, you won't," she said. "Not until you've bound the muscles tight to keep them still. Your ribs won't mend properly until you do, especially if they're cracked."

She understood so much now: his surliness on the boat, how he'd hung back instead of helping her, even the way he'd kept away from her, nursing his pride more than these battered ribs. And all the time she'd been blaming herself. Surely male stubbornness must be the most pigheaded vanity on earth!

"At least none are broken outright," she said gently as a kind of consolation, "or you would most likely have already died from a nasty hole wheezing in your lung."

He grumbled, a deep rumbling sound of suspicious displeasure better suited to a wounded dog than to a man, particularly a captain. "A surgeon in petticoats. Exactly what this voyage did *not* need."

"I have my reasons for keeping you in health, too, you know," she said. "I, for one, do not wish to trust myself at sea to the judgment of a captain who cannot bear to lift his arm and stand upright at the same time. And as for that selfsame man becoming my husband—well, we shall not discuss *that* at present. Now, where do you keep bandages and such? Or is that, too, beyond your blind colonial trust?"

"You'll find a small box of things for physicking in that chest," he said, resigned to enduring her minis-

trations as a kind of penance, at least to a point.
"There, lass, below that bulkhead."

"Bulkhead." She looked at him blankly. "I know
both the words *bulk* and *head,* but the two combined
make no sense, particularly as a direction."

"Lubber," he said with weary scorn.

She didn't need a translation for that. Though the
exact definition might evade her, his tone implied
meaning enough, and it wasn't flattering.

"The bulkhead, Joshua," she said patiently.
"Where, pray, is the bulkhead?"

"That paneled bit of woodwork standing upright
between the two decks," he said. "With the looking
glass pegged to it."

"The *wall.*" With an impatient sigh, she headed
toward the chest, moving with arms outstretched to
counterbalance her uncertain steps, as if walking on
ice instead of the slanting, shifting deck. She *was* a
lubber, decided Joshua as he watched her tottering in
her high-heeled mules, but a mightily fair little lubber
at that.

As she knelt to open the chest, he silently opened
the cabinet behind him to retrieve a small, treasured
bottle of Rhode Island rum, poured a healthy dose of
it into the mug of coffee, and swiftly returned the
bottle to the cabinet, all before she returned to the
table.

He drank deeply of the coffee, finding comfort in its
amplified warmth. If she was so blasted determined to
fuss over him, at least he would be properly fortified.

She returned with both a roll of torn linen strips
from the chest and his breeches from the peg on the
door.

"Here," she said, handing him the breeches and
then turning her back. "Make yourself respectable."

"Aye, aye, mistress," he said. He was glad she

wasn't watching, not so much as for modesty's sake as so that she wouldn't see how stiffly he had to bend to pull up his breeches. "Respectable it is."

When she turned back toward him, he was still fastening the last buttons on the fall of his breeches. They were an improvement over the coverlet, true, but the way the weather-softened linen clung to his hips still automatically drew her gaze and made her blush all over again. Lord help her, even the man's legs, bare below the knee, were beautiful, thick and strong as tree trunks. How much better it would be to have him safely covered with shirt and waistcoat and coat and hat—and breeches and stockings and boots as well! Then, at least, he'd be merely handsome and without this devastating effect he seemed to have over her sense—and her senses.

"I know it's going to hurt, but you'll have to raise both your arms and keep them there so I can wrap the bandages tightly," she said, striving to be briskly efficient. "Perhaps if you stood by the wall—I mean the bulkhead—and braced yourself against it, you might not be quite so uncomfortable."

His expression skeptical, he emptied the mug and went to stand where she'd ordered. The left arm went up easily, but the right arm was a slow, agonizing trial. But at last he succeeded, his arms outstretched like a bridge, and gradually, as the muscles grew used to the position, the pain, too, lessened.

"This won't take long, will it?" he asked with a certain wariness, shaking his hair back from his face so he could watch what she did. "I should've been topsides to check on the wind an hour ago."

"The wind will either have changed or it won't, and your minding it won't make a speck of difference." She ducked with the long strip of linen already in her hands and came up between his outstretched arms. "I shall try to be as quick as ever I can, and not to hurt you, either. You'll be rather like my own Maypole to twist 'round with ribbon, won't you?"

Her own Maypole: there was no way under heaven that he'd comment on *that*.

In any other circumstances, he would have delighted in their positions, with her trusting and trapped between him and the wall, his arms above her ready to swoop down and carry her off. But now she was the one giving orders, and it felt entirely backward and wrong, a heinous crime against the natural order of things.

With the lightest of touches, she ran her fingertips across the swollen, angry bruise. "He kicked you, I'd vow," she said sadly. "Oh, Joshua, how vastly sorry I am! First for causing this to happen to you, and then for being such a coward about coming here, to tend to you as I'd promised!"

" 'Tis not so very much, lass," he lied. Though she'd barely touched him, that feather of a caress from her was as potent as the rum in his coffee. To be touched by her yet to be unable to touch in return, to have her soft little hands upon his bare skin, was as fine a definition of *torture* as he could conceive.

"How did a grand lady like yourself come to know such things?" he asked, struggling manfully to lead his thoughts down other, safer paths.

"My brothers," she said absently, circling around him as she wrapped the bandage, tugging it close. "You sailors are not the only men to fall into scrapes, you know."

"Your infernal brothers again," he said, gritting his teeth against the pain. The growing pressure of the bandage did, however, have a wonderfully deflating effect on his randiness. "But I'd wager a nobleman's sons were coddled and prodded by a costly learned physician, leastways a surgeon."

"They were if my father learned of it," she said. "Faith, Joshua, can't you be still?"

"Aye, aye," he said with a dutiful sigh that was nearly a groan. Yet as painful as it was, he liked watching her work so close to him, the serious expression in her eyes and the way she pursed her lips as she concentrated. Though she'd dressed her hair herself in a haphazard knot, it still was redolent of the same violet scent he remembered from the first night he'd met her, a scent that, because of her, now held an endlessly seductive power. If he could, if he dared, he'd reach down and pull the pins from that knot and bury his face in the violet-scented hair as it tumbled over her shoulders.

"That's better," she said, unaware of his thoughts. "My brothers soon learned that as soon as the physician had left, Father would come and thrash them for whatever misdeed had caused the injury, whether fighting or climbing trees or tumbling from a horse. Father was dreadfully stern about such things with boys, you know. So no matter how badly they were hurt, my brothers would rather drag themselves up the backstairs to the old nursery for Mama or our nanny to patch them back together. Later, I learned to do the same."

"They were—*ah!*—fortunate to have you as a sister." More fortunate, he added mentally, than in their father. The viscount sounded like a right royal bastard; at least he seemed to have kept away from Anabelle.

"Oh, I'm not so sure they'd agree with you, most times. You know how brothers and sisters can be." She laughed softly as she tugged the end of the bandage taut. "There, we're almost done. I expect your mother—Mam, wasn't it?—had her sorting out to do in your family, too."

He went instantly still. "I've never told you that."

"No," she said slowly. "No, I suppose you haven't. But when I first came in, I heard you speaking in your sleep, and you said her name then. Does she still live in Appledore, too?"

He never spoke of his mother to anyone, not even to Samuel. In Appledore, most people knew the shameful way his family had been broken apart—it was too small a place for secrets—but they also knew better than to mention it before him.

But Anabelle wouldn't. How could she? And how, in turn, could he blame her for it?

"My mother is dead," he said as evenly as he could. "She died long ago, when I was nine."

"Oh, Joshua, I did not know," she said sadly, reaching up to lay her hand against his unshaven cheek in empathy. "No wonder you were so kind about the cradle! But, oh, who would guess we'd share such a sorrow in common?"

She was finished with the bandage, and he could have stepped free of her, turned away from the warmth of her hand and her understanding if he'd wanted to. He'd always been his own man, one who took care of his own problems and troubles without burdening others.

"It's an old sorrow now, long done, may God rest my poor mother's soul," he said at last. "I pray she's at peace now, beyond the reach of those that hurt her when she lived."

"Amen," said Anabelle softly. "But how proud your mother would be of you now to see the man that you've become!"

She could speak of the man, but it was the grieving

boy inside him that heard her now, and that boy longed to weep with the bittersweet comfort her words brought to his sorrow. Appalled by his own weakness, he couldn't fathom how a charming, frivolous creature like Anabelle Crosbie could understand him so well. What had he done to betray himself like this to her? What part of his careful guard had he let slip, leaving a gap yawning widely enough for her to creep inside? He felt as defenseless as if he stood on a rocky point in the face of a gale, open to the kind of pain and suffering that no amount of linen bandages could ever bind up and soothe.

And he could not do it. He looked down into her small, round face turned up so hopefully toward his and he knew he could not risk giving up that much of himself, not to her, not to his wife, not to anyone.

He lowered his arms carefully, breaking the barriers that had bound her in. "You were right, Anabelle," he said. "You've managed to ease the pain with your swaddling, just as you promised, and thanks to you, I may make old bones yet. Perhaps I've shipped a surgeon with me after all, eh?"

He saw the confusion flicker through her eyes as she struggled vainly to follow his change of thought. Self-consciously, she took a step back, away from him, and turned the hand she'd held to his cheek back to rest against her own breast. The gesture drew his gaze to the beguiling cleft above her tight lacing, and he let it linger there, both from pleasure and a definite sense of relief.

This response to her was better. This he could understand. Admiring her beauty and desiring her body, taking amusement in her conversation and satisfaction in the way she'd nursed him: all these were things he sought in a woman, and, now, in a wife. *His* wife.

He reached for his shirt and drew it over his head, stuffing the tails into his breeches. On the deck overhead, he could hear the bell that marked the change of the watch and the thud of the men's footsteps as they rushed to obey. He was eager to join them, and he thrust his feet into his sea boots without pausing to bother with stockings.

"Where are you going?" she asked, though it was obvious enough.

"On deck, sweet," he said, hurriedly buttoning his waistcoat and stuffing his watch into the pocket. "I've left those rascals untended long enough, and the devil only knows what mischief they may have found for themselves."

He bent over her just long enough to brush his lips across her cheek, and, gratefully, felt no more than appreciation for the soft velvet of her skin: one more reassuring proof to himself that he'd wrestled his passing weaknesses back into place.

"You may stay here in my cabin," he said, feeling most generous, "if that pleases you better than to sit in your own quarters. Perhaps, if the weather allows it, we could share supper together later, eh?"

"No, I think not," she said, her voice crackling with angry resentment, "because I'm coming with you now."

He stopped, his hat raised halfway to his head. "Anabelle, an open deck is no place for a woman, certainly not for a lady. I thought you understood."

"Oh, yes, I understand completely." She seized her shawl from the back of her chair and flung it around her shoulders. "But damnation, Joshua Fairbourne, I'm not going to let you run away from me again!"

His surprise turned into the blackest glower. He didn't care for her swearing—no Appledore women swore, not even the girls in the tavern—but he cared even less for this foolishness about his running away. He was not a coward and he'd never run from anything.

"It's for your own safety, Anabelle," he said sternly, "for your own good and the good of the ship and her company."

"*Damn* the ship and her company," she said, her own expression a murderous match for his own. She sailed past him—albeit sailing with the unsteady rudder provided by her mules—and threw open the cabin door. "*I* am going up to the deck, Captain, if *you* wish to join *me*."

She kicked off her mules before she reached the companionway, racing up the steps in her stocking feet with her slippers in one hand and her skirts bunched in the other. Miraculously, she managed to reach the deck before Joshua, standing breathless at the top of the companion ladder as her shawl flapped like another sail around her.

"Miss Crosbie!" An astonished Samuel Worden rushed across the deck to take her hand. "Miss Crosbie, what the dev—that is, what are you doing here?"

"What a *vastly* common question that is becoming!" she said, but taking the tartness from her words by flashing him one of her most winning smiles and clinging gratefully to his arm as they made their way to the rail. "I am here to take the air, Mr. Worden, to walk about and see the sights."

Samuel's smile was more uncertain, verging on downright doleful. "Are you certain, miss?" he asked, his glance sliding around her to the companionway as he clearly looked for Joshua. " 'Tis not a very pretty day for ladies."

Even Anabelle could see that his evaluation was hardly an understatement. Although the sun shone brilliantly in a cloudless sky, a stiff east wind was driving the *Swiftsure* hard and fast as she heeled through the waves. The deck sloped at a heady angle to the larboard, and the breaking waves washed up over her sprit and across her forepeak.

But Anabelle's anger made her stubborn and left her no easy way to retreat. "'Tis fine enough, Mr. Worden," she insisted. "Come, show me about, if you please."

"Aye, Mr. Worden, show Miss Crosbie about," said Joshua behind them, his great thundering voice ringing effortlessly across the deck. "And be sure to hand her your glass so she can see that landfall there to the north. That's the last she'll see of her blessed England for a good long while."

Anabelle tucked her mules beneath her arm and took the offered spyglass from the thoroughly miserable Samuel.

"You are too kind, Mr. Worden," she said, raising her voice so that Joshua would be sure to hear it over the wind. "Although Captain Fairbourne misremembers that my home was in Ireland, not England, I shall be most happy to see the last of England. The sooner I see England means the sooner I'll see the last of *his* blessed ship and sea."

"Miss Crosbie misremembers a good deal more if she thinks this voyage is nearly done," thundered Joshua. Every man on board could hear him, and every man was listening, but Joshua was too angry to care. "You might ask Miss Crosbie, Mr. Worden, if she is perhaps planning to *walk* the rest of the way across the water?"

Somewhere in the rigging far above, a man guffawed loudly, only to be stifled in an instant by his mates.

But not, alas, before Anabelle had heard him.

With humiliation ladled over her anger, she whipped around to face Joshua, her shawl blowing out straight behind her.

"I trust you are most satisfied," she said. "Most satisfied, *Saint* Joshua of Fairbourne."

There was nothing saintly about Joshua's expression now, and with his long black hair flying wild in the wind, he looked more like one of the devil's own specters than a saint. "Are you done, Anabelle?"

"That depends on you," she snapped. "I've no intention of being the laughingstock for you and your men. None at all, do you understand? I'm not a fool. I have seen maps and charts. I know that Massachusetts is not so very far from England.

"Not far, miss?" asked Samuel doubtfully. *"Not far?"*

"Not far at all," she answered impatiently, and shoved back the billowing shawl. "I said before that I am not a fool. However far could Captain Fairbourne's wretched Massachusetts Colony be from England?"

"In *New* England, Anabelle," said Joshua deliberately. "In the American colonies. On the other side of the Atlantic, on the far side of the world. More than three thousand miles."

She stared at him defiantly, not wanting to believe him. She remembered the globe in Grandfather's library, and Grandmother's bony finger jabbing at the pink blotch that she had said was Massachusetts. If had not seemed that far on the globe, two or three inches at most. How could three inches become three thousand miles? If only she'd stopped to think before she'd let her temper speak first! And how would she ever survive on this ship for that long? She had nursed him and coddled him with coffee and asked him of his family, all things that would please most any man.

But once again, Joshua had chosen his ship over her. Once again, all she'd found was hostility and bitter loneliness in place of the love and happiness she'd sought.

Once again, I've tried so hard to please and failed. Oh, Lord, help me, it's like being at Kilmarsh with my father, where nothing I did was ever good enough.

One of her slippers tumbled from her grasp to the deck, and almost in a daze, she bent to retrieve it. Her stockings had soaked through with spray from the sea, her toes showing cold and pink through the wet silk.

"One month's voyage if the winds smile on us," said Joshua, his face so hard against her she wanted to weep, "two or even three if they don't. And pray to the dear Lord, Anabelle, that we both survive."

❧ *Ten* ❧

"Nothing to speak of," said Samuel, handing the glass to Joshua. "Wind's the same, and we're following the same course, except for a mite of trimming to hold her steady. Asa marked a topsail to the east, but it vanished without showing more than a speck of white."

"Well enough by me," said Joshua, idly sweeping the horizon with the glass. Even with its aid, the last tip of the English coast, Lizard Point and Land's End, was no more than a dark ripple on the horizon. Such mundane certainties calmed him, making him forget his anger toward Anabelle, and he drew in another deep breath of the cool, sharp air. "The less company we have, the better, I say."

"Oh, aye, I expect you would," said Samuel with studied carelessness. "Considering how the company's been faring on board, the less we find elsewhere, the better for us all."

Swiftly, Joshua swung the glass down to look

squarely at his first mate. "What the hell's that supposed to mean, anyway?"

"You know exactly what the hell I mean, else you wouldn't be squawking at me like a rooster with wet tail feathers," said Samuel evenly. "What was all that sorry business with Miss Crosbie, anyways? Do you mean to marry her or lash her up to the gratings for a flogging?"

"Marry her, you interfering bastard." Joshua scowled, his newly recovered contentment evaporating fast. "Not that it's any concern of yours."

"It is when your temper turns the whole ship on its end, Josh. You're always a-worrying what the men are thinking or saying about you. Well, you gave them a right bushelful of contemplation just now with how you bellowed at that poor little lass."

"Poor lass, hah," said Joshua decisively. "Her tongue's sharper than my cutlass. You heard her, Sam, calling me names here where everyone and his brother could hear them. I can't allow that to stand, not even from Anabelle. Nay, especially not from her."

Samuel cocked one sandy brow. "Oh, aye, Saint Joshua. A great insult, that."

"Now don't you go taking her side, Sam," cautioned Joshua, but already he could feel his displeasure shifting from Anabelle to his own broad shoulders. "It was her own blessed fault, making me rage on like that."

Samuel nodded sagely. "I 'spect she understands that now, the way she run below. I 'spect she's weeping her eyes out now from sheer mortification."

"Not Anabelle," grumbled Joshua. "I've never once seen that woman cry."

"You might not see it, but that's only on account of her not wanting you to." Samuel held up his hand to tick off his reasons. "One, she's female. Two, she's scarce more than a child. Three, she's in love with you. Four—"

"Samuel," warned Joshua ominously. "Do not push me."

"Well, then, three's enough. The poor little miss is crying, no mistake." He waggled his three raised fingers at Joshua and sighed. "Three reasons, Josh. I never thought I'd see the day when I'd be offering advice about women to you."

"You haven't seen the day," said Joshua. "Not in its entirety, and if you keep on with your blessed advice, I can promise that you won't last until sunset."

With an unmistakable smugness, Samuel silently lowered his offending fingers.

But Joshua's conscience continued the conversation, and most admirably, too. He hadn't intended to speak so sharply to Anabelle. It had been his temper talking, not him, but she wouldn't know that. Likely she wouldn't know that he preferred to keep his private conversations private, too, and not trot them out for all his people to see like yesterday's dirty shirttails. No crew would respect a captain who didn't. The sad truth was that she didn't know much about him, not after the scant time they'd spent together.

But he could have explained everything quietly, when they'd been alone together, instead of letting the whole blasted conversation explode like gunpowder on deck. As her future husband, it was his responsibility. It must fall to him to teach her how he liked things done and where she'd fit into his life, the way his father had done for his mother. He must remember that.

But instead he found himself remembering other, more pleasant things, like the shy, eager way she'd smiled when she'd told him how she'd fixed his coffee. The coffee: aye, now there was one of his preferences she'd figured out on her own, without a lick of guidance from him, and most handsomely, too. And binding up his ribs so cleverly: that was another. She'd done a wonder by him with that. Tentatively, he raised and lowered his arm a fraction, testing it. The best testimony to her skill was that for the first time since they'd cleared London, he hadn't given such a movement a thought.

But most of all he remembered the expression on her face when he'd grudgingly spoken of his mother. He hadn't wanted her sympathy and he hadn't sought it, but he'd basked in it just the same. What was it she'd said? "Who would guess we'd share such a sorrow in common?" He'd always believed sharing to be a bond that brought people together. For proof, he'd only to look at that wretched cradle of hers, handed down from her mother and grandmother. But could the long-ago unhappiness that plagued his dreams serve such a purpose between him and Anabelle?

It could, perhaps, if she loved him.

He took a deep breath, uneasily letting the notion settle on him. Samuel wasn't a fool, for all that he often spoke too freely. Maybe Anabelle *was* in love with him. He didn't know, himself. Love had always been a hazy place he'd steered clear of with any of the willing girls in Appledore. Several of them had claimed they'd loved him, but beyond moony-eyed simperings and allowing agreeable freedoms in the meadows, he hadn't seen much to recognize again. He'd loved his parents and he loved his two brothers and his sister; he loved the *Swiftsure* and a following wind, strong rum and rare roast beef, fancy stockings

on a well-turned leg and "The Rakes of Mallow,"
played lively and loud on an Irish fiddle. But as for
falling *in* love, he'd no notion of that at all, and
powerfully thankful he was, too.

He did want his wife to love him. Aye, that was
proper. Yet to have Anabelle be in love with him
already wasn't something he'd expected. He wasn't
prepared for it, not yet, and neither, he guessed, was
she. He thought again of how wickedly she looked up
at him with her head tipped to one side, and then how
her laughter bubbled out of her, the merriest thing a
man could ever hope to hear. He hadn't heard it
nearly enough these last days. Poor, dear, wicked,
charming Anabelle. Had he really made her suffer so
very much?

He sighed again, deep enough to rattle the buttons
on his coat, and clasped his hands resolutely behind
his waist. "You believe I should go to her, don't you,
Sam?"

"That's for you to decide, not me," said Sam flatly.
"But I will tell you that afore you go, you scrape a
razor over your face and a comb through your hair,
unless you want to scare the little lass silly. You look
like the road to Hell on a bad day."

"Mr. Worden," said Joshua, "shut up. Now."

Yet though he'd made up his mind to talk to
Anabelle, it took him a good long time before he went
below. There were so many other things to tend to
first: the wind veered away to the northwest, requiring
a change in their course; while trimming the courses,
a greenhorn landsman tumbled from the sheets and
sprained his ankle and had to be carried to his
hammock below; Ezekial wished him to view an
improvement he'd made in the wheel; and empty
pages of the ship's log, ignored during the first hectic

days of the voyage, now needed to be filled with the neat, careful entries that were his special pride.

By the time this last was done to his satisfaction, the bell for the end of the second dogwatch and the beginning of the next had already rung, and the candles in the lantern over his desk had burned to half their size. The remains of his supper still sat beside the logbook, the plates nestled securely against the rail along the table's edge to keep them from crashing to the deck, and next to them lay his old pewter watch, open to show the time: half past ten.

Wearily, he dropped back in his chair and sighed, rubbing his hand across his eyes. Was it too late to go see Anabelle now? If she still kept London hours, then she'd be awake, but if not, if she were already asleep, he'd no wish to rouse her. Perversely, his mind pictured her that way, blissfully asleep and unaware, her dark hair tumbled across the white pillow slip, her night rail slipping off one shoulder, the sheets kicked back so her bare legs would . . .

With a great effort, he forced his thoughts back to more respectable paths. He couldn't afford to let himself consider Anabelle that way, not with six long weeks or more at sea before they'd find a minister to wed them. He'd lost control of himself and shamed her once in that damned artist's house, and he was determined not to do it again.

The people of Appledore weren't going to be particularly impressed by the peers scattered through her family tree, but they would be quick to count the months between the day they married and the day their first child was born. As it was, one look at that ridiculous cradle coming down the gangplank was going to give the gossips a running start. He didn't want that kind of scandal attached to his name, and he certainly didn't want it trailing after his wife. And the only way to be sure was to keep his baser passions dowsed with a bucket of icy seawater.

Now, God help him, if only Anabelle could manage to do the same.

He raked his hair back from his face with his fingers, searching through his pockets for the thong he used to tie it back. Damnation, he should shave, too; Sam had been right about that. He ran his hand along his jaw, cursing the half a week's worth of black whiskers that bristled beneath his palm. On land, to look his best, he often scraped a razor over his face both morning and afternoon, but at sea, most days he didn't bother beyond once a week, particularly when the weather was rough. Few sailors did. But with Anabelle on board, he'd have to be more conscientious. Sam had been right about that, too. A high-born lady like Anabelle would be the first to smoke him for not being a gentleman.

He stripped off his shirt and shaved quickly, not bothering to call and wait for hot water from the galley. When he was done, his cheeks were as smooth as English steel could make them. They were also quite pink beneath his tan, having been scraped raw and splashed with the chilly water standing in the pitcher, but now he had at least an air of gentility. He put on a clean shirt without any darns, wishing the linen didn't already smell so fusty from being stored in his sea chest. Beneath the collar he tied and knotted a watchet scarf that brought out the blue of his eyes, or so the shopkeeper who'd sold it had promised.

Not half bad, he thought with satisfaction as he shrugged into his coat before the looking glass. Not half bad at all.

Still, he felt nervous and awkward as a plowboy fresh from the farm as he stood before the paneled door to Anabelle's cabin. He could hear men speaking and laughing quietly among themselves farther forward between the decks, and he prayed no one would see him waiting here like some moonstruck puppy. He rapped quickly, not so loud as to wake her but loud enough, he hoped, to be heard within.

But the force of his overeager knuckles betrayed him, and he winced and swore to himself as the thumps seemed to echo like cannon fire in the narrow companionway. What if she were asleep, he thought uneasily. Or worse, if she were awake and chose not to answer, or berated him shrilly through the closed door, or decided she never wished to see him again, or—

The latch inside rattled and the door swung open. There stood Anabelle, staring up at him with heavy-lidded, befuddled eyes.

"My, my, Joshua," she murmured sleepily, not bothering to stifle an open-mouthed yawn. "It's you, isn't it? La, what a vastly peculiar time for you to come calling."

"I'll come back later, then," said Joshua hastily. "I did not mean to wake you. Nothing I have to say can't wait until morning. I don't wish—"

"Oh, bother and hush, Joshua, and come in." She stepped back to let him enter. "Only let me find the striker and light the candle so you won't stumble over yourself. Or me, for that matter."

She vanished momentarily into the gloom, reappearing with a flash of sparks as she lit the single candle in the gimbal over her bunk.

"There," she said with a still-sleepy smile. "That's better, isn't it?"

It was, and it wasn't. It was, because Joshua could see the little cabin and Anabelle in it clearly now, and it wasn't, for exactly the same reason. She stood bathed in the candlelight, her night rail sliding off one creamy shoulder exactly as he'd imagined it, the fine Holland linen doing precious little to hide the rest of her. She shook her hair back over her shoulders without one whit of self-consciousness, leaving him to make out the sharp little nubs of her nipples through the linen, and the darker skin around them, enough to tempt Lazarus to rise from his grave, and right smartly, too.

"Anabelle," he said, unable to say much more as he struggled to remember whatever foolish resolution he'd made not a quarter of an hour before in his cabin. "Anabelle. You have the most beautiful—most beautiful—*hair.*"

"Hair?" She looked at him queerly, then laughed as she climbed up onto the edge of her bunk. "I vow there is a great quantity of it, but beyond that, there's little credit I can claim. If one doesn't cut one's hair, then one's hair shall grow, and one cannot truly be praised for what nature, not calculated artifice, does for one. Or this one can't, anyway."

She smiled again, hoping to encourage him to leave the companionway and join her. Now that she was more awake and knew she wasn't dreaming, she realized how rare this moment likely was aboard the *Swiftsure,* and she'd no wish to frighten Joshua away before he'd said whatever he'd come to say. She doubted it was an apology—she wasn't that optimistic, or that foolish, either—but from his newly shaved face, here in the middle of the night, and the tidy watchet scarf and the strangely strained look upon his face, she doubted he was going to bark at her again.

In fact, if treated well, he might actually be quite

human again, quite Joshua-in-London-ish and not lordly, hateful Captain Fairbourne. But she'd have to use great care, else she'd lose him again like she had this afternoon, and she wasn't sure how many such second chances he'd be willing to give her.

She drew her knees up beneath her night rail, hugging her arms around them. "Please do come in, Joshua," she said. "There's a wretched draft with the door ajar like that."

"Oh, aye," he said, nodding wisely. "The draft."

He looked over his shoulder as if he expected to see the ill-mannered draft like a dog sniffing at his boot heels, ducked his head to avoid the low beam, and walked directly into the cradle. With a grunt of surprise, he pitched forward across it, barely catching himself against the edge of the bunk with his hands close beside her thigh.

She watched as he scrambled to untangle himself, then clucked her tongue. "Oh, Joshua," she said sadly. "I did so *warn* you not to stumble."

"What is that double-damned piece of useless flotsam doing in here?" demanded Joshua furiously as he rubbed his knee where he'd struck it on the heavy carved oak. "Why isn't it in the hold with the rest of the dunnage?"

"Because I wanted it here," said Anabelle promptly. "I didn't trust it in your hold. I wanted to be sure it was safe, here with me. Our daughters will be vastly cross with me if I don't."

"What about our boys, eh?" said Joshua, in no mood for mildness yet. "Or are you going to treat them as shabbily as you treat me and leave them out to fend for themselves in the stable?"

"They'll sleep in the cradle when they're babies, peaceable as angels, exactly as my brothers did," said Anabelle. "I only mentioned the girls because they're the ones who'll have the cradle next, when they're grown. I intended no slight toward the boys. I'm rather partial to boys, you know."

The purring emphasis that she put on the word *boys* sounded alarmingly all-encompassing to Joshua, suggesting males of more advanced ages of twenty or thirty—or even forty. He hoped he himself was there at the top, deserving the lion's share of her partiality. Certainly the way she was speaking so freely of all these sons and daughters they were to produce together inclined him to believe so.

It was also inclining his hapless imagination back to places it didn't belong, places with more inclining and reclining, too, without any difficulty. Reluctantly, he dragged his gaze away from the tiny, fascinating bow that held the drawstring at the neckline of her night rail and to the cradle at his feet.

Aye, the cradle, he thought with relief as he crouched down beside it. *That* was safe enough. Now that he saw how it occupied nearly all the deck space in the tiny cabin, he wasn't surprised that he'd tripped across it. More likely, it would have been impossible to avoid. While the decision was hers to have the wretched thing here with her instead of stowed in the hold where such furniture belonged, he still couldn't deny that the cabin would be cheerless and cramped even without it.

Nestled as it was into the *Swiftsure*'s frame, the bunk was a lopsided platform with the curved beams arching overhead, the well-worn wool-stuffed mattress offering scant comfort against the hard planks beneath. A pine-framed looking glass and a wedge of a table, bracketed to the bulkhead beside the bunk, were the sum of the cabin's other furnishings, with Anabelle's sea chest stowed under the bunk. There was neither a port window for air nor a glass light to filter in sunlight from above, and the single candle in the tin lantern pegged to the bulkhead was smoky gray tallow.

For Samuel Worden, who expected no more than a closet for a first mate's privacy and a place to sleep between watches in relative peace, the humble cabin served well enough, better than those found in many other merchantmen. But to Anabelle, raised in a house grand enough to have a name, surrounded with luxuries of every kind, the place must seem a dismal hole indeed. If there were any other, better place for her on board, he'd grant it to her in an instant, but the only more suitable spot would be his own cabin, and that wouldn't be suitable at all.

"Did you come here for a purpose, Joshua?" asked Anabelle softly. "To play turnabout, and catch me asleep as I did you? I cannot blame you if you did, for that was a barbarous trick to play upon the captain. Though I did bring you a pot of coffee."

"And most fine coffee it was, too," he said, ignoring her question because he wasn't sure of his answer, not anymore. Lightly, he touched the carved face of the cherub on the cradle's bonnet, and through the twisting glimmer of the candlelight, the wooden lips seemed to smile winsomely for him alone. "Most fine."

"And your ribs," she continued, almost coaxing. "They are faring better, too? Your pain is less? The bindings will work loose, so you must be sure to tell me when they do, so that I might wrap you up tight again."

"Nay, nay, your handiwork stands," he said, "and most fine it is, too."

"I am glad." She smiled down on him fondly, though he wasn't looking her way. She liked to see him touch the cherub's face, his finger tracing the carving the same way hers always had for as long as she could remember. Maybe the cradle could weave the same spell over him, if he let it. Grandmother had spoken of mother to daughter to daughter again, but was there any reason for the father, the husband, not to be a part of the magic as well?

She pulled the coverlet from the bed around her shoulders and hugged her knees more tightly to her chest, watching him. She loved his complexity, the way his rumbling voice could roar out an order loud enough to be heard over a gale, then whisper soft as a butterfly for her ears alone, or how the same big, rough-hewn hands could have both the power to knock a man flat and the gentleness to caress a cherub's cheek.

He wanted so badly to be thought a gentleman, and she'd seen enough of real, high-born gentlemen in her life to know he'd never succeed. But what he didn't realize was that he was better than a score of London gentlemen: more handsome, more honest, more honorable, more just, more trustworthy, more—faith, Joshua was simply *more*. Truly, that expressed it all.

She smiled, thinking how he'd bluster at that. Strange how sure she'd been that he would be the one she'd marry, the one who'd be the father of her children. With him, she would be happy. From the first moment she'd kissed him, she'd been certain of it. Even when she'd accepted Henry Branbrook, her heart had been with Joshua Fairbourne. She didn't know why, and she couldn't explain it, but there it was, and there she was with it.

Or rather, she hoped, with him.

"I missed you," she said softly. "When my brothers went away to school, sometimes my father would not notice me for a fortnight at a time. There were, oh, scores and scores of people at Kilmarsh, but I was always alone. That's what it felt like again, to be here by myself on this ship and be of no reasonable use or interest to anyone. And what I said about going mad alone in this little place, with no one to see or talk to—it was you I missed most, Joshua. With you, I believe I could bear anything."

He looked up at her then. The candlelight washed over the strong bones of his face, his wide, open brow and the jaw to balance it, his eyes an intense, startling blue. He rose slowly to his feet—in the small space, there wasn't room to move swiftly, anyway—and held his hand out to her.

"Come with me, Anabelle," he said, his words a rough growl. "Come now, and I'll show you freedom enough to fill your soul."

She slid down from the bunk, her gaze never breaking with his. She hadn't a clue as to what he intended, but the way he'd said it, that wild, rough command, was enough to make her heart quicken with anticipation.

"I should dress," she murmured, though she made no move to begin. "It's bad enough of me to let you see my night rail, but if we're to go—"

"No one will say aught to me." He reached over the cradle and lifted her up across it before she'd realized what he was doing. She gasped with surprise, but she linked her arms around his shoulders without a pause. By now, she was becoming accustomed to this sort of demonstration from him, though she knew she should be mindful of his ribs.

"You shouldn't be doing this, Joshua," she did say as he carried her toward the companion ladder, the coverlet trailing over his arm. "You are still injured, and I do not want to be the cause of your hurting yourself further."

"'Tis nothing," he said easily.

"'It' may be nothing, but I most certainly am something," she said, wriggling as judiciously as she dared against him as she tried to get down. "Though I may be a short woman, I am not a frail one."

"The hell you're not," he said, lifting her a fraction higher as proof. "You're a mite to me—aye, no more than a capful of thistledown."

"You've thistledown between your ears, Captain Fairbourne, if you believe that," she insisted, though without much conviction. She'd seen the swelling and bruises on his side with her own eyes, but there was no denying that he was holding her easily enough now. She particularly liked the way his arm felt beneath her, warm and secure and strong around her hips as he climbed effortlessly up the ladder to the deck. "You would not dare say such—*oh!*"

She had never imagined there could be so many stars in the sky. Without the lights of a city or town to diminish them, without a tree or spire to narrow the horizon, the whole world seemed bright with stars, a million brilliant diamonds scattered over the blue-black velvet of the night. The wind that had blown with such whirling force earlier had fallen off with dusk; so that while the *Swiftsure* still cut her way through the waves, her progress had become instead an easy glide. The wind thrummed and sang through the taut rigging overhead, while the water *shushed* against the sides, all of it music to go with the wide beauty of the sky overhead.

"Oh, Joshua," whispered Anabelle. "Oh, I've never seen anything so beautiful in my life! Please, please put me down so I can see better!"

Obediently, he set her down on the deck, watching the radiant smile on her face as she twirled about on her pink toes, as free as a child, with her long hair dancing behind her in the wind. The whole ship would talk of nothing else tomorrow, but for now he did not care.

"Come aft with me," he said softly, taking her hand to lead her. "You'll be free of the sweep of the mainsail then."

He guided her to the quarterdeck, past Robert Stark at the wheel. The man nodded but didn't speak, the bowl of his pipe glowing red beneath the cocked brim of his hat, and Joshua nodded silently in return. These quiet watches that ran through the night were often this way, with each seaman lost in his own thoughts and his place within nature. It was a rare, peaceful time when a sailor's life was nothing but magic, a magic Joshua now offered to share with Anabelle.

He wasn't good with pretty phrases or explaining his sorrows to others. He'd been in the habit of keeping such things to himself far too long for that. It wasn't like giving orders, simple and direct, without any of the eddying currents and riptides to twist his own words against him or draw him down.

Still, he wanted Anabelle to know that he'd understood all she'd said. He understood because he'd felt that way, too, on his first voyage, a homesick, seasick boy struggling to find his place in a man's world. His one solace had been to climb to the highest maintop, the one place on board where the loneliness was of his own choosing, and lose himself in the wild beauty of the sky and the sea far, far below.

He watched Anabelle now as she stood beside the taffrail, the *Swiftsure*'s churning wake creamy in the dark water behind her. How the devil could that wretch of a father ignore *her*? She seemed so small to him there with the coverlet as a makeshift shawl, so vulnerable to all that could go wrong in the world, yet at the same time so miraculously heedless of it. As if hearing his thoughts, she impishly glanced over her shoulder at him and laughed from pure joy.

"Faith, Joshua, is there anything more beautiful in all the world?" she asked. "No wonder you love it so!"

"Would that it were always like this, sweet," he said gruffly, delighting in her pleasure as he joined her at the rail. This was the merry Anabelle he remembered in London, and how much it pleased him, too, that the sea could restore her spirits the same way it did his! "There're more days and nights when the sea's contrary than when it's not."

"But then I would have you as my captain," she said promptly. "You would be there to guide me over the waves upon the sea and through the storms and across the ocean. Or should that be over the sea and through the waves and past the storms upon the ocean? Oh, help me, Joshua, which is right?"

Unfortunately this, too, was the Anabelle from London, and Joshua took his time answering. "As long as we don't go beneath the waves," he said carefully, "I warrant it's all the same."

"Oh, good," she said with obvious relief. "I can get so vastly *lost* in things like that."

So, thought Joshua, did he, but he preferred to keep his confusion to himself.

She gathered the ends of the coverlet before her into a lumpy rosette, looking from it up to Joshua without lifting her chin. "I am sorry to have been so headstrong about the length of our voyage," she said. "Truly, on Grandfather's globe it did not seem so very far at all."

"Well, it is," he said, surprised she'd admit to any error. "You'll see for yourself soon enough."

"I suppose I must." She sighed heavily. "But 'tis not the most grievous mistake I've made. When first we met, you know, I did believe you were a Scotsman, and that your Massachusetts was some manner of Scots county or parish."

"Scotland?" he repeated with open disbelief. *"Scotland?* For God's sake, Anabelle, the two places could not be more different!"

"Perhaps to you, yes, but only because you've been to both," she said defensively. "At Kilmarsh, in the laundry, there was an ancient bad-tempered Scotswoman, a crofter's daughter, she claimed, and she was forever speaking darkly of the 'blo-o-o-o-ody Sassenachs' whilst she boiled the linens. Just like that, too, with all those extra O's in bloody to make it especially rude. You must admit that Sassenachs and Massachusetts do have much the same sound in the ear. It really is a most understandable mistake on my part."

"Sassenachs and Massachusetts," repeated Joshua. He could almost see the connection after she'd explained it, and the fact that he could worried him no end. "I'll have to tell that to Samuel."

"Oh, do, please." Anabelle nodded vigorously. "But pray tell him I meant no affront to your home."

"Thank you," said Joshua. "But you should know where we're bound, Anabelle, considering it's going to be your home, too. And likely Massachusetts is a good deal larger than Scotland, though all you'll mostly concern yourself with is Cape Cod. That's where Appledore lies."

Her face went oddly stiff, as if she'd bitten a sourtasting lemon. "Perhaps I do deserve it, Joshua," she said reluctantly, "but you really shouldn't speak such untoward jests before me."

He frowned. "You're making no sense, lass."

"For all love, must I spell it out?" she said indignantly. "I do not know what is proper in your Massachusetts, but I cannot believe that it is considered genteel to make low jests about—about *cods* before a maiden lady."

" 'Cods'? Oh, sweetheart!" He laughed; he knew he shouldn't, but he couldn't help it. "The place is named Cape Cod on account of the fish the first Englishmen found there, a kind of large haddock. It has nothing at all to do with . . . ah . . . a man's dearest parts."

"Oh, hush, then. Stop laughing!" She looked askance, unconvinced. "Why am I to believe you, sir? Are you quite certain, and this is not some base trick to make me sound strumpety and ill bred among your people?"

"Nay, not at all," he said, finally mastering his laughter. "Cape Cod is the good Christian name of the place, and no one will ever judge you strumpety for calling it so."

"And is this Cape Cod truly so far away from England," she said, still skeptical, "or was that another example of your tavernkeeper's wit?"

"No wit, sweet, only the truth. Pray this wind holds, and I'll make the crossing as tolerably swift as we can."

She sighed mournfully, twisting her hands into the coverlet. "A month is a long time for a voyage, Joshua, especially for us. If we *had* gone to Scotland, we might already be wed and a respectable husband and wife. I'm not quite certain what I am now, neither fish nor fowl, the only lady here in the middle of the ocean with a score of men, but I do not believe it's respectable. At least I doubt that Grandmother would call it so."

"The day we land, Anabelle," said Joshua firmly. "The day we land, no matter what hour, I will take you to our meetinghouse and insist that Dr. Townsend marry us. You'll be the most respectable woman

in Appledore, and no one will ever say otherwise to
Captain and Mrs. Joshua Fairbourne. No one, mind?"

"That is reassuring." Her smile wobbled, clearly
not reassured in the least. "But isn't there some
cunning way that you as the *Swiftsure*'s captain can
serve as a minister, too?"

"What, and marry us myself, like some sort of
pagan lord? Nay, Anabelle, it's an agreeable notion,
but if you've a mind to be respectable, I don't think it
will stand."

"No. No, I suppose it won't. Your Dr. Townsend it
must be." She sighed again and hunched her shoulders against the wind, drawing the coverlet higher.
"For June, the air is most chilly this evening, don't
you think?"

At once, he began to unbutton his coat to give it to
her. "Forgive me, Anabelle; I give the winds no
thought," he said contritely. "Here, you must have
my coat."

"And leave you in the cold? No, better we should
share, I think." She slipped inside the front of his coat
where he'd held it open to take it off and eased herself
close to his chest. "There. You must agree that this is
much the better for us both."

He'd agree that it was better, aye, but not necessarily in the way she meant. Or maybe she did. For all
that she complained of being cold, she felt warm
enough to him, warm and wonderfully soft, and it
seemed the most natural thing in the world for him to
put his arms around her to hold her closer within his
coat.

"It's the ice floes," he said, striving, and failing, to
keep his mind from her scent, violets and sleep and
warm, willing woman. "From the north seas. Pieces
of the pole melt in the summer and drift south. It's a
deuced nuisance for sailors, for if you stray too far

north, you'll run afoul of the ice itself, chunks of it as big as an island—not to mention the fog."

"Oh, aye, the fog," she murmured, lightly resting one hand on his chest as she arched up toward him. "I vow never to forget the fog."

She might not forget the fog, but he would, and he did, the instant she kissed him. Her lips were chilled, as she'd claimed, but by contrast, her mouth was all the more dizzyingly warm. He could no more keep away from that warmth than he could stop his heart from beating, and recklessly, his mouth sank deeper into hers, adding his own heat, scalding them both. If he'd learned anything about Anabelle, it was that kissing her, simply pressing his lips to hers, would never be enough, and tonight would be no different. Even the constraints of standing on an open quarter-deck in a freshening east wind weren't going to lessen his desires.

He slipped his hands inside the rough woolen cocoon of his coat to find her, dragging her off her feet and into the crook of his arm. His lips slid down her bare throat, tasting the salt spray that had settled there upon her skin, salt and sea and skin and violets, all mingled together.

She clung to him, trembling with a need she'd come to connect with Joshua's kisses. He was like strong spirits, rich and potent on her tongue, and with the same ability to sweep her wits away from reality. She loved the way he tasted, she loved the way he felt, his scent intensified in the shelter of his coat. She burrowed closer into him, wanting more, wanting all, even though she'd only the vaguest notions of what that might be. But though her poor befuddled head held none of the wisdom that her body seemed so cunningly to possess, it did have an ally in her conscience, and that conscience spoke to her now in the imperious voice of the Dowager Marchioness of Auboncourt.

"Whatever am I doing?" she whispered to no one in particular. Particularly not to Joshua, whose blistering kisses on the hollow of her collarbone were still making her shudder with delight. Yet reason forced her eyes open, making her stare up over Joshua's sleek dark hair to the ghostly spread of sails overhead. How had she come to be nearly inverted, and not notice? "Oh, heaven help me, whatever *am* I doing?"

"What the devil d'you think you're doing, sweet?" murmured Joshua, the words hot upon the tender skin of her throat. "And you're not alone about it, either, mind? I'm here, too. And here."

He slid his open palm down the sweep of her spine, spreading his fingers to caress the fullest part of her bottom through the thin linen of her night rail. Oh, Heavens, he *was* there. If she didn't put an end to this now, while she still had a fleeting scrap of decency left, she'd end up losing her maidenhead this very night. After that, there'd be very little question about her relationship to the *Swiftsure*'s captain, and it wouldn't be as his wife.

"Joshua, please, I must stop this," she said breathlessly, twisting about as she struggled to right herself. "You must already think me too bold by half. Joshua. Joshua, *please.*"

"Nay, not too bold, Anabelle, not by halves, nor thirds, nor any other rule."

"Joshua, please," she gasped, beginning to panic. "Oh, what sorry kind of lady do you believe me to be?"

"Damnation, Anabelle, you *are* a lady," growled Joshua in return, his breathing ragged as he let her go. A *lady*—how had she guessed the one sure thing to say to make him stop? Appalled by his own behavior, he staggered back away from her, the heavy rhythm of lust still pounding in his ears.

Jesus, what had he been doing? He would drive her away in disgust, destroy any feeling, any regard she might have for him, and who would blame her? He had wanted a lady wife, and with Anabelle, he would succeed beyond his wildest hopes. Yet the moment she'd come trustingly to him, he'd gone mad as any rutting Liverpool Jack on liberty, groping and slobbering over her like she was some ha'penny trull. No wonder she wished to be safely wed, when he seemed so wretchedly incapable of controlling his base instincts!

"I am sorry, Joshua," she said, her voice so rushed and low he could barely make out the words, her head bowed with shame and her hair falling around her face. "Oh, I am so sorry! It is all my fault, to be so— so wicked. Look at me, strutting about in my night rail before you, as bold as the greatest harlot in Christendom! Grandmother always said I was wild as a hare, an Irish hare, and now I've gone and proved it to you and now you'll likely not want me for a wife, not after I've—"

"Stop it, Anabelle," said Joshua harshly. "Stop it at once. I'm the one needing to beg for forgiveness, mind? My God, I'm the vile bastard who can't be trusted alone with you for five minutes! You've done nothing wrong, and I won't hear you say otherwise."

"Oh, Joshua," she said forlornly, at last raising her face toward his. "All I want is to have a place in your life. And in your heart, too, Joshua, if you'll let me."

"That's all?" He stared at her, astonished and humbled. Didn't she realize she had that already? He would have given her anything in his power, promised her the world without a thought of the consequences.

She nodded miserably. "Truly. That's all I'll ever want."

It should have been the simplest thing imaginable to tell her then. The words should have come rolling off his tongue, easy and true and straight from his heart. He couldn't imagine his life without her in it; she was already part of him in a way that no other woman had ever been. So why the devil did he stand there before her, just stand there, as mute as if he'd been carved from wood? What demon made the words choke unspoken in his throat as her face grew more and more desperate?

"I know I'm always resolving to stop being so—so impetuous, Joshua," she said slowly, her voice squeaking upward as it broke, "but this time will be different."

How could he tell her that that wasn't what he wanted, not at all? He sighed, suddenly exhausted, and when he held his arms open to her, she came to him, resting her head against his chest.

"You'll see," she said. "I'll never behave ill again."

"You and me both, Anabelle," he said. "You and me both."

❧ *Eleven* ❧

Joshua stood at the helm, his feet wide spread to counter the *Swiftsure*'s long roll through the heavy seas. Though the waves this afternoon demanded a firm, strong hand at the helm, they'd at last broken through the worst of the storms that had plagued them these last ten days, one hard blow rolling in after the other.

Ten days of double watches and short sleep and tempers to match, ten days of wet clothes that never had the chance to dry, of water sluicing through the hatches and down the ladders, ten days of dowsed galley fires and no hot food or drink. If Joshua had needed proof that he'd dawdled in London too long, then these storms had been it, warning enough that the hurricanes of late summer and fall were not far behind.

But the storms had not been all bad. With the skies at last clearing, he'd finally been able to take a reading from the noon sun to determine their bearings, and to his overwhelming surprise—a surprise he was careful to keep from the crew, who regarded his navigational skills with awe—they'd scarcely been blown far off course at all. They had, in fact, made considerable headway, despite some days sailing under little more than a scrap of canvas, and he wondered if the ship had caught his bridegroom's fever of eagerness to reach home.

He smiled to himself, thinking of his bride as his hands on the wheel's spokes unconsciously corrected the course. These ten days had been a good time for Anabelle and him, too. While he had spent most of his waking hours in the driving spray and wind of the quarterdeck and she had been forced to stay below for safety's sake, he had insisted on sharing their supper together in his cabin each night. Without a fire in the galley, the meals were Spartan affairs at best, biscuit and butter, cold ham and steeped beans and onions, but Joshua could not remember when he'd enjoyed dining in his cabin as much.

Sitting across the table from him, Anabelle had been the very picture of an ideal wife: obedient and charmingly meek, resourceful and tidy. Though he hadn't expected it of her, for the first time it seemed as if Anabelle had actually stuck to her vows to be good.

She had seen that the table was agreeably laid, or at least as agreeably as possible when plates and forks could go flying at any moment, and from somewhere, she'd produced a pot of strawberry preserves that had gone far toward improving the ship's biscuits. She always asked after his day, as dutifully as if he'd spent it on a stool in a counting house, and then listened raptly as he'd regaled her with sails set and sails taken in, and which tack favored the *Swiftsure*'s sailing points the most. She'd asked an endless store of other questions, too, about topics from the workings of the telltale compass in the cabin to the kind of linen used in the sails, not only passing their evenings but also making Joshua feel like a wise and learned fellow.

If he in turn asked few questions about her day, well, that was to be expected. However she chose to pass it must be tedious stuff indeed, all lumped vaguely together in his approving mind as ladies' work, fancy sewing and whitework knitting and such. Though he'd given her the freedom of his cabin during the day, she was seldom there, preferring, he guessed, the close privacy of her own quarters.

Yet despite the tiny mate's cabin, despite the rough seas, she had always contrived to be prettily dressed for him by supper, a welcome sight after a day of seeing nothing but dripping sailors, and she'd been quick to help slip the coat from Joshua's shoulders and to tug off his boots.

She'd gone no further than that, though. While neither of them had mentioned that shameless, shameful starlit night on deck again, they'd both somehow silently agreed to keep clear of such temptations again. No kissing, no wanton caresses, with each staying resolutely and properly clothed at all times. If part of Joshua—primarily the part within his breeches—longed for a return to Anabelle's beguiling disarray in her night rail and a coverlet, then that same part was compelled to understand the dangers of such an arrangement. He was determined to control himself as completely as he controlled the ship in his command.

That cradle in her cabin was a potent reminder to him as well. Anabelle had been one of four children and Joshua's own mother had been brought to childbed six times before she'd been widowed at the age of twenty-five. Joshua would be a damned fool to ignore the warning of such prolific stock on both sides. He knew it, and so did Anabelle, and it didn't make the wanting one whit easier to bear. Hell, if he could, he'd signal ahead to have Dr. Townsend waiting for them on the dock, prayerbook in hand.

His smile turned wry, imagining what the response in Appledore would be to that. Dr. Townsend himself would probably perish of apoplexy. But there was only a sennight more with any luck, he thought with satisfaction as he gazed up at the sky. One week, that was all. Even he could survive that.

With Anabelle as his reward, he had damned well better.

He gazed down the length of the ship, the sun warm upon his back. It was fine enough this afternoon that Anabelle might enjoy coming on deck. As she'd proudly demonstrated to him each night at supper, she'd finally found her sea legs, and with him at her elbow to guide her, she'd be safe enough. Aye, she'd like that, and so would he, and he called for Hosea.

"Pass the word for Ezekial Webb to come relieve me here," he said as Hosea trotted aft. "Then take my compliments to Miss Crosbie and ask her if she'd like to take a bit of air on deck."

"Aye, aye, sir," said the boy instantly from habit. But he hesitated, shifting his weight uneasily from foot to foot. "I'll find Mr. Webb right quick, but Miss Crosbie . . . Miss Crosbie's not in her quarters just yet."

"No?" Joshua frowned. Taking Anabelle a tray with two meals a day should have been the sole extent of Hosea's contact with her. "And how the devil would you know that, puppy?"

" 'Cause Miss Crosbie never is, sir, not at this time o' th' day," said Hosea with a thoroughly irritating stubbornness. "She never is, sir."

"Then where in God's name is she?" thundered Joshua. By now, the boy should be trembling in his boots before his captain, and damnation, he was still standing chipper as a sparrow. It was almost as if, inconceivably, he were daring to take Anabelle's side against him.

"In the fo'c'sle, sir," said Hosea. "Miss Crosbie always—"

"In the *fo'c'sle?*" repeated Joshua. He didn't know whether to be disbelieving, stunned, or horrified; most likely a stupendous mixture of all three was appropriate. "What the hell is Miss Crosbie doing in the fo'c'sle?"

Though Hosea opened his mouth to explain, Joshua wasn't going to wait to hear him. He roared at Jemmy Clarke to leave off whatever double-damned rubbish he was about and come take the wheel. Jemmy obeyed with a fearful speed, and the minute his hands were on the spokes, Joshua was already halfway down the companion ladder. If afterward Jemmy swore to his mates that there'd been smoke—black smoke—and plenty of it puffing from the skipper's ears as from a chimney, it wasn't much of an exaggeration.

Certainly black smoke was as good a description as any for Joshua's temper as he went striding forward. He was not a captain who believed in hovering around the fo's'cle. He'd begun his career as a fore-mast jack, and he was all too familiar with the awful, bewildering majesty of a captain's descending unbidden into the crew's quarters. The fo's'cle should be the one place in the ship that was their sanctuary— just as his cabin was his—their place to eat, sleep, and spin yarns between watches.

But it was not, and never would be, the proper place for a lady, let alone one who soon would be the captain's wife. What the devil could possibly have drawn Anabelle there in the first place? He thought of his genteel little image of Anabelle in her cabin, bathed in candlelight, her head bent over some dainty hooped handwork, silk threads and linen in her smooth white hands, her feet in their elegant little mules tucked up on the rails of her cradle.

Then he pictured the fo'c'sle, the air forever thick with tobacco smoke and oaths and the stench of men with few opportunities to wash themselves or their clothes from one port to the next. There'd be the single battered table forever stained with grease, the backless benches that sometimes served as weapons, the lewd French print of a mermaid that someone had pinned to the bulkhead, and worst of all, the double row of bunks where the men slept, tumbled pillows and coverlets and stained, wool-stuffed mattresses, altogether a scene that would make any decent woman cringe and look away.

Or at least it should. With Anabelle, he was never sure what would distress her.

Damnation, what had happened to all her charming resolutions to reform, all her pretty shows of housewifery and wifely devotion? She'd certainly managed to make a fool out of him. God only knew what other mischief she'd hidden behind that sweet smile, those deferential little curtsies as she'd refilled his glass, her "Yes, Joshua" and "No, thank you, Joshua" and "Pray, what are your thoughts on this, Joshua?"

He was so angry by the time he reached the last door that he didn't bother to knock, instead using as much of his boot as he did his arm to shove it open wide, the poor battens flying back on their hinges to smash against the bulkheads. Through the filtering haze of his fury, he had only the swiftest impression of the fo'c'sle: as hazy with tobacco smoke as he remembered, a polished brass lantern swinging from the beams for light that he'd forgotten, the two rings of bunks, the blur of startled, guilty faces of the sailors gathered there—Robert Stark, Blue Andrew, Asa Hallet, and Samuel Worden, double blast him for playing the Judas—until, in the middle of them all, in the halo circle of the lantern's light, he found Anabelle and forgot everything else.

"La, how you astonish me, Joshua!" she said, turning slightly on the nail keg she was using as a stool. Despite her surroundings, she looked exceedingly proper, dressed in quilted petticoat and a light green jacket—*his* favorite light green jacket, the one with the silver braid, double blast it, too—with a neat white cap over her hair, her wrist arched to hold a small book and her eyes wide, the perfect picture of astonished innocence.

Innocence, hah. A triple blast to that. He'd caught her red-handed.

"You needn't look so fierce, you know," she continued, smiling as if nothing were amiss. "And even for a captain, cracking down doors like the mighty North Wind himself will earn you nothing better than broken hinges."

"Anabelle," he began, as good a beginning as ever while he tried hard, very hard, to keep his temper in control. "Anabelle. What under God's Heaven are you doing here?"

She grinned. "I do believe you've asked me that before, Joshua, though I cannot recall the circumstances. Perhaps twice, now that I consider it."

"This isn't what you're thinking, Josh," interrupted Samuel, the only man brave enough to speak. "Miss Crosbie here—"

"Miss Crosbie can damned well explain to me what this is." Joshua clasped his hands behind his back, partly from habit and partly to keep from throttling her pretty white neck. "If it pleases *her,* that is."

"Oh, stop acting like such a great ogreish bear," said Anabelle, perilously close to scolding. "We're not fomenting dark intrigues and mutiny, if that's what you fear. It's all vastly harmless. No, less than harmless, since for once I'm going quite beyond causing harm to doing good. You should be exceptionally proud of me, I think."

She slipped a ribbon into the book to mark her place and leaned forward to pat the sleeve of the sailor on the bench beside her. "Show the captain your wrist, Robert," she said. "I do not think he shall believe me otherwise."

But Robert Stark shook his head and looked down into his lap, his weathered face the color of cooked beets as every eye turned his way.

"Please, Robert," she urged softly. "Won't you do it for me?"

"Oh, aye, he'll do it," said Joshua, not liking that soft, cajoling tone of hers easing its way into ears other than his own. "But he'll do it for me, Anabelle, not you. Come, man, show me this great wonder."

His gaze still downcast, Robert Stark rested his left arm on the table and carefully rolled back the sleeve of his coat. His wrist had been splinted between two small boards, cushioned in lint and held in place by a carefully tied bandage, as pretty a job as any Edinburgh surgeon might do. As pretty, and as efficient; Joshua's own ribs had healed under just such admirable attention.

"He won't be back to rights for another week or two," explained Anabelle, "but by next month, I expect he'll be skylarking through the rigging again with the rest of you. Isn't that so?"

Robert Stark nodded solemnly, and so, to Joshua's amazement, did the other three men around the table.

"Miss Crosbie knows her physick, Josh," said Samuel evenly. "You can't imagine what a comfort she has been to the men, setting sprains and generally patching us back together, especially after that last stretch of foul weather left us so battered. She'll have your neighbors lined up at your kitchen door when word of her gifts gets 'round Appledore."

Joshua's jaw tightened. This was not the role he wanted for his wife, tending to his crew's every ill, real and imagined, and as for physicking all of Appledore from the white-painted doorway to his new house—well, that was simply not to be borne. He wanted his wife pouring tea for other captains' wives, not dosing every farmer and fisherman who turned up on their doorstep.

"Oh, bother, Mr. Worden, 'tis no great 'gift,' as you call it," she scoffed with a smile. "Only common sense, that is all."

"And I say you're too modest, Miss Crosbie," said Samuel, bowing as he returned her smile, and Joshua could have sworn the damned fool blushed.

"That doesn't explain what's happening here the rest of the time, Anabelle," he said, his temper raised another degree by Samuel's too-obvious adoration. "There's just so many smashed thumbs, even among these ham-fisted lubbers."

He glowered around the table at the men, until his glower stopped short at Asa Hallet. "What the devil is that you're working on, Hallet?" he demanded, not wanting to believe what his eyes told him the man's handiwork was.

His eyes, and now Hallet's mouth. "It is one of Miss Crosbie's petticoats," he said seriously. "Since she is no hand with a needle, I offered to put up her hemmings for her."

Anabelle's petticoat, for all love, her scent clinging to the soft wool where it had brushed across her legs, her thighs, *her* petticoat, here in the fo'c'sle for any man to touch.

"All my skirts are too long, Joshua," explained Anabelle blithely. "Without hoops, they all drag after me like yesterday's sorrows. But Asa Hallet here so kindly offered to shorten them for me, and you can imagine how I leaped to accept him. Such beautiful work he does, too—as fine as any tailor's in London."

Now it was time for Hallet to flush with pleasure, and Joshua barely stifled an oath of utter disgust. They were all besotted, all under her spell, a pathetic sight if ever he'd seen one.

"Why the devil didn't you tend to your own sewing, Anabelle?" he demanded. "Why waste my man's time with your women's work?"

"Why?" She tipped back her head and laughed, and his fond, domestic image of her bending over her needlework disintegrated in an instant. "Because I am hopeless with a needle and always have been. No one could ever teach me otherwise. Faith, your ham-fisted lubbers are nothing to me!"

"Nothing is, Anabelle." He took a step closer to her, then another. "But you still have not answered my first question. What under God's heaven are you doing here?"

"Why, reading, of course." She smiled brightly, and held the little book up for him to see. "It passes the time wonderfully, you know. We have been progressing through Mr. William Shakespeare's history plays, and we've only begun *Henry VI* this morning. Do you know that not one of your men had ever heard of Mr. Shakespeare? Can you conceive of such a thing?"

What he couldn't conceive of was that she came here every day, morning and afternoon, while he was occupied with running the ship, and in her clear, sweet voice read out loud by the hour to this adoring pack of ninnies. Read Mr. William Shakespeare, for all love. Henry the ruddy Sixth.

Hell, she'd never once read to *him*.

"There are no plays in Massachusetts, Anabelle," he said through gritted teeth. "There are no plays or players or theaters because they're considered idle, worldly fripperies. There are even laws against them."

She cocked her head slyly, tapping the book with her forefinger. "Oh, aye, aye, Captain Fairbourne, I'll believe that tale," she said archly. "Laws against plays! La, how vastly wicked you are to tell such lies!"

He moved so quickly that she didn't even realize he'd come toward her, not until she felt his hands on her upper arms, lifting her from the chair to her feet. He didn't say anything, and from the look on his face, she judged it wisest not to say anything either, at least not until they were in the companionway and out of the others' hearing.

"Let me go, Joshua!" she said indignantly. "I am completely capable of walking without your forcible assistance!"

"Oh, aye, capable of walking and talking, too," he said grimly, still keeping his hand locked firmly around her arm as he led her, stumbling, into the cabin. "Walking and talking and calling me a liar before my people. What the devil were you trying to prove, eh?"

"I wasn't trying to *prove* anything, Joshua. You said a foolish thing, and I merely pointed that out to you."

He let her go to slam the cabin door behind them, latching it for good measure. She had seen him angry before, so many times that she'd lost track, but she'd never seen the kind of black fury that filled his face now. If she'd any sense at all, she should have been frightened, but he'd provoked her to the point that her sense had fled, and her anger was rapidly swelling to match his own.

"It wasn't foolish, Anabelle. It was the truth." He pulled her chair from beneath the table and thumped it down on the deck before him. "Now you sit, and you tell me why, as soon as my back was turned, you went creeping off to the fo'c'sle, the *fo'c'sle,* for all love!"

Anabelle ignored the chair, sweeping around it instead to thump her palm flat on the table. "I did not go 'creeping off' Joshua. I was trying to do something that I thought would please you."

"Why are you so confounded concerned with pleasing me?" he growled. "Why don't you keep to pleasing yourself instead, eh?"

She stared at him, astonished that he could be so amazingly thick-witted. If she did not strive to please him—or Grandmother or Father or any other such person in her life—then she'd cease to be of any use to anyone, cease to be worthy of love, and cease, in a way, to exist. After that, what would be the point in pleasing herself alone? It all seemed entirely logical to her, but perhaps it was something that men couldn't understand. Certainly Joshua was one man who would never be ignored by anyone.

At least he certainly wasn't going to tolerate it now. Mimicking her, he struck the opposite side of the table, though with his fist, not his palm, and hard enough to make everything on it bounce into the air.

"Answer me, Anabelle. What the devil—"

"Oh, hush with your devil this and devil that!" she shot back. "Just hush, Joshua, and stop stomping about like the village bull, and *listen* to me!"

"I'll listen when you begin telling me something worth hearing!"

"Then listen now, Captain Fairbourne. I'm sure every other man in the *Swiftsure* already is, given your roaring." She paused, letting the truth of that sink into Joshua's dislike of audiences. At least it had scrubbed the know-all smirk from his face, and in record time, too.

"After I helped you with your sorry bruises, it seemed reasonable to do the same for the rest of the men on board, and so I went to the fo'c'sle and offered my assistance. Of course, being men, they balked at appearing weak before any woman, but when I told them how I bound your ribs for you, then——"

"You *told* them?" said Joshua, aghast at such a breach. As captain, he'd always prided himself on appearing invincible. The men expected it.

"Well, yes, I did," admitted Anabelle without a shred of regret, "and it helped convince them wonderfully."

"Better they'd stayed unconvinced." Again, he pounded his fist on the table. "Damnation, can't you see how wrong this is for a lady in your position? For you to go among my crew, hardly a party of saints at the best of times, tending to them in so intimate a way——Anabelle, you are going to be my *wife.*"

"Yes, that alone is quite reason enough to doubt my judgment, isn't it?" she said. "If I had married Mr. Branbrook or another like him, I would have been expected to go among the people on his lands, to know their names and their troubles and to help them as best I could. The *Swiftsure* is your holding, at least until we reach Appledore, the crew your people; you are the master, and when we are married, I will be the mistress. It all seems exceptionally obvious to me."

And to Joshua's dismay, her explanation seemed

obvious to him, too. He didn't want to admit how little he knew of how fine English ladies passed their time. He'd always thought it was in going to dressmakers and visiting other ladies and other genteel time-wasting, but he couldn't deny that Anabelle's version was much more worthwhile and admirable, too.

Not that he'd ever admit it. "Then why in blazes didn't you tell me what you were about, eh?"

"I never told you because you never asked," she said, permitting herself a wifely little smile. She could afford to give him that much. She was winning, and she knew it even if he didn't yet. "You appeared so occupied with your captain's duties that I didn't wish to bother you. Certainly you didn't believe I sat in that dark little cabin all day, as solitary as a hermit, pining for you?"

From the look on his face, she realized that that was exactly what he'd believed. She also realized, quite suddenly, the reason for the heightened state of his belligerence.

"You're jealous, aren't you?" she said, letting the delight of her discovery spill over onto him. "You, the almighty and splendid Captain Joshua Fairbourne, are jealous of your own crew, of the time I spend among them and not with you!"

"I am not," he said immediately. "Don't go leaping to such flattering conclusions, Anabelle."

"I do not have to leap, or even to hop," she said happily. He wouldn't be jealous if he didn't care about her, and her heart did leap with purest, giddy joy. "You have done all the work for me."

"I have done nothing of the kind, and if you— damnation, who is it?"

He turned to glare at the tentatively opening cabin door and Hosea's round, apprehensive face sliding from behind it. At least now the boy looked respectably full of dread, decided Joshua. Small satisfaction, that, but the way this day was going, he must be content with small victories.

"Well, Hosea, spit it out," he ordered. "There's only an hour or two left until nightfall, mind?"

Still silent, the boy twisted his knitted cap in his hands and glanced reluctantly toward Anabelle.

"Go ahead, Hosea," said Joshua. "I've no secrets from Miss Crosbie, at least none to compare to those she has from me."

"Very well, sir." The boy swallowed hard, concentrating on getting his message right. "Mr. Worden sends his compliments, sir, and begs to tell you there's a sail bearing hard to the east, and it won't go away."

Joshua nodded, considering. Likely the stranger's sail would vanish soon enough—given the *Swiftsure*'s overwhelming speed, they generally did—but he still wished the other ship weren't there at all.

"Tell Mr. Worden I'll be there directly," he said, and glanced meaningfully at Anabelle. "Leastways as soon as I'm finished here."

"Aye, aye, sir," said Hosea, and gratefully fled.

"You're finished whenever you please, Joshua," said Anabelle. "You need not linger to please me. But I do question that bit about your secrets. Yes, I do question that, considering what I've heard from your men."

For the second time, she'd managed to halt him dead in his tracks. She was beginning to rather enjoy herself. Besides, for reasons she didn't try to understand, Joshua was particularly attractive when he was angry—the angrier, the better. His eyes grew bluer, his voice stronger and more passionate, his whole body so tense and ready to fight that he seemed to fill the room. And she liked it—my, my, how she liked it.

"So help me, Anabelle," he said at last, "and you, too, if you've been prying and gossiping about me."

"There was no prying whatsoever. Everything was volunteered. And such things I did learn, la!"

"Mostly lies, I'll wager," said Joshua suspiciously. "Those men know a ripe cully for their tales when they see one."

"Oh, lies, lies, more lies," she agreed, grandly sweeping her arm through the air for emphasis. "For example, I learned that most of your crew has sailed with you for years, and they swear they'd never sign with another skipper. Such loyalty! Marlborough himself couldn't claim more."

"Marlborough doesn't sail out of Appledore," he said warily. He didn't trust her when she turned expansive like this. Generally, such a change meant she'd depend more upon her wit than her emotions, and he could counter the emotions a good deal better.

"Considering Marlborough is a general in the army, I'd vow he doesn't sail out of anywhere," she said, resting her elbows on the back of the chair between them. "But I heard you pay better than any other shipmaster in Appledore, too, perhaps even on Cape Cod, because of the extra risk. Your cargo, I heard, is not exactly as the customs gentlemen believe it to be. You don't let yourself be troubled by detailed lading bills and tariffs and other niceties. Smuggling, they called it, a rather wanton-sounding word for the practice. But I vow it was mostly lies, just as you say."

"Every last word of it," said Joshua. Damnation, he wished she wasn't wearing that snug green jacket, not in the middle of a quarrel, when it wasn't fair. "Was there more?"

"Faith, yes!" she said, rounding her eyes with a great show of wonder. "Strange how you've been so eager to tell me of your grand new house but never once have you mentioned watching after the families of your crewmen, particularly those who perish at sea."

He'd stopped noticing the green jacket. Somehow, she'd yet again managed to subtly change this quarrel, or conversation, or whatever the hell it was, and he didn't like this particular tack at all.

"A man gives his life in my service, and I'll make sure to provide for his kin," he said carefully. "'Tis fair enough."

"Especially fair when I learned what happened to your own family," she said softly. "Or was that more lies, too?"

Harshly, he sucked in his breath. "You heard that from Sam, too, didn't you?" he demanded. *"Blast him for a blathering Judas!"*

"He didn't betray you, Joshua, not the way you think," said Anabelle swiftly. Now that she'd come this far with him, she'd have to see it to the end. "And he wasn't the only one to tell me, either. But though what befell your poor mother was a tragedy, there was no sin, no shame in it that I can see, and it certainly was no fault of yours. The world is seldom as kind to widows and orphans as it should be. With you as her first son, I think she fared better than most. But for you to lose both her and your father when you were so young—oh, Joshua, how hard that must have been for you!"

"They were not 'lost,' Anabelle," he said sharply. "They died, mind? My father on the rocks at Marblehead, my mother a year later of a fever that claimed her while I was at sea. They *died.*"

"And do you believe they would have wished you to do this to yourself," she asked in return, "to hate yourself for living while they did not? They would never have wanted you to suffer, because they loved you, Joshua. They loved you."

And so do I, she added in her thoughts. *Oh, how I love you, Joshua Fairbourne!*

He turned away from her, unwilling to let her see the emotion that must show on his face. "Did you hear that between decks, too? Or is this more folderol come from that infernal cradle of yours?"

"Oh, Joshua." She came to stand behind, slipping her arms loosely around his waist. She rested her cheek against his broad back, letting the simple gesture say more than any words could. She felt his back stiffen briefly, fighting with himself, but in the end, he didn't push her away. She closed her eyes, savoring the warmth of his body against hers. She had missed this over these last weeks: not only kissing him, which she'd grant was most fine indeed, but the intimacy of being close to him like this. Hadn't he missed it, too?

"I didn't have to hear it from anyone else," she said softly. "I simply *knew.* From your fairness, your honor, your respect for others, even the way you try to bury your goodness by acting like such a great blustering ninny—I *knew.* You couldn't possibly have become the man you are now unless your parents loved you then."

He sighed, a deep rumble that she didn't hear as much as feel beneath her cheek.

Damnation, she was right. *She was right.* Not about him being such a fine and honest fellow, for he wasn't so cocksure as to believe that for a moment, but about his parents' loving him. He had always concentrated on the shame of having his family broken up, the boyhood agony of feeling helpless. But there had been so much more before that. His father's teasing and his mother's laughter as they'd sat around the table for supper, going out to fish with his father alone on the bay in a little two-man boat, the way his mother was always quick to knit him another mitten even as she scolded him for losing the last: all of that was part of him, too, and somehow Anabelle had known it.

"Easy enough answers for you, aren't they, sweetheart?" he said slowly.

"Nothing is easy, Joshua," she said firmly. "I should not have to tell that to you, of all people."

"Sometimes you should. Not often, mind, but sometimes."

"Truly?"

"Truly, sweetheart. You are so damnably wise some times it fair frightens the life from me. Aye, it does. But then I'll warrant everything comes easy when your father's a lord."

"An easy life," she said, her voice fading with a wistfulness he'd never heard from her before. "An easy, splendid life, with a father who cares more for his dogs and his porter and whiskey than he does for his children, and a mother whose only way out of a loveless marriage was to die of a broken heart. A house like a palace can be cold as a cave if there's no love inside to warm it. If that has made me wise, Joshua, then I should be frightened, too."

"Poor lass," he murmured, appalled by the life she'd described. How in blazes had a lighthearted creature like Anabelle survived such a dismal family? He thought back to the few times she'd mentioned her past, remembering, too, though she'd not mentioned it herself, the overbearing grandmother who'd been so determined to marry her to that capering numbskull of a lord. No wonder she clung so fiercely to her mother's cradle!

There'd been other unspoken clues scattered through her chatter, now that he thought of it, though he'd always been too caught up in his own affairs to pay much notice to hers. Yet she had always found time for his. Even here, now, it had taken his long-buried unhappiness to unlock the depth of her own.

Clumsily, he placed a rough, self-conscious hand over hers. Words—at least the words he knew—seemed woefully inadequate to console her, and for long seconds, the only sound was the muffled ticking of the watch in his waistcoat pocket.

"It was bad, wasn't it?" he said at last, and inwardly winced at how impossibly weak that sounded.

She sighed. "Parts of it, yes. And other parts weren't so very bad at all. My mother, while she lived, and my brothers, and our treehouse, and the stream and meadows around Kilmarsh—that was all rather fine, in fact. But all of it, good and bad, is done now, isn't it? It's done and can't be helped or changed, and that's an end to it."

His heart twisted at how hard she was trying to sound cheerful. She deserved better than she'd gotten from life so far. It was up to him to see that she received a good deal more in the future.

"I'm sorry, sweet," he said softly. "Though that means precious little, eh?"

"It means the world to me," she said fervently. "And so do you."

"Perhaps you're not so wise after all," he said gruffly, and with a deft turn of his wrist, he managed to pull her around to face him, holding her gently in the circle of his arms. He'd forgotten how neatly she fit there, as if she belonged nowhere else. Nay, no ifs about it; he never wanted her anywhere else, and it was high time he found the courage to tell her, too. "Perhaps you're—damnation, now what?"

Again, he swung around toward the door, though this time Anabelle was giggling as she peeked around his arm. Again, Hosea entered with obvious reluctance, reluctance mushrooming into outright mortification when he saw Miss Crosbie in the captain's embrace.

"Forgive me, sir . . . an' miss, you forgive me, too," he stammered, his face changing through every shade of red to a fine purple-crimson.

"Hang your forgiveness," ordered Joshua. "What the hell does Mr. Worden want this time?"

"He wants—that is, Mr. Worden sends his compliments and begs to remind you that your damned hide is still wanted on deck." Hosea swallowed hard. "His words, sir, not mine."

"Oh, I know that," said Joshua. "Tell him I'm on my way, and remind him, too, that he's not above a good ten lashes for impertinence."

The boy ducked and disappeared, and with a sigh, Joshua turned back to Anabelle. What he wanted to say would have to wait a bit longer, but at least that way he'd be sure of the right words.

"You see how ill-founded my discipline is," he said mournfully. "A week from home, and my word means nothing. If I don't go to Sam now, the devil only knows what he'll do next."

"I understand entirely," murmured Anabelle, running her forefinger lightly from one button on his waistcoat to the next and the next beyond it. "Besides, it could be important."

"Could be." Before he changed his mind, he gently took her by the wrists and freed himself. "You wait here. I'll be back as fast as ever I can. You have my word."

"I'd rather come with you, Joshua," she said. "Please."

Automatically, the same old reasons for denying her came to him—the dangers of an open deck, the distraction she caused, the impropriety of her simply being there on the quarterdeck—but this time, they seemed somehow less important. If she stayed with him, then he'd be able to speak to her all the sooner, and that, now, seemed most important of all.

"Please, Joshua," she said again. "I'd rather like to be with you."

"Very well, then, Miss Crosbie." He held his arm out to her, his smile crooked. "I'd rather like it, too."

❖ Twelve ❖

"Can you make her out yet, Josh?" called Samuel from the deck, up to Joshua high in the foretop. "What ship is she?"

But though Joshua squinted through his spyglass until his eyes watered from the strain, he still couldn't identify the strange ship that had been following them from yesterday afternoon through the night to where she lay now, a tiny black silhouette against the red ball of the rising sun. By the end of this watch, he might be able to make out more, but for now, there was little use in his staring any longer into the eastern sky. With an uneasy sigh, he tucked the glass into the front of his waistcoat and began the long hand-over-hand return to the deck, to Samuel and Anabelle waiting there for him, all the while wondering who in blazes was following them.

Lord knew Joshua had done his best to shake the ship. As soon as dusk had settled the night before, he'd ordered his usual precautions to discourage company. He had changed his course sharply to the north and then, around midnight, changed it back again toward the west. He had run out all his extra canvas, sailing as close to the wind as he could to eke out every last scrap of speed that the *Swiftsure* could muster. In the unlikely case that the stranger's eyes were sharper than theirs, he had taken in his English colors and in their place run up those of a neutral Dutchman, complete with a blue, white, and orange company flag for an Amsterdam merchant house. In the thick of the night, he'd even replaced his foretop sails, the ones that would peek over the horizon, with a set made from dirty gray canvas designed to blend into the darkened sky.

Yet here it was daybreak, and the proof that none of his deceptions had worked lay there on the horizon.

"Not yet, Sam," he said heavily, before the other man could ask again. "But I expect we'll learn soon enough."

"But *I* still do not understand why that other ship should wish to follow us at all!" said Anabelle indignantly. Although Joshua had urged her several times to go below to sleep, she had insisted on remaining on deck, by his side, throughout the long night. Her nose and cheeks were red from the wind and the chill, but her eyes were bright with the same fever of impatience that burned within everyone else on board. "We have as much a right to this ocean as they do!"

"That's not quite the point, sweet," said Joshua. "I doubt that other captain covets my particular bit of seawater."

"He certainly covets something," she declared. "Why ever else would he come traipsing after us in such a bold fashion?"

"Why ever and whoever and why the hell doesn't he go stick his bowsprit in someone else's affairs?" He sighed and fought the temptation to pull out his glass and stare at the strange ship again. He hadn't gone into the details of their predicament before this, not wishing to frighten Anabelle, but perhaps the time had come to be more honest. "Do you recall, sweetheart, that fine new word you learned in the fo'c'sle?"

"I learned a great many fine new words in the fo'c'sle," said Anabelle promptly, "most of which I fancy would not bear repeating in genteel company."

"I'd wager not," said Joshua hastily, ignoring the sudden coughing fit that had seized his first mate beside him. "But I'd like you to recall the one you said described my, ah, trade. Smuggling, it was."

Anabelle nodded, tucking her hands familiarly into the crook of his arm, as much to warm her fingers as from affection. Even though she'd changed into her kerseymere traveling habit and the gloves to match, she'd never before been so cold in July.

"Oh, yes, I remember that particular word perfectly, and its meaning as well," she said cheerfully. "The goods in the *Swiftsure*'s hold are considered smuggled because you didn't declare their true nature or worth to the trading authorities in London. Nor do you intend to do so when we reach Appledore. This makes these goods doubly valuable, on account of being untaxed and uninsured, for of course no insurance company can insure an article that doesn't legally exist. Therefore, we are all of us on this brig engaged in the act of smuggling, and you and Mr. Worden here are smugglers personified."

"Well, that nicks it all on the mark, doesn't it?" said Joshua, taken aback by the unexpected, almost alarming, clarity of her definitions. He wondered if she understood as much about all the new words she'd learned in the fo'c'sle. He rather hoped she didn't.

"I suppose it does, yes," said Anabelle mildly. "I can be reasonably clever if I set my mind to it."

He raised one black astonished brow; "reasonably clever" was one of the greatest understatements he'd ever heard.

"Now then, Miss Crosbie," said Samuel, "you should understand the two possibilities for that ship's identity. First, that they're pirates or other thieves, or second, that they're the king's men, revenue bastards from the navy."

"La, what a puzzle." Anabelle fumbled in her pocket for her handkerchief and dabbed at her nose while she mulled over the possibilities, the white lace fluttering before her face in the wind. "I do not know much of such things, of course, but it does seem to me that pirates are more to be found in warmer waters, are they not? Where their parrots will be comfortable? Where they can swagger about beneath the palm trees with their pirate wenches and bury their golden Spanish doubloons without worrying about great-coats and such?"

Joshua exchanged a sympathetic look, or at any rate an understanding one, with Samuel, who had less experience with Anabelle's bewildering notions. Parrots and greatcoats, Spanish doubloons and pirate wenches—how in blazes had she come by this picture, anyway? Yet like most of Anabelle's more peculiar ideas, a grain or two of truth did lie at this one's core.

"You're right enough, sweetheart," he said absently, coming to Samuel's rescue. "Few pirates venture this far north. But there aren't even many of them left in the Caribbean these days, with the worst of the lot hung in our grandfathers' time."

His gaze wandered over her head, back to the

strange ship that was still lost in the rising sun, still unknown. He knew he could not show his dread before Anabelle or his men, and he wouldn't. Yet it was impossible to deny its existence to himself: a cold, sick feeling that twisted in the bottom of his stomach, a feeling caused not by fear but by the certainty of fate. Aye, that was it. He should have known better than to revel in the happiness he'd found with Anabelle. Happiness like that was too fragile to survive in this life, and the grim, inevitable reminder was sailing there on the horizon.

"Then it is a navy ship that you fear?" asked Anabelle. "A British navy ship, coming after British citizens? How vastly froward of them!"

"A British navy ship coming after British citizens who are . . . ah . . . winking at British law by not giving the king his share," said Joshua. "We're naught but thieving rogues to that captain."

Though he'd meant it to sound roguish and daring, the lightness he'd intended evaded him. He saw his failure in the way Anabelle's chin ducked downward and how her brows drew together with perplexed concentration.

"Rogues, hah," she said scornfully. "They are the rogues, to chase us like this. You and Mr. Worden are no more rogues than I."

"Thank you," said Joshua, still squinting out toward the horizon, "though I'd wager that by being caught in our company, you'd find yourself called something a great deal less charming. Asa Hallet, here!"

The man came running, his bare feet thumping across the deck.

"Here," said Joshua, handing Hallet his own glass. "You take this up to the foretop and see what your younger eyes make of our shadow out there."

Anabelle leaned back, shading her eyes as she watched Hallet climb nimbly to the highest point to bear a man's weight on the *Swiftsure,* an easy sixty feet in the air above the deck. To watch Hallet or any of the other sailors skipping through the rigging made her quite dizzy and made her marvel, too, that she hadn't seen any more serious injuries than a few sprains and smashed fingers. Hallet hooked his knees around the spar and leaned forward, using his hands to hold and steady the glass instead of himself, and swiftly Anabelle looked away. Asa Hallet was a grown man, responsible for his own welfare, but that didn't mean she had to watch him tumble and crash to the deck on account of his own recklessness.

Instead, she looked squarely at Joshua, relieved that at least this time he wasn't the one pretending to be some Barbary ape. "What will these navy rogues do to us if they catch us?"

"Why," he answered, barely hearing her as he stared over her head to Hallet. "I expect they'd punish us."

She could sense the tension radiating from both Joshua and his first mate, the air on deck fairly crackling with the intensity of it as they craned their necks to follow the man aloft. Even the sky seemed to have grown uneasy, the clouds darkening and becoming more ominous by the moment.

She moved closer, lacing her fingers into his, and the fact that he didn't seem to notice worried her all the more. They could pretend to her that this strange ship was nothing but an annoyance, but the way Joshua was straining with every muscle to hear Hallet's announcement told her how very much was at stake.

"Exactly how will they punish us, Joshua?" she asked, her own voice higher as it echoed the tension around her. "Please don't coddle me, I beg you. I want to know. I *need* to know."

Without looking down at her, Joshua sighed, a deep rumble of unhappiness.

"If they are a navy ship," he began a last, his voice a harsh monotone, "and if they catch us—neither of which is certain yet, mind—they can claim the *Swiftsure* and her cargo as their prize, confiscate her and send her into port for sale and keep the profits. They can impress my men into their bloody navy and keep them there by force, never letting them again touch land or see home. They can put me in chains and take me back to London for trial, where they can keep me in prison the rest of my mortal days, or hang me, whichever suits."

Horrified, Anabelle shook her head in furious denial. "But they can't do that!" she cried. "How could they possibly hang you for mere *smuggling?*"

His smile was bleak. "Anabelle, sweet, you are too tenderhearted by half. London magistrates think nothing of sending children to the gallows for plucking a handkerchief from a man's pocket. Do you think they'd scruple over someone who's taken blessed revenue from the king himself?"

Beside him, Samuel swore with frustration. "But it makes no sense, Josh, no bloody sense at all!" he said, his despair clear. "Ten years we've been making this run, and in all that time, we've never once seen anything like this! It's not as if we were scuttling back and forth from France, dodging all the guns in the channel. You know that. There's what, but ten revenue cutters along our coast? Twelve at best? Think on that, Josh! That's a dozen ships for hundreds of miles of rivers and harbors and neat hidey-hole inlets, yet we have this bastard on our stern as easy as kiss my hand!"

He broke off, swearing again, before he could bring himself to continue. "Do you think it's Holme himself? Do you think he'd sell you to the admirals on account of his . . . of his . . ." He stumbled to an awkward halt, too late remembering Anabelle.

She smiled, though without the enthusiasm she would ordinarily have shown. Her heart was too heavy for that. "You need not be coy before me, Mr. Worden. I am perfectly well acquainted with the captain's previous *belle petite amour*. We have in fact conversed on two distinct occasions."

The unfamiliar but suggestive French made Samuel cough to mask his embarrassment. The three words had no meaning for Joshua, either, but then he was more accustomed to Anabelle's ways.

"Holme wouldn't betray us like this," he said firmly. "He'd stand to lose too much himself, and the old miser is a sight more fond of his profits than his daughter. He could have pulled his cargo from the *Swiftsure* in London, but he didn't, and if it came down to—"

"She's hull up, Cap'n!" bawled Hallet from aloft. "A frigate, Cap'n, no mistake!"

A frigate—even Anabelle knew what that meant. Frigates were not merchantmen like the *Swiftsure*. Frigates were navy ships, bristling with guns and blood-thirsty marines and fighting sailors. And frigates were known to be fast. Very, very fast, and her hope turned to ashes in her mouth.

"There you have it, Josh," cried Samuel with disgust as the word passed rapidly through the ship. "It's as if they had an invitation to follow us, written out neat and delivered. Not even you can say otherwise."

"What I say is that they haven't gotten us in range of their guns yet," said Joshua, purposefully raising his voice so that the men would be sure to overhear.

"And until they overhaul us—*if* they overhaul us—
none of this spleeny chatter is worth a tinker's damn,
mind?"

Anabelle listened and marveled at how differently
the two men responded. Samuel Worden seemed to
shrink before her eyes, bowed down beneath his
uncertainties and worries. Though he stopped complaining after Joshua's warning, the anxiety still
showed in the way he kept rubbing his hand over and
over the back of his neck, over and over and over.

But Hallet's excited bellow had had the opposite
effect upon Joshua. With his worst fear confirmed, his
physical presence seemed to expand to meet it, and
before Anabelle's eyes he grew even taller, his shoulders broader, his blue eyes flashing, somehow all of
him more alive in the face of the challenge. Joshua
Fairbourne was the *Swiftsure*'s captain, and no one
would ever dare think otherwise.

Her captain, she thought proudly, and more than a
little possessively, too. How vastly wise she'd been to
fall in love with him and to put her future in such
capable hands! He looked every inch the hero now,
with his handsome weathered face turned resolutely
into the wind and his long black hair streaming out
behind.

Well, she conceded, perhaps not entirely a hero, at
least not a *hero* hero. A hero would not have a day's
growth of beard blackening his jaw or have knotted
his neckcloth so carelessly; nor would a true hero have
shown quite such a damn-the-devil boldness in his
eye. Now that Anabelle thought about it, he looked a
great deal more like the pirate that Grandmother had
warned he was, or at least the savage, and the idea was
vastly pleasing indeed. For hero or pirate, or even
savage, the result would be the same. He would see
them through this trial, and just as he'd carried her

from Grandmother's house, he'd carry her home to Appledore and safety, and Anabelle almost shivered from the wonder of it. Faith, was ever any other woman blessed with such a brave and splendid man?

"Wind's coming 'round for us, and we're close to our home waters as it is," he said, gazing up at the sky and the skittering clouds, and he turned to call to the man at the helm. "Let's take her another point closer to the wind, Webb, and hold her tight on that course until we leave those sots behind."

"Aye, aye, sir," came the automatic reply, and with it the wordless humming of the ship shifting to obey as well.

At last, Joshua looked down at Anabelle, the corners of his eyes crinkling as he smiled at her. With a gallantry—and an openness—she'd never expected to see from him, he lifted her hand to his lips and kissed the back of her knuckles.

"What a monstrous pity I am wearing gloves!" she said, her smile a match for his. "Or perhaps it is not. The fire of your kiss upon my innocent skin, la! I should be completely undone, here upon your deck for all the world to see."

"Hang the world," he said, a dare if ever she'd heard one. She'd never seen his eyes so bright or his smile so wolfishly wicked. "When this is done, I mean to test every inch of that innocent skin of yours, and no hiding away behind gloves or jackets or petticoats. No las about it, either. You'll be undone, completely and thoroughly, and damned happy about it, too."

She laughed, delighted, even as she blushed. He'd never spoken this boldly to her before, and she rather liked it. No, she *quite* liked it. If this is what danger did for him, well then, she was soundly in favor of it.

He laughed, too, then let the merriment fade slowly away, keeping his gaze locked with hers. "You're not frightened, are you, lass?" he asked in his deepest, most rumbling voice, the one that she always felt as if it were a caress. "We're in a tight spot, no mistake."

She shook her head fiercely. "What should I care, Joshua, as long as I'm with you?"

He raised his brows with mock surprise. "You trust me that much, eh?"

"You've never given me the slightest reason to do otherwise," she declared, relishing the bond she felt so strongly between them. "Now, if you please, I'd like the glass to see the villains for myself."

"Aye, aye, Miss Crosbie." He handed her the spyglass, nodding with approval as she steadied it with both hands. "We'll make a proper sailor of you yet."

"I should like to see you try to make me a proper anything. No one else who's tried has had the least success. Consider poor Grandmother." She closed one eye and squinted the other, the way she'd seen the men do, and tried to find the other ship. Magnified, the waves bobbed up and down at such an alarming rate that she overcompensated and swung the glass up too high, suddenly focusing on ratlines that appeared as thick as a tree trunk.

Determined not to admit defeat before Joshua, she moved the glass again until she finally found the tiny frigate on the distant horizon. She understood now what Jacob Hallet had meant by "hull up," for with the glass, the ship's hull was now clearly visible above the horizon. At such a distance, her untrained eye could make out few other details: the bright tricolored blotch of the British flag, the great clouds of canvas with every sail set for the chase, and lower, just visible, the neat row of black squares against a white stripe on her sides that would be her gunports.

"There seem to be a great many guns, Joshua," she said, feeling considerably more sober as she lowered the glass. "I suppose they wouldn't be chary about firing them either at us, would they?"

"Nay, they wouldn't be," admitted Joshua reluctantly. "Leastways they never have been before. But generally, they fire one or two shots across your bows as a warning that they mean sterner business and give you time to strike."

"It's all so very dreadful!" she cried. "I do not understand how one set of Englishmen can fire upon another like that, as if we were no more than nasty, wicked Frenchmen or Spaniards! However can they *do* such horrid things and still consider themselves gentlemen?"

Joshua made a low rumble of disgust by way of agreeing. "I'm not sure how many of them do."

"Well, some do consider themselves exactly that," said Anabelle promptly. "I know that for an absolute fact. One of Mr. Branbrook's first cousins is a lieutenant on some ship or another, and though Mr. Palmer is only a fourth son, only an honorable, his father *is* the Earl of Carrollton, which makes Mr. Palmer undeniably a gentleman, at least by blood. I saw him once across the room at an assembly with a number of other officers, and Mr. Branbrook told me who he was. They certainly had the manners and appearance of gentlemen; their uniforms were vastly splendid, with a great deal of gold lacing, though I did not care overmuch for the cut of their hats. I thought they gave the gentlemen's heads a foolish, smallish sort of look."

She sighed, absently tapping her fingertips on the leather casing of the spyglass, until she realized that no one else was speaking, and that the look on Joshua's face had suddenly turned very grim indeed.

"Oh, dear, dear," she said contritely. "I've been babbling again, haven't I?"

"Anabelle," said Joshua, with unsettling care and uncharacteristic patience. "Do you mean to tell me that that bloody ass Branbrook had a cousin in the navy?"

She nodded vigorously. "Yes, he did. Or still does. That is to say, *I* did. Told you that, I mean, and just a very short moment ago, too. Lieutenant the Honorable Edward Palmer. Yes."

"Did you have any notion of how close they were?" continued Joshua. "Were they just kin, or mates as well?"

"Oh, close enough, as cousins went," said Anabelle blithely. "You know how it is. Their mothers are sisters, I believe, and so they went to the same schools and rode to the same hunts and visited one another's houses for holidays. That sort of thing. So I suppose that would have made them mates, in a way, wouldn't it?"

"Aye," said Joshua heavily. "Aye, it would."

Determined to control his temper any way he could, he released her hand to clasp his own behind his back instead, forcing Anabelle to hold out her hands on either side to keep her balance as the deck heaved back and forth beneath her feet. The seas had increased, the waves dark green and with a strange, almost oily sheen, an ominous match to the cloud-filled sky above.

"Tell me, Anabelle," he said slowly. "Would Branbrook have told this cousin when you disappeared with me?"

"Well, yes, perhaps," said Anabelle swiftly, the horrible realization of what he suspected—of what she'd *done*—beginning to dawn upon her. "If the mortification of a broken engagement wasn't too great for Mr. Branbrook's pride. I don't believe most gentlemen would boast of being jilted, and even though I tried to explain everything in my letter to show it was not his fault but mine, for becoming more attached to you and deciding to marry you and sail with you to Massachusetts, I do not believe—"

"You left him a blasted *letter?*" thundered Joshua with disbelief, his long-tried temper erupting at last. "You told him everything—*everything*—in writing? Jesus, Anabelle, have you any notion of what you've done?"

"I did not know!" she cried desperately, the shocking impact of her well-intended action almost beyond bearing. "Oh, Joshua, you must believe me, you must! I did what I thought was honorable, to tell Henry the truth! I never dreamed this would happen!"

"Oh, aye, *this* is honorable!" he said as he flung his arm toward the frigate, not bothering to hide either his anger or his disgust. "Betraying a score of good men to salve the pride of one worthless well-bred cockerel! Betraying *me,* Anabelle!"

"I swear to you I did not mean it to be so!" She reached out for him, and as she did the deck rocked again and she stumbled backward. He did not come to help her; she did not try again. "I swear to you, Joshua, by all that I hold dearest, that I would never do anything to harm you or the others! Oh, please, please, Joshua, you must believe me!"

He stared down at her, his fury too tangled with his emotions to think straight, to see anything beyond the fear and guilt mingled in her eyes. She had betrayed him, aye, but for what possible purpose? When he had told her all that could befall them if they were captured by the frigate, he had purposefully omitted what would happen to her. Now he could think of nothing else: Anabelle branded as his lover, his whore, but not his wife; Anabelle treated with scorn, disrespect, open cruelty, or abuse by those same gentlemanly officers; Anabelle in endless disgrace, finally married to that bastard Branbrook for her money alone.

Instead of to him. Lord help him, instead of to *him*.

In the end, it wouldn't matter that her thoughtlessness had done this. Like so much else that Anabelle did or said, this, too, had its own strange logic, and whether he liked it or not, he'd come to accept it about her. Nay, what mattered more was that he had sworn to protect her, to make her happy, and all he'd done was make her life infinitely worse. But he hadn't lost yet. However perilous, he still had a chance.

"Go below, Anabelle," he ordered, his mind racing ahead to weigh every possibility, every advantage that the changing weather might offer. "I don't want you on deck where I must worry about you."

"Oh, please no, Joshua, don't make me go below!" she begged, panic apparent in the way her voice wailed upward. "Please let me stay here with you!"

"Listen to me, Anabelle," he said, striving to make this as clear as he could. "If we can make out their flag, then they could just as easily see you in turn on our deck, and I don't want that to happen. Go below, now, else I'll have one of the men carry you."

She pressed her hand over her mouth, pressing back the tears and pain that threatened to overwhelm her. "If you do not believe me, Joshua," she said, one last plea, "then put down a boat and send me to the frigate! If it is only I that they want, if this is my doing and therefore Branbrook's, then let me pay the price, and let you and your men go free!"

He stared at her with disbelief, unable to understand how she'd ask such a thing.

"Nay, Anabelle, I'll never do that," he said slowly, and no one who heard him would ever doubt it. "You are mine, and I will never give you up."

Alone in the tiny cabin, Anabelle lay curled on her misshapen little bunk in the dark and listened to the endless creaking and groaning of the *Swiftsure*'s timbers as the sea dashed against her sides. Now that she'd burned all but the last candle she'd determined to save for an emergency, the black darkness seemed to make her hear such sounds more clearly, just as she seemed to feel more keenly every sickening plunge from the crest of one wave into the trough of the next.

She'd lost all sense of time and distance, of whether it was night or day or night again. Hosea had come to her once, with cold biscuits and cider, but she'd heard the calls for all hands to report to the deck or the pumps too many times to be surprised that he hadn't returned.

This might be only her first voyage, but in these last weeks, she'd sailed through enough storms to be able to judge which were merely inconvenient and which were more dangerous. This one—this one was different. The winds howled like the banshees in her old nursery stories and shrieked like souls lost in the wilderness of night, while the seas tossed and tore at the poor *Swiftsure* as if she were no more than a fragile cockleshell. How much longer could any ship withstand such brutal pounding?

When Joshua had asked if she'd been frightened by the frigate's guns, she had shaken her head in complete honesty, but now she *was* terrified, for her own sake and more especially for Joshua's. While the men in the fo'c'sle had listened eagerly to Shakespeare, she in turn had hung on their real-life tales of disaster and woe. In a storm such as this, a man could vanish over the side so swiftly his mates wouldn't even see him go, and he'd be washed away forever in an instant.

But not Joshua, she prayed, trying not to picture him standing so tall and so dreadfully exposed on the quarterdeck, at the wheel. Not now, not before she'd told him how very much she loved him.

She curled herself tighter against her fear and misery. Though the frigate's menace had disappeared with the storm—by now they could have been blown a hundred miles off course and away from the *Swiftsure*—her guilt and grief over what she'd unwittingly done would take far longer to go away, if indeed it ever did.

Certainly she would never forget the look on Joshua's face when she'd mentioned the letter, so carelessly, so foolishly, never dreaming of all the suffering she could have caused. Remembering how they'd laughed and teased one another only minutes before made it all the worse. Now they would never be happy. Lord help her, she might not even ever see him again, not in this life, and with a broken-hearted sob, she turned her face to her sleeve and wept again for all she'd lost.

She knew she was dreaming, because she knew she was in Appledore. She was standing before Joshua's house, her house now, and the apple trees that had helped give the town its name were in flower, the blossoms drifting like pink-and-white snow across the path to the front door. She tugged down a branch to pluck a sprig from the nearest tree, sniffing its sweet fragrance before she tucked it into the front of her bodice.

The windows were open to the warm spring day, the curtains ruffling through the sashes in the breeze from the bay, and through them, too, she could hear Joshua singing, his rough quarterdeck rumble turning the lullaby into something altogether different as he rocked the cradle with a rhythmic thump. But the baby—their baby—with him didn't mind at all, and Anabelle could hear the gurgling laughter even from here. Smiling in happy anticipation, she lifted her skirts with both hands to hurry up the white path of crushed shells to join them. But as she reached the granite step, the door swung open from within.

"So here you are at last, my beauteous Belle," said Henry Branbrook, patting his brow with the lace-trimmed handkerchief he'd drawn from his cuff. "Ain't you glad to see me, you naughty chit?"

She woke with a cry, a cry that was lost in the thundering echo of splintering, shattering wood from above. She groped in her pocket for her striker, her fingers shaking as her heart pounded. The motion of the ship had changed, growing heavier, and it seemed as if the water were not just crashing against the thick timbers of the *Swiftsure*'s sides, but seemingly inside her as well, in the companionway outside. She thrust her hoarded candle onto the candlestick's spike and somehow managed to light it. Even though the candlestick was mounted in its gimbal, its little flame bounced wildly back and forth with the motion of the ship, casting dancing shadows over the bulkheads. Still dressed in her woolen traveling habit, she slid from the bunk and plunged ankle-deep into icy seawater.

With a startled gasp, she seized the candle and held it lower to the deck, or where the deck would have been if it weren't awash. The cradle was covered to the tops of the rockers, and though she knew it must be no more than a trick of the candlelight, it seemed as if the fat-cheeked cherub on the bonnet had lost its smile forever.

Faith, she could not blame it if it had.

It took all her weight on the latch to open the cabin door, and when she finally did, more water rushed it, swirling around her, and the wind that came with it snuffed out her candle. But ahead of her she could just make out the companion ladder, more like a waterfall than steps, and as she waded toward them, two men came lumbering past her, carrying a large crate between them.

"Jacob Hallet!" she shouted at the nearest man, plucking at his sleeve to stop him. "What has happened? What are you doing?"

He stared at her stupidly, not stopping, too exhausted and numb to realize at first who she was. "We're lightening th' ship to keep her from sinking," he mumbled, shuffling past her to the ladder. "Cap'n's orders."

"Where is the captain?" she cried. If Joshua were giving orders, then he must still be alive, still unhurt. "Oh, pray, where is he?"

Hallet cocked his head wearily toward the top of the steps, then disappeared through the hatch with the other man and the crate. She *would* find Joshua, and with her sodden skirts dragging heavily around her legs, she followed the men through the streaming water and up the ladder.

The force of the wind and the spray made her stop at the hatch, crouching down low and clinging to one of the lifelines that had been strung across the deck and tied to the mainmast. The ship pitched and rolled, pitched and rolled, her bowsprit plunging deep into the foam-capped waves that then broke and washed over the heaving deck.

She could not believe the scene before her. Joshua's

pristine deck was a shambles, the larboard rail washed away and the foremast and all its sails were gone, with only a jagged stump to show where they'd been. Instead of hanging in neat coils, loose lines dangled from above to lash like whips across the deck, while torn bits of canvas jerked and waved in ghostly pennants from the spars. And just as Hallet had told her, the men were clumsily hauling up goods through both the hatches, crates and barrels and bound boxes, and heaving or shoving them over the side. To keep the ship from sinking, Hallet had said; could they really be at so great a risk?

Anabelle shielded her eyes to scan the deck for Joshua. He *had* to be here. He would never leave his beloved *Swiftsure,* not willingly, yet in the driving spray, she could not find him.

Two more men appeared at the top of the companion ladder, their shoulders bent over their awkward burden as they hauled it upward. Anabelle moved along the lifeline to let them past, then froze with shock, for in their hands, next in line to be tossed over the side and into the dark waves, was her mother's cradle.

"No!" she screamed. "No, you cannot! You must not!" Forgetting her hold on the lifeline, she ran stumbling across the pitching deck and toward the cradle. "Oh, please, you cannot do this!"

The ship lurched and she slipped forward, catching herself with both hands on the side rail of the cradle. She'd saved it, she thought triumphantly as her fingers tightened on the familiar turned oak. She'd saved it for the babies she'd have with Joshua.

But her weight on the cradle was enough to make the two men lose their grip, and with a thump, the cradle fell from their hands and began sliding down the sloping deck. Frantically, Anabelle tried to stop it, but her scrambling heels could find no purchase on the slippery, wet deck. Suddenly, there was no deck at all beneath her feet, and she and the cradle both were sailing through the air, hanging there, with the *Swiftsure* and her toiling crew before her like a theater's setting.

How vastly strange, she thought with amused distance, and beside her cheek, the cherub smiled again, too. How vastly, vastly strange . . .

She struck the rising wave with a force that stole her breath, washing over her, trying to claim her as its own. But desperately Anabelle clung to the cradle, and when at last they both rose to the surface, she was sputtering and retching but still alive.

"That's it, lass, clap on tight," ordered Joshua, settling his hands tightly over hers on the cradle. "Don't let go, mind?"

She twisted around to see him, his wet black hair and beard making him look like some great, sleek sea otter, come to rescue her. "You came," she gasped. "You came for me, Joshua."

He drew her head into the crook of his arm, raising her above the surface of the water as the waves swept them relentlessly away from the brig.

"I told you before, Anabelle," he shouted over the wind. "You're mine, and I won't give you up."

❧ *Thirteen* ❧

Whatever Anabelle was lying upon was cool and hard beneath her cheek, while all around her came the sounds of a dozen quarrelsome cats, mewing and squabbling crossly at one another. They made no sense, those cats, yet how impossibly difficult it was to drag open her eyes to see the cats for herself! Her eyes felt sore and swollen, as if she'd cried herself to sleep, and even opening them this tiny fraction stung. She saw no cats, only a hill of glittering white—snow, sugar, sand. Narrow lines of green crossed the white, bending over in the breeze to sway and scribe perfect circles at their roots.

Roots, she realized slowly, prodding her sodden mind to accept that much and continue: roots meant leaves, and the narrow lines sharpened into grass, tall, waving blades in clumps that poked through the sand. Sand, a beach, the distant crash and hiss of waves. She rolled herself over and forced her eyes to meet the blinding brilliance of the sun. Not cats, but white birds with wings tipped with black, yellow legs and beaks against a blue sky, white birds that circled and hovered as they called back and forth.

"Anabelle." The birds and the sun and the blue sky vanished, in their place Joshua's face, lined with concern. "Anabelle, sweet, tell me how you are."

She smiled, and the parched corner of her lip cracked. "Well enough," she said, her voice a dry croak, "because you are here with me."

He smiled then, too, albeit crookedly, and with a shocking suddenness the memory of all they'd survived came rushing back: the storm and the waves and the overwhelming certainty that she would die, drown, slide beneath the cold green waves that sucked at her and disappear forever. With a broken sob, she pushed herself upright and threw her arms around him, burying her face against his shoulder.

"There now, no need for that," he said gruffly, but the fierce way he held her close against his chest betrayed that his need, too, was very great indeed and infinitely more powerful than any words of denial. For a long time, they stayed that way, his hand gently stroking the tangled mass of her hair as it fell over her back, comforting her, comforting himself.

At last Anabelle gave a hiccuping shudder of a sigh and pushed herself away—not far, just enough so she might study him. The left sleeve of his coat was ripped at the shoulder, his neckcloth had vanished, and half the buttons from his waistcoat as well; the clothes that remained were salt-stained and damp and blotched with sand that had clung to the wet cloth; his hair was a dark, uncombed mass around his face, and his skin a little sticky from the saltwater, but otherwise he looked perfectly, gloriously like Joshua, *her* Joshua.

"You are not harmed yourself?" she asked anxiously as she lightly ran her hands over his chest to be sure. "You are not injured in any way? No vainglorious pretending to be stronger than you are?"

"Nay, I am well enough, well enough," he said with a great show of heartiness. "I should know better than to try to trick you otherwise by now, anyway."

She nodded. "Then I . . . I wish to thank you," she said haltingly, her hands still resting lightly upon his chest and her gaze concentrated on the front of his shirt to avoid meeting his eyes. "Not simply for saving me, you see, but for—for believing that I was *worth* saving."

"Oh, Anabelle," he said, appalled she'd even imagine such a thing. He would always be haunted by the image of her small, determined, bedraggled figure clinging to that infernal cradle in the middle of one of the worst storms he'd ever known; clinging to the cradle, clinging to her dreams of both her past and her future, even as she'd fallen through the air toward the sea and what had appeared to be forever from his life. "Anabelle, sweet, I don't want to hear you say such things."

"No, Joshua, you must," she said, shaking her head, "for I'm only speaking the truth. After what I did to you, with that letter to Mr. Branbrook and his cousin and all, the sorrow and suffering I could have caused, I could not fault you at all for thinking the very worst of me. How could you do otherwise? I had no right to expect anything from you."

"Hush, Anabelle," he growled. "I'll listen to no more of this nonsense from you."

"But Joshua—"

"Nay, you listen to me, lass. Mind your captain, eh?" Gently, he cradled her face in the spread fingers of his hands, tilting it upward so she couldn't avoid his eyes any longer. "I've told you this before, Anabelle. You're mine, and I will never give you up. Not to Branbrook, or the sea, or King George's entire blessed navy. Damnation, Anabelle, I can't give you up, because I love you. There now, I've said it. I love *you*."

"You do?" she squeaked with astonishment. "Oh, Joshua, you *do?*"

"Aye, I do," he said firmly. Now that he'd finally forced himself to part with the actual words, he realized how badly he'd wanted to say them all along, and how right, how natural they sounded. "I love you, Anabelle Crosbie, and I've never in my life meant anything more. I love you, mind?"

Her smile spread slowly, wide and giddy and endlessly enchanting. "Oh, aye, aye, I'll mind you, Captain," she said, "because I love you, too."

"Well, now," he said gruffly, overwhelmed by exactly how fine it felt to hear those same words spoken in return. "That is the way it's supposed to happen, isn't it?"

"La, yes," said Anabelle, her cheeks turning delightfully pink, "but I don't believe it does very often outside of theaters, and certainly not between people who are already to be wed."

"That's because most people don't share our luck." He kissed her then, not only because it seemed the proper thing, but because he wanted to as well. He wanted to do a great many things with her, and frequently, too. No wonder being in love was so highly rated; in his experience there wasn't anything that came close to bettering it, especially not when the woman was Anabelle.

"Oh, Joshua, I do love you!" she whispered breathlessly when at last their lips parted, that giddy smile of wonder instantly returning to her lips. "What a *vastly* fine life we shall have together! Yet when I think again of how close we came to not having one at all——"

"Nay, lass, don't," said Joshua hastily as he saw her smile begin to wobble. "It doesn't bear worrying over."

"That's because you are so much braver than I shall ever be. You think nothing of leaping into the waves, whilst I was—I was—" Her smile wobbled and shook again, more precariously this time. "I was horribly more frightened than I can express."

"Bravery didn't have much to do with it." He hated the thought of her being frightened, and he gently stroked his thumb across her cheek, hoping to comfort her. "You must recall that I was born to the sea, as much at home with it as any fish."

"Then come," she said with a little sniff. "Let me see your gills so I might judge for myself what manner of merman you are."

She slid her hands on either side of his neck, beneath his hair, pretending to hunt for his fish gills, but as she did, she found she had no spirit left for playfulness. She dipped her chin forlornly, her hair falling on either side of her face as at last the tears spilled from her eyes.

"Poor lass." Gently, he touched his thumb to catch a tear on her cheek. "Do you know this is the first time I've seen you weep like this?"

She looked up at him, her eyes wet and bright. "That cannot be true," she said, snuffling. "It cannot. I weep all the time whenever I'm distraught—oh, great oak buckets of tears."

She reached into the slit in her petticoat, fumbling for the handkerchief in her pocket. The pocket was filled with wet sand, a slippery clump of seaweed, her flint and striker, a small tortoise comb, and a handful of coins; the handkerchief, when she finally pulled it free, was crumpled and sodden enough to need wringing. But for lack of anything better, she still used it to wipe her eyes.

"Look at me now, blubbering away like a two-shilling mourner," she said in a quavering voice. "I am quite hopeless, Joshua, quite. I cannot stop. However can you say you've never seen me weep?"

"It's true," he said staunchly. "For a lady, you're damned near watertight. I'd even be willing to forget this time, considering the circumstances."

"Oh, Joshua." She found his insistence strangely touching, and fresh tears welled up in her eyes. "You see how ready I am to make a liar out of you."

His eyes searched her face with renewed concern. "You are certain you're not hurt?"

She shook her head, trying hard to control her crying as she wadded her soggy handkerchief into a hard little knot of linen in her hand. Her ragged nails snagged on the wet cloth; she had broken every one of them with the force of her desperate grip on the cradle.

Dear Lord, the *cradle*.

"Oh, Joshua, where is it?" she cried, scrambling unsteadily to her feet. "The cradle, Joshua! Oh, please don't tell me we lost it, please—"

But the cradle was there, sitting lopsided but undamaged on the sand behind Joshua, and she hurried to its side, brushing away the sand that clung to the dark wood.

"You kick me if I ever say another word against that blessed cradle of yours," said Joshua, coming to stand behind her. "I hauled it from the water right after you. It saved our lives by being there to hang on to in the waves, and most grateful I was, too."

"So am I." Lightly, she traced her fingertips over the cherub, which this morning seemed positively serene. "I'm sure somehow it was my mother's doing, watching over us and keeping us safe. She *would* wish that, you know. She would want us to live and be happy and have children in quite the worst way possible. I fancy your mother would, too. With the two of them to shepherd us along, no wonder we were brought to shore."

"Amen to that," he said gruffly. Perhaps Anabelle was right about her mother, and his, too. He'd never given any thought to such matters. But certainly something had saved them, whether the cradle or their mothers' watchful spirits combined.

"Amen, indeed," she said gently as she patted the cradle's bonnet. "But what, pray, will become of us next in such a deserted land, I wonder?"

For the first time, she looked around at the place where they'd been washed ashore, and in spite of the warmth of the summer sun on her back, she shivered.

They were alone: quite, quite alone. The storm tide that had brought them had receded, leaving a broad sweep of beach strewn with tangled heaps of driftwood and glistening clumps of wrack, fish bones and crab shells, broken timbers and shattered spars and a twisted length of canvas that must have been a sail from some hapless vessel. She thought of the poor, dear *Swiftsure* and the men aboard her, Samuel Worden and the Hallet brothers and Hosea and all the others, and when she looked up to see Joshua staring out across the empty sea, she knew he was thinking of them, too.

"Do you think they reached safety, too?" she asked wistfully. "If we found land, couldn't they—"

"Either they did or they didn't," he said curtly, his face shuttering against her, "and no amount of guessing by us will change that."

Joshua knew he'd done the right thing to save

Anabelle, and he would have done it again without a thought. But still, a captain belonged with his ship and his crew, no matter how good the reason might be for his leaving. Nothing could change the fact that he'd abandoned the *Swiftsure* in distress, and even the rare happiness he was finding with Anabelle could not help ease his conscience.

"But if the storm—"

"I said it's done, Anabelle. Now come, and pray we find fresh water."

She knew him well enough not to ask more if he'd no wish to speak, and silently, she took his hand and followed him along the beach and up the steep side of the dune. She hadn't realized how thirsty she was until he'd mentioned it, and now she found she could think of little else. Every muscle in her body ached from the beating she'd taken from the waves, followed by lying on the sand in wet clothes. But she wouldn't dream of complaining to Joshua, not now. What were such complaints compared with being alive?

They crossed through the tall, nodding grass at the top of the dune and half slid down the sandy slope into a low hollow of stunted, close-packed oak trees. Joshua walked swiftly among the trees and through the bushy undergrowth. The oaks gave way to sparse-limbed pine trees, taller and more widely spread, and then a kind of low, wild meadow or heath. Yet still Joshua didn't stop, and doggedly Anabelle followed.

"Do you know where you're going, Joshua?" she finally asked. Though her shoes had miraculously remained buckled on her feet throughout the time they'd drifted in the water, the now-stiffening leather rubbed her feet at every step, and already she could feel blisters blossoming on her heels. "Have you visited this coast before?"

"Nay, but for all its length, the Massachusetts shore

is so much alike that I almost feel as if I have," he said, stopping to give her a brief respite. "'Tis not that different from the land around Appledore itself."

"Massachusetts!" she cried excitedly, and looked around with fresh interest. "We are in Massachusetts?"

"Somewhere within the colony's boundaries, aye, though I cannot say exactly where." He sighed and rubbed his sleeve across his forehead. Away from the breeze off the water, the sun was hot, and he, too, was considerably more tired and thirsty than he wanted to admit. "There are a handful of little islands scattered along the coast, and doubtless we made one of them."

"An island." She frowned. "How would you know this is an island?"

"It's simple enough, sweet," he said. "Every day, the sun rises in the east and sets in the west. It is morning now, and yet where we sat, the sun rose over land—that is, in the east—which in these waters can but happen on a peninsula or a cape, which would surely be settled, or on an island, which wouldn't necessarily be. Thus, we were cast onto an island."

"Oh," she said faintly, not following his explanation at all. "I suppose that spotting islands is a simpleton's task for a sailor."

"Aye, it is," he agreed amiably, and too late, she noticed the teasing spark in his eye. "Besides, if you'd but lifted your head when we stood on the crest of the dune, you would have seen the water all around us. Ah, here's our pond, right where it should be."

She would have retaliated for that, but her thirst overcame her desire for revenge, and she hurried after him through the rushes and to the water's edge. Though three green-headed ducks, startled by the intrusion, flew straight up before them with a rush of wings, Anabelle didn't care as she knelt on the bank beside Joshua. Making a cup of her hand, she scooped up the cool water and drank in deep, sloppy gulps, and when she'd drunk enough, she splashed the water over and over her face, her throat, her arms, amazed how something so simple could feel so good. She pulled off her shoes and stockings and dipped them in the water, too, gasping as the cold took the sting from her blisters.

"How much more cheerful you look, sweet," said Joshua, returning to her side, and she looked up quickly, water still dripping from her face. She'd been so caught up in relishing the water that she hadn't even noticed he'd gone, she thought guiltily, a grievous transgression, considering how much she loved Joshua. She must resolve to be more attentive; she wouldn't want to mislay him completely.

He held out his cradled hands to her. "Blueberries," he said. "I found them growing over there. If we were so daft as to sail in hurricane season, then at least we were wise enough to be cast away in time for berrying."

"*Blue*berries," she said with relish, plucking one from his hands. "What a vastly fine name for a fruit. Blue has become quite my favorite color, you know, on account of your eyes."

He looked at her doubtfully. "My eyes are like blueberries?" He held one of the small round berries beside his eye for her to compare. "Hell, I hope not."

"I did not say that," she said indignantly. "I said your eyes are blue and these berries are blue, but that is the end of the likeness, as you know perfectly well. La, these are tasty! You say there are more to be picked?"

"There, beneath the pitch pine," he said, holding back the rushes so she could pass. "But mind you stay clear of that vine, there, the one with the three clustered leaves, else you'll itch and turn so red you'll wish you'd stayed bobbing in the ocean. Keep your skirts clear, too, for the poison can rub off."

"How very grim," she said, sweeping her petticoat away with an exaggerated twitch as she ate another handful of berries. "So far, your Massachusetts is nothing like my Ireland."

"It's nothing like Scotland, either," he agreed, and when she swatted his arm, all he did was smile. But she was grateful for that, too; she knew how heavy his heart must be, and she'd do anything she could to lighten his burden for him.

When they'd eaten their fill of the berries, Joshua found a large, curved piece of bark that they used as a makeshift basket, filling it with more berries to take with them for later. While he worked, Anabelle wandered from the bushes into what seemed to be an open meadow, covered with low gray-green heathers and silvery shrubs and dark pink wildflowers. It might not be Ireland, but it was beautiful in the same wild, rough way, and she could understand why Joshua would love it so much.

"Captain Fairbourne," she called. "Come tell me the name of these peculiar plants. I've never seen their like, but I don't dare touch them from fear they will turn me into a toad or something worse."

Running to follow her voice, Joshua found her standing in a small patch of stalks that towered over her. The stalks themselves and the long leaves were pale brown and brittle so late in the season, but the jutting, tasseled husks that held the plant's bounty were fat and ripe for picking. Yet Joshua frowned, unable to avoid wondering who had planted it here in such neat rows, and who might soon reappear for the harvest.

"What is it, my learned teacher?" Anabelle teased.

"Surely you can know the answer. Faith, I've never seen such an ungainly plant!"

"Anabelle," he said sharply. "You're not to leave my sight, mind?"

"But I only—"

"No arguments, Anabelle. You stay with me."

A flash of panic flickered in her eyes. "You suspect something, don't you? The navy men?"

"Nay, not the navy men," he said, striving to make her cautious but not frightened. "Not in particular, anyway. But 'tis better to be wary in a strange place than not."

She stood silent and unconvinced beside the corn stalks, and with a sigh, he reached up to break off an ear.

"This is corn, lass," he said. He pulled back the husk to show her the kernels—black, yellow, white, maroon,—that lay inside. "Not your English corn— we call that wheat or rye—but Indian corn. I'll show you how to roast it for our supper."

But Anabelle had stopped listening. *"Indian* corn?" she said, remembering what Grandmother had said. "Planted by true Indians? Is that what you fear, that we'll be set upon by savages?"

"Not at all," he said quickly. "'Tis only a name for the corn, that's all."

While he doubted that the corn had in fact been planted by any wandering Wampanoags or Narragansetts, not this far out to sea, corn was not a crop that reseeded itself or grew untended. Anabelle might see the island as deserted, but everywhere Joshua looked, he saw the hand of man: the stumps of trees that had been sawed for lumber, the scattered ashes of an old cooking fire, an empty bottle left in the rushes near the pond, and now this corn.

There was, of course, good to this, for it meant the island, though not permanently settled, was near enough to the mainland to be visited regularly, and the odds were that he and Anabelle would not be stranded long. But the bad news was that he'd no notion of who those rescuers might be, or whether in fact they'd be rescuers at all.

He sighed heavily, breaking off a half dozen more ears of the corn and stuffing them into the pockets of his coat for later.

"We won't starve, Anabelle," he said, "nor will we perish for want of water. But what I'd give for a plain-speaking flintlock musket and dry powder to go with it!"

"A musket?" she asked uncertainly. "Why, Joshua? What are you not telling me? Are we in danger?"

"Nay, not now," he admitted, inwardly cursing himself for speaking so freely. "But there are times when a musket can be wonderfully reassuring company."

She sighed. "Reassuring, perhaps, but I would not call a gun particularly *companionable* company," she said. "For that, I suppose you shall simply have to content yourself with me."

He would not quarrel with that, or with her, and for the rest of the day, before the tide rose again, they scoured the flotsam and jetsam and other rubbish that lay scattered over the beach for anything that might be of use or comfort. Among their scavenged treasures were a number of spars, a keg of ship's biscuits that was only a tiny bit damp, empty bottles that Anabelle refilled with water for drinking from the pond, and several lengths of cordage and rope.

But the most useful single discovery was an entire mainsail, stripped away by the storm from its mast with half a spar still intact, and though the huge piece of canvas has been torn into three pieces, it served Joshua's purposes admirably. He decided to set up their camp in the hollow behind the dunes, and with the largest piece of the canvas and several of the broken spars, he rigged a makeshift shelter for them among the oak trees.

The second piece he used to fashion a mattress over a pile of springy pine boughs, and with the last strip, he made a signal flag to fly from the tallest pine over the dunes. The pine wasn't very tall, and he worried that the pale canvas and the dunes were too much the same color for his flag to be seen, but he could still hope that some sharp-eyed lookout would spot the unfamiliar motion of the waving canvas and send a boat to investigate.

It was a great deal to accomplish in one day, especially when the knife he'd always worn in the sheath on his belt was his only tool as well as his sole weapon. Yet he welcomed the work, for it took his mind from the fate of his ship and his crew.

Beneath the July sun, it was hot work, too, and by midafternoon, he'd stripped down to his shirt and breeches. To his surprise, Anabelle had been more than ready to help in any way she could, and as he worked with the canvas, she'd looped up her petticoat and gathered wood for fires, dragging driftwood and fallen branches to a single pile on the sand.

"You don't have to toil so, lass," he said kindly when they paused to rest in the shade. Not only did she look hot and tired, but her nose and cheeks were pink with sunburn. "You've already done more than your share."

"More than you expected is closer to the mark," she said, bristling. "You'd rather do everything yourself, wouldn't you? Just because I am the daughter of a viscount doesn't mean I'm fit only for languishing genteelly in the shade."

"For God's sake, Anabelle, I didn't say that, did I?" he said wearily. What he hadn't expected was for her to insist on *working.* "I don't want you to overtire yourself, that is all. At least take off that woolen jacket so you don't keel over from the heat."

She drew herself up very straight, every inch a viscount's daughter despite the fresh blisters on her palms. "This is my bodice, Joshua, not a jacket," she said with surpassing dignity. "I have nothing beneath it except my stays and my shift."

"Then wear that alone, lass," he urged. "'Tis better than roasting alive."

Her backbone grew stiffer still. "I cannot, Joshua. You know that. What if someone comes to rescue us? What would they think of me, traipsing about in my shift like some slattern? No, it would be vastly improper of me. *Vastly* improper."

He hadn't the heart to tell her that her jacket—or rather, her *bodice*—already fell far short of propriety. The once-elegant plum-colored kerseymere was sadly faded and shrunken, and more than half the double row of buttons was gone. The few buttons that remained were tarnished from the salt and straining valiantly to hold the two sides of the bodice together and contain Anabelle within. At the top, the buttons had failed outright, and the gapping fabric only served to accentuate the deep, tantalizing valley visible between her breasts.

No, thought Joshua, dragging his own wayward gaze back to her face, the bodice wasn't particularly proper at all, and he didn't want any stranger gawking at his future wife's breasts any more than she did herself. But he didn't want her dropping to the sand from heatstroke, either.

"Aye, Anabelle, I wager you're right," he said patiently. "Even if there's not a blessed soul about to see you, you must be a proper lady. Aye, you must. Even if it would please *me* to see you like that, I must think of your propriety."

She frowned, and from her expression, he could see her conscience at war with itself. "It would truly please you, then?" she asked slowly. "To see me half dressed in the open air like that?"

Damnation, how could it not?

"I'm only a man, Anabelle," he admitted, "and one with wicked thoughts about you at that."

She considered only a moment longer before she began peeling the too-tight sleeves from her arms. "Very well, then, Joshua. Because I doubt that anyone else will come today, *and* because you say such a demonstration will please you, *and* because it really is most barbarously hot, I shall do this. But faith, you'll be asking me to leave off wearing my stays next."

He looked at the wide, rounded expanse of her breasts, pressed upward by the stays and barely contained as it was. The stiff canvas and whalebone and lacing were the only things unyielding about her, and he swallowed, swallowed hard. If she wanted any faint claim to propriety, she'd cling to that last bit of armor with all her might, especially around him.

"Nay," he said hoarsely. "Keep the stays."

That was all he said, all he could say, as he swiftly rose to his feet to return to his work and escape temptation. He stole a glance over his shoulder at her, bending over to pick up another piece of driftwood, and he nearly groaned out loud. He had sworn to keep her safe, but who was going to keep her safe from *him*? If he kept up like this, they wouldn't need to set a signal fire tonight. They could stake him out in the sand and he'd be burning just as hot and bright as any flame. *Only a man,* ha; right now he felt like such a damned rutting beast that being a mere civilized male seemed a completely unattainable goal.

And so, he thought morosely, until they were rescued, until they were safe, until they were married, was Anabelle.

❧ *Fourteen* ❧

"You were quite right, Joshua," said Anabelle as she nibbled the last kernels from the ear of corn. "I did like that, very much. Perhaps I was meant to be an Indian viscount's daughter instead of an Irish one."

Preoccupied by his own thoughts, he smiled faintly, contrasting in his mind Anabelle in a French silk gown and hoops with a Wampanoag squaw in moccasins and deerskin.

"I cannot see it, sweet," he said. "There's no such thing as an Indian viscount, nor do you bear much of a likeness to any Indian lass I've ever seen. They are taller, for one thing."

Anabelle tossed the cob into the fire before them and wriggled her bare toes into the sand. "Most everyone is. Taller, I mean, not a viscount. Viscounts of any height are rather more thin upon the ground."

Joshua didn't answer, and Anabelle sighed. She didn't particularly care one way or another about the Indian lasses, but she did care very much about

Joshua. He had grown more and more withdrawn as the day had gone by, until now, as they sat side by side beneath the signal flag made to attract passing ships, their backs pressed comfortably against the cradle's side, it seemed as if he'd barely spoken to her at all.

She told herself it could be any number of things: worrying and grieving over the *Swiftsure* and her crew or how close he'd come to drowning along with her or concern for who'd rescue them or even simply that he was exhausted after working so hard all the day long. Any one of these would be reason enough. All of them together must be overwhelming.

She glanced at him wistfully, longing for the right words to comfort him. Now that he'd told her he loved her, she did wish he'd confide in her and not keep everything roiling inside himself. Cautiously, she inched toward him, close enough to lay her hand over his.

"'Tis a beautiful night, isn't it?" she said as an opening. "So many stars in the sky! Do you remember how you promised me that in New England I'd see twice as many stars as I'd ever seen in London?"

He nodded, turning his hand slightly beneath hers so their fingers curled together.

"But where was this fine weather two, three days ago?" he asked bitterly. "Where were these kind winds then, eh? By God, if we'd had them instead of that double-blasted hurricane, we'd be in Appledore by now."

"Perhaps the *Swiftsure* already is," she said gently. "Mr. Worden seemed capable enough to have brought her in to port."

He tipped his head back against the cradle's rail, looking up at the stars instead of her. "Oh, Sam's a good enough sailor. He could have brought the *Swiftsure* clear from London if he'd a mind to. But that business with the frigate rattled him, and if she came back after my *Swiftsure*, well, I cannot say what would happen. I cannot say which would be worse—to lose the *Swiftsure* with all hands or to see her taken by the frigate. Sweet Jesus, I cannot."

She doubted his eyes were focused on anything now before him, yet she said nothing, letting him talk, letting him say what had to be said through the blanket of his despair.

"Sam had an older brother—Micah, his name was—who was pressed out of a whaler in the Greenland waters, him and four other Appledore men. Must be eight years ago now, but we've none of us heard another word from those men. Most likely they're dead, but never knowing for certain's been hard on their families, and Sam, well, he's never stopped hoping Micah would come back. Not that he speaks of it, 'course, but I know his thoughts. Aye, I know them."

He nodded to himself, and Anabelle wondered if he even remembered she was there beside him.

"And the Hallets, you know, they'd never fare well in a frigate's crew," he continued. "Quakers like them don't. They won't swear oaths to the king or take their hats off to an officer or drink spirits. Now I've never cared what a man believes so long as he does what I ask, but a navy boatswain would take offense to Asa and Jacob just from spite and make their lives hell. And Hosea—I took him on to please his widowed mother, even though he was such a little sprout he was no real use to me. It will break her heart if he's lost. It will indeed. I doubt she'll ever forgive me, her and all the other mothers and wives and sisters and daughters."

"Yes, they will," said Anabelle softly. "They will because they know you cared about their men."

He made a wordless sound of disgusted dismissal in his throat and shook his head.

"It's quite true, Joshua," she said firmly. "You want the world to think you're so fierce and damn-the-devil, and yet you're not, not really. You care too much about other people to truly be that way. Especially to your crew."

"Oh, aye, and a fine way I had of showing it to them, too, jumping ship in the middle of a gale!" His laugh was almost painful to hear. "I did that for you, Anabelle, yet I've failed you, too, haven't I?"

"Failed me!" she cried indignantly. "How ever can you say such a thing, Joshua Fairbourne? Faith, I would not be alive if it weren't for you!"

"And for what?" he demanded, at last turning to face her. By the firelight, his eyes glowed with a dark intensity that matched the flames themselves. "When I asked you to marry me, Anabelle, I could offer you a gentleman's house and a life where you'd want for nothing. Mind, I wouldn't have asked for you otherwise. You know that. But now I'm a captain without a ship, without a cargo, and I'll have to sell nearly all I have to make good on my debts. I'll have to begin again, Anabelle. I'm not afraid to do that, but you're a lady, and I've no right to expect you to suffer and scrimp and make do with me."

"Faith, Joshua, have we come roundaways back to that again?" she said fiercely. "That I am too genteel by half and half again even to—to *live?"*

"You *are* a lady, Anabelle!" he thundered. He yanked his hand free from hers, slicing his arm through the air for emphasis. "What kind of pinchbeck gentleman does this make me, eh? I've pulled you up from your roots like a rose from a garden, dragged you half way across the world and into the ocean, and for what? Damnation, for what?"

"For you, you great dunderhead!" she shouted, and before he could utter more foolishness, she scrambled on top of him, grabbing his shoulders with both of her hands to hold him steady, and kissed him, slanting her lips eagerly across his.

It was not gracefully done, pinning him down like this with her petticoats sliding every which way as she straddled him on her knees, but she was willing to sacrifice grace for the sake of keeping him still. At least he did not seem to object. As soon as she settled over him, she felt his hand clamp over the back of her waist, sliding up under her unbuttoned bodice to hold her in place, and if her mouth hadn't been otherwise engaged, she would have smiled with joyful triumph.

She had, of course, kissed him before, but not when he'd gone so long without shaving, and the bristle of his beard around his mouth and across his cheeks momentarily startled her, a different texture of him to learn. But then his mouth opened and sought hers, as hungry for her as she was for him, and once her lips parted in return, the familiar, exciting taste of him made her forget everything else. She grasped his face, spreading her fingers to comb through the rough fur of his beard to the softer tangle of his hair and she willingly lost herself in the dizzying depths of his kiss.

This night, she knew, was theirs by right, and all they'd have to do was take it for their own. The stars overhead, the tart-sweet taste of the wild blueberries that had stained her lips, the rush of the waves in the darkness at the edge of the shore, the flames that danced and flickered and licked through the twists of driftwood, all of it proof that she and Joshua were alive for another day, another night—wonderfully, gratefully alive. She longed to make him understand, and with that first kiss, she realized to her enormous relief that he already did.

He was the first to break away, tracing his lips along her cheek, her chin, her throat, while she let her hands ease down his chest, yanking the long tails of his shirt free from his breeches until she could slip her hands up inside to the warm, hidden skin and curling man's hair.

"What the devil are you doing, Anabelle?" he whispered hoarsely, though he made no more move to release her than she did him. "Damnation, Anabelle, don't."

"But I do, Joshua, and I will, and so will you," she murmured fiercely, her voice husky with longing. She was still a virgin, true enough, but she had overheard scullery maids, she had eavesdropped on her brothers bragging to each other, and while Grandmother's grim, dutiful admonitions had sketched in more details, a season in fashionable London, from clumsy kisses of her own to glimpses of the brazen couples in the gardens at Vauxhall, had brought her knowledge into full, ripe color.

But none of that had prepared her for the reality of Joshua and for how much she would desire him. She leaned over his chest to kiss him again, her hands roaming over his chest and his shoulders and back to the tantalizing narrowness of his waist, the touch made more vivid with her hands hidden beneath the linen.

"Anabelle," he groaned, her name becoming an animal growl as he arched beneath her. "Ah, Anabelle, you're a wicked, cunning lass."

She moved her lips close to his ear, her breath as warm as her words on his skin. "With you I am, Joshua," she said shyly, rapidly, like a magic chant of her own invention. "With you I am. You make me this way, you know."

His lips trailed lower, lower, to the doubled curve of

her breasts above the drawstring of her shift. "So this is all my doing, eh?"

"Yes," she whispered, her heart racing as he touched her. "Yes, oh, yes. You make me burn with fever and shiver with wanting and oh, la! so many other lovely Joshua-things you do, all at once and all for always. You made me wicked, love, and now you must make me yours."

"Nay, sweet, no orders." His fingers deftly undid the knot on the lacing on the front of her stays, zigzagging the cord through the eyelets. "Mind who's your captain."

"Aye, aye—*oh!*" she whispered, forgetting what came next as his hand pushed apart the halves of her stays to caress her breasts, filling his hand with the soft, full flesh. She gasped as he teased the dark rosebud of her nipple, unconsciously arching herself to move against his hand. He moved, too, accommodating her, and as he did, there came an abrupt thump, and then Joshua swearing, words that were stunningly new even to her.

"That—that infernal cradle of yours," he sputtered between oaths as he rubbed the back of his head. "Jesus, Anabelle, I thought your mother was supposed to be watching over us, not bludgeoning me on the head!"

"Perhaps she *is* watching over me," she said, unable to keep from laughing, though she knew she shouldn't. "Perhaps she doesn't approve of you."

"Well, it's too damned late for that," he grumbled, disentangling himself from Anabelle long enough to stand. "But I've no mind to stay here and let her have another crack at me."

Before Anabelle could answer, he'd swept her up in his arms and over his shoulder with a startled shriek of laughter from her. With steps that slid deeply through the sand, he carried her over the top of the dune and down the side, to their shelter among the windswept oaks. She was laughing still as he tossed her onto their sailcloth bed, sinking deep into the fragrant pine boughs that stuffed it, and laughing, deeply and throatily, too, as she shrugged away her bodice and stays and fumbled with the drawstring on her petticoat.

But as soon as Joshua came to join her, her laughter vanished. To him, she suddenly looked achingly innocent and alarmingly young, kneeling there on their sailcloth sheet with her hair a dark mass around her face and her shift sliding off one shoulder. If she changed her mind, he would stop now, though the effort to do so would likely kill him dead there on the spot. But it would be her choice; if it weren't, she'd likely spend the rest of her life hating him.

"Anabelle," he said, self-consciously keeping his shirt bunched in a ball in his hands before the front of his breeches to hide the obvious proof of how much he wanted her. "Anabelle, if you are doing this only to please me, then—"

"Oh, no, Joshua, do not think that!" she cried, shaking her head in furious denial. "That is, once you said—once you promised—oh, Lord, why can't I talk straight the one time it actually *matters?*"

"I understand, lass," he said, feeling unspeakably noble and entirely frustrated. "You do not have to speak. I can read your expression well enough. We had agreed to wait until we were decently married, in Appledore, and it is, ah, right of you to remind me."

"*That* is what my expression says?" she asked, her eyes wide with astonishment. "Faith, how *vastly* wrong! What I was thinking of was how you once promised you would do things to me that—that would please *me* so that I would be left—oh, how hideously bold that must sound now, after what you just said about being wed first!"

He didn't judge her bold, and certainly not the least bit hideous, especially as he drew her into his arms, warm and soft and marvelously willing.

"I don't recall exactly what I promised," he whispered as he slowly pulled apart the tiny bow on the drawstring of her shift, "but I'm certainly willing to try to remember."

"Perhaps you need a reminder," she said, tangling her fingers into his hair again to draw his face closer. "Perhaps I must do what I always do, which is to kiss you first."

"Aye, a good enough beginning," he murmured. "But I'll wager I can improve upon it."

He smoothed her hair back from her face and kissed her, kissed her *first,* deep, knowing kisses that made her cling to him, her fingers digging deep into his shoulders. He eased her back onto the sailcloth, the boughs beneath rustling, their piney fragrance mingling with her own.

Violets, he thought as he dragged his mouth hotly over the hollow of her throat, her pulse quickening visibly beneath his lips. After all they'd been through, how the devil did she still manage to smell of violets? Violets and her own scent, musky and sweet and altogether intoxicating as he breathed deeply of her skin, losing himself in her and forcing himself to forget how close they'd come to the awful finality of death, of never having this night to share.

She felt him tugging the neck of her shift lower over her breasts and she shrugged her shoulders to help him, his fingers cool where they touched her fevered skin. He rubbed his callused palm back and forth over the sensitive tips, and she shuddered as she pressed the soft weight of her flesh into his hand. His dark head moved lower, and as she threaded her fingers through his hair to hold him there, he drew the rosy crest into his mouth and the unexpected, rare pleasure of it raced through her blood to center low in her belly.

Impatiently, he reached for the hem of her shift, tangled around her legs, and swept it upward, baring her body to him and the night. He thought she blushed, but she didn't turn shy or coy, her arms still linked loosely around his shoulders as she watched him watching her with eyes dark from excitement.

He had imagined her like this, times beyond counting, but his imagination had never conjured the perfection of her skin, flushed now with desire and glistening where he'd tasted her, the soft, round curves of her flesh. Without the rigid whalebone of her stays, her waist was less sharply defined, her breasts less fashionably raised, but he preferred her like this, more womanly, more welcoming.

She smiled crookedly, her lips parted so her small white teeth showed, Anabelle supreme. "I told you, Joshua," she said as she wriggled closer to him, her breathing so rapid it rushed her words. "I cannot help myself with you."

"Then don't." He kissed her again, hot and demanding, running his hands along the length of her back, over her hips, his fingers spreading to cradle the fullest swell of her bottom.

Gently, his touch shifted forward to the dark triangle of hair, and he felt her gasp and press against him as his fingers eased between her thighs. He gentled her with his kiss, soothing her, as he pushed deeper, her legs twisting around his wrist. She was so small, so tight, but her body betrayed her eagerness, and his own blood pounded harder in his ears as he savored the proof of her desire. She broke away from his kiss, turning and pressing her cheek against his shoulder as she cried out, and he slowed his touch, giving her time to accustom herself to the rhythm of her need.

She closed her eyes, so overwhelmed by the intensity of the heat that roiled through her body that she could scarcely think, only feel. She'd lost all reason, that was clear enough, or she'd never be lying here with Joshua touching her with more sinful intimacy than she'd ever thought possible. Yet still she ached for more, more of him and his taste and his scent and the feel of his untamed maleness moving around her and over her and in her, to her soul and her being. Her heart was pounding, her entire self so coiled and tight with this strange madness that she felt as if she were teetering on the edge of a cliff. He began stroking her again, sliding deeper, and she writhed against him, demanding more.

"That is—oh, Joshua, what you *do*," she said, the words drawn out into a shuddering moan. "Please, Joshua, oh, *please!*"

Joshua felt her little hands slide possessively down his belly, following the path of hair toward his breeches. She fumbled with the buttons on the fall, and he sucked in his breath with anticipation of her touch. He covered her hand and pressed it over his hard length, barely contained by the linen.

"Oh, my," she whispered, her breathing ragged. "La, I pray—oh, I pray my mother's not watching over me now."

"She sure as hell had better not be," muttered Joshua as he rolled away from her only long enough to rip the buttons free on his breeches and tear them off. He had waited too long to delay any longer, and he prayed she had, too. He pulled her beneath him, touched her one last time, and then buried himself deep inside her with a groan.

"Anabelle, sweet, I'm sorry," he tried to say, as coherent as he could be in the circumstances. Though she hadn't cried out, he had felt her stiffen with painful surprise as he'd entered her, and with what little of his brain was left, he cursed his selfishness. He had wanted to be gentle, to be sure of her pleasure, too. But damnation, she was so unbelievably slick and tight as she held him that he didn't dare move, let alone try to make explanations. "Anabelle?"

"I am—I am fine," she said, muffled beneath him. She wasn't fine, not exactly. What had been fascinating beneath her fingers had lost much of its appeal when it was forced within her. She felt sore and stretched and she wondered where all the wondrous pleasure he'd given her before had gone.

But she didn't want him to be sorry. She wanted him to love her as much as she did him, and tentatively she raised her mouth to kiss him. That, at least, she knew how to do.

"Anabelle, love," he whispered hoarsely, slanting his mouth across hers. "Let me make it better, lass."

As he kissed her he shifted his weight from her, and she felt the trapped feeling begin to ease. He eased her legs over his hips, and she felt better still, the awkward pain beginning to fade away, and she felt her body relax to accept and welcome him.

Gently he began moving, stroking her again as his fingers had before, and slowly the pleasure began to return, too. From instinct alone, she began to move with him, her back now arching with a purpose as she met him, finding and sharing his rhythm as the irresistible currents rose up to claim her. She curled her legs tight around his waist, crying out as she found herself on the edge of the cliff again, but this time she wasn't alone and he was with her, and as she let go, she felt the waves of joy and delight sweep them both away into blissful oblivion.

"This is not how I'd wished it to be, sweet," said Joshua as he held her later, much later, her head nestled against his beard and her leg thrown wantonly over his. "First, of course, I'd meant to marry you. Then I would have carried you over the front step of our house like a proper bride, and up the staircase to our bedchamber."

"You did that, nearly," she said drowsily, curling herself closer to the warmth of his large body, "except you chose to go over a dune instead of up a staircase."

"But there would have been more, Anabelle," he continued, almost wistfully. He had wanted to give her so much, but with the *Swiftsure* lost, the house would have to be sold, too, and it grieved him deeply to know that this pretty story of his might be all he had. "Much more. I meant to have the bedchamber filled with every flower I could find in Appledore, with the hangings on the bed looped back so you could smell them and crushed lavender scattered inside the pillow biers for you to lie upon while I told you how much I love you."

"You still can do that, you know," she said. "I haven't tired of hearing it, or saying it to you, either. I love you, Joshua Fairbourne. I love you, oh, to a most amazing degree. There. Practice is the path to perfection, they say."

"And I love you, too, Anabelle Crosbie." He kissed her tenderly, prizing her. "Now will you let me finish my tale, eh? We would have eaten supper in the bedchamber so we could have watched the sun set, and I'd have had the food brought from the tavern on a tray with a bottle of sweet wine, so you wouldn't have to fuss over it."

"A good thing, too," she said with a yawn, "since you will soon find I am even less accomplished in the kitchen than I am with a needle."

"Hush, you wicked creature," he scolded, "for I'm not done. Because then I would have given you a gold locket on a chain that I found in London, a heart with our names engraved upon it, for you to wear always."

She smiled, though her eyes were already closed. "So vastly much to want for one wedding night, Joshua," she murmured. "And here all I wished for was you."

Captain Richard McCandless sat at the dining table in the great cabin of His Majesty's frigate *Corinthian,* trying to concentrate on his morning toast and tea instead of the provoking whelp of a lieutenant standing on the black-and-white-checkered floorcloth before him.

"A small party of men to comb these islands, sir, that is all I propose," said Lieutenant the Honorable Edward Palmer, with as much earnestness as he dared. "I would not presume to suggest that the ship—"

"No, Palmer, you will not presume," said McCandless sharply. He was a captain who had worked his way up through the ranks on his own merit and hard work, and he had little use for this foppish lieutenant with the influence in the House of Lords and the beautifully tailored uniform coat and that damn-your-eyes *honorable* thrust in the middle of his name, as if to say all other men were dishonorable by default. "You have presumed entirely too much and too often already on this voyage as it is."

"Yes, sir," said Palmer, unperturbed. "But if the storm destroyed the smuggler's vessel as we believe—"

"As *you* believe, Mr. Palmer," said McCandless, scraping at his toast as he wished to do to the lieutenant's smug, overbred face. "Flotsam on the water doesn't prove a thing. We have squandered far too much time on these so-called smugglers. If they are still afloat, then they have reached their snuggery by now and broken bulk, and there's an end to anything we can do to them. The bastards go free. You know the law, or should. Without the goods, your damned scraps of paper and bills are worthless. Worthless, understand?"

"Yes, sir. But there is still the question of the young lady, sir, and I—"

"Ah, yes, the young lady. Miss Crosbie, isn't it?" McCandless bit savagely into the toast. Personally, he could not fault the young lady's judgment in choosing to run off with a man—any man—other than Palmer's cousin, especially after he'd overheard an unsavory rumor about Palmer's expecting a finder's fee for returning the girl to London.

Yet the cousin's family was wonderfully well connected in the present government, and Miss Crosbie's brother was said to have the ear of the lord admiral himself. To employ his beloved *Corinthian* on such a sorry errand rankled McCandless and stuck in his throat like the dry toast. But influence was influence, and he and his career wouldn't prosper on chasing smugglers from the colonies alone.

"One of the men reported seeing smoke, sir," continued Palmer, "the sort of smoke that might come from a cook fire or signal set by the survivors. We should not like the young lady to suffer, sir, if she were among them."

McCandless glowered at the lieutenant, wishing with all his heart that the navy rewarded officers for decent acts of bravery and initiative instead of for chasing after double-damned blue-blooded trollops.

"Very well, Mr. Palmer," he said with a resigned wave of his hand. "You may have the pinnace and four men. And pray to your maker that you are right, entirely right, about the young lady."

❧ *Fifteen* ❧

"Oh, la, Joshua, you must see the prospect from here!" called Anabelle as she waved to him. She had climbed to the highest of the rocks that made up an outcropping at the tip of the island, a place they'd come to explore only that afternoon. The tide was on its way in, and the way the surf crashed and boomed far below her bare feet made her feel grand and all powerful, like some sort of ancient goddess in a play or poem. She smoothed back her hair and lifted her chin higher, more nobly, and spread her arms as if to command the very waters.

Now *this,* she thought with satisfaction, this was how that silly Mr. Rowan should have painted her, not with some trumpery bow and arrow.

"Mind yourself, Anabelle!" shouted Joshua. "Those rocks can be slippery!"

"Mind yourself *yourself,*" she called back cheerfully. He tried to glower back at her but fell to smiling instead, and she felt her heart swell close to bursting with joy. Lord, what had she ever done to deserve such a man? When he gazed up at her like this, his eyes as blue as the sea behind him, his shirt billowing all around his magnificent chest, and his handsome face so filled with love and concern for her alone, for *her,* and when she remembered all they'd done last night, and that afternoon, too, she couldn't believe such happiness was hers. Not even an ancient goddess could improve on her life this day, and she lifted her skirts to dance a little jig on the flat stone.

"I mean it, Anabelle! This isn't some blessed assembly room!" shouted Joshua again. He was farther down among the rocks, barefoot, too, and closer to the water, cutting out clumps of the dark blue mussels for their supper. "None of your scatterbrained foolishness on those rocks!"

But without shoes, she felt surefooted as a little wild highland sheep, and all she did at his warning was to wrinkle her nose and laugh. She flicked her hair back from her eyes and looked beyond him and out to sea. This was where they should have posted their signal fire and flag; from here, she was sure she could see for miles and miles and miles, particularly on so clear a day. In the distance to the west, she could just make out a faint, low line on the horizon, and she wondered if that could be the mainland of Massachusetts, maybe even Appledore and her new home.

"Joshua!" she shouted excitedly. "Oh, Joshua, you must come here directly!"

The concern she saw on Joshua's face nearly made her laugh again. Lord, what did he think was wrong, anyway? She watched as he thrust his knife back into the sheath on his belt, and with the mussels knotted into a sailcloth bundle over his shoulder, he hurried to join her, bounding over the rocks. He was, she decided with amusement, like an exceptionally large and potent ram, and she laughed again as she tried to picture him with a splendid set of curling horns. She could scarcely wait to tell him that tonight, when she could pretend to be his little ewe and make him laugh, too.

She glanced at the sea again, and in that quarter second that she looked away, she heard a scraping of rocks and Joshua swearing, and when her head whipped back to look for him again, she saw Joshua sitting sprawled on one of the rocks below her, clutching at his ankle.

"Joshua!" she shouted, the ram and the ewe forgotten as she went running and sliding down the rocks to reach him. "Oh, Joshua!"

"I told you not to run, you little fool!" he growled at her as she knelt down beside him.

"Oh, yes, and pray, who has tumbled over like an overburdened hay cart?" she said promptly. As long as his temper was so vigorously intact, she figured he could not be too badly hurt. But already his ankle was beginning to swell in a most evil fashion, the skin scraped raw across the ankle bone where he'd slid against a rock. "Can you waggle your toes?"

He glared blackly at her. "Jesus, Anabelle, I'm in no mood for your games!"

"This is not a game, you great ninny," she said. "I need to know if this is but a sprain or something worse. Now do as I say."

"I'll take no orders from you or anyone else," he grumbled, but still he did as she said, moving his toes without any difficulty.

"At least we've crossed that particular bridge," she said, frowning with concentration. "But I'll wager you cannot put your weight upon this foot, can you?"

"I will not be one of your cosseted cripples from the fo'c'sle, Anabelle," he said, grunting as he tried to stand. "I will not lie meekly by and sip gruel from a papboat while you—damnation, Anabelle, stop hovering about me!"

She stepped back, her arms folded across her chest and her eyes flinty. "Very well, then, Captain Fairbourne," she said tartly. "I should vastly like to see how you fare without me."

She saw, and the answer was exactly as she expected. He could barely balance on one leg while holding on to the rocks behind him.

"How exactly do you propose to leave here, Captain?" she asked drily. "Or will stubbornness and swearing support you well enough?"

"Hell and damnation, Anabelle!" he thundered. "Would you have me beg? Is that what you want?"

She smiled sweetly. "It would be an entertaining amusement, yes," she said, considering. "We could sell tickets, you know, the way they do at Vauxhall for their silly tin waterfall."

"Anabelle," he said, his expression as black as his beard. "Anabelle, so help me—"

"Well, that is what I wished from the start, wasn't it?" she asked. "To help you? Now come, you sit here. Give me your knife, if you please."

Awkwardly, he sat on the rock she'd pointed to and looked at her suspiciously. "Why the devil do you need my knife, eh?"

"To cut off your leg, of course." She looked heavenward and sighed. "Faith, Joshua, what do you think I'm going to do with your precious knife? I must bind your ankle tight to keep it from swelling from here to China. Regular linen bandages don't seem to be in much supply here, so I must fashion them from my petticoat instead. Your knife would be a great convenience in cutting this kerseymere, but I shall contrive to manage without it if I must."

"Take the damned knife," he muttered, handing it to her. "And be quick about this, too. I don't like us sitting out here on these rocks like a pair of pigeons waiting for the hunters."

"You should have thought of that before you began hopping about," she said as she began to cut and tear the hem of her petticoat into long strips. "Besides, I rather thought we wished to be seen, so that we might be rescued whilst I still have a shred of clothing to my name and over my body, too. Now let me have your foot. Oh, stop twitching, I won't hurt you, not if I can help it."

She began to wrap his ankle in the plum-colored wool and he gritted his teeth, determined not to flinch no matter how much it hurt. And hurt it did, hurt like hell and damnation and more devils than even he could name. No wonder surgeons were always male. At least then a man could swear and thrash about all he pleased in dignified peace without worrying about shaming himself before some woman.

"Oh, I'll grant you that it's been most pleasant here on this island with you," she continued, "including last night. Particularly last night."

She tied the bandage tightly, tucked the ends into the top, and then quite wickedly slid her hand up the inside of his leg, letting it rest on the twitching muscles of his thigh long enough to make other things twitch as well before she rose and brushed her hands briskly together as if she'd performed nothing more than a charitable act.

"*Most* particularly last night," she said again, altogether evenly, though the smugness of her sudden grin betrayed her, "and even more particularly this morning, and if I continue to be fortunate, the particulars will only increase with each night and morning, and other times, too, if possible."

"Of course it is possible," he said, trying to look stern, while the pain in his ankle was being rapidly displaced by a more agreeable ache. Perhaps there were certain advantages to a female surgeon after all, especially one that he loved as much as he loved Anabelle. "Even likely, if you wish it. But not now, not here."

"Oh, my, no, neither here nor now, not in your weakened state." She slung the bundle of mussels over one shoulder as she let her gaze roam frankly over him. "Still and all, it is a good thing that I am going to wed you, Joshua Fairbourne, and end the havoc you must have wrought among the maidens of this colony. I expect an especial wedding gift of my own from the grateful fathers. Now come, lean on me, and together we'll contrive to move you as best we can."

He swallowed his pride and let her slip her shoulder beneath his arm. The sensation of having her tucked beneath him was a pleasant one; the pain that shot through his leg each time he tried to put any weight on his ankle was not. Their progress down the rocks and across the island was slow, his dependence on her at once humbling and humiliating.

"I cannot fathom it," he complained irritably, wiping the sweat of exertion from his brow as he hobbled along beside her. "I've always considered myself a strong man, in my prime, and yet since meeting you, Anabelle, I have become a quaking, staggering wreck."

"I've been accused of having that enervating effect on men before, yes," she admitted, "though Heaven knows that has never been my goal. Consider what would have befallen you had you not been such a splendidly virile scoundrel before we met. At least this sprain of yours is not fatal, and with any luck, you shall be completely restored after only a few days' rest and idleness."

He glared at her. "You know damned well I cannot lie about like some Oriental pasha, Anabelle," he said impatiently. "Someone has to keep you from mischief."

"Oh, yes, and who will keep *you* safe?" she retorted. "Faith, when I consider—oh, Joshua, look! *Look!*"

"Not again, Anabelle." He winced at her excited jostling and twisted about to follow her gaze, indulgently prepared to see one more herring gull or snail shell or whatever it had been that had made her exclaim—and him go sprawling—before.

But his indulgence disappeared in an instant. There, in the distance, rode a small sailboat, a pinnace or a smack, and from the set of her single sail, Joshua was sure her course was set for this island.

Their island, and for them.

"Oh, Joshua, we'll be rescued!" cried Anabelle happily. "We could be home—*home!*—in next to no time now! How long do you think it will take that boat to come to us, Joshua?"

"Not long at all," said Joshua, without a shred of her happiness or excitement as he pushed her along across the sand. "Hurry, Anabelle—over the dune so they can't spy us."

"But what if they miss us?" she said anxiously. "Shouldn't we try to signal them now, to get their attention? Oh, what if they miss us? What if they pass us by?"

"There's no way in Heaven they'll do that, not with this breeze," he said. The men in the boat could be cod fishermen or coasters or even seamen from another deepwater ship like the *Swiftsure*. But the suspicion that lay heavy as a bar of lead in the pit of his stomach told him otherwise, suspicion so strong it felt like dead certainty. "Damnation, what I'd give for a decent spyglass now!"

"I don't understand you, Joshua," she said plaintively. "The people in that boat must have seen our flag, and they are coming to rescue us. Why does it matter who they are?"

"Because it does, damn it," he said, unwilling to worry her. He'd trusted his instincts all his life, but he wasn't sure how to explain them, not even to Anabelle. "It just *does*."

She stopped so abruptly that he nearly toppled over. "Then you *just* tell me what's making you act this way," she said, her round face uncharacteristically earnest. "I may not be as brave as you are, Joshua, but I'm not a ninny, either. It's only fair for me to know if we're in some sort of danger."

"Anabelle, sweet, I don't—"

"Tell me, Joshua," she said urgently. "If you love me, really love me, you will. And if you don't, I shall let you fall quite on your face into this dune."

He sighed, a deep sigh of resignation, and uneasily thought again of the coming boat. There'd been a time when he wouldn't have dreamed of confiding in any woman, but Anabelle was different. What was more, she was right. She did need to know, since she'd be in the thick of whatever happened. She was right about that, even if she was wrong about the rest. For she *was* every bit as brave as he was, and on some days, probably braver.

Besides, he'd no wish to fall face first into the sand the way she'd promised.

"Well enough," he said slowly, "I will. But keep walking, mind? I'll wager a guinea that that boat belongs to the frigate, and in it will be Branbrook's cousin, come to fetch you back to London."

"Mr. Branbrook's cousin? In that boat?" She

clicked her tongue in dismissal. "La, however could you tell at such a distance?"

" 'Tis a feeling I have, no more."

Anabelle considered this. "Even if it were so," she said, musing, "the Branbrooks wouldn't want me in the family now. I'm too thoroughly ruined by now for them. We've seen to that quite nicely, haven't we?"

She grinned. Joshua didn't. She might not realize how much was at stake, but for him, even that irrepressible, inappropriate grin of hers was a stabbing reminder of how much he stood to lose.

"The size of your dowry hasn't changed," he said grimly, "and besides, even a dim-witted noddy like Branbrook isn't going to want to give up a first-rate woman like you without a fight. You shouldn't underestimate yourself, Anabelle."

Her grin widened and her cheeks grew pink. "Why, Joshua, how very sweet of you! 'First-rate' is very sweet indeed; but you in turn must take care not to overestimate Henry. I'd be vastly surprised if he'd taken things as far as you seem to think, speaking to Mr. Palmer in the first place."

"Well, he must have," said Joshua, "and the devil take him for it. Now hurry, I want to reach those oak trees so we can spy on them properly."

But by the time they did, crouching so they'd be hidden in the tall grass and low brush by the shadows of the overhanging branches, the wind had veered around, and the little boat was being forced to tack widely, back and forth, to keep on its course.

"That's a sorry hand on the tiller if ever I saw one," said Joshua scornfully. "Only one sail and four men to do his bidding, yet the worthless lubber can't even mind that. Jesus, I could do better than that myself alone."

"Do you think they'll go away now?" asked Anabelle hopefully, her voice an unnecessary whisper as she leaned closer to him. "It looks as though they will, doesn't it?"

"Never trust the wind or the navy, lass," he said firmly, "for they'll both play you false."

Anabelle frowned. "How can you be so vastly sure it *is* the navy?"

"Why, because there's an officer," explained Joshua, fair bristling with contempt. "Look there, the dull, pasteboard figure with the braid on his coat, the fellow who considers himself too fine a gentleman to lift a finger to help his own vessel. *He* makes it a navy ship, no mistake."

"I see," said Anabelle, wishing she didn't as her heart sank. She hoped the pasteboard officer wouldn't turn out to be Mr. Palmer and make all this even more complicated and unpleasant. She hadn't dreamed that Henry Branbrook would be so—so *petty* as to send someone clear across the ocean to track her down like this, as if she were some sort of wretched fox he was bent on hunting. That was exactly how she felt now, a poor bedraggled vixen hiding in the brambles at the end of the day.

She sighed unhappily and edged closer to Joshua. "What shall we do when they arrive?"

"Don't know," said Joshua, an admission that he hated to make. He liked plans, he liked being prepared, he liked being in control, and right now, lying on his belly in the brush, he was none of these. "I'd as soon keep out of their way altogether if we can. That would be best. Not the bravest, I'll grant you that, but the best. For now we'll have to wait them out and watch and decide then."

"Then I'll go fetch us water and something to eat. At least I can do that much for us." She liked the idea of hiding. Hiding meant that no one would be hurt, that Joshua would manage to keep himself from blustering and swinging his fists and generally behaving like a man, and she liked that even more. Her spirits rising, she gave him a swift kiss on his unshaven cheek. "I won't be gone but a handful of minutes. You stay here and think upon how vastly much I love you."

"Damnation, Anabelle, wait!" he growled, but she had already wriggled through the brush and into the trees, back toward the pond. He knew he couldn't follow her, not the way his ankle was throbbing in furious protest now, and with an unhappy oath, he pulled himself upright. He hated being dependent on anyone, especially on Anabelle, and especially now. She should be looking to him for support, he thought with angry despair, not the other way around.

If he could fashion some sort of walking stick or crutch, then maybe he could manage better for himself, and with one last look at the boat, he hopped and stumbled and swore his way to the pile of wood they'd gathered for the fire. The first branch he tried snapped beneath his weight, but the next one held him steady and would do, even to the convenient fork that would slip beneath his arm. All he'd need to do was trim the ends a bit, and automatically, he reached for his knife.

The sheath was empty.

At once, Joshua remembered seeing the knife lying on the rocks beside Anabelle as she'd bound his ankle, the polished blade glittering in the sun. Then she'd smiled and teased him, and hellfire and damnation, they'd left it behind without another thought. Their only tool, and worse, their only weapon, was gone.

"Anabelle!" he roared. "Anabelle, get yourself back here *now!"*

He heard her coming through the brush, the swish

of the leaves and branches against her skirts and the rustle of her footsteps over dry leaves and her singing, *singing* for all love.

"There you are," she said when she reached him. In her arms were some of their carefully hoarded stock of biscuits, more blueberries, and an old bottle they used to carry water. "You cannot conceive of the amusing little animals I just came across, Joshua, snuffling about in the blueberry bushes. A mother and several half-grown babies, the size of a fat tabby and her kittens, ebony black except for two white stripes down their backs to the most perfect plumes of tails, and—"

"Skunks?" asked Joshua incredulously. Dear God, hadn't they trouble enough without having skunks tossed into the mix? "You found *skunks* amusing?"

"Yes, if that is what they are called, and why ever not?" she asked. "La, what a disagreeable name for so cunning a creature! I fed them some of the berries and they seemed vastly grateful."

"You should be the one who's grateful, to come away unharmed," said Joshua. "Skunks have a mightily disagreeable habit to go along with their disagreeable name. If you provoke them—even if you don't—they'll turn tail and spray you like a tomcat with the foulest-smelling stench you've ever smelled. Blinds you, too, if you get close enough."

"How dreadful." Anabelle's eyes widened. "They hardly seem capable of such ill-tempered behavior. But only if they are provoked, you say?"

"Aye, only if provoked," rumbled Joshua, pulling the knife's empty sheath around to show her. "Just as I am provoked now. Anabelle, do you recall what became of my knife?"

"Oh, my," she said softly, staring with obvious remorse at the sheath as she set the food and water bottle on the ground. "Oh, my, oh, no. It was—no, it must still be—on the rocks where we were earlier. Oh, Joshua, I am so vastly sorry!"

"Sorry isn't going to bring it back, Anabelle," he said angrily. "Here we are with that blasted boat full of men breathing down our necks and nary a weapon—"

"Then I shall go fetch it directly," she said with immediate resolution, gathering up what remained of her petticoat in one hand as she prepared to go. " 'Tis all my fault that the knife was lost, and now it is up to me to bring it back."

"The hell you will, Anabelle!" rumbled Joshua heatedly. "Do you truly believe I'd let you go off on your own like that, you little ninny?"

She lifted her chin higher, tossing her hair back over her shoulders with an air of wounded defiance that didn't please him at all.

"Of course I believe it," she said tartly. "Otherwise, Captain Fairbourne, you wouldn't have mentioned the knife at all. But I shall do as you wish and set everything to rights."

"To wrongs is closer to the mark," he scoffed. "Why the hell would I wish you to do anything more?"

"Oh, yes, why indeed?" she asked, the heat of her words a scorching match for his own. "I'll go now, *Captain* Fairbourne, before you can swear at me again, and return with your infernal knife in more than sufficient time for you to cut out the rest of my heart!"

This time she didn't pause to kiss him, and as she spun away on her heel, he was too awkward and slow to grab her arm to stop her.

"Anabelle, come back here!" he shouted, crashing clumsily after her as best he could with his improvised crutch. With all the walking he'd already done, his ankle hurt more now than when he'd first sprained it, making each ungainly step and lurch forward the purest agony. "Damnation, Anabelle, you can't go alone!"

But she wouldn't turn around. She would not give him that satisfaction, and if anything, she increased the pace of her steps, her bare feet sinking and sliding in the sand as she climbed up the dune. She had admitted she'd made a mistake, a most disastrous mistake, true, but one that anyone could have made in the same circumstances, and now she would fix it. What more could he wish from her?

And no one, not even her grandmother, had ever called her a ninny. A *little* ninny.

No, she certainly wasn't going to look back at him now and let him think that all his swearing and roaring had changed her mind, any more than she was going to let him see the hot, angry, wounded tears that were already spilling over and sliding down her cheeks.

She reached the crest of the dune and began hopping down it, her head lowered to watch her steps and keep from stumbling. A twisted ankle for her, too, was the last thing they needed, and impatiently she shoved her hair back from where it clung to her wet cheeks. If she were a little ninny, then he was a great, huge, hulky—

"Ahoy, Miss Crosbie, good day!" called a man's voice before her. "Miss Crosbie, there, good day to you!"

She stopped dead where she stood, unable to move or speak from shock and panic. The boat that had seemed so far out to sea was now not twenty feet away, with two men taking down her single sail while the others had already climbed over the side and were splashing their way through the low waves to her.

To *her*. Oh, Lord help her, whatever was she going to *do?*

The first man ashore was the pasteboard officer, the braid on his coat alarmingly bright at this close range, every brass button polished to blinding perfection. She could see his resemblance to Henry Branbrook in that, for Henry liked perfection in his dress, too. The softness beneath the chin was Branbrookian as well, as was the exaggeratedly upright way he held his head to compensate. But as he walked slowly toward her with his hat tucked beneath his arm, smiling with an aggressive, almost belligerent, intensity, she could tell this man had none of Henry's foolishness, none of his weakness, and that she'd be a fool herself to think otherwise.

"Lieutenant the Honorable Edward Palmer at your service, ma'am," he said as he bowed, clearly striving for the proper balance between charming London manners and a curt military air, a balance that teetered away from charm when Anabelle failed to answer. "I say, you are Miss Crosbie, aren't you?"

"Yes," she said slowly. "Yes, sir, I am."

And she *was*. She had to remember that, for that and her wit were the only weapons she had to use against his sword and pistol and the four other seamen now falling in behind him. She was the daughter of a viscount, the granddaughter of a marquis, a lady born of two of the greatest noble families in Britain, but most of all she was soon to be the wife of Captain Joshua Fairbourne.

Was Joshua watching her now? Had he forgotten the hateful words they'd spat at one another, and was he there in the shadows behind her, watching her and watching over her, ready to defend her if she faltered, if she showed any fear? Was he waiting for the right moment to offer his life for hers? For that is what it would be if he came to fight for her now: five against one, five armed with pistols and cutlasses against one with nothing, five who'd sooner that one were dead. And oh, dear Lord, she knew Joshua so well, loved him so well, and knew, too, which would be his choice.

But she could stop it. If she did everything right, she could save them both.

She drew herself up tall and straight, the special way she'd learned from Grandmother, and composed her face with the expression that would let her look down her nose at men twice her size. Even in the tattered remains of her clothes, even with her bare legs uncovered clear to the knees and her bodice held together over her stays by two sorry, straining buttons, even with the fear and panic gripping tight around her stomach, still, she could muster the power to stare down this pack of insolent, low-bred sailors. She could, she told herself fiercely, and she would.

And, somehow, she did.

"Pray, lieutenant, what has made you tarry so?" she demanded imperiously. She did not smile nor offer him her hand, though he clearly expected her to. The Auboncourts and the Crosbies were far older families and far better connected than the Palmers, and it was well that he be made to realize that. "I have been waiting and waiting, la, ever so long for even the hint of a savior to show himself."

She saw how quickly he backed away, not only from the slight step that he took in the sand but the wariness in his eyes that registered the emotional distance that she'd gained. That was good, she thought with satisfaction. She'd need that, for she hadn't the slightest notion of what to do next.

"You are alone then, ma'am?" he asked with surprise, looking past her to the tall grass and wind-stunted trees. "There were no other survivors?"

"I do not know, sir, nor do I care," she declared with icy finality. "When the storm took hold, the base rogues quite abandoned me. I was washed to this place alone by the winds and the sea and survived only through the mercy of Heaven."

"There was no boat, ma'am?" asked Palmer incredulously. "A gentle lady like yourself, cast on her own into the sea?"

"It was that, or perish," she said with a mournful relish. "Certainly there was no fine vessel such as you yourself have."

With a faint show of interest, Anabelle glanced around him to see the boat. The men hadn't bothered to haul it out onto the sand, not intending to linger on the island, but instead had used some sort of light anchor to keep the boat moored in the shallow water. Joshua had said that he could sail such a boat himself, and better, too. Had he meant it, she wondered desperately, or had it been no more than idle boasting? If they were somehow able to steal this boat away, could the two of them actually sail it together to the mainland?

Palmer stood shaking his head. "I still cannot imagine it, ma'am," he said, "how you survived a storm like that!"

"It was the cradle, Lieutenant," she said with a sudden inspiration. "Come and I shall show you."

She led them across the dune to where Joshua had set their signal fire and flag, and pointed grandly to the cradle sitting at the base. "This was my mother's cradle, and my grandmother's before that, and only by the greatest miracle did I survive by hanging to its side through the waves."

"To be sure, a great miracle," agreed Palmer respectfully, and behind him, one of the sailors crossed himself with genuine awe.

"Thus, you will understand, sir, that I must take the cradle with me," she continued, resting her hand possessively on the cradle's bonnet. "It is the only one of my belongings to survive, and I could not return to London without it."

Palmer coughed with feigned delicacy into his hand. "May I conclude then, Miss Crosbie, then you are, ah, unattached?"

She could not mistake the predatory gleam in his eye. "I wish to return to London under your captain's protection, yes," she said, though nothing could be more distant from the truth. "Might your men be persuaded to place the cradle into your boat for me?"

"Of course, miss. The work of a moment." He beckoned, and two of the sailors came hurrying forward to lift the cradle and carry it back to the boat. Palmer smiled, and for the first time, she smiled in return. She could afford to grant him that much, for he'd just unwittingly done her an enormous favor, sparing Joshua the nigh-impossible task of hoisting and lashing the cradle into the boat himself. One step closer to freedom, she told herself firmly, and tried not to consider that, if things did not go as she hoped, it could also be one step closer to London instead.

"The work of a moment," repeated Palmer idly, and his inquiring gaze wandered back to the cold signal fire. "But it seems to me another sort of miracle that you have made yourself so much at your ease here on this island. This flag, this fire—few ladies, ma'am, would have done so much on their own."

"La, sir, but I am not like other ladies." She smiled winningly even as she quaked within. He was a clever man, this Palmer, and she must not drop her guard before him, even for a second. "But surely Mr. Branbrook has told you as much about me?"

Palmer bowed stiffly, nonplussed by the reference to his cousin. "Henry Branbrook has told me many things, ma'am, not all of which I believe, having now had the honor and inestimable pleasure of meeting you for myself," he said, inching toward her. "But I can assure you, Miss Crosbie, that if you ever are in need of a champion, on our voyage or in London, at any time, you may depend upon me to the fullest."

It took all of Anabelle's will not to recoil with disgust. She'd seen that same expression on scores of men in Dublin and London and heard the same meaningless pledges, and the Honorable Edward Palmer was no different from any of the others. He wanted her fortune, or the fortune he believed her still to possess, and he'd cut out his own cousin to get it.

Only Joshua had never cared for the money she'd bring. Only Joshua loved her for herself alone, and what will it took, too, not to turn and run and find him and tell him again and again and again how much she loved him!

"How vastly kind of you, lieutenant," she murmured instead. "Too kind indeed. But surely our voyage shall not begin this night? The shadows are long, and 'tis nearly nightfall. Am I destined to remain one more night upon my little island?"

"One more night, Miss Crosbie, that is all, and then we shall rendezvous with my ship in the morning," he said, his smile creeping so suggestively close to an out-and-out leer that Anabelle longed to box his rascally ears. "But you need fear nothing, not with the full protection of my men."

"Then you all shall be my guests this night," she said with an eager welcome she certainly didn't feel.

The thought of these men in the special place that she and Joshua had made and shared beneath the oaks revolted her. Yet if she could somehow keep them there, out of the sight of the water and the boat, then perhaps she and Joshua might have a chance of escape.

And as Joshua slipped back into the woods ahead of them, his thoughts were almost exactly the same. To steal the boat must be their goal, and though Anabelle had done so much to set things in place, he still was at a loss for what to do next.

This was hardly the first time he'd had to deal with unlikely odds; even before he'd turned to smuggling, he'd survived his share of uncomfortable situations while fighting the French in the last war, and he'd always been able to thank his luck and his stars for seeing him through. But then he hadn't been lame and he'd always had a pistol or two to trust as well as his luck, and more importantly, he'd never had a woman to watch over as well as his own skin. Nay, not only a woman; he'd never had Anabelle, and that difference meant all the world.

He watched her later, when the deeper shadows of the night let him creep close, and saw her sitting primly beside the fire while that ass of a lieutenant fawned over her. She'd tried to tuck her legs beneath her petticoats, but with so much torn away—torn away to make bandages for *him*, blast her endless kindness!—there was still a good measure of pale skin on display in the firelight. He himself had grown very fond of Anabelle's legs, her trim little ankles and her plump, full calves, but after last night, he'd grown possessive of them as well, and he didn't want any other man enjoying the view. Now that he thought of it, he felt possessive of Anabelle in her entirety, from the parting in her hair to the tips of her tiny pink toes, a deep and unquestioning feeling doubtless brought about by loving her as much as he did.

And he did love her. There wasn't any help for it, and he didn't want any, either. He simply could not imagine his life now without her in it, any more than he could picture his bedchamber without that oak monstrosity on rockers of hers, complete with a handsome (or beautiful, depending on whether it was a son or daughter), squalling little sprat tucked within. Or perhaps two. Or three. Or Lord only knew how many; he and Anabelle would be doing their best in the oversized bed on the other side of the fireplace. Anabelle was part of his life now, because, somehow, she'd become part of him.

So why the devil had he let her run off like he had this afternoon? Why in his frustration had he said the things he'd known would drive her away? He looked at her now, surrounded by his enemies, and he knew he'd never forgive himself. He'd never do it again, that was certain. His only redemption might— *might*—come when he figured out a way to save her. He knew she was counting on him to do exactly that, knew from how often she glanced furtively about the trees, looking for him. And Lord help him, he would not fail her.

Yet as Joshua watched the five men finish their supper and waited as they bedded down for the night, their weapons in an accessible ring around the fire and one man at their head to act as guard, he still had no plan, and his despair grew by the moment. He watched and fought back an oath as the lieutenant lifted Anabelle's fingers to his lips in a good-night salute before she retreated to the bed made from pine boughs. At least she was somewhat removed from the others, though still not so far from the guard that she could slip away unnoticed. No, thought Joshua despondently, he was going to need something more than that.

And then, as he ate the last of the blueberries one by one from his pocket, that something appeared beside him. She was small, about the size of a cat, and all black except for the two white stripes down her back, and Joshua could scarcely believe he'd ever rejoice so much over a skunk. Or more precisely, five skunks, the mother and her offspring—Anabelle's skunks—and Joshua's conscience nipped at him when he remembered how short-tempered he'd been when she'd tried to tell him about the "cunning little animals."

Cunning, aye. They'd be cunning enough in the nest of sleeping sailors. The mother skunk came closer to Joshua, sniffing eagerly at the blueberries in his hand, and he could have laughed aloud from pure joy.

Instead he tossed the first handful of blueberries down into the circle of sleeping men. The berries landed with the lightest of thumps, unnoticed by the drowsing guard but loud as a clarion bell to the skunks. With an eager squeak, the mother waddled toward the camp with the food in the middle, and her children hurried after her. None of them wished to miss the berry treat, and like an indulgent parent, Joshua tossed another handful into their midst. He wanted them happy now, so they'd be thoroughly irritated to have their party cut short. He picked up a rock from beside him and with a smile of anticipation lobbed it into the camp directly before the sleepy sentry's foot.

"What—who goes there?" he sputtered loudly, jerking upright and fumbling for the pistol that had slid from his lap to the sand. The mother skunk squeaked and stamped her front feet with frantic alarm in return, a high-pitched cry that was echoed by her children. Almost in unison, their tails rose and their bodies arched, and suddenly every man in the camp was instantly, horribly awake, as the air was overwhelmed with the stinging, foul-smelling mist from five frightened skunks.

"Oh, most charming, perfect animals!" cried Anabelle with delight as she watched the skunks lumber away with great skunkish dignity. The sailors were not so fortunate, screaming and swearing and gagging and rubbing their hands furiously over their eyes as they ran and staggered blindly from the camp through the woods toward the pond and relief. Though there was no way to avoid the stench, Anabelle herself had been clear of the direct spray, and she now found herself wonderfully, unexpectedly alone. Swiftly, she rolled from the mattress to her feet, ran from the copse, and began to scramble up the side of the dune.

"Joshua?" she shouted wildly, her heart pounding and her only thought to find him and then the boat. He had to be here; he *had* to. *"Joshua!"*

She heard footsteps behind her, a man's breathing, and she turned eagerly. "Oh, Joshua, I—"

But it wasn't Joshua. It was Palmer, and before she could run again, he had grabbed her arm and jerked her close against his body, her back against his chest and the polished brass buttons of his coat and the cold, sharp blade of a knife pressed flat against her throat.

"No other survivors, were there, Miss Crosbie?" he said with a fury cold enough to match the steel blade. "All alone on your little island, you say? Then who the hell is Joshua, you lying little bitch?"

She gurgled with fear, the knife too tightly against her skin for her to speak.

"Call him again," he ordered. "Call him to you."

She would not do that to Joshua. She would rather die herself than betray him. Within the tiny circle of motion she could make, she shook her head and, trembling, remained silent.

But oh, she did not want to die! She wanted to live to see Appledore and marry Joshua and have his babies and love him—oh, how much she wanted to live to love him!

"Damned obstinate slut," said Palmer, practically spitting the words as he jerked her back harder against his body. "Do it, I say! Call him and—*unh!*"

He staggered forward, struck hard by something from behind, and as soon as Anabelle felt the knife slide away from her throat, she broke free, stumbling away. She felt Palmer's hand snatching at her skirt, and as she gasped and twisted around to pitch forward and avoid him, she saw Joshua looming behind him, the branch he'd used as a crutch held high in his hand.

"The knife, Joshua!" she cried desperately, her voice strained from where the knife had pressed into her throat. "He has a knife!"

But Palmer had already swung around to face Joshua, and in the split second that they faced one another, the lieutenant saw the bandage around Joshua's ankle. Without hesitation, Palmer kicked Joshua's ankle as hard as he could. Joshua roared with agony, doubling over and loosening his grasp on the branch. Instantly, Palmer lunged forward, hurling himself against Joshua. Yet somehow Joshua mastered the pain in his ankle enough to make his hand seize Palmer's wrist with the knife, and they wobbled against each other, a tense, unsteady dance on the sand as they fought, before they finally toppled backward. Over and over, they rolled down the slope of the dune, each man twisting and struggling and kicking sand as they struggled for the knife.

On her knees, Anabelle watched, the sick horror of what could happen—what *was* happening—growing every second. Not Joshua, she prayed, not Joshua, not here, not now on this beach while she watched, while she *watched*. But she wouldn't let it end like this, not without her help, and scrambled across the sand for the branch that he'd let drop. Holding it clumsily in both hands, she rushed toward the two men, the branch poised over her shoulder. They were still twisting and rolling and she was terrified she'd strike Joshua by accident. But she couldn't wait, she couldn't let it go any longer, and with a broken sob, she swung the branch down as hard as she could across the back of Lieutenant the Honorable Edward Palmer's head, and saw him jerk once and lay still.

"Oh, Joshua!" she cried as she helped him to his feet. As soon as he was upright, she threw herself about him with such loving force that he nearly fell backward again. "Joshua, love, what if you'd been— what if you'd been—"

"Well, I wasn't," he said, still gasping to catch his breath as he slipped the other man's knife into his own sheath. "But this must wait, Anabelle. Come now, give me your shoulder. Hurry, we have to reach the boat!"

They staggered across the beach, weariness and urgency combining to make them clumsy as they waded into the water. The tide was coming in, the water nearly to Anabelle's shoulders, and she fought back a little sob of fear as she remembered how closely she'd come to drowning before.

"Here now, lass, up you go," ordered Joshua as he

pushed her up into the boat. "Settle yourself there in the stern, beside the tiller, and hold it steady for me."

He reached deeply into the water to dislodge the mooring anchor and pulled himself over the side. As swiftly as he could, he set the single sail, knowing the preciousness of each second. Every inch of his body ached and twitched with exhaustion, yet all he felt was triumph as the wind caught and filled the sail and the boat leaped to life beneath him.

"Oh, Joshua, we're moving!" cried Anabelle. She was holding onto the tiller with both hands, her hair blowing back from her face and her dear little face bright with delight in the moonlight. "We're moving, and we're free! Oh, Joshua, how much I love you! How vastly, vastly, *vastly* much I love you!"

"And I love you, Anabelle," he called back, his smile so broad it almost hurt. "And right *vastly* at that. Now steer for home, love. Steer for Appledore."

❧ Epilogue ❧

Because the winds favored them, they made the sheltered harbor at Appledore by noon the next day.

"That white spire, there, that belongs to the meeting house, the finest one in Barnstable County," said Joshua proudly, pointing out over the water, and for once, he didn't scold Anabelle when she stood upright in the bow to see better, even though she'd been warned again and again never to do so in an open boat.

"And that is the blacksmith's," he continued, "new last summer, and those shops, too, along the wharf are new as well. But Rodger's windmill, the one with the gray shingles, is as old as blazes—older than I am, anyway. Now look, there, higher on the hillside beyond that little sliver of a pond—that's Merriminac Pond, sweet, you'll learn the names soon enough— the fine house with the gambrel roof and the twin chimneys and the apple trees on either side of the door is mine. Is *ours.*"

"And there, of course," said Anabelle promptly, "is the *Swiftsure.*"

And there, of course, the brig was indeed, sitting contentedly at her home mooring, at least as contented as a ship can be that was as battered as the *Swiftsure.* But she'd suffered nothing that could not be mended, and already workmen from the shipyard were toiling to put her to rights. Or they had been, anyway, until the first man spotted the pinnace with Captain Fairbourne and the captain's bride and the largest, grandest cradle anyone had ever seen. The man shouted to his mates and the mates called to their friends, and now the *Swiftsure's* rail was lined with people, and others were running to the wharf, too, men and women and boys and girls, shouting and laughing and cheering and tossing their hats in the air.

"What a vastly splendid welcome," declared Anabelle, sitting on the cradle and waving with a genteel graciousness that greatly became her tattered clothing. "One would believe, Joshua, that you are quite the first gentleman of Appledore."

But instead of agreeing, Joshua only shook his head. "This isn't how I wished things to be, love," he said with a wistful sigh. "I'd thought our homecoming would be on board the *Swiftsure,* and that you'd be standing beside me on the quarterdeck rigged out in one of your best London gowns, all silk, you know, and that we'd—"

"Oh, hush, Joshua, just hush," said Anabelle, leaving the cradle to come sit on his lap. "Whenever will you learn, you great dunderhead, that all I ever wanted was you?"

And when she slipped her arms around his neck and kissed him, there for all Appledore to see, he knew, with Anabelle, he'd never again wish for anything more.

**POCKET STAR BOOKS
PROUDLY PRESENTS**

Cranberry Point
Miranda Jarrett

**Coming Soon
in Paperback
from Pocket Star Books**

**The following is a preview of
Cranberry Point. . . .**

Off Cape Cod
1720

Everything had vanished.

The pale strip of beach, the rocks above it, the ragged wind-bent pines on the far side of the dunes, even the wheeling, diving gulls that had followed her this morning— all of it was gone, swallowed up in the wet, gray nothingness. Who would have dreamed a winter fog would come in this fast?

Serena Fairbourne held the tiller of the little single-masted sailboat as steady as she could, her fingers numb with the cold despite her heavy mittens. She knew she shouldn't have waited so long to leave Denniman's Cove for home, no matter how good her reasons had been for lingering, just as she knew she was something dreadfully close to a fool to be out there now, alone on the bay. At least she hoped the dark green water that lapped at the boat's sides belonged to the bay, and not to the ocean that lay beyond. Please God she hadn't strayed that far with the ebbing tide, or she'd never find home again.

She shoved the hood of her cloak back from her face, straining to hear any sounds that might guide her toward the shore: the bell from the meetinghouse on the hill, a fisherman's call, even a dog barking for its supper.

But there was nothing.

Nothing.

She swiped a mitten across her forehead to brush her damp hair back from her forehead, the fog wet and chill upon her skin. The worst thing she could do in a boat was to panic. That was what her oldest brother, Joshua, always said, anyway, and he'd been sailing as long as she could remember. She took a deep breath to calm herself, determined not to be afraid. Fairbournes weren't afraid of anything. Her brother said that, too.

But still her breath hung in nervous little puffs before her face, and her heart thumped painfully within her breast. Now all she could remember were Joshua's horrifying tales of those lost at sea, swept overboard into the icy waters, struggling vainly in the waves until—

"Ahoy, there, y'infernal bastard!" roared the man's furious voice from the fog. "Shove off now, less'n you mean to haul us all down to the devil wit' you!"

Instantly the steep, black side of a deep-water sloop loomed out of the fog before her, the black-painted side rising high as a wall as its path angled across hers. With a gasp Serena threw all her weight against her boat's tiller, desperately trying to sheer from the path of the much larger boat.

"Shove off yourself!" she shouted back, her fear swallowed up by anger as her boat bobbed precariously in the other's wash. "And may the devil take you as one of his own!"

"By all the saints, it's a woman!" A second man appeared behind the first at the rail. He was a tall man, all in black, his face hidden by the wisping fog and the shadow of his hat's brim. "Haul aback, I say! Haul aback directly!"

"Haul aback yourself!" retorted Serena. She'd barely managed to turn in time, and now the two boats were sailing side by side on the same course, the space between them not more than a dozen paces. "Where are your lights, sir? Your bell? What kind of foolish ninnies go about silent as the grave in a fog such as this?"

The first man, the bearded one, swore impatiently. "And

what manner o' sorry female would go out in a boat on her lonesome in such a fog? Answer me that, ya yowling, dim-witted strump—"

"Enough, Davis," said the tall man, his voice deep and easy with the certainty of being obeyed. "The lady needs our assistance, not our insults."

"Thank you," said Serena stiffly. Too late she realized that the captain's order to haul aback—for surely the tall man must be the master—had been directed at his own crew and not at her, for the sloop had slowed to keep pace with her little boat, the distance between them narrowing further. Why, why had she let her temper get the better of her again? Shrieking insults across the water like a fishwife was not something to be proud of, and the tall man in black was being generous—*very* generous—to refer to her as a lady. And the dear Lord help her if Joshua ever learned of this!

Self-consciously she tried to smooth her hair, aware of how bedraggled she must look in her salt-stained cloak and muddy petticoats and hairpins sticking out every which way, and in a boat so small as to be called a peapod. She wished she could see the man's face as clearly as he must see hers, and the unevenness of her situation made her feel doubly vulnerable, bobbing alongside in the water a good ten feet below him.

"I have rather lost my bearings in this fog, sir," she began again, this time with a certain belated primness, "and if you would be so good as to advise me as to the proper direction to the harbor at Appledore, then I shall be quite on my way myself."

"Appledore," repeated the man, rolling the name off his tongue with a booming flourish. "Come aboard, sweetheart, and I shall carry you there directly as my guest."

"Oh, but I mustn't!" said Serena hastily. After spending all her life in a seaport town, she knew too well the perils to women who trusted strange sailors. While this captain seemed gentlemanly enough, his accent marked him as an outsider, a foreigner, not from their county, and as for that cavalier "sweetheart"—ah, she must be wary, wary indeed. "That is, your offer is most kind, sir, but not necessary at all."

"Not necessary, you say." He shook his head, perplexed. "Yet I cannot in easy conscience let you simply vanish away into the fog."

Serena nodded eagerly. Clearly the man didn't like being refused, but then, what man did? "Of course you can. Your pilot can tell me the way to Appledore, and that will be more than sufficient. You needn't worry over me. I am quite skillful in a boat."

That was not the truth—neither the *quite* nor the *skillful* nor any combination of the two—and Serena's conscience twitched uneasily. Like most Appledore women, she could handle a boat well enough in fair weather, but she did know when she'd crossed her own limitations as a sailor. Yet a dubious truth did seem preferable to being kidnapped and ruined and sold to some Martinique brothel, or whatever other untoward fate this man might wish for her.

"Doubtless Appledore lies just through that fog," she continued, nervousness rushing her words. "Likely no more than a stone's skip away."

But the tall stranger had no interest in skipping stones. He motioned to the sailors behind him, and instantly two long boat-hooks appeared over the side of the sloop, catching Serena's little boat and pulling it snugly against the sloop's dark planks.

"No, no, you cannot do this to me!" cried Serena with growing panic, swinging her mittened fist at the nearer boat-hook. "I told you I didn't wish to come aboard, and I still don't! I *don't!*"

Swiftly she bent to grab her only weapon, the long-handled rake she'd used for scalloping. If she could smack away the boat-hooks, then perhaps she could push herself clear enough to escape. That was her best chance, her only hope.

But now even the rake seemed to be against her. The wooden teeth snarled in the single sail's lines, forcing Serena to struggle to work it free as her heart pounded with frustration and fear. Abruptly the line gave way, and with a startled gasp she tumbled backward into the puddle in the bottom of the boat, nearly losing the rake over the side in the process.

"Let me help," said the man as he dropped into the boat with alarming agility. "Here, take my hand."

"I'll take nothing from you!" cried Serena, settling awkwardly onto her knees as she tried to untwist her tangled cloak. Her hood had flopped over her eyes, and all she could see of the man now was his buckled shoes. "And who gave you leave to be in my boat, anyway?"

"You refused my hospitality, so I took that as an invitation to try yours instead. Now come, give me your hand and we'll set you upright. There's a good lass."

She swatted away his hand so hard that the boat rocked back and forth in clumsy sympathy.

"The devil take you," she declared, trying to sound braver than she felt as she struggled to find her footing, hampered by the rocking of the boat and her twisted petticoats and the way her hood had once again fallen forward over her eyes. Blindly she groped for the rake, her fingers finding and tightening around the oak handle. "And I am *not* your good lass!"

But before she could lift the rake, the man put his foot squarely over the handle, trapping both the rake and her hand with it.

"Your goodness, or lack of it, is of no concern to me," he said. "Which is fortunate for you, seeing as you seem to have precious little of that admirable quality, particularly for a woman. *Especially* for a woman. Now come, up you go."

Before Serena realized what was happening, the man took her by the wrist and swung her up onto the bench to sit beside him, with only the tiller between them. His fingers on her cold skin were warm and strong, his touch disturbingly proprietary. With a frightened gasp she finally managed to shove the hood back from her eyes, then nearly gasped again as, at last, she saw the man's face.

"There now," he murmured, his voice low, as if sharing a

special confidence with her alone. "That's far better, isn't it?"

"Better?" repeated Serena foolishly, unable to bring more than that single word squeaking to her lips. *"Better?"*

She was twenty-two years old, old enough, she'd believed, to have seen something of the world and the men that ruled it. But she'd never seen a man such as this one, not even in Boston, a man so supremely, outrageously sure of himself: a strong mouth and a stronger jaw, an arrogant hawk's beak of a nose, black hair and black brows and black lashes, and eyes that were bluer than a summer-bright sea. And, oh, the size of him beside her, so much larger, so much more grandly *male* that he seemed to fill the little boat entirely.

"Yes, better," he said with a mild patience that proved he was completely aware of his debilitating effect on women-folk as a rule. "Or would you have preferred to continue drifting out to sea?"

Her first inclination was to strike him silly, to smack her open palm across his smug, handsome face. She had precious little patience for male condescension. But she'd lost her temper once already, squalling and squawking when she'd feared their boats would collide, and she wouldn't give the man the satisfaction of doing it again, any more than she wished him to know of the strange puddle of warm confusion he'd momentarily reduced her to.

No: reason and a calm, measured demeanor would be her best weapons now. Her only weapons, really, since he'd kept his shoe firmly across the rake.

She dared to meet his eyes again, dared herself to remain unaffected. "I wasn't drifting out to sea. I was perfectly in control, excepting for the fog."

"Oh, yes, the fog." He nodded agreeably, but the glint in his eyes showed he no more believed her claim than she did herself. "So you said earlier."

She pulled one mitten off to tuck a wayward lock of her hair back behind her ear, wishing her fingers and nose weren't so red with the cold and her clothes so bedraggled. Not that she cared what the man thought of her, of course— she reminded herself sternly that she didn't care in the least—but in comparison he looked as if he'd just stepped from a carriage in London instead of dropping into her boat from a sloop in the fog on Massachusetts Bay.

His greatcoat and breeches were beautifully tailored, the superfine wool a deep, midnight blue, nothing homespun, and not the black she'd first thought. The buttons on his waistcoat and at the sides of his knees—very large, masculine knees, leading to equally masculine, muscular thighs and other masculine things she shouldn't consider—were polished brass, stamped with tiny flowers, and his linen was the best holland, better than most men she knew could boast for Sabbath wear, finished with a neat pleated frill at the cuffs. To dress like this he must be a prosperous captain indeed, especially considering he could not be much older than herself, and self-consciously she once again smoothed her rumpled skirts over her knees.

"It is very bad today, most dreadfully bad. The fog, I mean," she continued, hoping she wasn't really babbling as badly as she feared. "Far worse than I can ever remember at this time of year. Nigh as thick as clabbered milk."

"Indeed." The corners of his mouth twitched upward, something that Serena suspected happened often. " 'Thank you' would be sufficient, you know," he said. "Or is the custom different here in your colony?"

"Of course we thank others in Massachusetts," she said defensively. "But only when they deserve it, and I do not believe that you do."

"Even when I've done exactly as you wished?"

"If you'd done as I wished, you'd have stayed aboard your own vessel!"

He sighed deeply, too deeply for any man not suffering from blackest melancholia, and far, far too deeply for Serena to regard him with anything other than outright suspicion.

"And here I'd thought I'd come to your rescue," he said mournfully. "Playing the gallant hero and rescuing the fair maid from her distress."

"I am not in distress," she said sternly, "nor am I this wretched fair maid you fancy awaiting your rescue."

"No?" His raised one brow with feigned surprise. "Ah, sweet, how sadly then you've misled me!"

Serena's cheeks grow hot. *He* was not the one who'd been misled. She should have known better than to refer to herself as a maid, or rather to deny that she was one, which was not what she'd intended at all. Blast him for twisting her words about so! No man in Appledore would ever presume to speak to her like this. But then, this particular man wasn't from Appledore, and he'd clearly no notion of how one addressed Miss Serena Fairbourne, unless one wished to be addressing her brothers next.

And in an oddly perverse and confusing way, Serena was almost glad he didn't.

"I have not misled you, and I wish you would stop pretending that I have," she said with as much dignity as she could muster. "Now please go back aboard your sloop and leave me in peace."

"Not possible, I fear." He sighed again, and settled his arm comfortably on the tiller between them so that his sleeve brushed against hers. "I'm not enough of a sailor to go dancing across the waves, even at your bidding, sweet. Can't you see how we're already well on our way? But once we reach your Appledore, I'll be happy enough to oblige."

Belatedly Serena realized that the boat was moving through the water, drawn by a tow-line that bound it to the larger sloop. With a little cry of dismay she twisted around on the narrow bench, her face to the wind as she stared back out over the stern at the white-flecked wake they'd churned through the waves. How could she possibly have let herself become so distracted by the man beside her that she hadn't noticed?

From the wind she guessed they were in fact heading toward Appledore, as he said, but in Appledore her problems would only grow worse with him beside her. After what she'd done earlier this day and where she'd been, she needed to slip back into the harbor unnoticed, to return this boat she'd borrowed and run back to her house along the back paths through the marsh to Cranberry Point so she wouldn't be seen or questioned. But to be towed in instead like a prize for everyone in town to remark upon would bring questions she didn't wish to—no, *couldn't*—answer, and it would all be this man's fault.

"There now, didn't I tell you I'd rescued you?" he said, his smile widening to a wickedly satisfied grin as he watched her stare at the dripping tow-line.

"But you cannot do this!" she cried indignantly. "Hauling me off against my will as if I were no more than an old piece of lumber! It's kidnapping, you know, pure and simple! *Kidnapping!*"

"Oh, aye, and I'm the wickedest old Turk in creation for trying to help you. Now come, lass, sit neat beside me and tell me of this Appledore."

She glared at him, wishing he were not as big, not as charming, not as strong, not as comfortably settled in her boat as if he owned it instead, so that she could shove him over the side as he deserved. "What I'll tell you of, sir, is the stout new gaol where you'll be spending the night. Double walls and iron bars, and a brick floor, too, to keep you from burrowing out."

"What a disheartening beginning." He swept off his cocked hat with a flourish, holding it with both hands in his lap, and frowned a bit as if to concentrate. "Let me offer this instead:

The nymphs of Appledore are most wondrously fair,
With Neptune's own gold in their gossamer, ah, hair,
Mermaid-daughters of the mariner's keep,
Where salty zephyrs bring fresh rose to their damask
  cheek.

At least that fits you, sweetheart."

"What it's fit for is the rubbish heap," declared Serena promptly, but not before her own damask cheeks flushed hot to betray her. She'd never heard such nonsense before, not from a man's lips, anyway, and she wasn't prepared for the effect. Yes, that must be it: unfamiliarity. That must be *all.* Empty compliments were empty compliments, no matter how prettily they were phrased or how handsome the messenger.

So why, then, could she not bring herself to break her gaze with his?

"Rubbish?" he asked with a showy, heartfelt sigh of disappointment that still couldn't undermine the merriment in his eyes. "Faith, considering I'd no time to beckon a muse properly, I judged it rather fine."

"Then you misjudged. 'Mermaid-daughters of the mariner's keep,' indeed! Whatever does that *mean?*"

"But you remembered the line, didn't you? My humble effort cannot be so appallingly bad then, can it?"

Lord help her, he had dimples, too, charming little brackets to a smile that held altogether too much charm already. And she wished he'd return his hat to his head, so she wouldn't be distracted by the way his thick, dark hair streamed back from his forehead, the black silk ribbon on his queue fluttering in the wind.

"Oh, yes, it can." She narrowed her eyes, striving not to be distracted. "I still say you misjudged, and badly at that."

"I don't in matters of literature," he said, tapping his forefinger on the crown of his hat, "nor among ladies, either. I'm considered a deuced fine judge of both."

"Then you should know better than to go about calling decent women 'nymphs,'" she declared, but somehow her words seemed unable to convey any of the primness she'd mustered earlier. It had been much easier to do when she'd been frightened of him, and now, somehow, she . . . wasn't. "I am not quite sure what a nymph may be, but I'm certain it's wicked. It sounds that way. *Very* wicked. And we are respectable women in Appledore. Excepting perhaps some of the sluttish ones that serve at the taverns."

"I shall remember that," he said without the least contrition. "Every word. Especially that part about the sluttish ones."

"Rubbish," she said, slipping back onto her seat on the bench beside him. "Everything you say is. Honey-sweet words with nothing behind them. 'Tis all naught but rubbish."

"Then we must agree to differ, lass," he said. He brushed her cheek with his thumb, sweeping away a stray bit of her hair with a touch that was perilously close to a caress. The merriment faded from his eyes as his fingers spread to cradle her cheek against his palm. "For you *are* a most agreeable mermaid-daughter."

The last thing Serena expected him to do then was to kiss her. Or maybe it wasn't the last, but the first. Maybe she'd expected it from the beginning, deep down behind her conscience, for otherwise she would have slapped him outright, the way he deserved, or at least shoved him away. She wouldn't have let her eyes flutter shut as his face neared hers, or tipped her head to one side for her mouth to meet his, or parted her lips for the last, helpless sigh of protest to escape and vanish over the waves.

To let a stranger kiss her like that was undeniably wrong. Yet the longer his mouth moved against hers, the more right it felt, making her heart race and her blood run faster in her veins, and her head turn as dizzyingly light as the wisps of fog surrounding them. He might think of a dozen elegant ways to describe that kiss, but she knew only one: *magic*.

Yet when at last they broke apart, he had no elegant, teasing words to offer. He wasn't laughing now. Instead, his expression seemed curiously confused, almost bewildered, as he searched her face, his fingers still lingering across her cheek.

Serena's heart fluttered oddly in her breast, a strange mixture of hope and joy. For all his teasing airs, perhaps he was no more in the habit of kissing strangers than she was herself. Could he perhaps have felt the special magic between them, too?

But if he had, he didn't admit it, instead only shaking his head. "I should not have done that, sweet," he said softly. "If you but knew the promises I'd made, and now have broken . . ."

Swiftly she drew back from his hand, her cheeks stained

bright with shame. She had been too occupied with her own position to think of his. He could be betrothed or even married, someone else's sweetheart or husband or father.

"What you must think of me," she said, her words stumbling over themselves. "Lord help me, I've never been so bold, and I must beg your forgiveness, surely I must, and—"

"Hush, sweet." He placed his forefinger across her lips to silence her. "No begging, no apologies. A practice of mine, born of much experience, you see. I should not have kissed you, no, but I cannot in truth say that I regret it. Nor, I pray, should you."

"Nay, you do not understand—"

"But I do, lass," he said gently. "I understand everything."

He smiled then, a smile that turned his charm bittersweet with the regret he swore he did not feel. "Now come, speak to me of other things instead. That fine bucket of cockles, shall we say?"

"Cockles?" she repeated, as much confused by his abrupt transition as by the unfamiliar word. She followed his gaze to the water-filled oak bucket of fresh shellfish that sat wedged in the boat's bow before them. "Ah, you mean the scallops."

"If that is what they're called here," he said, leaning away from her to look into the bucket.

"Scallops," she said again. No regrets, he'd said, no apologies: if he could do that, then so could she. She'd intended the scallops to be her alibi when she returned to Appledore, and they could just as easily serve the same purpose now. "I raked them myself this morning. 'Tis the season for them to be sweetest, you know."

"I didn't." Heedless of his fine linen cuffs, he plunged his hand into the bucket, running his fingers through the water and across the heaps of fluted shells—rose, lavender, pale lemon, deep blue—with undisguised fascination. "All the ones I've seen at home were only white, but these—these are much more handsome. Almost like wildflowers. But what's this?"

He held his dripping hand outstretched to her. In his palm lay a pair of shells of striated pink, shading like a sunset from deepest plum to pale rose. Though the two shells were still joined together at the hinge like wings, the animal within was gone, the concave interior empty and clean.

"A sorry catch this makes for fisherfolk," he said, tossing the twin shells lightly in his palm. "No prize for the market here."

"Oh, don't throw them away, please!" she cried, lunging for the empty shells before they vanished over the side of the boat. "I know they're worthless, but I kept them because—because they were beautiful."

"Then so shall I," he said, his fingers closing over the shells. "To remind me of you, for the same reason."

Over his hand their eyes met again, the power of his gaze alone enough to make Serena's breath tighten in her chest. He was welcome to the shells. She'd need nothing extra to remind her of him.

But no apologies, no regrets . . .

"Appledore, sir, a point to the starboard," called the sloop's pilot from over their heads.

"Ah, sweet, so your home beckons at last," said the stranger, breaking the spell between them. Carefully he tucked the scallop shells into the pocket of his coat as he rose to stare across the water. "And a fair place Appledore looks to be. No marvel that you are so fond of it, and so eager to return. What better time for us to make our adieus?"

"But wait, Captain, please," said Serena quickly as the men in the sloop pulled her boat closer. "Please, I—"

"Not 'captain,' lass," he said as he prepared to untie the line that held the two boats together and climb back aboard the sloop. "I've no right to that title or any other, by birth or by merit. Except, of course, as a rogue. That's the one title I've earned."

"But you never told me your name!"

"And neither, sweet, did you." With the rope in his hands as a guideline, he swung himself away from her boat and climbed up the shallow footholds carved into the sloop's sides. Over his shoulder he smiled at her one last time, a smile that failed to reach his eyes. "In my heart you will always be my misplaced mermaid, beckoning from the fog, and you can think of me as your gallant savior, rescuing you against your will."

Already the two boats were separating, carried apart by the wind and currents, and belatedly Serena hurried to set her own course for the shore. By the time she could look back, the sloop was slipping away into the fog, and she could just make out the stranger's face and the hat waving in his hand.

"Farewell, Mistress Mermaid," he called, "and may Neptune always watch over you in my place."

She waved her hand in return, staring after the sloop long after it had disappeared. At last she lowered her hand, carefully touching her fingers to her lips where he'd kissed her. Then with her head bowed, she steered her course for home.

. . . and no regrets.

Look for
Cranberry Point
Wherever Paperback Books
Are Sold
Coming Soon from
Pocket Star Books